For Mina.

NECESSARY EVIL

FLETCHER & FLETCHER, PARANORMAL INVESTIGATORS: BOOK ONE

DAVID BUSSELL

This is a work of fiction. Names, characters, businesses, places, events, and incidents are either the products of the author's imagination or used in a fictitious manner. Any resemblance to actual events, or to actual persons living, dead, or undead, is purely coincidental.

uncannykingdom.com

FLETCHER & FLETCHER

PARANORMAL INVESTIGATORS

1

NECESSARY EVIL

CHAPTER ONE: GHOSTED

NIGHT-TIME. Smoky shafts of neon light filtering through the slats of a Venetian blind. A shady lady with legs up to her armpits and lipstick the colour of wet blood. That's how detective stories are meant to start.

Not with some irked bloke sitting alone in a dank pub, waiting on a client who doesn't even have the decency to show up. Who'd read that? Who wants to follow the story of a pissed off loser watching a closed door, standing by for a job that's never going to happen? A case that ain't to be.

Cursed.

That's what he told me, this no-show of a client. Said he'd been hexed, and that nothing good could come his way until the spell was lifted. He didn't know where the curse had come from, or who'd dealt it, but he was sure there was black magic involved. *Sure of it.* The ones who come my way always are. It's never down to their shitty life choices. Never their habit of using the free will they were given to always, *always* make the wrong decisions. Oh no. Black magic, that's the culprit every time. Lose a bundle on the nags? Cursed. Passed over for that promotion? Cursed. Got steaming drunk, ran a red light, and ended up with some old dear's brains painting your mud flaps? Double cursed.

Or maybe I was wrong. Maybe the guy I was waiting on really did have a monkey on his back. Maybe he had every intention of showing up tonight… at least until he fell down a lift shaft to the distant sound of a cackling gypsy. From my perspective, it didn't much matter. Well, not really. The job was a write-off, and I'd wasted an entire evening doing sweet FA. Those were the facts.

Unless…

Walking through the pub door came a man, middle-aged and wearing a face like a dropped flan. Was this my jinxed client? Was this the man who was going to pull me out of my professional slump and offer up some decent work to chew on?

Nope.

The feller with the face shuffled by me and took a seat at the bar before ordering a pint of something brown and bubbly. Lenny, the landlord, reluctantly heaved his elbows off the bartop and obliged.

I just realised I haven't really set the scene for you. Sorry about that. Give me a sec and I'll paint a proper picture. Okay, where to start? Tell you what, why don't we kick off with my favourite subject: me. My name's Jake Fletcher. I'm six-feet tall, easy on the eye, and I dress in a tidy black suit (a nice one, not something off a Moss Bros clearance rack). At this point in the story, I'm in The Beehive, specifically The Beehive's saloon bar. The bar is a sort of speakeasy; a place for a certain… subset of London society to relax and tip their elbows among their own kind. I'll get into the details later; right now, let me just give you some atmos.

The room I was sat in was packed full of wonky furniture and booths with Gaffer tape-patched upholstery, all propped up by a floor so sticky you'd think someone had gone arse-over-tit with a bucket of glue. Lenny, the aforementioned landlord, was a rafter-scraping man-mountain with cro-magnon features covered in a dusting of iron-filings stubble, and a voice that made him sound like he'd swallowed a lawnmower.

He leaned around the man at the bar and fixed his deep-set eyes on me. 'Been stood up, Fletcher?'

'Leave it out, Lenny, I'm not in the mood.'

A smile quirked his lips. 'Horrible to watch. Just horrible.'

A new punter hailed Lenny from the other end of the bar, and he trudged off to serve her.

I wasn't up for banter. Work had been thin on the ground lately, and I lacked the energy to act as if that didn't bother me. The manners, too. Far as I was concerned, Lenny could take a hot dip in a wet shit.

I felt a buzz coming from the inside pocket of my suit jacket and plucked out my phone. Was *this* the client?

Please let that be him, please let that be him...

It wasn't.

I stared at the name on the screen. Vic Lords. Vic fucking Lords.

Vic was what you might call a local entrepreneur, but could more accurately be described as a brothel owner, drug dealer, money launderer, gunrunner, human trafficker, and all-round shady geezer. Originally born within earshot of the Bow bells, Vic now presided over a criminal fiefdom that reached from east to west London and both sides of the river. As well as running scores of illegal enterprises, he was known to be a closet Satanist who dabbled in the very darkest corners of the occult. I'd seen some evidence of this myself but had yet to witness first-hand proof of any of the more outlandish rumours associated with his name, by which I mean cannibalism, communing with demons, and a penchant for human sacrifice. In any case, whether the gossip was true or not, Vic Lords was a bad man. The kind of man who should be accompanied by the theme tune to *Jaws*.

I cancelled the call, but no sooner had I returned the phone to my pocket than the thing started up again. It had been ringing red-hot ever since curiosity got the better of me and I picked up the first of Vic's calls two days ago.

'Jakey boy,' the voice on the other end of the line had said. *'How you keeping?'*

'What do you want, Vic?' I spat back.

Him and me had a past. One I'm not going to get into here. For now, let's just say we did some business together once, and that we didn't part on the best of terms.

I heard the creak of cheap vinyl as Vic rocked back in his office chair. *'Got a proposition for you, me old mucker.'*

'Oh yeah?'

'Yeah. Thought I'd chuck a job your way. Put a bit of dosh in your back pocket. You in?'

'Thanks for thinking of me, Vic, but I'd rather clean Camden with my tongue.'

He unleashed an ugly, phlegmy laugh. *'Why not, Fletcher? Did you lose your bottle? Or are you too busy for the likes of me?'*

Something about the way he asked that question suggested that he knew I wasn't. I didn't care for that. Had he been digging into my business? Keeping tabs on my comings and goings? I wondered, did he have eyes on me at that moment, sat there kicking my heels up at a boozer when I should have been out there chasing pavement and righting wrongs?

'You've got nothing to offer me, Vic,' I told him.

'Well, if it's not cash you're after, what do you want? Just name your price, my son.'

I could feel his shark fin circling. Vic had been on my case for years, trying to tempt me back into the fold with increasingly generous offers, but I was having none of it. I'd turned over a new leaf, and no amount of honeyed words were going to win me back.

'I already gave you my answer,' I told him. *'Now give it a rest and lose this number.'*

'Haven't I always done right by you, Fletcher?' he went on, undeterred. *'Haven't I helped you out of some jams? The least you could do is hear what I have to say.'*

'Don't act like you've done me any favours, Vic.' My thumb hovered over the End Call button, but refused to pull the trigger.

'I gave you work when no one else was offering. Paid you a fair price for it, too. What do you call that except for a favour?'

'A mistake,' I replied.

I heard a couple of strokes of a Zippo, then Vic took a long drag on what I knew from first-hand experience was a cigar that smelled worse than a burning mummy. *'Why don't you have a think on it, Jakey boy? Take some time to consider my offer properly. For old times' sake.'*

'Okay, I will. I promise.'

'Seriously?'

'Sure. Hey, you know what, I just thought about it. Fuck you, Vic.'

He laughed again; a laugh like he knew something that I didn't. *'You're your own worst enemy, Jake, you know that?'*

'What's that supposed to mean?'

He hung up before I had a chance to find out.

Back in the here and now, the phone rang again. Again, I cancelled the call. I should have put a block on Vic's number two days ago, but knowing how inept I am with technology, I'd probably have ended up finding a button that set the phone on fire.

I waited for the mobile to ring again, but this time it stayed quiet. Ten minutes passed, and the device sat idle on the table in front of me. What was all that about? Had Vic finally given up, or had he decided that he was done asking nicely? People who said no to Vic had a habit of winding up preserved in concrete and propping up motorway flyovers, or—as one oft-told yet never verified story went—cut up and sold to local kebab shops for meat. Had I just made the mistake of a lifetime?

I thought about that all the way back to my office in Chalk Farm.

The building I was based in was a gin warehouse originally, but had since been converted into a residential block. Well, half-converted; the work was never officially completed, which is how I came to grab a sweet top floor corner office with an impressive panoramic view of the borough.

I took the shuttered lift to the fifth and headed left, only to find the door to my office slightly ajar. I pulled to a stop.

'Hello?' I called out.

No answer.

Was someone snooping around in there, or had they shown up looking for my services? Maybe the bloke who left me in the lurch at the pub arrived here instead, wanting to talk about his curse. Not likely, though. Chances were he got lucky at the races and knocked the whole "hexed" theory into a cocked hat. Poxy timewaster.

So who was it, then? Who'd let themselves into my office? Had a potential client come knocking and made himself comfortable in my absence? Maybe this was good news for a change. I could certainly do with a dose of that. It had been a good long while since I sunk my teeth into a nice, juicy case, and I was hungry for another bite.

I approached the doorway to the office and looked down to see splinters of wood on the ground, just beyond the threshold. The doorframe had been shattered, no doubt the result of someone kicking their way inside. Guess that blew my "good news" premise out of the water.

'Hello?' I repeated. 'Who's in there?'

Again, nothing.

Whoever it was that had broken in, they were either gone or hiding. And if they were hiding, they definitely weren't on my friends list. What was I looking at here? A burglar? A junkie looking for someplace dry to shoot up? Or was it one of Vic Lords' goons, come to twist my arm? Maybe even punch my ticket for good.

I stepped sideways through the door and switched on what I generously called "the lights". The building's electricity had been cut off a while back, leaving me to make do with a scattering of battery-powered lamps. I switched on the closest and lit up the front half of the office, not that there was much to illuminate. A desk, a battered office chair, an old filing cabinet—empty—and that was about it. Some visitors have referred to the decor as "spartan", or "were you robbed?". Me, I prefer "uncluttered".

The back half of the office remained robed in shadow, but as my eyes adjusted to the dim light, I could just about make out something that shouldn't be there: the silhouette of a figure, stood motionless in the darkness. Ice spiked my veins. It was a real squeaky bum moment.

'Whoever you are, this is your last chance to skedaddle. I've got a shooter, and I'm more than happy to use it.'

I was bluffing, but with any luck, I'd managed to put enough steel in my voice for the lie to ring true.

But no. The figure remained, still as a statue, so quiet that I couldn't even hear him breathing.

'If you're one of Vic's dogsbodies, you can piss right off. I already told him I'm not for sale.'

Then again, on second glance, the figure didn't look big enough to be one of Vic's bully boys. No, the profile was all wrong for a heavy. Who was this bloke? I was desperate to get a proper look at my mystery guest, but the lamp that lit the remainder of the room was out of reach, at least without moving into grabbing distance of the intruder.

I briefly wondered if the trespasser was of the supernatural variety, but I'd long since taken precautions against those. I had a protective ward in place that locked off my entire floor to Uncannies. A ward composed of a concoction of my own design that I call my "secret herbs and spices": a proprietary blend of silver oxide, rock salt, iron filings, wolves bane, desiccated chicken blood, and anything else that keeps the beasties out.

The trespasser moved suddenly, lurching forward a step and letting forth a deep, guttural moan that made my scalp crawl. I backed up a step, but the figure kept coming, shambling towards me with an ungainly, shuffling gait, arms out like a cartoon sleepwalker.

A zombie.

No special powder for that. No magical protection to ward off the walking dead. At least, none that I knew of.

The bones in the zombie's stiffened neck creaked as it groped its way in my direction, shuffling into the pool of light cast by the nearby lamp. It wore a decomposed black suit that was a surprising match for my own. I saw its face and heard a gasp escape my throat.

Is that...?

I couldn't correlate what it was I was seeing. The logical part of my brain tried to convince the lizard part that it was a trick of the light, a mental glitch, anything that made sense. Something that explained this impossible sight away. But the lizard part of my brain knew the truth.

I was looking at my own reanimated corpse.

Now, that's *definitely* not the way a detective story is meant to start.

CHAPTER TWO: THE TWO JAKES

Did I mention that I was a ghost? A phantom spirit, marooned on the physical plane. I didn't? What am I like, eh? I tell you what I look like, describe the clobber I'm wearing, but forget to declare that I've been six feet deep since the noughties.

At least I thought so. Apparently, my old body had gone walkabout and decided to pay what was left of me a visit. And from the way it was moving, it didn't look like it was bringing me in for a hug.

I stared back in horror at my evil twin, its face sallow, cheeks sunken, jaw snapping at me hungrily. Instinctively, my legs took over, transporting me at speed from the approaching menace. The zombie wasn't to be deterred, though, and pursued me around the office, hot on my heels. I dodged to the other side of my desk, putting the hunk of wood between me and my attacker, but the zombie turned it over like it was flipping a pancake.

Just what in the name of sweet Bruce Dickinson was going on here? My body was long gone, delivered through the black, spiked gates of Camden Cemetery and patted down with a shovel. I should know, I saw it happen when I attended the funeral. So you can imagine how surprised I was to see my animated carcass in the (rotting) flesh.

'Calm down,' I said, palms out, desperately trying to deescalate the ridiculous situation I found myself in. 'Let's talk about this.'

At this point, you might be asking yourself what exactly I was so scared of.

You're a ghost, Jake; an immaterial apparition. What are you doing worrying about some vengeful sack of blood and bones? What good is a physical being against a disembodied spirit?

Well, here it is. See, despite being incorporeal, certain things can still affect ghosts. Two such things are magic, and certain creatures possessed of or powered by magic. A zombie would be a prime example of the latter. Yup. There are things out there that can even kill the dead. Who knew? Certainly not you, but that's okay, you're new to this. Don't beat yourself up about it.

Speaking of beating yourself up...

My reanimated corpse made a lunge for me, snatching up a fistful of lapel and lunching on my collar. I lashed out defensively, getting a couple of sloppy punches in, but nothing that made a dent. By way of a thank you, the zombie balled up a fist, cocked its arm, and delivered a brick to my face that sent me reeling.

How was this happening? Who'd raised my body from the ground and pitted it against me? What sick fuck does a thing like that? I racked my fevered brain, but I had no idea who'd be capable of that kind of voodoo. Here's what I did know: I wasn't going to beat the zombie in a brawl. Best I could do was put as much distance between me and it as possible.

Thankfully, getting gone fast is very much a specialty of mine. As well as possessing the usual suite of ghost powers—invisibility to the living, being able to pass through solid objects, the ability to totally freak out Scooby-Doo—I had a couple of powers that not many phantoms did. One that got a regular airing, and proved invaluable in the event of an unwinnable fight, was translocation, otherwise known as the "Brave Sir Robin" manoeuvre. Translocation allows me to instantly vanish from one position and reappear at any point I'm familiar with. In other words, goodbye *Walking Dead* reject, hello escape hatch to anywhere else.

Up, up and away...

I went to warp out of there, but when I tried to translocate, nothing happened. I looked down at my hands and tried again, but instead of vanishing, I saw my mitts come apart like a couple of misaligned transparencies before snapping back together again. Not good. Not good at all.

As my flesh and blood doppelganger came lumbering at me again, I decided to give it the slip a different way. Like I said before, the zombie was perfectly capable of doing ghosts harm, but that didn't mean it could do the things I could, for example, walking through walls. Just because something was stopping me from translocating, didn't mean I couldn't rely on the classics.

'Not today, silly bollocks.'

I offered my shambling likeness the middle finger, then dashed to the other side of the office and whistled through the wall like wind through a keyhole. I arrived in the adjoining room, the empty kitchen space of an unfinished apartment, bare but for some half-assembled units, a workbench, and a few discarded tools. Safe at last. Or so I thought.

Over my shoulder, I heard an almighty crash as the zombie came ambling through the wall and appeared in the apartment wearing a coating of brick dust.

'Shit. I guess you can walk through walls after all.'

It was just then that I noticed a broken copper pipe sticking out from the demolished wall and heard a suspect hissing sound. Apparently, gas was the one utility in the building that had yet to be cut off. Great. Now the block was being flooded by highly combustible fumes. This was turning out to be a real gold star day.

Of course, there's always room for things to get worse when you're being pursued by a zombie, so it came as no surprise when my decomposing assailant accidentally knocked a chisel off a workbench that sparked on the concrete floor and lit the gas pumping into the room. I'm guessing, ordinarily, that it would take a while for a gas leak to reach sufficient density that it caused an explosion. For it to occur this quickly would take a very special set of circumstances, say a main gas pipe being torn in half and venting like mad into a pokey London-sized kitchen with its door closed, which —*whoops*—is exactly what happened.

'Balls,' I managed to say, right before a fireball tore through the room, setting alight a pile of Linseed oil-soaked rags that had been used to varnish the kitchen counter.

The next thing I knew, the place was blazing, flames licking up the walls, all the way to the exposed wooden rafters. The whole building was about to get incinerated, my office included, and there was nothing I could do about it. I had no way of putting out a fire. What was I going to do, blow on it? I'm a ghost, I couldn't put out a birthday candle.

Then again, being a ghost meant I couldn't be burned alive, either, which was proving to be quite advantageous given the severity of the situation. Or at least it would have been, if fire was the only threat I was facing. As if to balance out that point in my favour, I felt a sudden vice-like grip as the zombie closed its cold, dead fingers around my throat. My feet departed from the ground, tracing tiny circles above the floor as I dangled in the monster's clutches.

'Get off me!'

I firmed up my fists and threw a couple of swings at the bastard, but I might as well have tried punching my way through the hull of a battleship. I was done for. Finito.

It's funny, really. I always suspected I'd be the death of me, but not like this. My money was on a fondness for cigarettes and booze being the culprit, not the claws of my reanimated corpse. There you go, though. It's a funny old world.

I saw my zombified body unhinge its jaw, ready to nosh on my neck, and felt my eyes roll back in my skull. Time to die. Again. Shame, really. I was just starting to enjoy being semi-alive.

CHAPTER THREE: PHANTOM PAINS

MUCH TO MY SURPRISE, my throat remained noticeably intact. I peeled open my eyes to find out what the hold-up was and saw a new visitor had arrived on the scene. The figure entered the room through the hole in the apartment wall, framed by a wreath of fire and looking like the Devil himself.

Vic Lords.

Unaffected by the flames, and wearing a smile of shark-like proportions.

How to describe Vic to the uninitiated? Let's try this... If Doctor Frankenstein decided to make a monster assembled entirely from human malevolence, Vic Lords would be the end result. Need more? Okay. If a kid saw Vic on the street he'd say, "What's wrong with that man's face?" then he'd curl up and die. Vic Lords was a monstrosity. A creature grown somewhere dank and moist. A bloated dwarf with blue cheese skin and a rug of Brylcreemed hair that sat on his head like a stubborn oil slick.

Ordinarily, Vic wore a cheap, ill-fitting suit devoid of any unnecessary decoration. This evening he'd elected to dress somewhat differently: clothed in a floor-length red velvet robe. The bloke was really giving it the big 'un. I expect the duds were meant to impress me, but honestly, they only made him look like a low-rent Hugh Hefner.

'Nice dressing gown,' I managed to squeak through the zombie's steely grip; the zombie that was obviously under Vic's control. 'You come straight from the shower?'

Vic made slits of his eyes. 'I reckon you know this is a wizard's robe, Fletcher.'

I did. Vic dabbling in the occult was no secret to me, but this was the first time I'd seen him really walk the walk. Not only had Vic managed to stroll into a burning building unscathed—which suggested the use of some decent protection magic—he'd also succeeded in getting my carcass up on its feet, which meant he could add necromancy to his CV, too. That all added up to some pretty serious voodoo. No wonder I couldn't translocate; the near presence of another source of magic, if strong enough, had a habit of nullifying that power completely.

'Nice party trick,' I croaked. 'So what now? Are you just going to stand there waggling your pentacles at me?'

Vic nodded to the zombie, which closed its grip on my neck, digging its fingers into my throat and bringing my windpipe dangerously close to collapse.

Now, if I can just stick a pin in the narrative here for a moment...

You're probably wondering how me and Vic Lords came to be acquainted in the first place, right? I did say up top that the two of us did some business together once, but I was being a bit coy there. Fact is, I worked for the feller for years, back before I became a detective. Back when I was alive.

In those early days, when I was still pulling air, I used to ply my trade as an exorcist. Yeah, an exorcist turned ghost – don't worry, the irony isn't lost on me. A man who used to evict spirits for a living, cursed to remain on Earth as the very thing he used to eradicate. You couldn't make it up.

Back then, if I saw the likes of me loitering somewhere they weren't wanted—a detached soul scaring away potential renters—I'd have sent me packing in no time. No notice given, no second chances, take your marching orders and sling your hook. I didn't mess around in those days, I was good at my job. Give me a haunted house and a couple of sprigs of burning sage and I'd have that place looking clean as a whistle.

Considering how good I was at being an exorcist, and how few other people could do that kind of work, you'd think I'd have made more money at it. And I might have if I wasn't working for Vic Lords. Vic's finder's fee for pointing me in the direction of a haunted property ran to 70%, which meant a big wet bite out of my profits. No wonder I wasn't living the high life. Still, Vic's was the only game in town. It was work for him or join the bread line.

Back then, I didn't know Vic Lords was going to become the man he did. He had his pudgy fingers in a few shady enterprises, I suspected that much, but he paid on time and he always had repeat work. I don't know, maybe if I hadn't turned a blind eye to Vic's dodginess, I wouldn't have wound up in the mess. Maybe I'd still be alive. Maybe I wouldn't be stuck walking the Earth as a ghost. All I know for sure is, Vic's shadow has loomed over me for a long time. My life on both sides of the grey veil is braided with Vic Lords.

But let's get back to the exorcist thing. How exactly does a working-class tyke from the East End of London wind up banishing apparitions for a living? Well, I was kind of born to it. As a kid, I realised I had a preternatural insight that I later learned was called The Sight. It gave me the ability to hone in on a frequency that very few could detect. To see the world beneath your world; the world that you tune out. Oh, you might think you're hip, you might think you're woke, but in reality… well, reality is exactly where you're stuck. Don't feel bad about it. Reality—what we call the waking world—is a fine place to be. In reality, you don't wind up being strangled by your own rejuvenated corpse. Which reminds me…

The zombie squeezed my neck so hard I thought it was going to turn into butter.

Vic grinned. 'Didn't I say you were your own worst enemy, Fletcher?'

He nodded to my rotten doppelganger, which released its grip and left me on the bones of my arse. I sat there, watching the flames close in around us, listening to the crackle of burning wood as the fire ate up the building from the inside out.

'What do you want?' I wheezed, rubbing my neck.

Vic leaned over to look at me, head tipped to one side like a painter admiring his handiwork. 'Like I said on the blower the other day, I need a favour, and you're the man for the job. You might be done with the past, Fletcher, but the past ain't done with you.'

I sighed. 'It's possible there are more polite ways of asking for help than digging up a man's carcass and giving it the old abracadaver.'

'Could be, but since you mugged me off on the phone, I reckoned this would be a good way to get your attention.'

He certainly had it. Burning down my office, raising the dead, strolling into my life dressed like a mad cultist on a Satanic Hootenanny... the man was centre stage for sure.

'What's the job?' I asked, not because I planned on doing it, just because I was curious, and asking bought me some time.

Vic motioned to the zombie, which produced a cigar from its pocket and handed the thing to its master. Vic lit the business end of the stogie on the encroaching flames, took a long, deep drag, and exhaled a thick lance of smoke. 'I need your knack of getting into places you're not supposed to be.'

'You want me to steal something for you?'

'In so many words, yes.'

I folded my arms. 'Forget it. Get your goon here to kick the door down. I'm not getting you shit.'

He laughed. 'You really are the most stubborn bastard I've ever met, Fletcher.'

'I'll take that as a compliment.'

Vic wasn't getting his way. He could torch my office, he could have his meat puppet throttle me, but I wasn't climbing back into bed with him. Our alliance was over, and it was never getting rekindled.

Vic straightened the hem of his robe and offered an unknowable smile. 'I'll be back in touch when you're in a better mood. One way or another, you're going to take that job, son.' He wheeled about and headed for the hole in the wall, back the way he came.

'Leaving so soon, Vic? I was just about to put a brew on.'

'Another time. I've got business to attend to.'

'Oh yeah?' I said, scrambling to my feet. 'I hope you're not leaving because your piss-weak protection spell is about to give out and leave you at the mercy of this bloody great fire you started. Because that would be awful.'

As a ghost, the flames would have no effect on me, but protection magic—the kind humans were capable of, anyway—came with a time limit. The best conservation spell known to man had the shelf-life of a peeled banana.

Vic spun on his heel, setting his robe swinging; a robe that was beginning to show the first signs of charring. This time he wore a face that was very much knowable. The face of a man who's number had been well and truly got.

'I'll leave you to your ashes, Jakey boy. Don't worry, we'll talk again soon.'

And off he went.

I turned to my reanimated cadaver, which stayed rooted to the spot, abandoned.

'Oi! What about the Living Dead over here?'

'What about it?' Vic asked over his shoulder.

'You're just going to leave your zombie behind?'

Vic shrugged. 'How is it the Yanks put it? "That sounds like a *you* problem".'

And off he toddled into the burning hole, vanishing through a sheet of flames.

CHAPTER FOUR: DEARLY DEPARTED

Vic Lords clearly meant business, but I wasn't about to do his dirty work just because that boiling cauldron of arseholes told me to. Not that Vic was my biggest concern in that moment. Priority number one was figuring out what to do about the fact that my office was burning down around my ears.

I surveyed the carnage. The fire was well beyond the point of being extinguished, that was for sure. Matter of fact, it looked as if the entire block was about to start coming down on my head. Not that a collapsing building presented any danger to a ghost, but still, it was probably time to make a move. If I've said it once, I've said it a thousand times: there are always better places to be than the inside of a fire.

'What are you waiting for?' I shouted at the zombie. 'Are you just going to stand there like a lemon?'

It did exactly that, remaining perfectly motionless as the flames edged ever closer.

I found myself wanting to help the poor sod. I mean, it was my body, even if it was little more than Vic's automaton now.

'Come on, leg it, you handsome tit.'

My corpse just stared at me. I knew I should have been cremated. Hey, it looked like I was going to get my wish after all.

'Fine then, have it your way.' I wavered for a second, but what exactly could I do? Damn Vic Lords for abusing my body in this way. For turning my remains into this ghoulish marionette.

I closed my eyes, concentrated on an arrival point, and translocated outside, appearing on the pavement just out front of the building. I stayed there for a while, painted by the fire's golden glow, standing by helplessly as my office burned to the ground.

'There goes the resale value on that place,' I said to no one in particular.

I wondered what would be left of the old, physical me. Would any part of my body be found after the fire was put out? And if it was, would forensics be able to piece enough of it together to figure out who it belonged to? Because if they were able to get their hands on my DNA they were going to have some serious questions, starting with, I would imagine, *"Why is this the second time this corpse has wound up on our slab?"*

Glowing embers leapt and cascaded from the building, raining down as flakes of ash and settling on the ground like dirty snow. High above, a giant, greasy plume of smoke corkscrewed into the night sky, blotting out the moon. The building was a goner, that was for sure. Soon there would be nothing left of it but charred remains.

Bugger.

I loved that office, I really did. Conveniently located, oodles of square footage, and best of all, completely rent-free. How come? Well, when I said before that construction of the building was never completed, it wasn't because the money ran out. The reason the contractors downed tools was because the property was declared haunted. Apparently, some ghost who shall remain nameless spooked the hell out of anyone wearing a hard hat who dared set foot in the place. Real spritz-your-pants stuff: power tools starting of their own accord, loose lumber mysteriously rearranged into impossible teetering stacks, threatening messages spelled out on dirty surfaces in front of a witness's eyes... enough to drive anyone out. The building just sort of slid into disrepair after that. Terrible business. What can I say, a ghost will really mess with your real estate value.

Anyway, that's how I came to be in my place of business. Doubtless not much of a surprise; ghosts and haunting go together like bangers and mash. A bigger surprise would probably be the fact that a dead man was able to run a business in the first place. I mean, you never hear about Casper the Friendly Ghost holding down a nine-to-five (then again, he had all that Richie Rich money to play with – Google it). So how exactly was I able to hold down a steady job in the first place?

Okay, here's the Reader's Digest version: since I took a trip to slab city, I've been a phantom, dead as a doornail, but still able to function on the material plane. Unlike the majority of my peers, I can "push", which is ghost lingo for making yourself just tangible enough to manipulate physical objects (to a limited degree at least). I can pick up a phone, search records, even pour a dame a stiff drink. That's how I've managed to operate as a detective all these years, despite having popped my clogs a long time ago. Look me up. The Spectral Detective: the busiest dead man since Tupac Shakur.

That was before. Like I said up top, things had taken a real downturn of late. Even when my office wasn't on fire, getting people through the door had been getting harder and harder. I guess some people just prefer doing business with a detective who's alive. It's discrimination is what it is.

But enough of all that boo-hoo

A silhouette appeared in the ground floor entrance of the burning building.

'Well, bugger me sideways…'

Out came my old corpse, shuffling from the inferno to join me on the forecourt, a bit singed around the edges, but otherwise fine. I guess it must have decided it didn't want to be toast, and its survival instinct kicked in. I get that. I'm dead too, and self-preservation ranks mighty high on my list of priorities.

'You're one triple-hard bastard,' I told the zombie. 'You must get that from me.'

I found myself feeling a little relieved. Which was weird. A minute ago, that hunk of meat was throttling me, and now I was grinning because it was still up and about. This whole situation was really doing my nut in.

The wail of a siren cut through the sound of the burning building. Shit. The authorities were on their way, and standing on the street, bold as brass and lit up like a Christmas tree, was a creature that shouldn't exist. The stuff of campfire stories.

Now, you might think a wandering zombie wasn't my problem, but you'd be bang wrong on that score. Sure, as a ghost I was invisible to the hoi polloi, I had nothing to worry about, but it's still my job to make sure the normals don't get wind of the Uncanny. That job falls to all of us who exist outside of the common spectrum. Us ghosts and goblins like to keep our business away from the regular folk. It's a kind of code. Honour amongst thieves, if you like. Pull back the curtain on my world and the whole apple cart turns over. Mass panic, rioting on the streets, the guys in tin foil hats knowing they were right all along. Can't have it. A zombie showing up on the front page of the tabloids would be the start of World War Weird.

So somehow I had to get this walking bag of fertiliser off the streets before the rozzers showed up.

'Oi, numpty, time to go home. Come on, stop fannying about.'

The zombie went nowhere. Just stood there like a post-apocalyptic shop mannequin.

'Get cracking,' I cried, 'the pigs will be here any minute.'

Nothing.

I slapped him on the forehead. 'You deaf, mate?'

The zombie got moving, but not in the way I intended. Instead of running for cover, it made a lunge for me.

'Braaaiiins!' it groaned, and went to take a chomp out of my skull.

Fans of hot dead-on-dead action will be disappointed to learn that I managed to duck the attack just in time to avoid losing a chunk of cranium, and gave the zombie a clump of hair to chew on instead.

'Blech!' complained the baffled zombie, and spat the hairball on the floor.

'You done?'

Apparently, I wasn't quite the meal the zombie had in mind. Could be I was low in fibre, or maybe ectoplasm isn't to everyone's taste. Either way, it looked like I was off the menu tonight.

I gave the zombie a shove, but it remained unshakeable.

'Wait a sec, what am I thinking?' I said, slapping my own forehead this time.

Why was I going to all the effort of trying to shift the zombie physically when all I had to do was climb inside of it, take control of its body, and walk it down the street that way? That's another power of mine, you see: possession. I know, I know, I'm laying a lot on you at once here, but that's just the way it's going to have to be. I wish there was a better way of parsing out this steaming great info dump, but it's a complicated business, being a ghost. Not only do you have to explain that you're dead in the first place, there's a whole list of rules and regulations you need to get straight. So I'm sorry if what I'm telling you reads a bit dry, but in my defence, we're only a few pages in and I've already given you a zombie attack and the towering inferno. What else do you want? Space aliens? A robot uprising? A new season of *Fawlty Towers*?

So where was I? Oh yeah, possession. Ordinarily, I use my ability to take charge of a person's physical form so I can interact with the waking world. Most often, it's so I can communicate with the living and contribute to society in some meaningful way. Sometimes it's as simple as wanting to manipulate a physical object that I'm having trouble with in phantom form.

I ran my eyes over the stubborn zombie. As much as I wasn't jumping at the idea of stepping into the driver's seat of a rotting corpse, it beat trying to shove the thing down the street like a tramp's shopping trolley. I also had to admit, even if it was falling apart at the seams, that the idea of being back inside my old body did have its appeal. They say you can never go home again, but why not give it the old college try? Yeah, possession was definitely the way to go.

You might be wondering why I didn't try this trick back in my office while I was being throttled, but believe me, that wasn't happening. Imagine trying to hotwire a car while someone yells maths problems at you, and the person who's yelling is kicking you repeatedly in the nuts. That's what it's like trying to possess someone when they're busy making a balloon animal out of your windpipe.

But this was different. Even with the pressure of the approaching sirens, taking possession of a static subject that was putting up no resistance was pretty much an open goal.

'All right, lover boy,' I whispered into the zombie's ear, 'bite down hard, 'cause I'm coming in dry…'

I manoeuvred my way around the back of the thing, made my body as intangible as could be, took a step forward—

And met with a brick wall.

Apparently, taking possession of a zombie wasn't as easy as I thought it was going to be. I couldn't say for sure what it was tripping me up, but I suspected it was Vic's magic; the spell he'd used to raise the creature, keeping me locked out. That or possessing zombies was a no-go. Maybe I could only use that power on the truly alive.

The sirens were accompanied by the approach of flashing lights now.

'You stubborn bastard,' I said, giving the zombie another fruitless nudge.

I yelled at it to shift its arse, but still it stayed fixed to the spot, a sleeping cow. I got nose-to-nose with the thing, my eyes boring into their glassy, lifeless twins, drilling deep, deep down. I glared at the vacant look reflected back at me, the slack expression on that gormless, wet face, and I saw myself. That belligerent refusal to listen. That maddening pig-headedness. That unwillingness to do the one thing that was in its own self-interest. Inside those eyes I saw the very worst of me. And something just snapped.

I gave the zombie a belt across the chops.

'Look at yourself! You never did know what was good for you, you dozy piece of shit.' I was a drunk man ranting at himself in the bathroom mirror, but I didn't care. 'Got yourself a dead-end job working for a gangster. Got yourself murdered. Couldn't even make it to forty without dying. Well, sod ya. You wanna stand here and get picked up by the pigs, be my guest. See how I care.'

The sirens were deafening now. If I had the means to go with the intention, I'd have put a bullet in that zombie. The authorities would have had some questions about the mouldy carcass lying face down on the pavement with a gunshot wound in its head, but better that than them coming face to face with a walking cadaver. Still, what choice did I have? I'd done everything I could to shift the bugger. At this point, I could only hope Vic's voodoo wore off and the zombie fell down of its own accord, which, come to think of it, was a distinct possibility.

I gave my doppelganger one last elbow, then turned about and went marching off down the road.

Clomp.

A noise behind me.

Clomp. Clomp. Clomp.

Footfalls of the heavy variety. Had someone finally showed up to see who the firebug was? I spun about. No, it was the zombie, following behind me like a baby duck. I took another step and my walking carcass did the same. What was it that got through to the thing? Was it something I said? Had that little heart-to-heart triggered something in its walnut brain?

I didn't spend too long wondering. A splash of headlights from around the corner announced the arrival of the first paddy wagon, swiftly followed by the pulsing blue lights of a fire engine. I searched for the quickest escape route, eyes falling on a pedestrian side street that cut between a couple of nearby office buildings. A side street that conveniently led in the opposite direction of the emergency services, which were rounding the corner and applying their brakes.

'Go on then, shoot your chuff through there,' I told the zombie, and to my relief, it stepped into the side street as ordered, leading with its jaw.

It says a lot about my life that walking side-by-side with my own reanimated corpse might not be the strangest thing that's ever happened to me.

I shuffled off down the side street with my new companion in tow, and off we bled, into the night.

CHAPTER FIVE: A NEW HAUNT

By the time we left the rising column of smoke behind, the darkness was already beginning its surrender to the approaching dawn. I had to get the zombie off the streets before the new day broke and Camden woke up. At this time, we only had a few drunks and derelicts to deal with, but in an hour or so, the streets would be filling up with the rest of the borough's weird and wonderful denizens. There are tribes of people in Camden Town that you'd be hard-pressed to find anywhere else in the UK: original '80s punks, cyber goths, crusties, nu-metallers, and die-hard hippies. Name a fad and it died here. I'm not the only ghost in this town. Camden is a graveyard for things that should have perished a long time ago.

With the sun just cresting the horizon, I ushered the zombie around the rear of a boarded-up building. Wasting no time, I ghosted my way inside, unlocked the back door from the opposite side, and quickly escorted my shuffling companion indoors.

The building I'd broken us into was a place of business once, a funeral home that had since been shuttered. It wasn't my first time there; I paid the place a visit a while back. I was actually instrumental in seeing the building closed down. Trust me when I tell you the proprietor had it coming. The fact that his property was now vacant and made for a handy hideout is entirely coincidental.

We were in the back half of the building, the part that wouldn't have been on show to customers, and with good reason. Because this wasn't the proud, traditional kind of funeral home that had been handed down from generation to generation. There was no shiny black carriage parked out back, no immaculately-groomed black horses bedecked with tall plumes. This was a place that even the dead were too good for.

We pushed through the gloomy interior, cobwebs billowing in the draft caused by our arrival. The walls were flaking and spotted with continents of black mould. The ceiling sagged and bellied out. Hung from it was a forest of long, sticky fly traps, studded with dead bluebottles.

This would do for now. Hey, I've stayed in worse places. Actually, scratch that, this place was the pits.

The zombie followed me to a moth-eaten velvet curtain separating this part of the building from the front portion of the property where the bereaved would have made funeral arrangements with the now-departed undertaker.

'Ladies first,' I said, and the zombie shuffled hesitantly through the doorway.

We arrived in the showroom portion of the funeral home. Mint green wallpaper clung tenaciously to the walls, refusing to disengage despite the creeping damp beneath. Vases of dusty plastic flowers decorated the alcoves, and lacquered coffins sat on wooden trestles, thick with grime. Ever since I died, I've hated places like this. Hated the way our culture handles this part of the mortal process. Perish in the western world and your body will be whisked away from the place you died to a funeral home like this one. It all happens off stage, in private, because death is a distasteful thing, shameful even, and must be dealt with in secret. To a ghost, this comes as something of a slap in the face. It's one thing to be marooned on the physical plane, forced to exist alongside the living yet unable to be a part of their world, but it's another entirely to watch your earthly remains crammed into a casket and tucked away, out of sight and out of mind. Treated like something embarrassing, a dildo buried in the bottom of a dresser drawer, only remembered in passing.

Talking of only being remembered in passing...

I felt my phone buzzing and fished it out of my jacket pocket. The caller ID named the person on the other end of the line as DCI

Kat Stronge. Stone the crows. Now, there was a name I hadn't seen grace my screen in a while. Stronge was what we in the trade call an "Insider": a regular citizen who's aware of the Uncanny world and knows to keep it to themselves. It doesn't happen often. Most normals who take a walk on the wild side end up in a rubber room, but a few—a rare few—live to tell the tale. Stronge was one such rarity.

It wasn't so long ago that she'd been a regular fixture in my life. Sure enough, though, she'd gone the way of every other breather I knew. The two of us had worked together in a professional capacity for a while, long enough that I thought we'd developed a firm friendship, but the radio silence of the last couple of years had thoroughly disavowed me of that notion. Whatever our relationship was, it didn't extend beyond the job. If Stronge was calling, it was only because she needed my help with something, and right then, I wasn't feeling too charitable.

I hit the red X on my phone and declined the call.

'Wrong number,' I told my silent companion. No idea why.

I took a seat on an antique chair and cast a fresh look around the showroom. It was grimly fitting, I supposed, a ghost and a zombie haunting a funeral home. Although the irony of a former exorcist being forcibly expelled from a building did chap my arse a bit.

I looked to the zombie. 'So, what do you wanna do with the rest of eternity?' I asked.

Would he last that long? Would my body forever shamble around, a brain-hungry drone? Maybe Vic's magic would wear off at some point and I'd see my old body crumple to the floor, lifeless once more. Which would be better? Weirdly, I wasn't sure.

The zombie stood there, arms slack by its sides, saying nothing. I studied its waxy face, examining the features that used to be mine but had since fallen into disrepair. A powdering of dust coated its unblinking eyes, making my own itch in sympathy. Patches of hair were missing from the top of its head, leaving a scattering of pale mottled craters in its scalp. The ravages of decomposition hadn't all been negative, though; death had given my corpse a set of cheekbones that I hadn't seen since my teenage goth days.

Not that I'd have traded places with the feller. Being a ghost, I don't have a sense of smell, but I had to imagine the zombie reeked to high heaven. Speaking of which, why was there anything left of me to cause a stink? I was buried back when faux-hawks were still fashionable, shouldn't my carcass have been reduced to a skeleton by now? How long ago had Vic dug me up? Had he been keeping my body on ice this whole time, waiting for the day he saw fit to raise it from the dead and send it crashing into my unlife? I wouldn't put it past him. Vic Lords had always been a full 360 degrees wanker.

And yet this little stunt of his had the potential to backfire on him quite spectacularly. As far as Vic was concerned, his attack dog had gone up in smoke along with my office. Instead, it had saved its own skin and ended up here with me. With a bit of effort, perhaps I could tame the thing and boomerang it back in Vic's direction. Instead of sitting around waiting for him to show up on my doorstep again, making more demands, I could take the initiative and use the free ammunition he'd given me. Use it against him. Put that prick down once and for all.

If I could just make the body mine again.

I placed my palms on the zombie's shoulders and looked deep into its soulless eyes. 'Budge over and let me in,' I demanded.

I butted my forehead against its corporeal mirror image and willed my mind to penetrate the zombie's thick skull. Willed our minds to merge, to become a single entity, under my control. But to no avail. Try as I might, I couldn't gain access, couldn't break through to the other side. And the worst part? I could tell now, here in this safe haven, away from the wail of sirens, that I'd been wrong before. It wasn't Vic's magic keeping me out, and it had nothing to do with the fact that the creature I was trying to possess wasn't alive. The reason I couldn't get inside the zombie's head was simply because it didn't want to let me. I could feel it, deep in my gut. My own body was throwing up the velvet rope and telling me I wasn't welcome. Jesus. There's rejection, then there's *rejection*.

Still, it was probably for the best. I mean, who needs a body, anyway? What is it really but a packet for your ego? Plus, taking possession of a corpse is just a fancy way of saying "necromancy", and that's black magic; the blackest of the black. The kind that God took a very dim view on, and getting right with the Big Man was priority number one, no matter how tempting it might be to wrap a pair of rotting hands around Vic's throat.

Why do I care what God thinks?

Fair point.

Despite being an exorcist once—the kind of person you'd expect to see wearing a white collar and carrying a briefcase full of crucifixes—I was never the religious sort. I believed in a higher power, sure, but I didn't believe in any one god enough that I was prepared to worship them alone and piss off the other few thousand. Better to not play the game than to take that kind of gamble. Besides, it's not necessary to nail your colours to any one mast in order to have the faith required to rebuke unwelcome spirits. Faith comes in many flavours. There's faith in the Almighty, faith in totems, faith in yourself, any one of which, employed correctly, can be used to see off infernal invaders.

Except…

Well, as I discovered after I got put inside of a graveyard fence, us ghosts aren't all wrong-'uns. In fact, very few are. Technically speaking, most phantoms are nothing more than the detached souls of the dead clinging to a locality, waiting to transmigrate to the afterlife. For that to happen, the ghost has to be satisfied in some way. It might be that there's one final puzzle they need to solve; a riddle from life that needs figuring out before they can move on. More commonly, it's that the stranded spirit needs closure on their death before they can head Upstairs, which typically means finding out who killed them.

That's where I come in.

As a spectral detective—well, *the* Spectral Detective—I help my fellow phantoms answer the questions keeping them moored to the material plane and send them off to the Good Place. Why do I do that? I do it because I have a stink on my soul. Because I did some stuff in life that's left me trapped in this purgatory, and the only way I get my ticket to the Great Clubhouse in the Sky is by cleaning my slate and getting good with Him Upstairs.

What's this "stuff" I speak of? Blimey, you are just full of questions today, aren't you?

It all comes down to what I used to do for a living, back when I evicted spooks for lucre. Not that I thought there was anything wrong with that. An honest job for an honest wage, that was my thinking at the time (well, if you ignore the fact that I was taking my pay cheques from a Satanic gangster, which I certainly did). As far as I was concerned, I was doing the world a favour, relieving the living of their ghostly infestations while helping earthbound spirits find their way to the afterlife. In my mind, I was a working-class hero, a humanitarian exorcist, which, as it turns out, is sort of like describing yourself as a pacifist war criminal. Because, unbeknownst to me, I wasn't helping those earthbound spirits get anywhere. I was only helping them die. Die for good.

Instead of sending those poor buggers to their final reward, I had in fact been obliterating them. Wiping them off the map. Off *any* map. It wasn't until I died and became a ghost myself that I realised the truth of it. I was a killer. A serial killer. Sure, I could claim I didn't understand the consequences of what I was doing, but there had to be a price to pay for rubbing out that many innocents. So that's why I'm here, beating the mean streets of Camden as a phantom PI, saving souls the *right* way this time. Help enough wayward spirits and who knows, maybe I can farm enough karma to get right with God and earn my own final reward. That's the plan, anyway.

Now, some of you might be wondering why I want to clear my debt. I seem to have a life of sorts, why the rush to get to the Great Hereafter? Two reasons...

One: Every day I worry that this is gonna be *the* day. The day the folks Upstairs decide my time is up and come get me, ready or not. What if that happens and I still haven't evened out my balance sheet? Yeah. I go the other way. Downtown. And red really isn't my colour.

Two: Well, it's weird. Ever since I died I have this sort of… ache to move on. Not a physical ache—being a ghost I can't actually feel an ache—but one I just sort of sense. This need to step out of the physical plane at last and join the rest of my kind. A soul isn't meant to stay on Earth, it's meant to pass on, to be judged. Every day that goes by, the need to leave this mortal plane behind claws at me a little more. It's an itch I can never scratch. Can you imagine how torturous that is?

One day I'll be moving on, whether by choice or by force. I could only hope I was doing enough good in this world to keep me out of the Bad Place.

My companion shuffled from one foot to the other. 'Braaaains,' it droned.

I wondered what the Big Man would make of me hanging out with a flesh-eating zombie. Was this going to cost me Brownie points? Was I placing even more air miles between myself and the Promised Land? Then again, what else was I meant to do, given the circumstances? Turf the guy out on the street? Surely that was a bit "no room at the inn" for the bloke who dictated the Good Book.

'What am I going to do with you?' I asked the zombie absent-mindedly.

The creature's mouth hung open horribly, catching flies. Like, literally catching flies. Its decaying flesh was attracting them like mad. A couple strayed too close to the zombie's orbit, only to pay the ultimate price for invading its personal space.

I was caught in a bit of a pickle. Seeing my decomposing body shuffling around the place gave me a serious case of the heebie-jeebies. If I wasn't going to shove the zombie out of the back door, maybe I should find a way to lay my old bones to rest.

Then again…

There was this other part that wanted to find a way to make this mockery of me blow up in Vic's face. Wanted to see his eyes snap wide in surprise as my corpse tore him limb from limb.

Guess which side won that argument. Come hold me, sweet, sweet revenge.

If I was going to keep the zombie around, I needed to figure out a way to stop the rot and keep it from turning putrid, because the way it was going, it wouldn't be long before bits started dropping off the thing.

'Braaaiiins!'

'Yeah, yeah, I heard you the first time,' I shot back.

Typical. I go donkey's yonks without a decent conversation, and when someone finally does show up to talk to, he's got the vocabulary of Donald Trump. God, I missed a good chinwag. Being a dead man is a lonely business, particularly at night, when the living slumber and the seconds telescope into hours. We ghosts don't sleep; for us, life is one long, unending day. I'd have given just about anything for a decent, adult conversation. A talking zombie would have solved all of my problems. Is that really too much to ask, universe? Okay, I suppose it might be considered a bit narcissistic to spend hours literally talking to myself, but it would beat the endless evenings spent alone, waiting for the world to kick back into gear.

'Honestly, mate, it drives me mental,' I told the zombie, voicing my train of thought out loud. 'Sometimes I just wanna climb the walls...'

And that's when something entirely unexpected happened.

To my surprise, the zombie did a sloppy pirouette, marched off to the far end of the showroom, and began clawing frantically at the wall.

'What are you up to?'

At first I was just curious, then concern set in as chunks of wall began to rain down under the zombie's frenzied onslaught.

'Easy, tiger,' I cried, but the zombie continued unabated, throwing its feet into the mix, making the whole wall crumble and shake. 'You're gonna have the roof down on us, you nutter.'

I sprinted across the room in a bid to leap on the zombie's back and wrestle it to the ground, but before I could get there, the wall it was busy destroying came crashing down in an enormous cloud of brick dust. Out of habit, I waved my hand in front of my face to fan it away, but I needn't have bothered, it passed right through me. Finally, the dust settled and I surveyed the damage. The remains of the wall lay scattered across the floor, just chunks of broken mortar and plaster now.

'Bloody hell,' I said, giving the zombie a dig in the shoulder. 'Just as well that wasn't load-bearing, eh?'

That's when I noticed something through the opening it had created.

A small room.

A secret room.

'Well, well. What do we have here?'

CHAPTER SIX: DAYLIGHT ROBBERY

STUDYING THE WRECKED WALL CLOSER, I saw two lengths of twisted metal that would have acted as hidden runners, designed to allow the false portion of the wall to be slid to one side. No doubt if I sifted deeper through the rubble I'd have found a switch—a mechanism to release the secret door and open it into the concealed chamber—though doing so would have been the definition of pointless. The zombie had already made a perfectly effective entrance of its own.

'Not so useless after all,' I said, slapping my rotten doppelganger on the back and knocking a shower of red dust off its shoulders.

The zombie stood there, eyes glazed over, immune to my flattery. I shrugged and made my way inside.

The room was all but empty. What was it doing here? Seemed a bit sparse for a man cave. Except for a couple of bits of bric-a-brac, there really wasn't much to look at. Well, so long as you ignored the large, cube-shaped object propped against the chamber's far wall and draped with a thick sheet.

I yanked off the cover, whipping up a swirling, grey blur of dust. Beneath, I found a heavy-duty combination safe that looked to be at least a hundred years old, maybe two. This was no man cave. This was a vault.

'Interesting,' I said, patting the top of the safe and finding it solid to my touch.

The box was painted jet black and sported a large brass handle. I looked for a nameplate so I could determine the brand of the safe, but this wasn't the kind you bought off the peg. This was a custom build, constructed by a locksmith with knowledge of the arcane. The kind that would be entirely uncrackable to a common thief.

I examined it closer. The safe's combination dial was surrounded not by numbers, but by squiggly little symbols that most would have dismissed as scribbles. Not me, though. I recognised them as a mixture of runes and glyphs.

'*Very* interesting,' I told my silent companion.

The undertaker the funeral home belonged to before I broke in wasn't your regular Joe, so it came as no big surprise that he kept his valuables secure using unconventional means. Unconventional, but pointless.

I placed a hand on the combination dial and played it like Chopin at the symphony, fingers dancing, spinning it this way and that as I whispered an invocation of unlocking. Within seconds, I hit the sweet spot and heard a telltale click as the safe's inner wheels snapped into place, disengaging the lock.

'Open Sesame.'

It's called kleptomancy in case you were wondering, or robbing magic to the uninitiated. Like Vic said, I'm pretty good at getting into places I'm not supposed to.

I pulled the safe's brass handle counterclockwise and swung open its heavy iron door. Inside, I found cash, wads of the stuff, the sum of the undertaker's ill-gotten gains.

'Happy days.'

You might be wondering what use a ghost has for money, what with us not requiring even the basic necessities in life. It's true that, for the most part, the dead have no use for cash. We don't need food or shelter, and when it comes to the rest of life's little annoyances—settling bills, paying taxes, chipping in for Debbie in Accounting's retirement present—we find ourselves blessedly unburdened of responsibility. That said, it never hurts to have a few sheets going handy, especially when your new lodgings look like they're about to fall down around your ears.

I heard a noise from over my shoulder and turned to see the zombie shuffling around in the rubble. In all the excitement, I'd almost forgotten how I'd come to find the hidden safe in the first place. Hm. What had gotten into that big lug? One minute we were having a very one-sided conversation, the next he was tearing down—

Wait...

Climb the walls. That's what I said. That was the trigger. I spoke those words and the zombie did just that. It wasn't trying to bring the wall down, it was attempting—in its own, heavy-handed way—to scale the thing. It was doing what I'd told it. Obeying my instructions. To the letter.

'I wonder...' I snapped my fingers and the zombie twisted my way. 'Do something,' I told it.

The zombie blinked at me slowly, drawbridge-mouthed.

I was going to need to be more specific.

'Okay then, do the Macarena,' I commanded.

Without hesitating, the zombie began shaking its hips and swinging its arms, palms down, palms up, jumps from side to side, the whole horrible routine. Interesting. Somewhere, lodged in that creature's head, was an ill-fated university summer ball I'd ironically attended. So ironically that I'd learned every step of Los Del Rio's hit song, and remembered it even after I took the big nap. At least some of my old memories were still lodged inside my physical brain. That was a weird thought. What are you if not your accumulated memories? Could this rotting puppet really have some broken-down version of me rattling around inside it? I wasn't sure how comfortable I was with that idea. Best to try and forget it altogether.

'That's enough,' I told the zombie, and it stopped dancing.

I thought persuading it to follow me from the blaze had been a one-off, but apparently not. This situation had some real potential. I didn't need to possess the thing, after all, I could just click my fingers and tell it what I wanted. Vic had it coming now. Oh yes. Thanks to him, I had a henchman, a cooperating corpse, able to bust through walls and throttle my enemies at will. A whole new world had opened up to me. After years of being a ghostly apparition, I had a ready pair of hands to handle the physical stuff that I found so challenging. My own personal muscle. The mind boggled with possibilities. Horrible, bloody possibilities.

I noticed something slim and white lying among the red rubble. Wait, what was that? Was that… a human finger? I cut a glance to the zombie, only to find it missing a digit from its left hand. Just a ragged stump remained where its pinky should have been. It must have torn a finger off when it clawed down the wall. Jesus. When I said I was worried about bits dropping off the thing, I wasn't expecting it to happen this soon.

'You silly sod,' I muttered.

The zombie didn't seem to mind, though. Its blood spattered the floor, a dark red stain, almost black, but the old dog wasn't barking about it. Then again, my body had suffered far worse before now. Last time I saw it in the flesh—before it was raised from the dead—it was lying on a mortuary slab in four separate chunks. Yeah, mine wasn't exactly a gentle death. It's a wonder they managed to make me presentable for the funeral at all, considering, but then morticians can work wonders these days. The things they can do with pickle and paint.

I scratched my chin. If a pro could fix a mess like that, surely I could bodge one little finger? I looked around for something I could use to reattach the severed digit—a needle and thread, a staple gun, some Gaffer tape—but nothing presented itself. What a ball-ache. I thought I'd gained a henchman, but here I was stuck playing nurse. So far, this revenge idea of mine was turning out to be a right load of old bobbins.

A buzzer sounded, cleaving through the silence like a cheesed-off rattlesnake.

'What the hell…?'

The buzzer sounded again, a long blast this time, as if someone were holding their finger down on the doorbell. Who could that be? The funeral home had been closed for months, and even in its heyday, I couldn't imagine anyone showing up shopping for caskets at the crack of dawn.

Buzz.

Maybe it was a couple of Jehovah's Witnesses. A couple of early bird Jehovah's Witnesses. A really persistent, early bird, couple of Jehovah's Witnesses.

Yeah, I wasn't convinced either. After all, there's really only one person it could have been. Vic Lords. Who else? Who else but Vic had the power to shine a light into my hidey-hole? Who else but the monkey that had been riding my back since the day I died?

He must have followed me somehow. Probably tracked me here magically; extended his psychic tendrils all over town until one groped its way into my lair. Christ, that man really was the patient zero of arseholes.

No doubt he'd come to press his job offer on me again. I wondered what he was going to do to try and persuade me this time. Who had he dug up and reanimated now? Father Ryan from the seminary? My junior school headmaster?

Another stab of the buzzer.

I nodded to the zombie and then to one of the caskets. 'Get in,' I told it. 'Quickly.'

The zombie climbed inside the box as ordered, and I closed the lid behind it. There was a chance that Vic didn't know the zombie was still in play, and if that was the case, I very much intended for it to stay that way.

Buzz.

I rushed back to the secret room, threw the sheet over the safe, and set a vase of plastic carnations on it, disguising it as a table. Okay, enough tarting about, time to say hello to my visitor. I marched out of the showroom, across the lobby, and stuck my head through the building's exterior wall so I could get a look.

It wasn't Vic.

'Hello, Fletcher,' said DCI Kat Stronge.

CHAPTER SEVEN: PAST LIFE

STRONGE STOOD ON MY DOORSTEP, arms folded, hip cocked. As usual, she wore a sharp Mary Quant bob, a pair of impressive shoulder pads, and the kind of face that made her look like she was in the process of doing kegels.

'Well, aren't you going to invite me in?' she asked.

Stronge had The Sight, so she had no problem seeing ghosts. Since making my acquaintance, she'd witnessed things that had opened her eyes to the weirder world, and yet, where most would have crumbled, Stronge came back twice as tough. The woman was formidable. A real spitfire.

'I wasn't expecting company,' I said.

'I called but you didn't pick up.'

I felt like giving her an earful. I mean, how dare she give me the cold shoulder for months on end, only to come knocking the moment she needs my help. The neck on her.

Then again, this was hardly the time to get into a row. The last thing I needed was a rozzer snooping about the place when I had a zombie on the premises. There weren't many cops who'd put up with someone keeping a flesh-eating monster for a pet, and Stronge had always been a by-the-book sort. Better to fob her off and send her on her way, that's what I figured.

'Come on Jake, can we just go inside?'

Try as I might, I couldn't think of a reason to say no. I just had to hope I could keep her away from the showroom. Away from the coffin with the killer zombie in it.

I opened the front door.

Stronge stepped through into the lobby and cast a wary eye about the place. 'So, this is new.'

'How did you know to find me here?' I asked.

'I'm a detective, it's my job to know.'

I arched an eyebrow at her.

'Okay, your frozen tramp told me,' she admitted.

Ah, Frosty.

Frosty was a ghost I knew; my informant, my man on the street. Like, literally on the street. Since the day he died, Frosty's been stuck to a patch of pavement like a tongue to a frozen lamp post. He was homeless at the time, and a cold snap took him one winter's night. Froze him through so bad they say it took three days to thaw out his body. Poor bastard.

'So what brings you to my door?' I asked Stronge. 'Don't tell me, you wanted to snap a selfie with the city's greatest detective. Sorry, you're out of luck, luv. I don't show up in photos.'

I was putting a brave face on it, but inside I was sweating bullets. The longer Stronge stayed, the sooner she'd notice something was up. She was an understanding woman, sympathetic to my situation and aware of the weird waters I swam in, but keeping a brain-hungry walking cadaver under my roof would take some explaining. Even if I could convince her that Vic Lords had revived the zombie to hassle me, there'd be no convincing her that it wasn't a menace to society. It tried to take a bite out of a ghost for Christ's sake, what was it going to do if it caught a sniff of a breather? What would it do if it smelled *her*? That dumb bastard would have Stronge's brain out with an ice cream scoop, or get its skull bashed in for trying. No, I had to keep the two of them apart while I figured out how to bring this meeting to a swift close.

'Don't I get a tour of the place?' she asked.

Perfect. Just perfect. Of all the lousy times for Stronge to walk back into my life, why now?

I shrugged like I was absolutely fine showing a police officer around my zombie-infested squat. 'Whatever floats your boat.'

And off we went. I made sure to keep Stronge in the front portion of the building, well away from the showroom. As I hustled her through, I pointed into various dilapidated side rooms: a toilet, a waiting area, a cluttered office. It was a real whistle-stop tour.

'So what do you think of the new digs?' I asked.

'They're, um... interesting,' she replied.

'What are you saying? You don't like the feng shui of the place?'

'I'm just saying you could use a decorator. Or a flamethrower. Talking of which, care to share what happened to your old digs?'

Jesus, it's hard keeping secrets from a copper.

'That fire was nothing to do with me.'

Stronge regarded me cooly.

'Well, it was *something* to do with me, but it wasn't my fault. Honest injun.'

She took in my new gaff. 'A burnt-out husk might actually beat this place, you know.'

I plucked a piece of loose wallpaper from the hallway wall. 'Give me a chance, I only just hung up my hat. A couple of weeks and I'll have this place looking cushdy, trust me.' I thought of all the money sat in the safe next door and my brain lit up. 'I'm going to turn this mouldy old pit into an office, that's what I'm going to do. A premium PI agency.' I pointed inside the cluttered box room the previous occupant had been using for a workspace. 'Picture it, Kat: Venetian blinds on the windows, an open bottle of Bushmills on my desk—just for the look—and right there, on the door, frosted-glass with my name stencilled on it. '

She bit down on the edge of a smile. 'Yeah, I can see it now: Jake Fletcher, Dead Dick.'

'Don't say it like that.'

'What?'

'Dick.'

'Why not? It's short for detective.'

'Yeah, but it doesn't exactly sound flattering the way you say it.'

She laughed and I felt my blood run hot. Suddenly, I'd forgotten all about the zombie playing Jack-in-the-box next door. 'Remind me again how many murders I've helped you solve, Kat,' I said. 'Are we talking double or triple figures now? Seriously, if I had to carry you any more I'd be wearing you in a papoose.'

She folded her arms. 'You've given me some tip-offs and I'm grateful for it, but come on, Fletcher, you can't be serious about making a business out of this. You haven't paid your dues. You're a chancer, not a PI.'

'Are you serious? I'm the Spectral Detective. That's my whole thing!'

'You can't just flip a switch and decide you're a detective. You think that's what I did? I worked hard to get where I am. Twice as hard as any man. I've got certificates on my office wall, Jake, not mould.' She rapped a patch of damp plaster and left a dimple in it.

'Well, it's been lovely seeing you, Kat,' I sighed, gesturing back the way she came. 'Maybe you can pop by in a few months and tell me some more about how shit I am.'

Instead of doing the polite thing and fucking right off, she stood on her tiptoes, craning over my shoulder and squinting in the direction of the showroom.

'What's through there?' she asked.

'Nothing.'

'Come on, I can tell there's more to see. Aren't you going to finish the tour?'

'That's just the back end of the building,' I replied. 'If you think this part's bad, you don't want to see the arse of the place.'

'Go on, show me. Unless you're hiding something. Something you don't want me to see...'

The woman was a dog with a bone. Much as I hated to admit it, she knew her job. DCI Stronge had detective running through her like the words in a stick of Brighton rock.

'Okay then, let's get this over with,' I groaned. 'Step lively.'

A quick squiz at the showroom to satisfy her curiosity, keep her away from the occupied coffin, and send her on her way. Bish bash bosh, nothing to worry about. So why were the alarm bells in my head ringing like Chinese gongs?

'Wow,' she said, clapping her eyes on the room with all the caskets. 'A spook haunting a funeral home, eh? Bit on the nose, isn't it?'

I shrugged. 'It was this or the ghost train at the funfair.'

Stronge stepped deeper into the showroom, moving slowly, her sharp eyes drinking in every detail. I tried not to glance at the coffin with the zombie in it. Tried not to raise any suspicions. I just had to pray Stronge didn't stray too close to it and wake the dog in its kennel.

'What happened here?' she asked, nudging the rubble of the collapsed wall with her toe.

'Oh, that. Thought I'd get started on the decorating early and knock that wall through, open the place up a bit. Give it some flow.'

'I see,' she said. 'And how does a ghost do that exactly?'

'You know me, Kat, if there's one thing I'm good at, it's ruining things.'

Her eyes searched my face. 'Right.'

It was as though she were looking directly into my soul, which, given that I don't have a shell to contain the thing, was technically correct. My eyes sank to the ground to avoid Stronge's gaze, and caught sight of the zombie's severed finger lying amongst the rubble.

Shit the bed.

I firmed up my foot and gave the appendage a swift boot, kicking it to the other side of the room where it disappeared under a wooden trestle. I looked back up at Kat, who thankfully remained oblivious to my subterfuge. Unfortunately, the reason she remained that way was because she was busy across the room, inspecting the casket with the zombie in it.

There were those gongs again.

Stronge stroked a stripe of dust from the coffin lid. 'You taken a look in this thing yet?'

I examined my cuticles. 'Yeah. Nasty vampire in there. A real biter. I'd steer clear if I were you.'

Stronge scratched her chin. 'I've never seen the inside of a coffin before. Not in real life.' She tapped a fingernail on the casket's blank brass plaque. 'Mind if I have a gander?'

'Maybe another time. I've gotta get cracking. Need to see a man about a dog.'

'Don't I get a brew before I go?'

'Sorry, I'd love to make you a cuppa, but I don't have a kettle. Or electricity. Or a body.'

I placed a hand on her shoulder in a bid to steer her to the front door, but she remained steadfast.

'What's the matter, Fletcher?' she asked semi-jokingly, patting the lid of the coffin. 'You're not keeping a dead body in there, are you?'

I laughed, accidentally pitching my voice just a little too high.

Stronge clocked my nervousness and her muscles tightened. Her eyes narrowed and tracked around the room before settling on something at her feet. There on the ground, sat upon the brick dust like wet rubies, were droplets of blood. Apparently, the severed finger wasn't the only evidence I needed to dispose of.

'Is that…?' Something in Stronge's head clicked into place and she took a couple of steps backwards, her hand instinctively reaching for the hip she kept her Taser on and placing a finger on the holster's quick-release buckle.

'What are you doing? Are you off your rocker?'

What she thought she was going to achieve by shooting at a ghost I had no idea, but then that wasn't my main concern. Of much greater importance was the fact that she was crouching down, dabbing at the blood, and rubbing it between her fingertips.

'Bit of rusty water, I reckon,' I said, faking a chuckle.

Stronge was less than convinced. 'That's not what this is,' she said, her weapon hand not straying from the Taser. 'What did you do, Jake?'

She took a step toward the casket.

The jig was up. The coffin was about to be opened, its secrets revealed. Stronge was going to flip that lid, and then, when she saw what was inside, flip her own. I had no idea what would happen when she clapped eyes on the walking corpse I was hiding, but chances were someone was leaving this place with less brains than they came in with.

I took a step between Stronge and the coffin. 'Let's talk about this, Kat…'

With a practised snap of her fingers, she flicked the release buckle off the holster and placed a hand on the Taser's grip. 'Get out of my way. Right now.'

I stayed where I was, barring her progress. 'No.'

I didn't present much of an obstacle. Stronge marched right through me, giving my eyeballs the full Grey's Anatomy of her insides.

'Stay there,' she demanded, drawing the Taser.

'Unless that's a magic stun gun you're carrying, this whole stand-off is a bit theoretical. Can we please just sit down and have a civil conversation?'

But I could tell she wasn't going to back down. Not now she'd literally smelled blood.

'Kat, please—'

With her eyes fixed firmly on mine, she reached for the casket and heaved the lid off with one sharp shove—

Only to find the coffin empty.

I don't know which of us was more surprised.

'Oh...' Kat mumbled, trailing off.

I stared at the casket's white satin lining in disbelief. 'There. Happy now?' I spluttered, wondering what in the name of Christ had happened to my reanimated cadaver.

That's when I noticed a breeze rustling the velvet curtain that led to the rear of the building and realised the back door was open. The zombie must have made itself scarce while I was busy chit-chatting with Stronge in the hallway. Go on, my son!

Except...

Now there was a zombie on the loose, rampaging freely around the streets of Camden. Not good. A real mess. A total omnishambles, if I'm honest.

But then, I wasn't the only one who'd made a cock-up today.

Stronge holstered her weapon. 'I really thought that was blood. This job... it can get to you.'

'Don't worry about it,' I said, brushing it off. 'Could have happened to anyone.'

She stared at the blood on her finger, confounded and embarrassed.

'Okay then,' I chirruped, clapping my hands together and giving them a brisk rub, 'I really do have to get going now, so if you don't mind...'

'That's okay,' Stronge replied, 'we can talk on the move.'

'Talk about what?'

'The homicide we just caught.'

A new case to crack. A soul to save. On any other day I'd have been chuffed to bits, but not this time.

'So let me get this straight,' I said, 'you show up uninvited, draw your gun on me, and now you want my help?'

'That's right,' she replied.

'*My* help? The chancer? The dead dick?'

Stronge offered an uneasy smile. 'Any port in a storm.'

CHAPTER EIGHT: I AIN'T GOT NOBODY

I TOLD Stronge I didn't have time for a side gig. That I had work of my own to do. Pressing business I needed to be getting on with that I couldn't put off any longer. Obviously, I didn't tell her that the business I was referring to involved tracking down an escaped zombie before it sank its teeth into a member of the public. Some things are better left unsaid, I reckon.

'What is it you're working on exactly?' she asked.

'There's a reason they call it "private" investigator, Kat.'

'Well, whatever it is, drop it. This is the job now.'

'What do you need me for? You can see ghosts, just ask the vic who did the deed and bring them in.'

'That's the problem,' Stronge replied. 'There is no ghost.'

That was indeed a problem. A rare one, too.

'Look, Kat, I'm sorry, but I just can't spare the time. You're on your own with this one.'

Her hands slapped against her hips. 'Either you come with me right now or I have this place of yours bulldozed. Trust me, I know people in Building Control who'd have this rathole torn down in a second.'

Could she do that? I wouldn't have put it past her, the woman definitely had clout. Saying no to her presented a real dilemma. If she was able to have this place demolished, I'd have nowhere to hide the zombie (assuming I managed to find the thing before she did). I had no choice but to play along. Somehow, I needed to fool Stronge into thinking that she had my undivided attention, and at the same time stop Camden Town from turning into a George Romero film.

'Okay, I'll do it,' I said, a plan already forming in my head.

'It's nice that you think you had a choice.'

I fell in step with her as she marched from the front of the building, heading in the direction of her car. 'Of course, I'll need my meat suit,' I added.

'What?'

'If we're visiting a crime scene, I'll need a body.'

A borrowed physical form that I could use to attend the murder site in three full dimensions.

'We don't have time,' Stronge fired back.

'Give me half an hour, tops. Unless you don't mind me playing backseat driver...'

We'd done it before on a previous case; me standing invisibly off to one side, yapping in her ear like the off-camera producer of a daytime chat show. Needless to say, it had not gone well.

'Okay, go get your man,' she told me, 'his mug's nicer to look at anyway.'

Stronge gave me the address of the crime scene, then I gave her the old cockney wink and left her for dust, warping away to a new location.

I wasn't really on the scrounge for a meat suit, though. Not yet. Not until my wandering cadaver was hunted down and locked up good and tight. I'd help Kat with her case, sure, but the corpse she was looking out for was already cold. Unless I intervened, my corpse was likely to create a fresh one.

Bleedin' Aida. I've heard of chasing your own tail, but this was ridiculous.

I reappeared a short distance away, just around the back of the funeral home. I needed to pick up the zombie's trail, and since I knew that this was the way it had exited the building, this would be my starting point. I surveyed the scene. I'm no tracker, but the trail of destruction the shambling lout had left in its wake was easy enough to follow, starting with a flattened fence that led through to Eversholt Street. The next clue I happened across was a crashed car, which had veered off the main road, most likely in an effort to dodge the zombie as it lumbered through traffic. The dazed driver had climbed out of the vehicle and was pointing off into the distance, no doubt after the figure that had caused the accident.

I focused on the area he was indicating to—a traffic intersection up ahead—and translocated there, closing the distance in a cocaine heartbeat. My sudden arrival went unnoticed by the people walking the high street, but upset a flock of pigeons feeding from an overflowing bin, sending the panicked birds flapping into the air and circling the nearby statue of Lord Cobden. I scanned my surroundings, looking for the next breadcrumb, but the path had gone cold. The zombie was nowhere to be seen.

A gruff voice barked at me. 'Am I seeing double, Fletcher, or is this the second time you've gone tearing down this street?'

I spun about to see Frosty—the dead dosser who told DCI Stronge about my new gaff—frozen to the pavement on his permanent spot under the cash machine in front of the mini-Sainsbury's. The patch of pavement he called his living room. I'd forgotten how close the funeral home was to his final resting spot.

As ever, Frosty looked as though he'd spent a week trapped inside a fridge freezer. Icicles clung to his whiskers and his skin had the pallor of old meat dipped in a bath of liquid nitrogen. He wore a pair of ripped jeans, but out of necessity, not because they were fashionable. Atop his head, he wore a tattered fisherman's beanie that was more hole than wool.

'Where did he go?' I asked. 'The zombie.'

'Don't know what you're talking about,' he said, obviously lying. Obvious because there's nothing that goes on in the NW1 postcode that Frosty isn't au fait with.

Contrary to what you might expect, being sat in the same spot day in day out hadn't made old Frost ignorant. Far from it. For reasons none of us understands, Frosty came back from the dead with a unique ability: the power to know everything that goes on in this borough the second it happens. Dying took away his freedom, but it turned him into Camden's own oracle. I'm telling you, if there was a way to unstick him from the pavement and drag him to a pub quiz, you'd clean up.

'Come on, Frost, I don't have time for the frenemy shit today. Tell me where he went or someone's going to get hurt.'

He laughed and coughed up a wad of phlegm, discharging it on the pavement. 'Chasing zombies, eh? What have you gotten yourself into this time, Fletch?'

The globule of ectoplasm slithered downhill like a fat green slug. I lifted a foot to let it roll beneath the sole of my brogue. 'Frosty, please. Be a mate and show a bit of professional courtesy, eh?'

He wasn't biting. I cast out another line.

'Come on, what's the world coming to when even the dead won't help each other out?'

A deep trench appeared in his forehead. 'Might know something. Depends whether you've got anything for me. Maybe a little breakfast sharpener to jog my memory.'

Frosty and me had a long-standing deal: he gave me gossip, and in return, I gave him booze. It's a game we've played for many a year. So long as I brought along the odd can of bruiser juice, Frosty was only too happy to share his secrets.

I patted down my pockets. 'I don't have anything on me. Not right now.'

'Shame,' he replied, folding his arms and pursing his frostbitten lips.

I doubled down. 'Just point the way and I'll come back here with so many tins you'll die for good this time.'

'Pfft. Chance would be a fine thing.'

I crouched down beside him, palms pressed together, my face a mask of pure earnestness. So earnest that if anyone walking the street had been able to see us, they'd probably have mistaken the gesture for a marriage proposal. 'Frost, I'm begging you. Lives are at stake here. Real lives.'

He let forth a long, gusty sigh, raised an arm, and aimed a feculent fingernail in the direction of Hampstead Road. 'There.'

'Cheers, pal,' I said, jogging away. 'I'll be back later with those cans.'

'Get fucked, Fletcher.'

'Thanks, mate, I knew I could count on you.'

And off I went. The zombie couldn't have gone far. Even taking into account the time I'd wasted bickering with Stronge and Frosty, it could only cover so much ground moving at the speed it did. I just had to find that dumb mutt, slap a leash on it, and drag it back to the funeral home before anyone got too familiar with the thing. It looked human. Human enough. So long as no one got a real close gander, there was a chance that I could put the genie back in the bottle. Unless that brain-hungry monster took a chomp out of someone first. Then all bets were off.

I rounded Mornington Crescent Station and found a *Big Issue* seller staring at a mangled hole in the railings of the fence surrounding Harrington Square Gardens, an impoverished scrap of nature tucked into the urban sprawl. There, at the improvised entrance leading into the park, I saw leaden footprints punched into the lawn that could only have belonged to my quarry. I looked up and saw figures off in the distance, obscured by the early morning mist, their voices raised but unintelligible.

'Please don't tell me he killed someone,' I muttered to myself before jumping to the scene of the disturbance.

What I found there wasn't what I was expecting. Not one bit. Four young men had gathered around my zombie likeness—four men in hoodies—surrounding him on all sides. One of them had a flick knife.

'Oh shit.'

The zombie looked to each of the muggers in turn, a dumb look on its face as it slowly dawned on its dimwitted brain that it was trapped.

'Give us your fucking wallet,' demanded the hoodie with the cutter.

'And your phone,' said another.

All at once, my sympathies switched. These fellers weren't victims. They weren't innocent bystanders about to be set upon by a bloodthirsty monster. They were shark-eyed robbers who deserved everything coming their way.

'Are you deaf, blud?' asked one of the hoodies, barging the zombie with his chest.

'What the fuck's wrong with you?' asked another, giving it a shove from behind. 'You on bath salts, mate?'

'He smells rank,' said the one with the knife, putting a sleeve to his nose. 'You a fucking tramp, bruv?'

This was liable to turn ugly fast. I waded in, waving my arms about and shouting, trying to break them up, and in doing so, briefly forgot I was a ghost. Unless one of them happened to have The Sight, which they didn't, I was stuck doing an invisible man impression for an audience of none.

The youths hassled the zombie some more, laughing and knocking him about like an undead pinball. One of them gave it a kick in the back of the knees, flooring the thing, then all four gathered around to put the boot in.

'Leave it out,' I yelled impotently.

The hoodies continued to batter away, adding punches to the mix, until finally the zombie let out a mournful roar, grabbed one by the shoulders, and hoisted him off his feet. The zombie screamed in his attacker's face, eyes wide, spittle flying.

'Get 'im, Ty!' cried the terrified teenager.

The kid with the flick knife lunged in from behind, sinking his blade into the zombie's back. By way of a thank you, the zombie dropped the teenager it was holding, grabbed Stabby by the throat, and took a nice big bite out of his cheek.

Christ.

By this point, the other three were away on their toes. The one missing a portion of his face was quick to follow, palm pressed to his cheek hole, leaving agonised screams in his wake.

The zombie tilted its head in my direction and offered a lopsided smile, a blood goatee on its chin. It gnawed on the cheek meat like a cow chewing cud, jaw moving from side to side.

'Oi, spit that out,' I cried.

The zombie hung its head and gobbed the flap of cheek on the grass like a naughty schoolboy being made to give up his bubble gum.

I wagged a finger at it. 'We don't eat people, okay? Got that? That's rule number one.'

The zombie nodded sorrowfully.

This really was all a bit of a mind fuck. That was me, my body, taking chunks out of people. The only way to try and wrap my head around it was to keep reminding myself that this was Vic's doing. Access to a few memories or not, I wasn't in there. This was an empty corpse. A zombie; nothing more. No part of me was hungry for human flesh. And yet still, looking at my own face with another man's blood dribbling down its chin… it gave me the collywobbles.

'You realise you probably just cost me a bunch of Brownie points, don't you?' I groused, shaking my head as I imagined my ladder to the Promised Land losing another set of rungs. 'Bang goes my retirement plan.'

The zombie's head hung low, eyes dipped to its feet.

'What am I going to do with you, eh? Get you chipped like the bloody family dog?'

Except… well, I could hardly blame the poor sod for wanting to stretch its legs a bit, could I? I wouldn't fancy being stuck in a casket either. Obviously. I mean, show me a ghost who does.

'If you've started a zombie epidemic I'm going to be so annoyed with you.'

I firmed up my hand, plucked the knife from its back, and tossed it into a nearby bin.

'Braiiiins,' moaned the zombie.

'Yeah, yeah, that's your answer for everything.'

CHAPTER NINE: BEEF SLEEVE

'STAY,' I told the zombie. 'Good boy.'

It was really more of a demand than a request, what with the fact I'd handcuffed the thing to the cast-iron radiator in the funeral home's dilapidated bathroom.

I was late meeting DCI Stronge at the crime scene, so in terms of security, this was going to have to do for the minute. Given time, I'd come up with a better solution for keeping my rotten runaway indoors, but for now, I was satisfied that the manacles would keep it from going AWOL any time soon.

The homicide job was important, and not just to Stronge. If I could bring the victim's killer to justice, maybe I could win back some points with the Big Man. That would be a real coup. I'd just been responsible for a zombie taking a bite out of one of His flock, so my halo could definitely use a polish. Yeah, this case had the potential of being a real win-win.

But first I had to get that body.

Mark Ryan was my go-to guy whenever I needed a physical form to possess. So long as I was working with the boys in blue, it was Mark's face I wore, his mitt that made the handshakes. Not that he knew it. Even though I'd borrowed his bones a thousand times, Mark had no idea that he was my meat suit. My skin sock. My human glove puppet.

Now, you might think picking on one particular bloke every time

I had a public appearance to make was a bit out of order, and in some ways, you'd be right. After all, I was enslaving a living person to further my own selfish needs, wasn't I? Well, no, not exactly. That might be the clickbait headline, but the truth was a little more nuanced. To put it simply, Mark Ryan had it coming, and then some. Why? To understand the reason I felt justified using Mark as my mule, you'll need to know the long and storied history I have with the geezer. So here goes...

Me and Mark went way back; all the way to our school days. We weren't friends. Far from it. For three long years, week in, week out, he was my bully. My personal tormentor. Back then he made my life a living hell—the kind that left scars, some mental, some physical—so these days, whenever I needed a living body, he was my weapon of choice.

Sometimes, I'd feel a twinge of guilt about carting him off without his permission and putting him in harm's way, but not often. I mean, didn't Mark deserve some retribution for the way he treated me back then? Wasn't he owed some payback? Why should I be the only one subject to the laws of karma?

It wasn't hard to find Mark. It never was. I've been inside his body so many times since I died that I've developed a sort of... well, let's just call it a link. Wherever he is, no matter how far or how deep he goes, I can home in on him. Not that I really need a psychic bond to find the berk, what with him Instagramming his whereabouts every mealtime.

I found him in a Soho strip club. Of course, I did. It had only just gone half ten in the morning—they hadn't even brought out the breakfast buffet yet—and yet there he was, watching a bit of crumpet with an epic prow perform aerial yoga on a greasy metal pole.

I guess this was his day off. Mark was a hedge fund manager by profession: a corporate wraith who contributed nothing to society and sent most of what he made up his soon-to-be-collapsed snout. Like most bullies, Mark was a shitty kid who turned into an even shittier adult.

I watched him from across the club as Def Leppard's *Pour Some Sugar On Me* shook the speakers. He had the collar of his pin-striped suit popped and wore a pair of Prada sunglasses. Indoors. He'd styled his hair into a man bun today, which I knew for a fact was nothing more than a futile bid to disguise a rapidly-developing bald patch.

The club was almost deserted at this hour, but the emptiness wasn't blunting Mark's enthusiasm any. He sat right by the stage, straddling the back part of his chair like a football manager giving his team a half-time pep talk. In one hand he held a sloshing JD and Coke, in the other he waved a folded tenner, pointed in the direction of the dancing girl.

'Hey, you,' he brayed. 'C'mere.'

At this point, can we all agree that me making use of Mark's worthless hide was not only justified but worthy of applause? I mean, seriously, has the phrase, "Life is wasted on the living" ever been more appropriate than when describing Mark frigging Ryan?

The dancer slid off the pole and moved haltingly in Mark's direction. He tucked the note into her g-string and beckoned her ear to his mouth.

'Don't worry, I won't bite,' he yelled over the din.

I moved in closer and watched as the dancer reluctantly dropped to her haunches and settled into a crouch. 'What do you want?'

'Give me your digits and there's another tenner coming your way,' he told her.

This guy. Did he really think twenty quid was going to persuade that poor woman to let him throw a dick in her? Honestly, you could die a death falling from the bloke's arrogance and landing on his IQ.

'Piss off,' said the dancer. She did a sharp heel turn, making a squeak that set my teeth on edge. 'Wanker.'

'Hey, I'm sorry, okay?' Mark blurted as she strutted away and slipped through a curtain backstage. 'Okay, fine, be a bitch, see if I care.'

Nice. A real tabloid newspaper apology, there; written in small print and buried in the footer of page twenty-two.

But our boy wasn't done yet.

A waitress came over to his table and gave him a nod. 'Can I tap that?' she asked.

Mark looked her up and down, evidently liking what he saw. 'Play your cards right and maybe you can,' he replied.

The unsmiling waitress gave him the kind of look that leaves a mark. She produced a card reader from behind her back and nodded to his wallet, which lay on the table beside him. 'I meant can I tap your card? With the machine. So you can pay for your drinks and go.'

It was painfully obvious to everyone but Mark that he had grossly outstayed his welcome. Right on cue, I saw a bouncer made of gristle and fists start in the direction of the disturbance, cracking his knuckles as he went.

If Mark carried on the way he was going, he was taking a trip to the hospital. Was there ever a more deserving patient, you might wonder, and you'd get no argument from me if you did. Quite honestly, I feel roughly the same amount of affection for Mark as a bomb disposal officer might his remote-controlled robot. Except, like that same officer, I know the robot, used correctly, has the power to do good. To save lives. So, much as I'd have liked to, I wasn't going to stand by and let Mark get his brains kicked in just for being a dickhead.

Was I?

Sigh.

No.

I surged forward and seized control of Mark's body. It wasn't hard. Even if the bloke had wanted to fight me, he'd have been onto a loser. After all, you know what they say: *possession* is nine-tenths of the law. Ha, I kill me (not literally, of course, someone already beat me to that).

Mark's senses fused with mine, sending a barrage of signals my way in a great, heady rush. I tasted bourbon on his tongue and felt the dull throb of last night's hangover prodding at his brain meat. Through his half-caved nostrils, I caught the first whiff of my surroundings: stripper sweat mixed with the smell of stale beer, hoppy and sour and cut through with a janitor's cheap detergent. Most of the time, I consider these rare moments of having a corporeal form a blessing. On this occasion, not so much.

Having fully taken possession of Mark, I stood up, swiped his wallet off the table, and settled the bill with his personal credit card (not the company one). With that done, I smiled warmly, pulled out every note he had, and handed the whole mess to the waitress.

'That's for you,' I said. 'Oh, and please make sure the young lady who performed for me gets this...' I tugged Mark's Rolex off his wrist and placed it on the waitress' silver tray. 'Thank you very much, and have a lovely day.'

The waitress and the bouncer stared at me, eyes agog.

I winked, threw down the last of Mark's drink, and left.

CHAPTER TEN: BIZARRE NOIR

THE ADDRESS of the crime scene Stronge gave me was a leisure centre on Durward Street, way out in Whitechapel. It was getting on for midday by the time I got there, and the sun was burning a hole in the sky.

The old bill had set up a secure perimeter around the grounds in front of the leisure centre. Guarding the barricade were two uniforms in hi-vis jackets.

'Morning,' I said.

I flashed Mark's pearly whites at the constables, who radioed the brass for clearance before consenting to me ducking the police tape. They knew the face I was wearing. Knew it well. I'd attended dozens of crime scenes dressed as Mark, each time under the guise of a "psychic consultant". How else was I supposed to explain my unerring knack for drawing the authorities to the all-important clues that led to a killer's untimely downfall? Tell them the victim's ghost had told me who their murderer was? Yeah, that'd go down a treat.

Up ahead, I saw an evidence tent, erected to conceal a dead body. The murder squad were already on the scene. A huddle of forensics officers in white boiler suits crowded the area, milling about like sheep in a paddock. I stood out like a sore thumb, but somehow I still felt like I belonged. I've always been comfortable around crime. In life, there was only one thing that intrigued me as much as the supernatural, and that was murder. I was a sucker for true crime stories, but my real thing, top of the totem pole, was classic noir. Raymond Chandler, Dashiell Hammett, James Ellroy; I read the lot. Then there were the movies: *The Big Sleep, Key Largo, The Maltese Falcon*, basically any old Bogey flick where he puts on a long coat and smokes like a chimney. Show me something with a cynical detective, monochrome lighting, and a visit from a dame with a killer set of gams, and I'm all yours.

I always fancied myself as a bit of a sleuth, so it's only natural that I took this career turn. Okay, I may not be your typical PI, but despite what Stronge thinks, I've got the goods. Just because I don't have a taciturn personality (bit of a blabbermouth, actually), I'm not morally ambiguous (too busy proving I'm a good person), and I'm not technically alive (dead as a doornail, mate), doesn't mean I'm not detective material. I've as much right being part of a homicide investigation as any copper. Although, there are those who disagree...

'Well, if it isn't Mystic Meg,' growled a voice at my rear.

DI Maddox, Stronge's walking erection of a partner. Maddox was a cynic of the highest order. A born pessimist. The living embodiment of a closed door. Needless to say, he was no fan of mine, the so-called psychic consultant.

The shadow of his bulky frame fell across me like an angry storm cloud. He was dressed in a thick camel overcoat, his bald head buffed to a mirror shine. In short, he looked like a cue ball sat on top of a dog turd.

As much as Maddox hated me, I didn't bear him any ill will. Well, not much, anyway. Not since he had an on-the-job accident that sent him to the infirmary with a shattered arm and put him in extensive therapy; physical and mental. The trauma he suffered caused what shrinks call a "dissociative fugue": a blackout coupled with severe amnesia that flares up like PTSD and requires regular psychiatric counselling. Maddox doesn't talk about it—not to his fellow officers, not to his partner, and certainly not to me—but every once in a while, he quietly disappears from active duty and goes on a bout of "administrative leave" to get his head straight. That's how deep his injuries run, and yet no one knows exactly what happened to him, or who was responsible. No one except me and Stronge, but we'll get to that later.

'How you doing, Madders?' I chirped. 'Been a while.'

He looked at me with knives in his eyes. 'How am I doing? The vic should have been tagged and bagged hours ago, Fletcher, and I should be tucked up in bed. Instead, I've had to stand here waiting for you to show up since the crack of dawn so you can pull off your con trick.'

'Right. But besides that?'

I caught a noxious waft of his rancid aftershave as he squared up to me and jabbed a meaty finger in my ribs.

'Listen to me, you scamming little toe rag. You might have the guv fooled, but you and me both know you've got no business being here.'

'That's not true. I bet I know a lot more about your line of work than you think I do.'

'Is that right? Then why don't you tell me what the Golden Hour principle is, eh?'

'It's um... when the sun's at a high point and you get the best photos.'

Maddox gave me another jab. 'You're a ghoul, mate. Admit it, the only reason you show up at these places is so you can get your grubby little rocks off perving at dead bodies.'

'Yeah, that and showing you how to do your job so killers actually go to jail.'

Maddox's fleshy lower lip stuck out obnoxiously, giving him the appearance of a chubby baby spitting up his num-nums. 'You know what I think? I think you know too much. I think there's a reason you show up every time a dead body does, and it's got nothing to do with being psychic.'

This wasn't the first time Maddox had intimated that I had blood on my hands. That my mystical powers were bullshit, and that I had a part in the very murders I was helping the police solve. I suppose he was half right.

'You know who else has a spooky habit of appearing every time a dead body bobs up, Maddox? You do. Does that make you a killer?'

'I've got a badge. What the fuck have you got?'

'About twice your IQ and a face that doesn't look like ten pounds of boiled arse.'

Maddox took a step forward and mashed his nose into mine. 'Let's go, Fletcher. You and me, right now.'

'Pack it in,' said DCI Stronge, grabbing her partner by the shoulder and pulling him off me. 'I'm sure Mister Fletcher could do without a noseful of your godawful aftershave.'

'Yeah, I was going to ask why you honked so bad. What happened, Madders? Did you take a roll in a Porta-Loo?'

He made a lunge for me, eyes wild, but Stronge kept him at bay.

'Go do something useful with yourself,' she told him. 'Canvass the locals. See if anyone around here saw anything.'

'I'm not done here,' Maddox snarled.

'Take a walk,' she ordered, pulling rank. 'Right now.'

The power dynamic between Stronge and Maddox was a strange one. Despite being partners, Stronge was a superior officer, which made Maddox less of an equal than a right-hand man. One who got the brush-off far more than he liked.

'Yes, guv,' he huffed.

Unless Maddox wanted to spend the rest of his professional life buried in an evidence room living off Greggs' steak bakes, he'd do as he was told. Scowling like a gargoyle, he ducked the police tape and strutted away before he did something he regretted but very much enjoyed.

Stronge turned to me so sharply that it looked like an invisible assassin had crept up behind her and snapped her neck. 'Why do you always have to argue with him?'

'I wasn't arguing.'

'You said he smelled like a Porta-Loo.'

'In my defence, I only said that to piss him off.'

'You *existing* pisses him off.'

I smiled. 'Can't help that, luv.'

Stronge's lips thinned. 'You realise that's the second time you've called me that? Did you not hear about Me Too? How about Time's Up? No, of course you didn't, you're a bloody ghost.'

'Oi. Just because I kicked the bucket a few years back, doesn't mean I'm stuck there.'

'Says the guy who wants to turn his office into something from an old gumshoe movie.'

Hm. Hard to argue with that. Maybe Stronge had a point. Was I really stuck in the past? It's hard keeping your edge when you're always one step removed from the waking world. Was this how it was going to be for me, I wondered. Slowly carried out by the tide, the future getting smaller and smaller until it became a dot on the distant horizon?

But this wasn't the time for navel-gazing. I had a job to do. A murder to solve.

'What are we doing all the way out in Whitechapel?' I asked. 'Isn't this a bit outside of your jurisdiction?'

Stronge's shoulders hitched into a shrug. 'Tower Hamlets is backed up so we're out here on loan.'

'Right,' I said, 'and this far from home you'll be over the distance threshold for expenses, which means you're onto a nice little earner.'

'Why, Jake Fletcher, you old cynic,' she replied.

Stronge steered me to the crime scene hotspot and pulled back a flap of an evidence tent to let me inside. Contained within the tent was a metal bike shed coloured bottle green.

'She's in there,' said Stronge.

Presumably, the murder had happened in the lock-up so the killer could carry out his work in privacy. So he could really make a mess.

I detected a lingering odour in the air. Something putrid.

'What is that?' I asked, wrinkling my nose.

'We're thinking a backed-up drain,' Stronge replied. 'The boys are looking into it.' She went to open the bike shed door, but hesitated. 'You ready for this?'

I nodded back at Stronge and we stepped into the shed, the detective leading the way.

The first thing I noticed was the blood. Lashings of the stuff, painting the walls as if hurled by the bucketful.

'Jesus.'

In the centre of a spreading red pool on the floor, lit by a portable floodlight on a short yellow tripod, were the waxy remains of a young woman. Pieces of a person. A human life reduced to a butcher's scraps. I dared myself to look closer and saw that the victim's throat had been slashed from side to side, then I tracked down further and saw her belly yawned wide open, parted by a deep, jagged wound. I felt a sudden wave of nausea and tasted bile in the back of my throat. When I said I was comfortable around murder before, I didn't mean I wasn't human.

Crouched down by the mutilated body was a heavy-set man in a white boiler suit, thick latex gloves, and black wellies. As Stronge approached him, he took to his feet.

'Ma'am,' he said. He wore an easy smile on his face and a keen glint in his eye. Apparently, neither the smell nor the horror were of much concern to him.

Stronge nodded a greeting at the man, then looked to me. 'Fletcher, this is Officer Pedersen, head of dabs.'

Pedersen saw the confused look on my face and explained. 'Chief Scene of Crime Officer. SOCO. I'm here to process the body.'

He flashed me a *Police Staff* badge in a black leather wallet.

'Oh. Well, don't let me get in your way, Officer.'

He didn't. Pedersen got right to work, firing up a dictation app on his phone and giving it his report.

'The body is badly dismembered,' he told the device, stating the painfully obvious. 'The jugular is severed by two cuts, and the lower part of the abdomen has been dealt a deep, horizontal incision before being ripped open.'

He hit stop on the recorder, pulled out a pad, and jotted down some notes.

'Nice pen,' I said, noting the ballpoint he was using, which was far from police-issue.

'You like it?' Pedersen asked, holding the pen up so I could get a good look at the lady on its side. 'Old school, right?'

He turned it upside down and the cocktail dress the lady was wearing vanished, revealing her naked body.

Stronge rolled her eyes. 'Is that really appropriate for the scene of a homicide?'

'I doubt she cares,' replied Pedersen, aiming the nib of his pen at the mutilated carcass. He said it with a feral smile that showed a few too many teeth.

There was something off about this bloke. About *all* of him, top-to-toe. Accompanying the weird smile, he wore his hair in an amateurish bowl cut—the kind a thrifty mother might give—and had dark, empty eyes that seemed to drink in the surrounding light.

He tucked the ballpoint behind his ear before craning over the body and restarting the dictation app on his phone.

'The wound to the neck has completely severed all tissues down to the vertebrae. The large vessels on both sides are severed, too. The incision is about eight inches in length and caused by something long and sharp. Something used with great violence.' There was real relish to the way he said that last part.

'If you wouldn't mind,' Stronge told him, 'Mister Fletcher and I would like a moment alone.'

'Of course,' he replied, dutifully switching off his phone and shuffling out of the shed. 'I'll be outside when you need me.'

I waited for him to leave. 'What did you say that feller's name was again?' I asked Stronge.

'Pedersen,' she replied.

'Worked with him before?'

'No, first time. Why?'

I considered saying something then dismissed it. 'No reason.'

Stronge took a couple of steps towards the body, careful not to disrupt or contaminate anything. 'You take my point about the missing ghost,' she said.

'Yeah,' I replied, surveying the scene. 'Something ain't right.'

Ordinarily, the best place to look for a murder victim's dislocated soul is the location they suffered their fatal trauma. For them not to be present there, one of three things had to happen...

'Here are the options,' I said, holding up a finger, 'number one, your vic went to the Bad Place.'

When it comes to claiming what's his, the Devil doesn't muck about. If someone's an undeniable reprobate—I'm talking murderers, rapists, people who use the word "methinks" in conversation—they get a one-way ticket to damnation. No delays, no paperwork to fill out, just a trapdoor to the Great Lake of Fire.

'Unlikely,' said Stronge. 'We've ID'd her already, and she doesn't seem the type.'

'Don't throw the idea out so soon. Bad people are on the rise, take my word for it. I blame Brexit.'

Stronge blew out a puff of air, sending her spirit level-straight fringe into brief disarray. 'What else?'

I held up another finger. 'The second option is that she's gone feral.'

Some ghosts don't go quietly into the night. Stuck in limbo for too long, most spectres become what we call revenants: roaming, unquiet spirits that wreak havoc on the living. Chain-rattling, spookshow phantoms that can scream so loud it's like having drill bits driven into your eardrums. Eerie, malevolent apparitions that kneel at the foot of your bed while you slumber, whispering the means by which you'll die. Basically, dickheads.

'I thought you said it took time for that to happen,' said Stronge. 'For a ghost to go ballistic.'

I had told her that. The amount of time it took varied from individual to individual, but I'd never seen it happen this quickly, not in all my time saving souls.

'Then there's only one option left,' I said, holding up a final finger, 'the deceased's spirit was exorcised in some way.'

'You mean like you used to do, back when you were alive?'

'Could be. Or it could have happened some supernatural way.'

There are creatures out there that eat human souls. Things that can slash a person's essence to ribbons. The spirit ain't eternal, you know? I'd have a much more laissez-faire attitude about my future if it was.

Stronge's eyes drifted to the body. 'So what's our next move?'

'We do it the old-fashioned way. We follow clues and we chase down leads.'

There was a good chance we weren't going to be able to give the deceased passage to the great hereafter, but we could still bring her killer to justice. That had to be worth something, right?

'That's it?' said Stronge. 'That's all you've got? We do police work? That's my job, Fletcher. It's what I do. I don't need you to help me run a homicide case. Sometimes I think Maddox is right and I'm mental working with you.'

A man less sure of himself might have been offended by that, but I knew something Kat didn't.

'I may not be a cop, but I've spotted something you haven't.'

'What?'

'This is Durward Street,' I replied.

'I know that.'

'Well, did you also know that Durward Street used to be called Buck's Row?'

'Is this going somewhere, Fletcher?'

I rolled my eyes at her. 'We're on Buck's Row in Whitechapel, and that woman's been slashed to bits by a knife. See where I'm going with this?'

The blank expression on her face told me she didn't.

'The Ripper,' I sighed. 'That body down there is a dead match for the first victim they pinned on Jack the Ripper.'

CHAPTER ELEVEN: DEATH MARCH

I HAD no idea how Jack the Ripper figured into this case, but I did know one thing for sure, Stronge wasn't quite the seasoned detective she thought she was. Of course, I took no pleasure in pointing this out to her. No pleasure at all. Okay, maybe a bit. All right, it warmed my cockles right the way through if you must know.

I left the crime scene in Mark's body with every intention of parting company on the way back to the funeral home. I'd drop him off someplace safe and sound with a few fabricated memories to cover the time he'd been on loan. Happy memories. I'm not the malicious type. Not anymore. Back when I first started using Mark as my meat suit I'd have some fun with the bloke once he'd outlived his usefulness. My favourite trick was to fill him up with booze and leave him in the toilet of a gay bar with a used condom in his pocket and no idea how he got there, then I'd skip out before the hangover kicked in. Classic japes.

But this time, I'd do the decent thing: leave him in a bar and let him think he'd spent a nice morning ogling strippers and flirting with barmaids. And to think this was the guy who used to make my life a living hell. Somewhere in Heaven there was a table with a *Reserved For Jake Fletcher* sign sat on it. Had to be.

I was half an hour from the bar I planned on parking Mark in when I felt a strange sensation in my skull, a sort of psychic prickle. It was a sensation I recognised. I was being probed. Observed from afar. Someone had their eye on me, and they were using magic to do it.

I've been around magic for a long time. Back in the day, when I was alive, I studied just about anything I could get my hands on. If it was esoteric and had a smack of the mystical about, I was into it. I'm talking theurgy, thaumaturgy, auric reading, ley lines, numerology, tarot, the Qabalah, the I-Ching, mentalism, Neo-Paganism, all washed down with a healthy dose of Hitchins to balance out the bollocks. Then there's the next-level stuff I learned later: chaos magic, psycho geometry, Enochian chants, necronomics, Left-Hand occultism, cryptozoology, and, of course, kleptomancy. I even took the time to learn something called ichthyomancy—a divination method that uses fish behaviour, fish heads, and fish entrails to augur things to come—so if you ever catch me craned over a sloppy mess of fish guts, now you know why.

All this might sound like a lot of information to hold in one brain, but being a ghost comes with certain advantages, one of which is time. *Lots* of time. There's really no limit to what you can turn your mind to when you're awake twenty-four hours a day. *Sleep when I'm dead,* my arse. You've got a lot to answer for, Jon Bon Jovi, you poodle-haired ponce.

Anyway, while I know a few things about magic in theory, my actual powers don't extend much beyond simple cantrips and such. I can pop a few locks and show you a bit of razzle-dazzle, but nothing to melt your face off. I do know a few handy tricks, though, and one of those is knowing when I'm being spied on by some dirty bugger with a scrying pool.

I was still on my way to the bar about twenty minutes later when I looked up to see a man with the physique of a silverback gorilla bearing down in my direction, knuckles practically dragging on the ground. He wore clothes that covered every square inch of his body, including his hands and face. Wrapped around the lower portion of his head, leaving only his eyes on show, was a plain, black mask. It was chilly out, but not that chilly, which meant the bloke was either sensitive to the cold, or up to no good. Given the amount of muscular insulation he wore, I was willing to bet it was the latter.

The ape-like stranger stepped in front of me, blocking my path. I had no idea who he was, but he definitely had my attention.

'I work for Vic Lords,' he said, his voice strangely muddied, like he was gargling a mouthful of marbles.

I was confused. How did this bloke recognise me dressed up in my meat suit? The best I could come up with was that Vic was the one spying on me, the person who gave me the heebie-jeebies earlier, and had told his goon who to look for when he sent him my way. Sneaky bastard.

'What does he want?' I asked.

'He wants you to pay him a visit. Right now.'

'Didn't we just have words?'

'He'd like to continue the conversation. Pick up where you left off.'

Was I ever going to get a minute to myself? *Rest In Peace*; isn't that what they tell the dead? Didn't I deserve that much?

'What if I already have plans?' I asked the goon.

'Mister Lords insists.'

I laughed in his face. 'Oh yeah? You gonna make me come with you?'

He leaned in close. So close we practically bumped corneas. 'Yes.'

I don't know if it was the reduced proximity or a change in the wind, but I caught a sudden whiff of the bloke and recoiled in disgust. He *reeked*. I gagged, sinuses stinging from a choking stench that smelled like rotten eggs with a top note of raw sewage.

'Do you wanna take a step back, mate?' I asked, fanning the air between us. 'You smell like Bear Grylls' ball bag.'

Despite all my posturing, I was shitting it. The bloke looked like he could snap Mark's body in half if the mood took him, which was sure to wind the Grand Fromage right up. I'd never succeed in balancing the books if I got one of His precious sheep killed. Mess this up and my ledger would be redder than Lenin's insides.

I was starting to wish my zombie was here to give Vic's messenger boy a good kicking, but I was better off keeping it in hiding. Vic would assume the thing had burned up in the office fire, and I was fine with that. That was some handy ignorance I could use to my advantage later, when the time was right. I'd wait until Vic's guard was down completely before I brought my secret weapon into play, then he'd find out exactly what happens when you push a dead man too far.

'I was told you might need some extra motivation,' said the henchman, 'so you should know we've taken a friend of yours.'

I chuckled. 'Nice try, but I don't have any friends,' I said, as though that was something to be proud of.

'The frozen tramp who sits under the cash machine,' said the goon. 'He's ours now.'

A proper laugh bubbled up me this time. 'Frosty? That's your leverage; a dead bloke?' Tell your gaffer he's going to have to work a bit harder if he wants me by the short and curlies.'

'Mr Lords had a feeling you might not come easy,' replied the goon.

He reached into his coat pocket—for a weapon, I assumed—and for a second I thought he was going to do something deeply unpleasant to Mark's kneecaps. Instead, he produced something that looked like a ball of wool. A ball that I quickly realised was actually a woollen hat.

Frosty's fisherman's beanie.

The hat was solid in the goon's hand—a physical object, not just an ethereal residue—and yet every detail about it was a match for the one Frosty wore. Every hole, every stain. Somehow, Vic's muscle had separated it from the dead tramp's skull and brought it here. That shouldn't have been possible. A ghost's outfit is made of the same stuff they are: ectoplasmic energy (sometimes called "necroplasmic"). Without getting too technical about it, a phantom—their outfit included—is a projection of a person who died. More specifically, it's a projection of that person exactly as they were the moment they died. Take me for example; I carked it wearing a black suit, which is why I'm stuck looking like I'm on my way to a funeral for the rest of eternity. This suit is part of me now; there's no getting rid of it. Taking it off would be like trying to peel off my own skin. Not possible. I'd bitch about it, but it could be worse. I know one ghost who had a heart attack on the crapper with his trousers around his ankles. Now there's a grievance you can hang your hat on.

'What have you done with Frosty?' I asked.

'He's fine,' the goon replied through his mask, his voice still curiously garbled, 'but if you want to see your friend again, you'll come with me.'

"Friend" was a bit of an overstatement maybe, but Frosty and me were definitely more than just casual acquaintances. Sure, we've had our ups and downs over the years, but he didn't deserve to meet his end at the hands of Vic Lords. No one did.

An idea occurred, but the goon read it on my face.

'Don't bother,' he said.

'Don't bother what?' I replied.

'Jumping out of that body and making a break for your pal. Trust me, you won't like how it ends.'

He was right. If I gave him the Irish goodbye and translocated directly to Frosty's whereabouts, I'd be leaving Mark behind and putting my best meat suit through the wringer.

I squared up to the goon, giving it the large, acting a lot tougher than I felt.

'Come on then, you big lump. Let's go.'

CHAPTER TWELVE: THE BEAST FROM THE EAST(END)

'THIS WAY,' said the henchman.

'But Frosty's patch is down there,' I replied, pointing off in the opposite direction.

'Not today it ain't,' the goon replied, heading the other way. 'He's moved.'

Impossible. Like I said before, Frost wasn't exactly what you'd call a frequent flier. Like those poor souls who froze to death at the top of Everest and became landmarks for future climbers to navigate by, Frosty was a permanent fixture. He was frozen to the patch of pavement he died on, and forever would be. That was his point of departure, to which he was eternally bound. He didn't just "move".

Then again, removing a ghost's clobber shouldn't have been possible either, and yet I'd seen first-hand proof of that when the goon showed me Frosty's fisherman's beanie. Apparently, impossible was on the menu today. That got me deep-down worried about what kind of state Frost might be in.

'Lead the way,' I said.

The masked goon conveyed me to his employer's office, which sat on the bank of Regent's Canal, not far from Camden Lock. Not that I needed a sherpa to make that journey; I'd been to the place so many times I could have found it blindfolded.

By the time we hoofed it over to the canal, the sun was burning hot and syrupy. No sunbathers out this way, though. Nothing green to lay a towel on; just a grey expanse of warehouses and chop shops, every one of them gang-tagged. But not Vic's building. Even the wildest of the jackals who roamed this part of town knew better than to deface his property.

'You know the way,' the goon prompted as he directed me into the building.

Being indoors with his rotten egg stench wasn't going to be any easier on the nose, but there was no going back now.

He ushered me up a short flight of stairs, then through the door to Vic's office. It was situated above a knocking shop, because of course it was. Vic Lords was the dark heart in the centre of this town; wherever bad things happened, Vic was never too far away. Not that the law could do anything about that. Vic should have had a rap sheet thicker than a vicar's bible by now, but he was too smart to let anything stick. He was canny enough to make sure he maintained enough layers of insulation between himself and his wrongdoings that the law could never touch him.

'Young Fletcher,' said Vic, sat behind his desk looking very satisfied with himself indeed.

He was dressed in a simple two-piece suit this time; a pile of spoiled luncheon meat poured into human clothing.

'Vic,' I replied, matter-of-factly. 'Needy is not a good look on you.'

I guess I must have been expected to tug on my forelocks or genuflect or something, because his henchman gave me a hard, corrective shove from behind.

'Oi. Mind the whistle,' I cried.

One of these days, I'll have to teach you a bit of cockney rhyming slang. Until then, you can ask Jeeves or whatever it is you people do these days.

'That is a nice suit,' Vic remarked, referring to the meat sock I was wearing. 'Be a shame if something were to... happen to it.'

Refusing to be drawn in, I avoided Vic's eyes and scanned his office instead. It was the same disgusting little grotto it always had been, every surface covered in clutter and cigar ash, its ceiling painted the colour of gravy by decades of nicotine. It was the kind of place you wouldn't touch wearing gauntlets.

There was one noticeable addition to the room since my last

visit, though, namely the alcove in the corner containing a magician's shrine. The makeshift altar contained shelves heaving with all manner of mystical gubbins: a silver scrying bowl (aha!), pewter talismans studded with strange crystals, a bunch of ostrich feathers bound by a single copper ring, a stone goblet, assorted animal skulls, and a triad of black candles that gave off a smell like a gangrenous wound.

'Where is he, then?' I asked, checking Mark's watch then remembering that I already gave it away. 'Where's Frosty? I haven't got all day.'

'I'll get to that,' Vic replied, 'but first I want to show you something.' He turned to his henchman, who stood blocking the door behind me. 'Take it off.'

The goon ambled closer and came to a halt. With some hesitation, he put a hand to his face and slowly peeled off his mask.

'Christ on a bike,' I heard myself say.

The man was horribly disfigured. I'm talking drunk Picasso bad. His face was nowhere near symmetrical, his features arranged seemingly at random. A jutting, caveman forehead shelved two sunken eyes, black as the darkest ditch of night. The bottom of his face was framed by a mangled jaw that rendered him incapable of showing any facial expression beyond anger, and the pit of his mouth was filled by a mess of jagged teeth, chipped and bent in like broken piano keys. No wonder he sounded like he was talking with a gobful of broken glass. And yet, despite all of his disfigurements, I recognised him. Not for what he'd become, but for the man he used to be.

'Wait a second, aren't you...?'

Vic's doorman, Kojo, the seven-foot murder tank he used to keep people out of his hair. I'd bumped chests with the bloke before, but he hadn't looked anything like this. This was one hell of a transformation.

'What happened to you?'

His eyes slanted to the side, avoiding the question.

'I did,' said Vic, a devil's glint in his eye. '*I* happened to him. Whenever he disobeys an order or does something I don't like, the curse I placed on him leaves a fresh mark. Ain't that right, Kojo?'

The goon nodded solemnly. 'Yes, Mister Lords,' he slurred from the side of his lopsided mouth, then quickly replaced his mask.

From the looks of it, the bloke had put up quite a fight before Vic broke him in. I don't think I've ever felt sympathy for a henchman before—especially not one who smelled like he did—but no one deserved that kind of treatment.

I looked to Vic. 'You must really hate this guy.'

He flicked some cigar ash on the fag-scarred carpet. 'Just the opposite, actually. Kojo here is a good friend of mine. The two of us go back years. Gave a speech at his wedding, I did. Shame how that ended up, God rest her soul.' His eyes locked onto the goon's. 'Still, if you've got sticky fingers, you've got to be prepared to suffer the consequences, ain't that right, Kojo?'

The goon caved in like someone had punched him in the gut. 'Yes, Mister Lords.'

The bottomless depths of Vic's corrupt soul never ceased to amaze me. Even his evil had evil. His wickedness was fractal.

He rotated his chair in my direction and ran a paw through his oil slick hair. 'Now, if I'm prepared to do that to someone I like,' he said, aiming a sausage-link finger at his deformed henchman, 'what do you reckon I'll do to someone who's disappointed me a hundred times over?'

The threat was a hollow one. 'Do I look like I was killed yesterday? Curses don't work on ghosts, Vic.'

He formed a smile that reached all the way to his forehead. 'Who said anything about curses?'

Vic sat up with a squeak and signalled to his goon. Kojo opened the office door and stepped aside.

'Come with me,' said Vic. 'Downstairs.'

I'd never been to the basement before. I knew Vic ran a brothel out of that floor, populated by hookers he trafficked in from abroad, but I'd never seen his den of iniquity with my own two eyes. I wondered why I was being taken there, and how Frosty figured into the visit.

On the way to the cellar, we passed an assortment of raw-knuckled goons, each of which snapped to attention at the sight of their employer. As far as muscle went, Vic used to make do with just

Kojo. Going by the band of toughs I was seeing now, he'd seriously stepped up his operation.

'I see you've been hiring,' I said.

Vic chuckled. 'You know me, Fletcher. Forever creating new employment opportunities.'

'Oh yeah. You're a real pillar of the community.'

We arrived at the basement. It stank. The sour taste of sweat and blood combined with other bodily fluids assaulted my senses, making me light-headed. Escorted along the floor's uncomfortably warm central corridor, I heard various moans and screams—some motivated by pleasure, others by pain—seeping beneath the two rows of private curtains either side of me. The place was a hub of sordid activity. From behind one partially-opened drape, I saw a naked prostitute splashed across a filthy mattress with blister-pocked lips and an empty needle in her arm. She wore a strung-out look on her face, her eyes showing less life than the zombie shackled to my bathroom radiator. I saw other things, too. Things I didn't even want to think about, but I knew would come back to haunt me later.

I should have done something about this place a long time ago, but somehow I'd succeeded in compartmentalising that part of my life. The connection I had to Vic. Still had. Then again, why was I the one expected to shut Vic down? Why hadn't God done His bit and blown Vic off the face of the planet? Was He waiting for me to do it for Him? Was putting Vic out of business all part of my grand, redemptive arc?

From the basement, I was led into a sub-basement that I didn't even know existed. This floor stank even worse somehow; a sharp, choking aroma that met me in a single, noxious wave. The unsoftened echo of my shoes against bare concrete brought on a distinctly claustrophobic feeling that wasn't helped by a ceiling so low I had to bow Mark's head to avoid separating him from his man bun.

Vic's goon bulldozed me into a large, dingy chamber. The only light came from the corridor outside, so all I could make out within were bare concrete walls and chains dangling from the ceiling.

'What's with the decor?' I asked. 'You shooting a *Hellraiser* film down here?'

Vic grinned and tugged on a light cord, bringing to life a single bare bulb that dangled in the centre of the room.

We were in a fetish dungeon. A well-equipped one. Dotted around the room I saw a whipping post, a wooden crucifix with thick leather restraining straps, a clothes rack hung with Nazi paraphernalia, a wicker changing screen (a bit prudish, I thought, considering the boldness of the rest of the items on display), and a spanking bench, next to which was propped a paddle studded with sharp metal tacks.

But the real centrepiece of the room was the medieval rack, upon which, drawn taut as a rubber band, was someone I recognised.

'Frosty?'

His limbs were all stretched out, impossibly elongated, as though his body was made of wet chewing gum. Somehow, despite this, the old bastard was alive, or as alive as a ghost could be.

'Fletcher,' he hissed through gritted teeth. 'I might have known this would be your fault.'

Vic chuckled and slapped the side of the torture device. 'You like my new toy, Jake?' he asked, circling my way. 'Amazing what you can get on the Silk Road these days, isn't it? It's called a spirit rack. It's for serious submissives. For some people, physical pain ain't enough. Some folks need a stiletto ground into their *soul*.'

I was barely listening to him. I was too busy trying to figure out how he managed to get Frosty into the device in the first place.

Vic sensed I was caught up in my own thoughts and stamped a foot. 'How did I pull this off? That's what you're wondering, ain't it?'

I didn't want to give him the satisfaction of knowing he was right, so I stayed tight-lipped. He wasn't fooled.

'You ever pour gelatine into water, Jake? That's basically what I did, only with magic. I took a phantom and I made him solid, and when I was done with that, I shovelled him up like frozen shite and brought him here.'

Apparently, Vic had employed a spell of his own design, a necromantic incantation that somehow rendered ectoplasm corporeal. The wily swine had seriously levelled up since the two of us last had a run-in. How did he get so powerful so fast?

'So what do you reckon, Jake? You going to do this job for me, or do you fancy a go on the rack, too?'

I remembered a man I read about once; a man known as H.H. Holmes who was also fond of the rack. They called him the Beast of Chicago. Holmes was a serial killer who operated around the same time as the Ripper of London did, only his body count was much, much higher (some say as many as three-hundred people died by his hands). He spent a fortune building a house that the authorities later named his "Murder Castle". The property came complete with sound-proofed walls, gas chambers, acid vats, and a crematorium to dispose of his victims' bodies. In the building's basement, the police found a medieval rack, only Holmes didn't call it that.

He called it his "elasticity determinator".

I looked back the way I'd come to see the goon blocking the room's only exit.

'I'm still waiting on that answer,' said Vic. 'What's it gonna be: one last job for me, or a trip to the tailor's to get your trousers let out? Your choice.'

'Bollocks.'

'Pardon me?' Vic replied.

'I said, bollocks. If you wanted to do that you'd have done it already. But you can't. You can't because you need me to pull off this heist for you, and chucking magical gelatine my way ain't gonna make that happen.'

I saw his nostrils flare before he arranged his face into a smirk. 'You think I'm out of moves, Fletcher? Huh? How about this one, then?'

He placed a hand on the wheel of the rack.

'Don't do it.'

'I'll do what I like, son.'

He gave the wheel a ratchet, retracting the chains attached to Frosty's wrists and ankles. Frosty cried out, unleashing a scream that sounded like iron nails being dragged over a rock.

'How about that?' Vic asked. 'That incentive enough for you?'

I went to rush him, but felt the goon's tree trunk arms grab me around the waist, lifting me off my feet. For a man shackled by mortal flesh, this might have proved a problem. For a ghost who was able to possess the living, all I saw was an opportunity to seize control of a man with muscles big enough to pop Vic's head off like a champagne cork.

I jettisoned from Mark's body, bailing out like I pulled the lever on an ejector seat, the goon my human parachute—

Except, just like the time I tried to possess the zombie, I ran straight into a brick wall. The heavy was shielded somehow, his body off-limits, bouncing me right off. Realising I wasn't getting anywhere, I quickly leapt back into Mark and reclaimed control of my original host.

Vic laughed like the end of the *Thriller* video. 'Well, Jake?' he said. 'You gonna pull your finger out? You gonna be a good boy for once?'

I looked past him to Frosty, who lay there, stretched to the limit, fear etched into every crease of his grubby face.

I nodded at Vic, defeated. 'Okay, I'll do it, but first I get to check he's all right.'

Vic gave the steroid job a nod and I was set back on the ground. I rushed to Frosty's side and placed a hand on his shoulder.

'How you doing, you old dosser?' I said, forcing a smile. 'You look skinny. You been doing the Atkins?'

'Just get me the fuck... out of here, will ya?' he groaned.

'I will, Frost,' I whispered in his ear, 'I just need a bit of time, that's all.'

He shook his head, resigned. 'You owe me... Fletcher. Forget about... those cans you promised, I want... a whole fucking barrel. I want... that shit on tap. You got that?'

'I got it.'

He twisted his head to one side and coughed, only instead of ejecting an escargot of bile this time, up came a cascade of blood. I winced as it struck the ground by my feet with an audible splatter.

'You shouldn't have done this,' I told Vic, feeling my hands bunch into fists.

'What choice did I have? I tried getting your attention when I set your corpse on you, but you wouldn't have it. Now you've got some skin in the game.'

I felt my knuckles turn white. 'You went too far, Vic. Way too far.'

There was no way he'd have left himself open to me possessing him, but that didn't mean I was helpless against the bloke. Didn't mean I couldn't fight him another way.

'Last chance, Vic. Let Frosty go and pack this in, or I'm going to do you some damage you won't walk away from.'

The goon took a step towards me, but Vic held up a hand, stopping him in his tracks. He had this.

I returned my attention to Vic. 'Well, what's it going to be? You give up?'

He stood there, still as a church statue, a wicked grin plastered across his ugly mug.

I smiled back at him. 'Tell you what, why don't I rephrase the question?'

Leaping from Mark's body, I surged forward and thrust an ethereal hand into Vic's chest, reaching through his rib cage and closing my fingers around his dark heart.

I regretted it immediately.

The pain that ripped through me was indescribable, but I'll have a crack at it anyway. Touching Vic's heart felt like picking up a lit blow torch by the wrong end, only it wasn't heat searing my fingers, it was raw, lacerating cold. I've heard people say Vic's heart was made of ice before, but I never realised until now how close to the truth they were.

I recoiled, pulling my hand free of his chest and gripping my wrist to stem the pain.

Vic wagged a finger at me. 'Naughty, naughty, very naughty.'

He raised his palms to the ceiling and began chanting something in gutter Latin. I felt a sudden surge of mortality, then I was coming apart at the seams, my essence pulled thin, drifting away like tufts of pulled candy floss. Vic was exorcising me. Rubbing me out.

'You think I want this, Fletcher? I made you who you are. You're like a son to me.'

'Right,' I managed, 'just like those kids King Herod was so fond of.'

As Vic resumed his chant, my body continued to disintegrate under his unholy assault, particles spiralling away and drifting to the floor. It wasn't painful. In fact, it was a curiously numb sensation, like having your intestines pulled free of your body while under the effect of heavy sedation.

'How are you doing this?' I asked. Where was he getting this kind of power?

'Never you mind, my lad.'

This was way beyond anything I could do as an exorcist, even in my prime. Vic wasn't having to perform any rituals, wasn't wafting a bunch of burning sage about, he was casting me into shadow with his words alone.

'Last chance, Fletcher. Get with the programme or you're going down.'

I had no choice. I was proud enough to let him kill me rather than give him what he wanted, but my life wasn't the only one at stake here. If I let Vic finish rubbing me out, Frosty and Mark would be quick to follow.

'Okay, I'll do it,' I told him. 'Whatever you want, I'll do it.'

Vic lowered his hands and ceased his invocation, leaving it hanging in the air like an unresolved melody. 'Good lad. Now was that really so difficult? Bloody hell, Fletcher, you do play hard to get.'

He began to chant backwards, reversing his hoodoo, and as he did so my body started to reform, coming together like iron filings drawn to a magnet. It was an incredible feat of sorcery. The kind of thing that would make James Randi shit himself inside-out.

With my spirit whole again, I returned to the physical shell I'd been occupying and resumed possession of Mark, who'd been passed out on the floor in my absence. I felt flattened. My brain was in tatters, and I could hear myself panting like a wounded Staffy at the rough end of a dog fight.

'What exactly is it you want me to half-inch?' I gasped finally, bent double, hands on my knees. 'How much money are we talking about here?'

'No money. This is a big boy caper. What I'm after is a *soul*. A very particular soul.'

I gave him a dirty squint. 'Do I look like the Grim Reaper to you? Since when did I go around robbing people's souls?'

'This soul doesn't belong to anyone. Not anymore. The body died a long time ago, now only the spirit remains.'

'How?'

He moistened his lips. 'Because someone trapped it and locked it away for safekeeping.'

'You're telling me this thing's sat in a jar on someone's shelf?'

'That's how the story goes.'

I studied his face. As unlikely as Vic's little tale sounded, he certainly believed it.

'What do you need with a soul?' I asked. 'Besides the obvious?'

'That's on a need to know basis,' he replied, tapping the side of his bulbous, veiny nose.

'Seriously, what happened, Vic? Did you lose yours in a fiddle contest?'

He didn't laugh. Obviously, not a big fan of *The Devil Went Down to Georgia*.

I blew out a big plume of nothing. 'Just tell me where it is and I'll get it.'

'That's for you to figure out, Jakey boy. All I know is, it's in the city. Other than that, I can't pinpoint the thing, which means it must be shielded by some pretty tasty magic.' He stabbed a thumb in Frosty's direction. 'Even the oracle over there doesn't know where it's hiding.'

'That's it?' I shot back. 'That's all I get to go on?'

'Oh, there is one more thing,' he replied. 'The name of the soul is Cimeries.'

'A name. You're giving me a name?' I offered him a taut laugh. 'The whole of London, and that's all I've got to go on? Fucking hell, Vic, do you want me to fetch you the horizon while I'm at it?'

His expression greyed. 'Wind your neck in, Fletcher. Do the job, and fast, or the dead tramp goes to the great soup kitchen in the sky.'

I looked to Frosty, stretched thin on the rack, mercifully passed out from the pain. What choice did I have but to shovel Vic's shit? None, that's what.

'I'll get you your soul, but after this we're square, you get me? A hundred percent copacetic.'

Vic showed me his teeth (smiled wasn't the word) and delved into the pocket of his jacket. He produced a small pouch and tossed it my way. 'When you find what I'm looking for, put it in here and bring it back to me.'

I turned the pouch over in my hand. It was made of skin—human skin if I wasn't mistaken—and decorated with a white, bone clasp. I wondered briefly about the unfortunate who sacrificed his hide for the thing, then decided I'd rather not know.

'How does it work?' I asked.

'Nothing to it,' he replied. 'Open it up, point it at the soul I'm after, and it's done.'

I opened the pouch to look inside and felt a hungry, sucking void from within that almost swallowed my hand before I managed to pull it free.

'Careful, son,' said Vic. 'That thing'll have your arm off and then some.'

I decided to pocket the pouch before I ended up inside of it.

'Leave Frosty alone and you'll get your soul,' I said, and went to leave.

As I reached the door, Vic called out. 'Don't let me down, Fletcher. Mess this up and I'll snap your little mate in half.'

I gave him a sour nod. I could protest all I liked, but Vic had me over a barrel. It was do or die. Again.

CHAPTER THIRTEEN: WHEREVER YOU GO, THERE YOU ARE

I DITCHED Mark like a snake shedding its skin and translocated back to the funeral parlour to check in on the zombie. Babysitting my reanimated corpse. Life can take some funny turns.

I appeared in the neglected bathroom, relieved to find the creature where I left him, handcuffed to the cast-iron radiator. Zombie-me looked up at real-me with its big, empty eyes. But just how empty were they, really?

I got to thinking about his little dance earlier; how he accessed one of my old memories, and a deeply buried one at that. Was that a blip, or evidence of some underlying humanity? Were my memories —or what remained of them in my decaying brain meat—still there for this undead interloper to rifle through?

And here was the biggie. The question I wasn't entirely sure I wanted the answer to. Did that mean this hunk of rotting flesh I had chained up like a slave was, in some way, still me?

'You know,' I said to the zombie, 'you might just come in handy. I'm being pulled in two directions at once here, and I could use a double to lighten the load.'

The zombie didn't react to my musing, just gazed off across the room, its attention captured by a cockroach scuttling across the edge of the bath.

Time to run a little test; see how much me was still rattling around in that broken-down bonce.

'Who was my first kiss?' I asked.

The zombie's brow creased and its jaw moved like a ruminating heifer. 'Braaaiiins.'

'Ha! Not even close, pal.'

Actually, the first girl I locked lips with was called Briana, so it was *kind of* close.

'Okay, let's try again. What number house did we, I mean, *I* grow up in?'

At first, the zombie did nothing. Then, ever so slowly, it began to raise its free hand. What was it doing? I watched as its fingers moved up and down uncertainly. Three? Was it trying to hold up three fingers? I did live at number three… was this sack of worm food actually going to—

'Braaaaiiinnnssss!' it brayed as its hand dropped back down.

I smiled and shook my head. No, I was the only me. The original and best and *only* Jake Fletcher. What happened before was just an involuntary twitch. An old memory firing off as my biological brain turned to soup in that automaton's head. Because that's all he was, surely. Just a corpse powered by magic. It didn't think. There was no true life, soul, or person hiding inside of that knackered old chassis.

Couldn't be.

My phone started shaking like it was having an epileptic fit. I thrust a hand into my jacket pocket and fished the thing out. The caller ID read *DCI Stronge*.

'I've gotta take this,' I said.

The zombie gave me an obligatory, 'Braaaaaiiiins,' as I turned and walked out of the room.

I swiped the slider thingie to answer the call, but the phone continued to rumble. I hated that thing, always had. I swiped it again and got nothing. What is it with these new-fangled contraptions? Why can't we go back to good old-fashioned buttons? Now everything has to be paper-thin and smooth as a glacier and too bloody complicated for its own good.

Aside from the technological trouble I was having, you might be wondering how a ghost was using a phone in the first place. I mean, surely the more traditional way of communicating with the dead is by ouija board, right? Ha, well done you, mate, have yourself a biscuit.

But yeah, all joking aside, I can take phone calls. I can make them, too. I could even send a Tweet if I had any idea what one was or why people did them. Consider me a special case. Very few ghosts carry a mobile. Matter of fact, I might just be the only one who does, and that's only thanks to a friend of mine who specialises in enchantment magic. One of her many talents is being able to imbue everyday objects with the jiggery-pokery required to make them solid to ghosts. It's the reason I can make phone calls, and how I went about acquiring the cans of Special Brew I knocked Frosty's way. Again, this brand of magic is called enchantment, which is a whole other animal to the voodoo Vic was using to torture phantoms. Vic's magic was the black stuff. Dark-side-of-the-moon black.

The phone continued to buzz in my palm. In all the excitement, I'd almost forgotten about the dismembered body we saw on Durward Street. The Ripper killing.

I went to terminate the call. I didn't have time for Stronge, not while an innocent man was trapped in Vic's clutches. I tried to hit the hang up button, but my thumb wouldn't let me. Despite the afterimage of Frosty drawn out on that torture rack still being imprinted on my brain, I knew I had to work the homicide. Me and Frost had a history, but he'd already had his chance at life, no matter how tragic and short-lived it turned out to be. The Ripper killer had murdered a breather, and if he planned on following his precursor's MO, he was going to go after more of them. Living souls have more weight than a ghost's, which made the Stronge case a clear priority.

I answered the call. 'Give me two shakes, Kat.'

I translocated to Kentish Town Police Station and arrived smack dab in the middle of Stronge's office.

'Jake Fletcher, reporting for duty.'

'Christ,' she groused, 'what did you have to come here for? Honestly, you're like one of those people who answers a text with a call, only worse. Don't you know anything about phone etiquette?'

'Sorry if I'm a bit behind the times,' I replied, 'I've been a touch busy being dead.'

I had no choice but to show up as a ghost, anyway. I couldn't have jumped straight back in Mark again, it was too soon. I was only able to possess an unwilling body for a limited time—a couple of hours at most—after that I get spat out like a wad of flavourless gum. Rules of the game. Don't ask me why.

Stronge shook her head with frustration, got up from her desk, and began shutting her office blinds.

I caught a glimpse of DI Maddox's shiny bullet-head looking in from outside before a blind dropped in front of his face and blanked him out. I was invisible to him in phantom form, but that didn't stop his eyes burning with suspicion the moment he saw his partner going dark on him.

While Stronge busied herself blinkering the office, I took a prowl around the room, taking in the sights.

'What's this then?' I asked, pointing to a plaque on the wall.

'A commendation,' she replied. 'One of those things they give actual detectives.'

I hoisted an eyebrow. 'What's it for?'

'Acts of bravery and heroism,' she replied matter-of-factly.

You might have expected me to dig deeper into that, but my mind was already on other things. 'Is that… wait, is that your real name?' I pointed to the inscription on the bottom of the plaque, which read *Katherine Mary Jane Stronge*. 'Your middle name is *Mary Jane*?'

A blush mounted her cheeks. 'My parents were hippies.'

I laughed, thoroughly tickled. 'A copper with a middle name that translates to jazz cabbage? Oh, that is rich. That is perfect.'

'Pack it in, okay?'

'Fine. Moving on.'

She took a seat and I pulled up a chair opposite her, ready to be brought up to speed on the case. The surface of her desk was sparse and uncluttered, and as she sat down, I noticed her adjust a sheaf of papers so they were in exact alignment with the edge of the desktop. Stronge's office was as sterile as an operating theatre, everything arranged just so, every item in its place, nothing out of line. It was the kind of workspace that a robot might keep; a robot cop called Optimus Crime.

Sorry.

I wondered why Stronge was the way she was. The kind of woman who irons creases in her jeans. The kind of woman who—I'd bet my life if I had one—kept a drawer in her kitchen filled to buggery with neatly-folded shopping bags that she was never going to use. Maybe maintaining a rigid sense of order was Stronge's way of rebelling against her bohemian upbringing. Of sticking it to her hippie parents. Who knew, maybe walking the straight and narrow was what led her to become a cop in the first place.

'You still with me?' she asked, sensing that I'd slipped into a reverie.

'Yup,' I replied, focusing up.

She pulled an old street map from a drawer and flattened it out on the desk in front of me. 'We checked out your Ripper theory and it looks like it might have legs.' She pointed at a spot on the map circled in red Biro. 'This ordnance survey map confirms that the Ripper's first kill and ours both occurred in the same location.'

'Because whoever did this is a copycat killer.'

'I said you *might* be right. We don't know for sure that we're dealing with a copycat. Not yet.'

'Come on, Kat, look at the evidence. Even the wounds are a match.'

'It could still be a coincidence. We can't rule that out.'

I leaned towards her. 'Give it up, love. Someone killed a woman in the style of Jack the Ripper, and chances are whoever did it won't stop at one.'

'Maybe, maybe not.'

'Kat, you've seen ghosts. Demons. Angels. Is some nutter rolling out the hits of a Victorian murderer really that hard to swallow?'

'I'm still on the fence.'

I felt a smile spread across my face. 'You already know, don't you? You know for a fact that it's a copycat and you're just too proud to say so.'

She held her breath, her face slowly turning the colour of a stop-light, until finally, she blurted, 'The dates.'

'What?'

'The dates are a match, too. August 31st, both murders.'

I snapped my fingers. 'I knew it!'

'God, I hate it when you're right,' she groaned, setting her head in her hands. 'Now wipe that smug grin off your face.'

'This is how I always look, Kat. I have resting smirk face.'

She laughed. It was an oddly kittenish sound, quite out of character. I sensed that we'd strayed from strictly professional grounds, so decided to capitalise on the moment and see what I could do to clear the air.

'I miss that laugh,' I said, placing a friendly hand on her forearm. 'What happened, Kat? How come things frosted over between us?'

She straightened up suddenly, pulling away from me, all business. 'We didn't have a dead body to talk about, that's all.'

'Come on, don't be like that. Talk to me. We used to be a team. What happened to the good old days? You know: chasing leads, bagging bad guys, classic scrapes.'

Her jaw muscles tensed. 'Last time we got into one of those *scrapes,* I almost died. Those scrapes leave scar tissue, Jake.'

I could tell we weren't going to mend any broken bridges just yet. Best to get back on track.

'What do we know about the victim?' I asked.

She cleared her throat. 'We did some digging and there isn't much to say,' she replied, settling back into the groove. 'We know she wasn't a sex worker like the Ripper's first victim. Record's clean as a whistle.'

That was a big deviation. Maybe our Ripper copycat wasn't such a slave to the details after all. That could make catching the turd a little trickier.

'What about enemies?' I asked. 'Anything there?'

'Nothing. Everything points towards her not knowing the identity of her killer.'

'You know, I always hated that phrase, "Her killer". Like the victim and the murderer were a team working towards some common goal.'

'You're getting philosophical in your old age, Fletcher.'

There was a sharp knock on the office door.

'Guv,' said DI Maddox, announcing himself.

'I'd better go,' I told Stronge. 'Looks like the missing link is getting restless.'

She nodded.

'Do what you do, Kat,' I said. 'In the meantime, I'm going to investigate an avenue of my own.'

CHAPTER FOURTEEN: SAUCY JACK

Good detective work isn't about sitting behind a desk, filing paperwork. Being a detective means feet on the street, chasing leads no matter how futile they might seem. Pounding the pavement, day in day out, until the soles of your shoes are thick with chewing gum. Some say that's where the word "gumshoe" came from in the first place. That's what it means to me, anyway. Results, but not without a lot of hard graft.

There was a Jack the Ripper walking tour that left Whitechapel Underground Station every day at 8 p.m., which left me just enough time to blink over there and tag along for the ride. I'd been on similar tours before, a long time ago, back when I was still drawing breath. You might say I'm a bit of a student of the Ripper; then again, show me a true crime nut who isn't. The Ripper story has everything an aficionado of the macabre loves: wild conspiracy, public scandal, taunting letters to the authorities, and of course, a mystery killer whose identity invites speculation to this day. Jack the Ripper is, in many ways, the granddaddy of serial killers.

That said, I'm no Ripperologist. I can spew a few factoids here and there, refute some of the wilder theories, and—on a good day—tell you the names of all five of the Ripper's canonical victims, but there's a lot about the case I don't know. A lot of holes to plug. If I was going to get a handle on this copycat killer and join the dots between the recent slaying and the historical ones, I was going to need a lot more information. I was going to need the ear of an authority on the subject, someone who lived and breathed Ripper lore, and who better than someone who walked in his footsteps each and every day?

The tour guide was in his late twenties, with a heavy-set build, a Van Dyke beard, and long brown hair that hung down past his shoulders. He wore leather trousers, a shiny black shirt, and had a silver crucifix necklace sat on his Adam's apple. It's fair to say he wasn't *quite* the mentor I had in mind when I decided to seek expert help, but then again, looks can be deceiving. I once saw a man transform into a giant wolf right in front of my eyes, so it's not entirely inconceivable that I could learn something from a bloke dressed like a struggling magician.

Right?

The tour guide and his procession of a dozen or so enthusiastic followers—mostly American tourists—took a corner down a cobblestone thoroughfare and wound their way through a warren of back alleys. I tagged along unseen, observing invisibly as we arrived on the street that used to be known as Buck's Row.

'My name is Dennis and I'll be your tour guide this evening. Thank you for joining me, ladies and gentlemen, and welcome to our first stop: the backcloth against which the birth of the Jack the Ripper saga played out,' he announced all of this in the voice of a professional Dungeon Master.

I took a look around. The area wasn't much to look at, but then I already knew that. As much as the guide tried to spirit us back to Victorian times, the street hadn't survived the unstoppable march of progress. These days it looked more like a building site than the scene of one of the 20th Century's most notorious murders. Not that this blunted the enthusiasm of the camera-happy crowd, who snapped photos of every conceivable nook and cranny.

The tour guide went on. 'It's the autumn of 1888, and a sinister killer is loose on the streets of Whitechapel. We're in the early hours of the 31st of August, and right here, in what used to be a stable entrance, a delivery man is about to make a gruesome discovery...'

The guide went on to briefly describe the victim, Mary Ann Nichols, who had shown up dead on the spot we were standing on after spending an evening drinking her doss money at a local pub. From there, things got… interesting.

'Who do you think the Ripper really was?' asked a gobby Yank with a tight, bleached perm, interrupting the guide's speech with a wave of her chubby hand.

Instead of showing annoyance, he returned a pale smile. 'The identity of Jack the Ripper isn't important to me. Never has been. I'm much more interested in the effect the Ripper had on the world at large than I am in knowing his name.' At this point, his voice leapt up a few decibels. 'Just think of what he achieved. He created havoc, terrorised an entire city—not just the slums—and caused divisions in communities that echo to this day. It's a legacy that's still with us almost 150 years later, and he managed all of this in the space of just a few months.'

'It almost sounds like you admire the guy,' replied the deflated Yank, her mouth caving into a cat's arsehole.

'How could I not?' asked the guide, really rhapsodising now. 'The things he did, they border on the supernatural. How could a man commit five heinous crimes, most of them out in the wide-open, without ever being seen? Without being arrested by the two different police forces working overtime to bring him down? Surely that can't be down to just luck?'

From there we were taken to Spitalfields, stopping off briefly at The Ten Bells pub and the soaring steeple of Christ Church, both of which loomed large in the Ripper mythos. Modern Whitechapel is one big homage to old Jack, boasting a Ripper museum, a hairdresser calling itself Jack the Clipper, and even a fish and chip shop called Jack the Chipper. A bit of fun, or monetising murder? You decide.

Finally, we reached Hanbury Street and arrived at the Old Truman Brewery, where the guide resumed his speech.

'The Ripper's second victim, Annie Chapman, was discovered on this very spot at around 6 a.m. on Saturday the 8th of September, eight days after the murder of Mary Ann Nichols. Ms Chapman's body was terribly mutilated. Her throat had been severed deeply, her torso disembowelled, her intestines thrown out of her abdomen and draped over each of her shoulders. And yet, despite the severity of her wounds, there was no evidence of a struggle having taken place.

The Ripper had proven himself nimble, methodical, and efficient. An apex predator.'

The guide was practically frothing at the mouth by this point, banging on about Jack the Ripper the same way a football fanatic cheers on their favourite team. Don't get me wrong, I've spent more time reading about Saucy Jack than is strictly healthy, but I wouldn't say I'm a fan of the bloke. This guy, on the other hand, probably had a framed picture of JTR sat on his bedside dresser. It got to me. To people like him, the Ripper wasn't a depraved maniac preying on defenceless women, he was a rock star. It was an attitude shared by many, but this bloke had taken it to the extreme. He'd made a career out of caring deeply about a multiple murderer, but had next to nothing to say about the man's victims. For the tour guide, the five brutally murdered women the Ripper left in his wake were nothing more than props in a never-ending one-man play.

Before the guide could continue waxing lyrical, another of the guests piped up.

'I read somewhere that it was the Queen's private surgeon who did it,' he announced with utmost certainty, despite looking like the kind of feller who regularly tripped over his own feet.

'Ah, yes, the *Quack the Ripper* theory,' replied the guide. 'Popularised by a certain "graphic novel". Never mind that Doctor Gull was over seventy years old at the time of the slayings, and of extremely poor health.'

Despite his sneering brush-off, the dismissal only served to encourage other members of the tour group to share their wild speculations. In rapid succession all manner of crackpot hunches were put forward: the Ripper was a painter, a famous writer, a Sioux medicine man, multiple killers working in tandem. And perhaps the most "out there" of all, put forward by the gobby Yank: a crazed midwife punishing whores for their earthly sins. I'd had enough. I came here for answers, not nutty pet theories. I needed to draw a line between the Ripper and whoever was aping him so I could get in front of the next murder.

I rushed the Yank with the perm and took possession of her sizeable body. Having locked in, I raised one of her chubby mitts and coughed for the guide's attention.

'Yes, Miss.'

'Thank you,' I said, taking charge of the conversation. 'I was wondering what you knew about Ripper copycats.'

The guide's mouth formed a patronising smile. 'That's an interesting question,' he said. 'While it is true that the "Ripper" sobriquet has been applied to other killers—most notably the Yorkshire Ripper—the comparisons have been strictly cosmetic. There has never been a real Ripper copycat, and I doubt there ever will be.'

'Are you sure?' I replied.

'Quite sure. It is a testament to the Ripper's mastery of his craft that not one person has had the audacity, intelligence, or skill necessary to truly mimic his work.' He paused for effect. 'Not outside of a Hollywood movie, anyway.'

A chuckle rippled through the crowd. They were laughing at me, and they were right to. This hadn't been a good use of my time. I'd come here hoping to spark a connection, to learn something that put me a step ahead of the Ripper clone, but I'd come away with nothing. The tour had led me down a dark alley and into a dead end, literally and figuratively.

There was no need to stick around for the rest of the guide's speech. I exited my flabby host, slipping out of her brain like a fading dream, and made my way from Hanbury Street, back in the direction of Camden Town. I was about to make the jump back to the funeral home when my phone began buzzing.

'Again?' I griped, tugging the thing from my pocket and answering the call.

'Mister Fletcher, this is DCI Stronge,' said the voice on the other end of the line. 'I'm here on speakerphone with Detective Inspector Maddox.'

That was a heads-up; code for, *"Don't talk about the weird stuff, Jake, my dipshit of a partner is listening"*.

Great. Maddox must have insisted on muscling in on the call, which only made the following conversation all the more challenging.

'How can I help you, Detective Stronge?' I enquired.

'I realise it's late, but I'm calling to ask if you've experienced any… psychic impressions of our killer.'

Again, code. This time the message translated to, *"Have you used your supernatural knowhow to make inroads into the murderer's identity yet, because we've got fuck all"*.

Given that I knew about as much as they did, I decided to palm her off with some broad but likely guesses. 'The picture hasn't totally come into focus yet, Detective, but the impression I'm getting so far shows me a man prone to animal abuse. A man with an unhealthy relationship with his mother.'

'That's... pretty general, Mister Fletcher. Do you have anything more specific?'

'I dunno,' I replied, 'maybe you could cross-reference that with people who hang their toilet rolls underarm style? Those guys are pure monsters.'

I heard a sigh on the other end of the line. 'I'm losing my appetite for sarcasm, Mister Fletcher.'

'Look, I wish I had more, but that's all I've got for now. Give me some time and I'm sure something will firm up.'

Now I was the one talking in code, specifically a code that said, *"Get off my back, Kat, I only left your office a few hours ago. What were you expecting, a bloody signed confession?"*

I heard Maddox's heavy breathing as he leaned in close to the speaker. 'If I had anything to do with this, we wouldn't even be having this conversation, Fletcher, but since you're on the payroll, listen up. Either you start pointing us in the right direction, or you go back to doing tarot readings and scamming grieving widows. Whatever the fuck it was you were doing before you landed in our lap. You hear me? Get the job done; we don't have time for your bollocks.'

'Except you do,' I replied. 'The killer's on the Ripper's calendar, which means we have eight days before he goes after his next victim.'

Well, what do you know? I guess I got something useful from that walking tour after all. Okay, okay, the killer was only *probably* on his calendar. He'd deviated from the script already, no saying he wouldn't again, but I needed to say something to put Maddox's nose out of joint. I know, I'm a petty little prick, ain't I?

Maddox went quiet, leaving his partner to pick up the slack.

'Eight days isn't a lot of time,' said Stronge.

'It's enough,' I replied. 'Give me forty-eight hours and I'll have our man. Trust me.'

I don't know if it was Maddox getting up my beak or Stronge's criminal lack of faith, but I was feeling cocky. Someone had to know this freak, and I was going to find out who. Despite Stronge's assertions to the contrary, I was a detective—a good one—and I was going to prove it by rooting out this lunatic before he struck again. Just because I didn't have Frosty to fall back on, didn't mean I was totally at sea. Someone in this town was going to talk, and I'd be there when they did.

'Put a couple of men on Hanbury Street in case our boy decides to scope the place out early,' I said, overstepping my bounds by a country mile and not caring one solitary fuck. 'In the meantime, don't call me, I'll call you.'

I hung up wearing the trademarked Jake Fletcher resting smirk.

CHAPTER FIFTEEN: GHOUL'S OUT FOR SUMMER

BEFORE I GOT on with either of the jobs on my plate, I decided I'd best check everything was okay with my house guest. Or as okay as could be expected of a warmed-over corpse.

I'll admit I felt bad leaving the dumb mutt to stew for all that time, alone and chained to a metal pipe. Back when I was at school, at the height of the bullying, Mark and a few of the other boys did something similar to me. They didn't do it to trap me, though, it was done specifically to cause harm. This was back when school radiators ran hot as the sun; hot enough to conduct through metal and cause a burn that left a permanent scar. And here I was, cuffing the corpse that wore that scar to a radiator, just like they had. What do you call that? Ironic cruelty, or the very definition of masochism?

Returning to the funeral home that night was like coming back to a cold meal that didn't look appetising when it was hot. There were plenty of other places I could have gone after my office got torched, but for some reason, this was the first that popped into my head. Unless it wasn't really my idea in the first place. I don't know, maybe I was meant to end up here. Was it fate that drew me to a place full of old coffins? I wonder a lot about this sort of stuff. About destiny. Was it inevitable that I ended up in a building that trafficked in the dead, the same way I chose a career that involved constant exposure to corpses? I've been asking myself these sorts of questions for years, but I doubt I'll be any closer to the truth an eternity from now.

But enough of the cod philosophising.

I arrived in the bathroom expecting to see my festering facsimile manacled to the radiator where I left it. Instead, I found a single bracelet attached to a dangling chain that had been snapped in half.

There followed some serious effing and jeffing.

I heard a scream coming from the direction of the lobby. It was a man's scream, a real blood-curdler, and it ran a chill through me like shitting a block of ice. I sprinted after it to find the zombie wrestling with an arm that had come through the front door letterbox. Evidently, my reanimated carcass had broken free of its yoke and chosen to snack on a wannabe burglar. This was, as my dear old gran used to say, a gold-plated fuck-up.

With a couple of long strides and a determined leap, I managed to get two hands around the front of the zombie's head and fish hook its mouth. Solidifying my feet so I could place them against the wall on either side of the door, I used my legs to lever the creature backwards. It was strong, though. Rock-solid. Trying to topple the thing was like trying to fell an Easter Island statue.

'Give it up, you bastard!'

As I struggled, I saw the burglar desperately trying to free his arm from the letterbox, but the yank he'd been given had the bloke wedged in tight. Honestly, I'm surprised the zombie hadn't ripped his arm out at the socket.

'Help me!' I heard him cry. 'Somebody help me!'

Great. If he carried on screaming, he was going to attract all the wrong kinds of attention. But that was only half of my problems. If I didn't pry off the zombie I was jockeying, it was going to deal the burglar a wound that was incompatible with living. It was going to sink its teeth into his arm and open up his veins like a sieve. Thief or not, that was the kind of blood I'd never scrub off. The kind that no amount of penance was going to negate.

The zombie strained against me, its head craned forward, teeth clacking together with a sound like marbles colliding, determined to get its literal pound of flesh.

'I said, give it up!'

Tapping into every bit of strength I had, I tightened my grip on the zombie's head and kicked out against the wall, rocking the beast back on its heels. With a final, exhausting flex, I felt the zombie begin to capsize, then the two of us tipped backwards and struck the ground in an ungainly heap.

The burglar's arm disappeared through the letterbox like a lizard retracting its tongue. This was quickly followed by the *slap-slap-slap* of shoe leather as he sprinted off the property, his footfalls rapidly evaporating into the distance.

I put my mouth to the letterbox and yelled after him, 'And stay out!'

With that established, I snapped my head to the zombie, which sat there on its backside like a toddler, a line of drool draped from its bottom lip.

'That's strike three,' I told it.

First, it attacked me, then it went for those hooligans at the park, now this guy. There was nothing for it, the zombie had to go. It was a liability, had been from the start. I'd been stupid to think I could change the nature of a brain-munching monster. That I could tame it and make use of the creature somehow. If I had a head on my shoulders I'd have dealt with the thing the moment I clapped eyes on it; pushed it back into my burning office and let the fire claim it. Instead, I took it home like a stray.

Well, if there was one thing this experience had taught me, it was that a zombie wasn't a pet, and putting a leash on it wasn't going to stop it from going walkies. The only thing that was going to stop it from lunching on someone's skull meat was putting it down. Before I did anything else, that zombie had to go back in the ground. You might think that's cruel, exterminating the thing like a lame dog, but it's what I had to do. You don't like it, I don't care. My body, my choice.

Under the curtain of night, I made my way to Camden Cemetery, the zombie at my elbow. It was lashing down with rain, and by the time we arrived at the graveyard's spiked black gates, my slack-jawed companion looked like something that had been dredged from the bottom of the Thames.

I pointed to the thick chain securing the entrance. 'Open it,' I demanded.

Without hesitating, the zombie pulled the chain apart like it was made of silly string. If only it did what it was told the rest of the time, but it seemed the moment I took my eye off the thing it went all *must-eat-brainsy* and became as controllable as a toddler with a sugar addiction. Sad, really.

'Heel,' I said.

The zombie tailed me beneath a couple of swaying sycamore trees, then together we cut across the neat lawn of the cemetery's memorial garden. Rows of tombstones stood left and right of us, some of them hundreds of years old, others smooth as bathroom tiles, fresh from the factory.

The rain was still sweeping down in stinging sheets as we joined a gravel path that led to a small burial plot containing a single grave. My grave. Unlike the ones surrounding it—some of which were covered in so many flowers that they looked like they'd placed in the Chelsea Flower Show—mine was bare. A straight man at a Pride parade.

I read the words inscribed on my tombstone: **JAKE FLETCHER**, followed by some dates that were way too close together for my liking. It stung, seeing those words. I always said I'd make a name for myself in this world, but I wasn't expecting to be reading it off a gravestone.

I jabbed a toe at the soupy soil beneath my feet. Somewhere, under that pile of sodden earth, was a distinct lack of my corpse. If I'd been smarter when I first showed up as a ghost, I'd have consecrated my grave to make sure my body stayed where it was planted. I should have known better, really, what with being an ex-exorcist, but I suppose I can be forgiven for being a bit distracted at the time. You know, what with the whole "being dead" thing.

I turned to the zombie and pointed to a shovel planted in the ground next to an open grave nearby.

'Pick it up.'

The clouds broke and lightning spilled out, painting the zombie's face bright white. In the flash, I saw the creature looking back at me with watery eyes.

'I said, pick it up.'

The zombie did as told, plucking the spade from the earth and holding it in its hands like some alien object.

It was time to undo Vic's little excavation. Time to put my body to rest once and for all.

'Go on, get to work,' I said, aiming a finger at the patch of ground at the foot of my tombstone.

I felt like a villain from an old-timey gangster movie, dragging his victim into a wheat field and forcing him to dig his own grave. It wasn't a good feeling.

I watched the zombie go to work, slowly at first, then gradually picking up the pace with each plunge of the spade. It bent low as it thrust the tool into the ground with its foot, then stood tall as it tossed each clod of wet earth over its shoulder. The deeper it dug, the more confident its shovel-work became, the steadier its rhythm, as though it was regaining familiarity with the process. As though it was remembering something forgotten.

I thought back to a winter I once spent working on a building site in my twenties, digging footings for a house extension. I recalled how hard the ground was, how the trench I dug would fill with snow as I went, how the work would get harder and harder the deeper I burrowed. Was that what the zombie was remembering, that little piece of my past? And if so, if I was really in there—even the smallest part of me—could I sacrifice it and still stay whole?

The rain had turned the ground to gravy by this point. The zombie was in the pit up to its chin, still tirelessly shovelling away, still flinging clumps of clay high and wide. Its suit jacket had split apart under the exertion, and its back showed through the wet white shirt beneath. I saw scars laced across its flesh, thick and pink and shocking. Scars that had once been mine.

I heard a thunk as the spade struck something solid, and peered over the crumbling rim of the grave to see what it was. Down below, I saw the first glimpse of a coffin. My coffin. The casket's lid was splintered and pulpy, made soft by years spent in the ground, soaking up rainwater. A better-constructed coffin would have been lacquered until it was clam-shell tough, but my burial was a budget affair, and the box that should have contained my body was turning to mulch.

'Open it,' I told the zombie.

It raised the shovel and brought it down on one of the latches, breaking through it easily.

'Again.'

A second thrust shattered the remaining latch.

'Now hand that to me.'

I firmed up my fists to accept the shovel, and did what I could to avoid the sorrowful look the zombie was wearing.

You're not killing it, I told myself, *it's already dead.*

But then wasn't I dead, too? Weren't all of the souls I obliterated as an exorcist? And yet I had to do this, because if I didn't, someone who hadn't seen their life through was going to lose it.

I felt a gulp travel up and down my throat. 'Get in,' I told the zombie.

With some hesitation, it reached down, swung open the lid of the empty casket, and took a step inside.

'I'm sorry,' I said, 'but you brought this on yourself.'

I raised the shovel and took aim at the top of the zombie's skull. Did I have what was needed to take it down in one? I didn't want it to feel any pain. Could it even feel pain?

Against my better judgment, I caught the zombie's gaze. The creature was shrunk back like a whipped dog, groaning pitifully, staring at me with big wet eyes.

'Don't look at me like that,' I said, the handle of the shovel trembling in my hands.

The image of a skull cracking open like a soft-boiled egg came into my head, and I remembered what it was like to die. What it was like to feel that light extinguished. Except, for me, death was just a phase. Something to be worked through. The zombie didn't have an extra life in the bank. The moment I brought down that spade, it was game over.

'Don't worry, big man, it'll be over in a second. You know what they say: happiness is a warm grave...'

I raised the shovel over my head like I was swinging a hammer at the funfair, but just as I was about to bring it down, the zombie did something that caused my non-existent heart to lurch.

It held up three fingers.

'What?' I said, my voice faltering as I looked at the three mouldy digits.

It couldn't be, could it? Was it answering the question I posed earlier? Telling me the number of the house I grew up in? That *we* grew up in?

No.

It didn't mean anything, surely. Just another twitch. Another old memory firing off in the dark. It didn't prove that there was really a life in there; an actual person who deserved to live.

Did it?

Shit.

I let the shovel slip between my phantom fingers and land in the slop of turned-over earth at my feet. Whether those three fingers proved anything or not, I couldn't do it. It didn't matter what the zombie was or wasn't, I couldn't kill it. I watched the shovel sink into the cold brown slush, until finally, it disappeared.

The zombie looked back at me as it lowered its hand, the corner of its mouth twitching into a skew-whiff smile. 'Braaaaains,' it groaned.

'Not today, Lurch. We've got to get you out of here before someone shows up.'

The sun was making an appearance, colouring the cemetery with the watery grey light of early morning. I reached down into the hole and linked hands with the zombie, and with a mighty heave, hauled my twin out of the grave. I'd figure something out. Some way of making this work. I had to. In the meantime, I needed to get my rotting companion somewhere nice and dark. Somewhere nearby. Lucky for us both, I knew just the place.

'Come on,' I said, planting a hand in the middle of the zombie's back, 'let's go get into some trouble.'

CHAPTER SIXTEEN: LEARNING TO LIVE WITH MYSELF

THERE ARE parts of London you can move around in with no one looking at you, and Kings Cross is definitely one of them. In the early morning, its streets are occupied almost exclusively by commuters, heads down, sipping their coffees and reading from their phones. And yet still, the hunk of haunted meat I was towing had begun to draw some looks, not least of all from a passing dog-walker, whose Golden Retriever had caught the zombie's scent and was barking furiously. Once again, I found myself in a real *Weekend at Bernie's* situation.

'Come on, Blue Lips, shift your arse.'

I shunted the zombie down the road before the dog decided he liked the look of my corpse's old bones enough to finish the burial I couldn't.

Having to steer the zombie clear of the general public wasn't my only problem, though. At any moment, Vic Lords could use his evil eye to spy on me. What a fine look that would be; me playing with my leftovers instead of hunting down the soul with the weird name that he was after. And yet, I understood enough about scrying magic to know the chances of us getting eyeballed were pretty slim. That particular brand of sorcery was extremely taxing, and couldn't be used with much regularity. After all, if scrying magic were easy, nothing would be sacred. There'd be no secrets left in the world. Every bit of information there was would be out in the open, available to even the most cack-handed of neophytes. No, I was pretty sure we were safe for now.

We arrived at a dilapidated magic shop tucked down a King's Cross back street. The shop sign read Legerdomain; a clever little pun that the proprietor had dreamed up back when she had a sense of humour. The owner of the shop called herself Madame Olena, but I call her Jazz Hands on account of her being handy with the old sorcery. Also because it winds her up, and there's precious little in this world that gives me more pleasure than getting that woman's goat.

'This should be good for a laugh,' I told my companion as I gestured for him to push open the shop door.

Jazz Hands didn't much like ghosts, so I could only imagine how she was going to react when I sent a zombie lurching into her establishment.

A brass bell tinkled overhead as we entered, an early warning system installed to detect civilians and Uncannies alike. A system that Jazz Hands had built personally.

I cast my eyes around the shop. The decor was the same as always: liver-red walls and bowed black shelves heaving with piles of magical wotsits and doofers, lit by the scant shafts of daylight able to penetrate the store's grime-streaked windows. Sat upon a frayed Turkish rug in the centre of the room was a rack festooned with all manner of alluring little objects: things that vanished, things that appeared from nowhere, things that floated in thin air. All of them stage tricks; Uri Geller shit. The real magic in Legerdomain was kept strictly behind closed doors.

Restocking the rack—a heap of magician's starter kits balanced precariously on one hip—was Jazz Hands. She was a short, pear-shaped woman who barely cleared the shop counter when she was at the till, and wore an outfit that had all the grandeur of a bin liner snagged on a barbed-wire fence. Hers was one of those confusing faces that could belong to a forty-year-old, or someone twice that age, depending on the light. Sat atop her head was a bird's nest of hair, brittle and straw-like and powdered with a thick dusting of dandruff.

She wheeled in my direction and peered at me through a pair of violet-lensed glasses that she referred to as her "spooktacles". She called them that on account of the fact that she was able to see phantoms through them, as well as other Uncanny types naked to the human eye. The specs were another of her inventions. As you might have gathered, Jazz Hands isn't one to take chances. She had some valuable goods in stock and had learned from bitter experience not to take chances with security.

Needless to say, Jazz was not thrilled about having a walking cadaver on her premises. Wearing a face like a bulldog licking piss off a thistle, she stomped over to the shop door and flipped over the Closed sign. This seemed a bit overkill to me, given that I'd never once seen a customer inside the place, no matter the time of day.

'Good Lord, Fletcher,' she cried, 'if you want a friend, join a book club. Don't go digging up your own carcass.'

Jazz was known to blow hot and cold. Mostly cold. Arctic, really.

'Here to drain your brain, Jazz, old bean,' I said before she could start yelling at me again.

'Let me guess,' she sighed, 'someone dredged up your dead body, reanimated it, and tried using it to kill you. Now you're attempting to figure out how to tame the thing so you can turn it around on them and get some payback.'

'That's... that's actually incredibly accurate.'

'It's a story as old as time itself,' she replied. 'So who's in the firing line? That old boss of yours? The shitbag gangster?'

'Vic Lords, yeah. Only, I've come to realise that Ol' Bitey here isn't quite the secret weapon I thought it was.'

Jazz approached my rotten doppelganger, entirely unafraid, and began inspecting it like a Crufts judge looking for the Best in Show. Okay, not exactly the reaction I thought I was going to get when I waltzed a sopping-wet zombie into her shop.

She grabbed the creature by the lapels and brought its head to hers so she could investigate its ears and teeth. For a moment, I wondered if she was going to reach down and cup the thing's balls before slapping a ribbon on it. Instead, she turned to me.

'Except for his outfit—which is an absolute disgrace by the way—I'd say he's in magnificent condition. I'm sure he'll do a fine job.'

'Trust me,' I replied, 'he's not up to snuff.'

The zombie was too wild, too unpredictable. Getting it to take out Vic would be like trying to operate a remote-controlled car catching cross signals. Chances were, its steering would drop out and send it slamming into a barrier before it got anywhere near the finish line.

'Plus there are other factors…' I went on.

I brought her up to speed on Vic's newfound powers and explained how he was going to drop Frosty through the trap if I didn't make good on his soul heist. It was only at the end of my speech that I realised Jazz's attention was elsewhere.

'Who's a good boy?' she cooed, rubbing the zombie behind the ear. It responded by kicking its leg like a dog getting a belly scratch. 'You're a good boy,' she confirmed.

'Jazz!'

'What?' she crowed, whipping her head in my direction.

'I'm trying to tell you how fucked I am here. Vic has magic, muscle, and a hostage. The bloke's got me painted into a real corner.'

'What are you saying? You're not seriously considering doing this job of his, are you?'

I shrugged. 'You got a better idea?'

She pouted in that special way that made her face look like a baboon's arse. 'It won't win you any points with Him Upstairs, you know that, don't you?'

Despite her spikiness, Jazz cared a great deal about my eternal soul. Sometimes I wondered if she was actually more invested in getting the red out of my ledger than I was.

'I realise this isn't an ideal situation...' I started.

'*Ideal*? You'll burn for this, Fletcher. Is that what you want? To be cast into a lake of fire with Lucifer and his demons?'

'What choice do I have?'

She paced up and down the shop, scratching the back of her head and dislodging so much dead skin that at the end of her march she was left wearing a pair of dandruff epaulettes. Eventually, she said, 'Maybe there's a way I can help you become more simpatico with your twin here. Make it so the pair of you can team up against this Vic Lords character and rescue your friend without having to do any dirty work.'

'I'm all ears,' I replied.

As Jazz racked her brain, she subconsciously returned to petting the zombie. In doing so, she noticed that one of its fingers was missing; the pinky it lost when it tore down the wall at the funeral home. Her eyebrows shot up like a pair of roller blinds. 'What happened here?' she demanded.

'Bit of an accident,' I replied. 'Not my fault.'

'You can't take care of anything, can you? Not even your own body.'

I was getting more than a bit miffed at the way she seemed to care more about my rotting corpse than she did me.

'Okay,' she said, returning to the matter at hand. 'Before we figure out your Vic problem, I need you to tell me everything there is to know about your relationship with our friend here.'

I looked to the zombie, then back to Jazz. '*Relationship*? With this thing?'

She didn't answer, just regarded me cooly over the rims of her violet-lensed spectacles.

'Fine.'

I gave her the whole story: how Vic had set my reanimated carcass on me, how I'd harboured it in an abandoned funeral home, the scraps of memories we shared, how it had broken free and attacked a couple of members of the public, and, yes, how I'd almost caved its skull in with the business end of a shovel.

'You did what?' she cried.

'What would you have done in my shoes? It was going to kill someone.'

'Is that right?' she fired back. 'And who are you? The zombie expert of Camden Town?'

I had to admit, I knew next to nothing about this particular breed of undead. I was a ghost guy. I also knew a bit about vampires, although that area mainly belongs to a teenage girl with a weird brand on her palm who calls herself the Nightstalker (a story for another time, perhaps). Zombies were pretty much a mystery to me. Voodoo shit. I had no idea they even showed up in this part of the world. Haiti, sure, parts of Europe, okay, even the occasional U.S.

shopping mall from time to time, but you didn't see many zombies out London way.

Jazz met me with her owlish gaze. 'Pay attention. Just as there is more than one type of person, there are different kinds of zombie. Yes, most are simply eating, killing machines, bred to destroy, but others retain a degree of sentience. If what you've told me is correct, this particular specimen exhibits a great deal of it. This is no mere empty vessel. No burned-out shell. For our friend here to be capable of the things you have described, there must be some vestige of a soul left inside.'

'You're saying this thing's alive?'

'As much as you are.'

'Bollocks.'

A stray snarl of hair dropped in front of Jazz's face. She blew it away. 'How else do you explain the way the creature retains your memories? Something of yours was left behind when you were separated from your earthly form. Call it what you will—mental residue, a scrap of your spirit—but that zombie doesn't just look like you. He *is* you.'

'So you're telling me this dollop of guts has as much right to live as I do? Even if he smells like a plague pit and looks like the cover of an Iron Maiden album?'

'Even then.'

I shook my head. 'Nah, I'm still not having it. For one thing, I don't go around trying to destroy people. Anymore.'

Yeah, all right, it does sound like I'm protesting a bit too much considering some of my own recent thoughts on the matter of my rotting doppelganger, but I wasn't altogether comfortable with the idea that part of me was in my decomposing body, looking back at me. Judging me.

'What makes you so sure our friend here is a killer?' asked Jazz. 'He's part you, remember? Would you deliberately kill an innocent person?'

I remembered the spade slipping through my fingertips. Remembered it disappearing beneath the mud. 'No.'

Jazz continued, 'I'm confident that any violent actions you've witnessed were reflexes brought about by Mister Lords' necromancy. Residue of the programming he implanted, which, from the looks of things, has all but worn off.'

'Braaaaaains,' droned the zombie, undercutting her argument quite spectacularly.

I looked to Jazz. 'Maybe there's a tiny bit of me rattling around in there, but so what? A zombie's an automaton, not a person. If I told this thing to crack open your noggin and gobble up the goo inside, chances are it would do it.'

To add weight to my argument, I ordered the zombie to pick Jazz up and lift her off the ground. It did so one-handed, scooping a paw under her behind and hefting her into the air like the bride at a Jewish wedding. It did this with enough force that it almost put the poor woman's head through the ceiling.

'Sorry about that, Jazzer, but you take my point? It's a puppet, that's all.'

Jazz cursed and rubbed the bump on her head. When she finally finished fuming, she resumed her argument. 'The zombie's obedience doesn't make him lesser, you cynical bastard. Loyalty is a fine thing in a man. A fine thing.'

'Is it a man, though? That's my point. A memory or two doesn't mean anything.'

That so, Jakey? Then why didn't you finish it off with the shovel?

An exhausted sigh fell from Jazz's lips. 'You keep referring to your companion here as an "it", but he's as much a "he" as you are, Fletcher. You think you're more of a person just because you can string a couple of sentences together? Get with it, man. He's real; you're a ghost. He's the original; you're just a photocopy.'

'How do you work that out? I'm the essence. Mouldy over there is just the packaging.'

'That's a theory, but not one I subscribe to. At least not in this instance.'

'Well, thanks a lot, Jazz.'

I mean, talk about kicking a man when he's down.

'I'm sorry, but you need to understand the facts if you're going to make this work. You think you're the genuine article, but he's the only one of you who's truly human. Be good to him, or Our Father certainly won't be doing you any favours.'

Now it was my turn to sigh. 'What am I meant to do exactly? Take him out on dates? Buy him a brain supper every Friday night?'

'Braaaaains!'

'Not now, okay?'

I wondered if this was another of His little tests. God's way of figuring out once and for all if I was a white hat or a black hat. He'd thrown some spanners my way already; could this be another one? Or maybe this wasn't a test at all. Maybe this was the way He wanted my afterlife to play out. Hell on Earth, forever and ever, amen.

I was in a real bind. If Jazz was right about the zombie having a soul—even a tiny shred of one—there was no getting rid of the thing. He was one of God's creatures, which meant I was left looking after him till the cows came home. What else was I supposed to do under the circumstances? Abandon him? Drive down the motorway and push him out of the passenger seat like a Christmas puppy? No. I was stuck carrying the bugger. A pallbearer for my own corpse.

I returned to Jazz. 'When we started this conversation you said you might know a way for me and stinky to get more in tune. Well, go on then, what's the secret?'

She thought on it for a few more seconds, then finally delivered the following: 'Be nice.'

'*Be nice*?

'Yes. If you want to make friends, be nice.'

'That's it? That's all you've got?'

'Pretty much.'

'I thought you were going to chuck some magic about. Be my Q. Build me some doo-dad that helps bring him in line.'

She gave me another look, her judgmental eyes magnified twofold by the violet lenses of her glasses. 'And what sort of "doo-dad" would that be exactly?'

'I dunno,' I replied, turning to the zombie, who stood so statue still that anyone watching would have thought he'd lost a fight with Medusa. 'An enchanted leash or something. You know, like dogs wear, but loaded with some hoo-doo that helps me break this thing in.'

Jazz ground the heels of her palms into her eye sockets. 'Haven't you listened to a bloody word I've said? He's not a pet to be house trained... even if I would prefer he didn't drool quite so much on my merchandise.' She plucked a handkerchief from her pocket and wiped a trail of saliva from the top of an ancient Paul Daniels magic set.

'Okay then, no leash.'

'No leash, no whip, no poxy cat o' nine tails.'

'So what then?'

'I do have something that will make him less conspicuous. Make it so he's able to move around in the world without attracting any undue attention.'

I scratched at my stubble. 'Well, that's a start at least. Okay then, go for it, do your thing.'

She smiled, reached behind the shop counter for a bottle, and doused the zombie neck-to-toe in Febreze.

'Ta-da,' she said.

CHAPTER SEVENTEEN: VIDEO NASTY

BEFORE I PUT Legerdomain in my rearview, Jazz Hands worked some magic on the zombie. Magic that proved a lot more effective than a spritz of air freshener. Specifically, she used a spell that sheathed him in a protective laminate similar to the kind she used to preserve her ancient books and grimoires. A sheath that would trap in the zombie's cracked-sarcophagus smell, and stop him from rotting to pieces.

She also provided some fresh clothes so I could take him out in public without drawing too many stares: a new suit, a hat, and a pair of oversized sunglasses to disguise his face. Why she had a wardrobe full of men's clobber lying around, I had no idea. An ex? A dead husband? Was Jazz Hands a widow, or did she have a string of lovers in her wake, a long queue of men leaving their clothes in her boudoir? I've known Jazz for years but knew so little about her. The woman was a total mystery to me. I once caught a glimpse of the inside of the safe she keeps behind the shop counter and saw a gold trophy for fencing. Never even thought to ask her about it. Fact is, I'm a self-centred bastard who thinks of little else but his own problems. It's the way I've always been, really. Probably another reason I stayed earthbound after I turned up my trotters.

I stole a look at the zombie shambling along beside me. With all the gear on, he looked pretty presentable. Okay, his mug was a bit gaunt, and his skin was a touch on the green side, but if you were prepared to let that go, he looked dandy. Give his hair a comb and slap a bit of foundation on him and he could even pass for healthy. Cancer patient healthy, anyway.

'Guess it's about time I gave you a name, eh? So what's it going to be…?' I flogged my brain for something suitable, but soon ran out of patience. 'How about... FrankenJake? What do you reckon? That work for you?'

'Braaaains,' he slurred.

'Had a feeling you might say that.'

The next thing I did was stash the newly-minted FrankenJake at the funeral home. I still had the Ripper case on my plate, which meant a visit to the cop shop, and as far as I was aware, today wasn't Bring Your Zombie To Work Day. No, FrankenJake would have to plant his arse for now. Okay, I was starting, reluctantly, to accept the idea that he was more than just a mindless killing machine, but I had a feeling Stronge might take a bit more convincing. Plus, I still wasn't totally persuaded that FrankenJake didn't pose a threat to the public, which left me with no choice but to keep him restrained.

I made a proper job of locking him up this time; two pairs of handcuffs shackling each wrist. I got the cuffs from Jazz Hands.

Top-quality, she assured me, *much stronger than the fancy dress pair I bet you used.*

When I asked her why she had so many sets of professional-grade handcuffs lying about the place, she flushed bright red and mumbled something about selling them to magicians for stage tricks. A dark horse, that one, for sure.

Stronge had instructed me to report to the station in my meat suit, so I had no choice but to make a stop-off on the way there and make use of my old bully, Mark Ryan. All this to-ing and fro-ing was wearing me out. On top of having a zombie to take care of, I had a copycat murderer to catch, and a whole other thing going on with Vic Lords. It was exhausting. I felt like I was being pulled in every direction at once, like poor Frosty, strapped to Vic's torture rack.

I jogged up the station steps, got the nod from the desk sergeant, and took the lift to the top floor. Stronge was there to greet me.

'About time,' she said, pointing to her office like a headmaster summoning a naughty student.

That gave me the royal hump, I won't lie. Manners had never been Kat's strong suit, but the way I saw it, she could at least stretch to a bit of professional courtesy.

'Jawohl Mein Capitan,' I said, firing off a sarcastic salute.

She followed me as I entered the office and took a seat opposite her desk. The room looked much the same as it had the last time I visited—everything in its place, the plaque on the wall commending Katherine Mary Jane Stronge hanging nice and level—but there was one notable addition. Maddox was there this time, standing off to one side, eyeing me warily. I hadn't expected that, and his presence made the room seem smaller somehow. Like the walls had closed in since my last visit. I could deal with Maddox out in the wild, but here, in his manor, I felt vulnerable. I'd spent half of my life indulging in, well, let's just say "extralegal" activities, so being cornered in the nick gave me understandable cause for concern. Not that I had much to fear from the law at this point, but still, the jitters were there.

'Morning, Maddox,' I said, faking a smile and doing my best to ignore his overpowering aftershave.

Maddox didn't answer, just stood there, arms crossed, looking at me like I was shit on his shoe.

'Suit yourself.' I turned to Stronge. 'So what am I doing here? You pinched anyone yet?'

'We're working on it,' she replied tartly. 'What about you? Has your investigation led anywhere interesting?'

'Not yet,' I confessed.

'Of course, it hasn't,' Maddox chimed in. 'There are magic 8-balls more reliable than you, Fletcher.'

Resisting the urge to tell him where to stuff his magic 8-ball, I looked to a whiteboard on the wall behind him. Scribbled upon its surface was a figure showing the number of days remaining until the next predicted Ripper killing.

Stronge opened a police-issue laptop and rotated it my way. 'Tell me what you make of this...'

I hunched over the screen like a hungry vulture. It showed a web browser with a video, currently on pause; just a greyed-out window with an unpressed play symbol.

'What is it?' I asked.

'The coroner found something on the vic's body.'

She showed me a photo on her phone. It was the victim's tongue, pulled free of her mouth by a pair of forceps to expose its underside. There on the base, carved very small, was a string of letters and numbers.

'What is that?' I asked. 'Some kind of calling card?'

'Christ Almighty,' said Maddox. 'What do you think it is? It's a URL.'

I hadn't used the web since I was alive, so it was hardly surprising that I didn't make the connection right away. Last time I was properly online, we still called it "surfing the net". Yeah. It had been a while.

'Right, a URL,' I replied. 'To the video. Sorry, bit of a Luddite.'

'What's this got to do with food?' asked Maddox.

It took me a second.

'You're thinking of a crudités, and that's not even how the word's pronounced. Fuck me, mate, try not to cut yourself on that razor-sharp mind of yours.'

Maddox took a step in my direction, his skin the colour of pickled beetroot.

'Stop it right now,' barked Stronge. 'Honestly, it's like watching a game of turd tennis with you two.'

She was right, and neither of us was coming away with a clean racquet.

'Go ahead,' I told her, affecting an air of professionalism, 'let's see this video.'

Stronge took a deep, sustained breath and reached for the play button. 'Okay then. Maddox, I want you looking for anything I might have missed the first time around. Fletcher… just let me know if it gets your psychic juices flowing.'

She stabbed the button and the video came to life.

I saw a minimalistic kitchen: uncluttered granite counters, scrubbed tiles, silent but for the quiet hum of a refrigerator. The camera was trained on a set of oven hobs with plenty of headroom for a chef, but no one present to take the role. I could make out a few more details here and there—various utensils hung from wall hooks, a professional-looking knife block—but it was too dark to make out much else. I searched the frame for clues, for something that might give away the kitchen's whereabouts, but found nothing. I wondered what the footage was recorded on. Was it shot on a phone or a camcorder? Was the camera on sticks, or was it set on a counter? Was the dingy light ambient, or was it coming from an artificial source? These sorts of facts might seem inconsequential to you, but when you're on a job, you never know what might come in handy later. What will help crack the thing wide open. Unfortunately, much as I struggled, I could find answers to none of my questions. I continued to stare at the video, which was beginning to look more like a still photo the longer I looked.

'Does anything actually happen in this thing?' I asked.

'There,' replied Stronge, just as a figure slid into view.

A heavy-set man entered from stage left and took his mark centre frame. He wore black clothes and an oxblood-red balaclava. The few parts of his face that the mask didn't conceal were obscured by the dim kitchen lighting. *Who* he was was just as much of a mystery as *where* he was. In any case, this was him. The copycat killer. The new Ripper.

Without announcing himself, he bent over the hobs and used a match to light one of the burners.

'There,' I said as the hob flared to life, briefly illuminating the suspect's face before he took a step back into the semi-darkness. 'Did you see that? Could you make out his eye colour?'

'I've paused it and had it analysed already,' Stronge replied. 'Too dark to tell, even when the contrast's been monkeyed with.'

Damn.

The mystery chef took an iron skillet from a hook, placed it on the burner, and greased it with a knob of butter. Nothing sinister had happened, nothing had been said, and yet still the video had a creepy anything-might-happen quality to it that set my teeth on edge.

I felt compelled to lighten the mood. 'What is this, eh? An IRA cookery show?'

Not bad for an off the cuff quip, I thought, but I bombed like Hiroshima doing its first open mic. Stronge and Maddox tutted, then the three of us returned to the video, the room heavy with silence.

On screen, the masked chef reached out of frame and came back with a glass bowl containing some kind of meat. It looked like offal to me, a large, bulbous thing with what looked like valves attached to it. A heart, maybe. A cow heart? The chef draped the meat across the now sizzling pan and pressed down on it with the back of a spatula.

There was something about the way he moved that wasn't quite right, I thought. His gestures were unnatural, twitchy, like an alien who was doing his best to pass for human but hadn't quite settled into the role yet. As the mystery meat crackled in the skillet, the chef turned it over periodically, ensuring that it was browned equally on all sides. As it cooked, he whistled.

'I don't get it,' said Maddox. 'Why send us this? What's in it for him?'

I had a theory. 'It's a message. The original Ripper left them, too. Sent letters to the press, wrote graffiti on walls. This must be a homage. A 21st Century remix.'

'If it's a message, what's it saying?' Maddox asked.

I didn't have an answer for that.

On the laptop, the chef used the spatula to scoop up the meat and set it on a porcelain plate. Using a knife and fork, he carefully carved off a slice, posted it into his mouth, and began to chew.

'According to the coroner, that's a human organ,' said Stronge.

'Jesus,' said Maddox. 'So we're dealing with a cannibal now?'

'You okay?' asked Stronge, pausing the video.

Apparently, Maddox hadn't long been returned to active duty since his last psychiatric meltdown. Maybe this was too much for him. Maybe he wasn't ready to chase monsters. Not since he chased down a real one; a demon called a soul feaster that left him so rattled it shook his brain like an Etch a Sketch and scrubbed the thing clean.

When I said before that I knew the truth about what happened to Maddox, this is what I neglected to mention. It happened years back, not long after I first started calling myself a detective. Stronge and I were on a case, chasing down a demon, when Maddox got caught in the crossfire. It was the demon who shattered his arm and put him in therapy. It was the demon who taught him that monsters were real, but unlike his partner, Maddox's mind had chosen to reject the truth. It's a common defence mechanism. Deny, deny, deny; that's what the brain does best when it's faced with the impossible. After all, if you accept that magic is out there, the dead walk the Earth, and fiends from the Nether are constantly clawing their way into our dimension, it's going to be hard to walk down the shops for a pint of milk afterwards, isn't it?

'I'm fine,' said Maddox, halfway embarrassed, halfway annoyed. 'Hit play.'

Stronge gave me a sideways glance and started the video up again. The home movie resumed and we watched as the chef went back to his meal. He hewed off another slice of meat before dangling it over his face and letting it fall into the hungry pit of his mouth.

'What exactly did he take from the vic?' I asked.

'That's the thing,' Stronge replied. 'He didn't take anything from the girl we found in the bike lock-up. What he's got there belongs to someone else.'

'A second body?' I said, sitting bolt upright. 'You're saying he already killed again?'

Stronge nodded grimly.

'This soon? But his next attack shouldn't take place until September 8th.'

'Apparently, he didn't get that memo,' she replied.

Maddox looked distinctly green around the gills now. 'What kind of organ is that exactly?' he asked, tapping the monitor as the killer enjoyed another slice of meat.

For a moment, it looked as though Stronge wasn't going to tell him—was going to spare him the details and save him from the truth—but that wouldn't have been professional.

'According to the coroner, what he's eating there is a uterus.'

CHAPTER EIGHTEEN: A BIG ASK

WITH SO MANY unanswered questions flitting around, and Frosty temporarily out of service, I needed a new source. An informant. A tip-off man. Someone with a set of ears that were tuned into the backchannel goings-on in this town.

Thankfully, I knew a good place to throw out a net.

I took FrankenJake with me. The destination was a way away, but it was dark out now, and it didn't seem fair to leave the poor sod mothballed in the funeral home all day and night. Besides, I wasn't worried about a zombie raising any eyebrows where I was going. Where I was headed, a zombie would fit right in.

The Beehive is the pub I was sat in when this little tale first kicked off. The one that my so-called "cursed" client stood me up in, back before Vic set my reanimated corpse on me, and some lunatic started slicing up women in the style of Jack the Ripper. More innocent times, you might say. Anyway, I didn't really describe the place in much detail on that occasion, so let me frame the scene properly for you this time...

The Beehive is situated down a blind alley off Ealing Broadway. Blind alleys are a sort of... crack in reality. An urban Bermuda Triangle, if you like. Regular folk can't see them, but they're there for those of us who know how to look. To people like me, such places are plain as day. Even as a kid I could sense them, not in full focus, but like the remnants of an old picture that had been painted over.

Faint outlines, parts peeking through from a buried layer, puzzling, intriguing, impossible, and yet right there.

Down the blind alley, the only evidence of The Beehive was a small, flaky picture of its namesake painted on a stout, wooden door. No swinging pub sign, no welcoming music, just a tiny, barely distinguishable mark, left there like a clue to some mysterious puzzle.

I instructed FrankenJake to push open the door, and as I stepped through after him, I felt the skin of a protective bubble part around me.

No Fighting, No Spells, No WiFi.

That's what the sign above the bar says, and in case anyone got confused about the second part, the dampening magic that permeated the place did their thinking for them. It didn't rob the patrons of their powers entirely, but it deadened any spells to the point that they weren't worth worrying about. It also ensured that scrying magic couldn't penetrate the pub's walls, which meant so long as I was inside, I was guaranteed to be off Vic's radar. As far as he was concerned, I could be just about anywhere.

Inside the saloon bar, sat beneath a rattling old fan that stirred nicotine-tinged air as thick as gravy, a gang of misfits indulged in a spirited hand of gin rummy. Sat around the table was a man in a colourful turban with nut-brown skin (likely a magician of some sort), a hollow-cheeked vampire, and what I'm fairly certain was some kind of werecritter in human form. A fairly typical night then. The Beehive is a place for the city's ghouls and goblins to let it all hang out. Every city in the U.K. has a place like it: a murky drinking hole where us Uncanny types can knock back a pint in peace, among our own kind and away from the prying eyes of the masses.

That didn't mean the patrons of The Beehive were my friends, though.

The card players regarded me suspiciously as I made my way to the bar accompanied by my walking corpse. You'd expect it would be the zombie causing a stir, but I was the one getting the hairy eyeball. A lot of people don't like ghosts, you see. To them, we're a walking, talking memento mori. A reminder that they too will die. And yet, apparently, the animated corpse accompanying me didn't inspire the same sense of dread. I don't know why. Maybe the simple fact that it had a physical form made it seem more human somehow. Or was it that the card players shooting me hate rays were fans of that American TV show? The one with all the zombies and the meaningful stares.

These were questions for another time.

I approached the bar and greeted Lenny, The Beehive's live-in landlord and resident giant. Anyone else might have enquired as to what a ghost was doing strolling around with his reanimated cadaver by his side, but not Lenny. He'd seen every freak of nature there was walk through his door, so instead, he stared back at me, poker-faced and saying nothing.

'I hear it's two-for-the-price-of-one night,' I joshed, nodding to my twin.

Not a sausage. I tried another angle.

'You got any decent cocktail rums back there, Lenny?' I asked. 'I was thinking I might get a Zombie for my friend here.'

A big, fat nothing.

I cast my eyes to the bar, defeated. 'I'll have a pint of the black stuff.'

Lenny nodded his mutton-chopped head, took a step to the right, and pulled a pump labelled *O'Ghouls*. Given the pub's rather eclectic clientele, many of whom were undead, Lenny had managed to perfect a brew that was potable even to the corporeally-challenged. So in case you were wondering why I put up with the bar's sticky floor, shabby decor, and total lack of customer service, now you know.

Lenny set down the glass of stout. It wore a collar so perfect and white that it looked like a man of the cloth in the presence of the Pope himself. Say what you like about Lenny, but the feller could pull a pint. But I hadn't come all the way to his establishment just to wet my beak. I was on the lookout for an informant. A trafficker of information. Someone who could look into a couple of burning questions I had and come back with some answers. And there he was, sitting in a booth on the other side of the bar: an eaves.

Eaves are a funny-looking lot. Imagine a mole rat that figured out how to stand on its hind legs and dress itself, and you're most of the way there. This one was a typical specimen of the species: a squat body with skin so white it was practically transparent, Spock ears, and an oversized mouth filled with two rows of sharp yellow teeth.

I clocked what the eaves was drinking and ordered a pint that matched. 'Wish me luck,' I whispered in FrankenJake's shell-like.

I strolled by the card players and plonked myself gently in the booth opposite the eaves.

'Chin, chin,' I said, pushing the drink his way and raising mine in salute.

He narrowed his bloodshot eyes at me, drained the last of his drink, then started in on the next one without clinking my glass.

I knew he wouldn't be so easily bought. An eaves collects news and hearsay and passes it on for a price, but the cost was going to be a bit steeper than a warm pint of Lenny's ale. The eaves trade in magic. It feeds them and enables them to conceal their dens from anyone bearing a grudge, and given that they're happy to grass on just about anyone, keeping their kith and kin on the down-low ranks pretty high on their collective agenda.

'What do you want?' the eaves hissed.

'Information,' I replied. 'The whereabouts of a couple of errant souls.'

'Do I look like a rat to you?'

Now that you come to mention it... I wanted to say, but kept my trap shut.

'Look, this isn't my first day on the job. I know how this works. Do you want paying or not?'

He tipped the last of the beer down his neck and let fly a long burp. 'You got the goods on you?'

I replied, 'I can get it.'

'How?'

'I know people. Believe me, I'll get you so much magic you'll be shitting the stuff.'

I was bluffing. I knew a spellslinger or two, but none of them owed me any favours, and chances were they had better things to do than spend their magic on this gossip merchant.

'You're full of it,' said the eaves, sniffing me out for the bull-shitter I was. 'And just so you know, we're not all tattle-tales, my kind. Some of us make an honest living, just like the rest of you.' He pushed away his empty glass. 'Thanks for the pint, ghost.'

The eaves slid out of the booth and off he trotted, over the hills and far away.

Balls. Big fat hairy ones.

It was crystal clear in that moment just how valuable Frosty had been to me. I guess I never realised quite what an asset he was before, not until he got kidnapped. That cantankerous old git had left some big old shoes to fill, no doubt about it.

I slunk back to the bar where FrankenJake was still stood, mute and unmoving, a silent sentinel.

'Well, that went down like a turd on a birthday cake,' I groaned, and ordered another pint of heavy.

Three more of those and I was having a proper conversation with the big lug. A very one-sided conversation, anyway.

'What am I gonna do, mate?' I slurred into his ear, one hand clamped on his shoulder, heavy as a trailer hitch. 'I'm stuck. Dead-ended.'

He looked back at me with those big doe eyes of his as if to say, *Don't give up, Jake. All is not lost.* Or at least that's what I inferred.

'You're right,' I said, wobbling on my bar stool. 'Someone's gotta know something. Someone's gotta have something meaty I can sink my teeth into.' I realised who I was talking to and regretted my choice of words. 'No offence.'

FrankenJake carried on lending his ear. Unlike most people, he wasn't just waiting for a gap in the conversation so he could jump in and say his piece. He really was an excellent sounding board.

An idea lit up in my head.

'How about you?' I said. 'How about *you* be my Johnny on the street? You're a good listener; I bet people would tell you all kinds of stuff. Okay, you don't really talk, so passing gossip my way is going to be a bit tricky, but we can work around that. Maybe get you a Speak & Spell like they did *E.T.* What do you reckon? You up for it, big man?'

He tipped his head my way, causing his jaw to fall wide open. 'Braaaains,' he drawled.

Okay, so maybe not my brightest idea, but then desperate times call for desperate measures.

Tiring of my less than verbose companion, I looked around the bar in search of more stimulating company. And Christ, did I find it.

Sat at a corner table by herself was a woman who practically defined the word "stimulating". She had a head of platinum blonde hair and the supple, willowy body of a Victoria's Secret model. Tucked under her table, crossed coquettishly, were two of the longest getaway sticks I'd ever seen.

'Where did you come from?' I muttered to myself.

Here I was, wasting my time trying to strike up a conversation with a brick wall, when the whole time *she'd* been sat there, lighting the place up. I wondered what kind of Uncanny she was. A witch? An angel? A siren? The last one, I guessed, because she was dragging me her way like a frigging tractor beam.

With a conspiratorial wink, I leaned across the bar to Lenny, who reluctantly stooped down and turned his ear to me.

'What do you know about the blonde?' I asked from the side of my mouth.

He grinned. 'She's something, ain't she? Adds a real touch of glamour to the place.'

'I'll say.'

Lenny aimed a torpedo of spit into a pint pot and polished it with an old rag. 'Doing wonders for business. Been seeing a lot more punters in here since she started showing up.'

'Is that right?' I replied, scratching my stubble thoughtfully.

As if on cue, a young man from a neighbouring table sidled up to the blonde and tried to engage her in conversation. He was quickly rebuffed.

'None of 'em ever gets anywhere,' Lenny said with a shrug. 'None of 'em ever will, I reckon.'

'Oh yeah?' I said, buffing my nails on my jacket. 'We'll see about that...' I nudged FrankenJake. 'What do you say, brother? Wanna be my wingman?'

His expression stayed the same: slack and vacant. 'Braaaaaains.'

'Suit yourself then.'

I watched the blonde out of the corner of my eye as she drew a pack of Winston's from the pocket of the long beige coat slung on the back of her chair and tapped out a cigarette. Time to strike. I gave Lenny a nod, took one more sip of beer—just enough to scrape up the nerve I needed for what came next—and made my move.

'Here, let me get that for you…' I said, swooping in and snapping my fingers.

An arc of flame leapt between my thumb and forefinger, lighting a cherry on the end of the blonde's cigarette. In magical terms, it was a cheap trick, but nonetheless, the extent of my pyromantic abilities. I guess what I'm saying is, don't get it into your head that I'm going to be lobbing bloody great fireballs about any time soon.

She took a drag on the ciggy and exhaled from her nostrils, letting the smoke fall into her mouth like a grey waterfall. 'Thanks,' she said in a distinctly American accent.

I wasn't expecting a septic.

Sorry, I just remembered you might not be from around these parts. Might even be a septic yourself for all I know. Just in case, I'll give you this bit of cockney rhyming slang for free: septic tank = Yank. Got that? Okay, on we go.

'So, you're an American, are you?' I asked the blonde.

'Among other things,' she replied.

Instead of explaining the meaning of this cryptic remark, she left it pending. It was hard to say whether she did that as a come-on or a sly rebuff, but I took a gamble and pulled up a pew opposite her. She regarded me cooly, drumming the surface of the table with the points of her cherry-red talons.

'Let me get you a drink since you came all this way,' I said, waving to Lenny. 'Barkeep, same again for me, and one of whatever the lady's having.'

I flashed Lenny a fifty. I was feeling flush, what with all the money I'd liberated from that safe, a wedge of which was burning a hole through the inside pocket of my suit jacket. I'd persuaded Jazz Hands to do her razzmatazz on a portion of the stash during my recent visit to her magic shop, meaning I could handle it as easily as if my hands were made of flesh and blood. I was excited. It had been a while since I had some walking money, and I was ready to spend.

Lenny delivered the drinks. The Beehive didn't offer table service, but the note Lenny snatched from my hand was enough to persuade him to make an exception.

'Come on then,' said the blonde, taking a sip of her negroni, 'let's hear this chat-up line of yours.'

I flashed her a grin. 'I don't have one,' I replied. 'I just came over to let you know—objectively speaking—that you're the best looking woman who's ever set foot in this hole, and you can trust me on that because I'm a real connoisseur when it comes to this kind of stuff.'

'Is that right?'

'That's right. So now you've got two choices: you can carry on this conversation, or you can tell me to piss off and brag to your friends later that some creepy bloke in a pub cornered you just to tell you how drop-dead beautiful you are. It's a win-win.'

She let slip a laugh that sounded like a feather falling through wind chimes. 'Listen...'

'Jake.'

'Jake, you're charming enough in an old-fashioned sort of way, but you and me... I just don't think we'd be a very good fit.'

'Why not?' I asked.

'Trust me on this one, okay?' she said, stubbing out her cigarette. 'Some things aren't meant to be.'

'Was it something I said? Where did I go wrong? Should I not have called myself creepy?'

'You didn't do anything wrong. I just prefer my men with a little more... substance.'

'Was that a ghost joke?'

'No.'

'Oh. Well, that's even worse, then.'

I tried to think of something clever to add, but nothing came out. You have to understand, I wasn't exactly operating at a hundred percent efficiency by this point. The effect of all those pints had finally kicked in, and I was drunk. Proper trousered. So much so that I was having to tip my head back to see under my eyelids, which had apparently been lowered to half-mast, and refused to be run up the pole again. It seemed I'd turned into a bit of a lightweight in my old age.

'Goodnight, Jake,' said the blonde. 'Take care.'

'But I haven't—'

I heard a voice over my shoulder, stonier than granite, and felt a mountainous shadow fall upon me. 'Is this joker getting on your wick?' Lenny asked the woman, whose name I only just realised I hadn't thought to ask.

'Don't bother,' I slurred. 'I'm leaving.'

I got to my feet with a stumble I thought was slight but probably wasn't, and called to the bar. 'Come on, let's go, FrankenJake,' I told my entourage, who was still busy staring into space and collecting dust.

The zombie joined me and we headed for the door. I honestly don't know which of us was staggering more at this point.

'Thanks for the drink,' said the blonde as I flung open the door to the alley beyond.

'Yeah, yeah,' I grumbled as I stumbled out.

Not my finest hour, I think you'll agree.

And yet, it gets worse.

CHAPTER NINETEEN: EVERYTHING YOU ALWAYS WANTED TO KNOW ABOUT SHIFTERS (*BUT WERE TOO AFRAID TO ASK)

I WAS DESPERATE FOR A PISS.

Ordinarily, I'd have translocated home and done my business there, but I was hammered, and didn't want to risk it. I've tried the old, "Beam me up, Scotty" after a few too many jars at The Beehive before, and instead of arriving home, found myself emptying my bladder in the throne room of Buck Palace. Right on top of the throne, in fact. Don't get me wrong, I'm no royalist, but there's no need for that.

In any case, I couldn't just pull a Houdini. I had FrankenJake to think about, and leaving him to make his own way home presented way too much of a risk. Then again, I was taking a whole other risk by walking the streets accompanied by a zombie I was trying to keep secret from Vic, especially given that his scrying magic was almost certainly recharged by now. Still, there you go. The disguise the zombie was wearing would go some way to shielding him from Vic's piggy little eyes, even if the rule I'd insisted upon on the way here—that FrankenJake trail ten paces behind me to make it seem as if we didn't know each other—had been all but forgotten now. What can I tell you? Right then, I was thinking about as straight as I was walking.

The light from the alleyway's only source of illumination, a Victorian-era gaslight, seemed to be duplicating itself as I shuffled to the darkest end of the alley to take a slash, my insides sloshing around like the drum of a washing machine. Typically, ghosts don't need to urinate, but then most of my kind spend their evenings haunting the living instead of propping up bars and necking micro-brewed ghost booze. More fool them.

'Stupid... zip.'

My fingers fumbled at my trousers, but no matter how hard I tried, I couldn't figure out how to get my fly down. Pretty sure I gave up and got FrankenJake to do it in the end. Not proud of that.

The sound of the zip coming down caught the attention of some local fauna, and a rat the size of a Jack Russell went tearing out from behind a bin and shooting from the blind alley. Any passing Londoner on the other side of the alleyway would have seen a giant rat spat from a solid brick wall, and yet chances were they'd just accept it. For most people—almost all of them when it really comes down to it—the impossible, even seen up close, stays impossible. The supernatural does not exist. *Cannot* exist. So when confronted with anything less than absolute cast-iron proof, what's your everyday Joe going to believe? That they've imagined something that isn't really there, or that there are invisible alleyways concealing magical speakeasies right on their doorstep? Not much of a contest, is it?

I heard the pitter-patter of piss at my feet and my thoughts returned to the here and now. What a night. Two times I put it all on the line, two times I crashed and burned. I was no closer to knowing the identity of the copycat Ripper, nor the whereabouts of this soul Vic was so keen to get his hands on. The visit to The Beehive had been a big waste of time. Time I didn't have.

'Fuck.'

You never see this bit in a film noir, I thought: the dashing detective, half-passed out around the back of a spit-and-sawdust pub, tackle out and pissing like a racehorse. I caught sight of my reflection in the puddle of urine at my feet.

'Well, well, if it isn't Sam Spade himself,' I slurred, then inclined toward my companion with a wonky grin on my face. 'Sam "dug up with a" Spade, more like.' I laughed, losing my aim and peeing all over my shoes.

And that's about the last thing I remember.

Well, almost. I recall hearing a squeak, wondering briefly if the rat was back, then turning around to discover that the noise was coming from the shoe leather of a hollow-cheeked vampire. There he was, lurking behind me, the overgrown mosquito I'd seen playing cards in The Beehive only moments before. *That* was the last thing I remembered. That and a fist connecting with the side of my face.

Bit of knowledge for you: vampires can hurt ghosts. I can't say why exactly, but I suspect it's because we're from the same undead family. Other ghosts can hurt me too, plus ghouls, banshees, gorgers, and—as we've already firmly established—zombies. Not that the undead are the only creatures capable of doing me a mischief. Demons, creepers, lurkers, even eaves; all of them are able to damage phantoms. What a rip-off, huh? I mean, what's the point in being dead if people can still kick the living shit out of you?

My memory skips ahead a little here and resumes with me waking up in a pool of my own piss and a headache so fierce it made my eyeballs pulse in their sockets. My fault, really, getting drunk as a skunk and splashing my cash about in a den of iniquity; what did I expect to happen? The Beehive may be a safe space, but outside—even a few feet outside—you're on your own.

'Thanks for the help,' I grumbled at FrankenJake, who stood off to one side, regarding me with dispassionate glassy eyes.

I patted down my pockets and found the wedge of cash I'd arrived with was no longer on my person. Naturally. No doubt the vampire had had a bad run at the card table, seen me lording it up at the bar, and spotted an opportunity to not go home empty-handed. And really, what better setting for a mugging than a seedy back alley in the dead of night?

'Looking good,' said a nearby voice I didn't recognise.

I struggled to my feet to find a tall man wearing a trench coat and a head of scraped-back yellow hair. I didn't recognise him, but from the way he was standing, it didn't seem like he was looking for aggro. All the same, I whistled to FrankenJake and summoned him to my side.

'I've just been sparked out by a Dracula,' I told the stranger, 'so unless you're planning on helping me, how about you jog on, mate?'

A cigarette danced on his bottom lip as he spoke. 'Helping you is exactly why I'm here. I understand you're looking for a shoe-shine man.'

I looked down at my piss-soiled brogues. 'Bloody hell, word gets around fast in this town.'

The stranger shook his head pityingly. 'I'm talking about an informant, a snitch… actually, before we go on, would you mind giving that a shake and putting it away, please?'

He glanced to my crotch, leading me to realise that I'd forgotten to zip up. Embarrassed, I tucked myself in and hoisted my fly (without outsourcing the job this time).

'Who are you?' I asked. 'And why are you earwigging in on my conversations?'

He placed a hand on his heart, mock outraged, his eyes flicking from mine to FrankenJake's. 'I'm wounded. Don't either of you recognise me?'

'Mate, I've never seen you before in my life.'

It was only then that I noticed something unusual about the hand fanned out on the stranger's chest. Nail polish. Cherry red nail polish.

'Wait a second,' I said, realising that I was also familiar with the long beige coat he was wearing. The outfit, the blonde hair, even the brand of cigarette he was smoking was a match. I rocked back on my heels. 'You're her, aren't you?'

'That's right, Cookie,' he replied, then transformed before my very eyes, his face reshaping itself like clay in the hands of some invisible sculptor.

The shapely blonde from the bar looked back at me, and for once, I was as slack-jawed as my brain-hungry partner.

'Or how about this...?' she said, before metamorphosing again, this time into The Beehive's lofty landlord.

'L-Lenny?' I stammered.

Only it wasn't Lenny, just someone pretending to be him. The uncharacteristic blonde hair was the giveaway.

'I'm just showing off now, aren't I?' said the stranger, affecting a pitch-perfect rendition of Lenny's bowel-loosening baritone.

The stranger transformed back to the blonde woman and offered a smile that made me sincerely regret having being caught with my tadger in the wind.

'It's cold out,' I said, offering a late and futile defence.

'Okay,' she said, confused. I couldn't tell if she was failing to follow my train of thought or just being polite.

I suddenly felt very sober indeed. Witnessing a beautiful woman transform into Lenny and then back again was a hell of a wake-up call. A real coffee enema.

I quickly reviewed the story so far, but tripped over upon recollecting my first encounter with the… whatever it was.

'But I… you and me... I mean, I was trying to…'

'... Chat me up? Yeah. See, I told you we wouldn't be a good fit.' She made eyes at FrankenJake. 'Now this is more my speed. What's your name, strong and silent?'

'Why is everyone so bloody taken with him?' I cried. 'He's just me with added mildew.'

I was getting hung up on the wrong thing. Here I was having a conversation with a breed of Uncanny I never even knew existed, and I was acting like some jealous teen.

I squinted, studying the blonde closer, looking for flaws, only there were none. There was no way of telling her apart from any other woman, except for the fact that she was far better looking than most.

'What you are…' I blurted, 'what you can do… it's insane.'

'Is it?' she replied, cocking her head to one side and exhaling a delicate wisp of smoke. 'There's a guy playing cards in there who can turn into a timber wolf. All I do is change into other people. Just think of me as a sort of... were*person*.'

I could just about wrap my head around that, but something still had me stymied. 'So what's your deal then?' I asked. 'Are you a bloke or a bird?'

'Neither. I'm completely gender fluid.'

By way of a demonstration, she transformed back into the blond man.

I raised my hands defensively. 'You can keep your gender fluids to yourself, mate.'

He gave a pitying smile. 'What I mean is, I have no real gender. I'm a man *and* I'm a woman. I'm both.'

'So you're, like... a paranormal tranny?'

'Ugh, knock it off, Adolf. No one says "tranny" anymore.'

'Hey, don't get all arsey with me just because I'm not up on the current lingo. Honestly, you millennials with your safe spaces and your dolphin-only bathrooms.' I tried to suppress a burp and failed. 'That's right, I know what's going on in the world, I read the papers.'

He sighed so hard that the resulting winds probably showed up in a weather bulletin. 'I just showed you that I can change into anyone, so what on Earth makes you think I'm a millennial? Also, are you telling me they still print the news on paper?'

I was so worked up that I couldn't tell whether he was joking about that last thing. All I knew was, I was confused. That blonde at the bar—her sultry voice, her knockout body—all of it wiped out in an instant by chin stubble and the prospect of two hairy balls.

'Why the sudden animosity?' he asked. 'You were all over me back at that bar. What changed?'

'You did. Into a big honking man.'

The stranger tutted. 'You need to update your thinking, buddy. Get woke.'

'Why should I? What was wrong with the way things used to be? When men were men and women were women.'

The stranger gave FrankenJake a knowing look. 'Is there anything worse than a ghost rambling on about how things were back in The Good Old Days? Honestly, how do you put up with this guy?'

That touched a nerve. First Stronge comes to my gaff and tells me I'm not an actual detective, now this herbert rocks up saying I'm barely a person. It's hard, okay, being a ghost and not becoming obsolete. I mean, how long can a dead man really be expected to stay relevant? Just because my spirit hangs around forever, doesn't mean my mind can keep up with an ever-changing world. It hadn't even been two decades since I went in the ground, and I was already losing track of what was going on. I was starting to feel like an ice statue, rapidly melting in the glare of a bright new day.

'Is there a reason we're having this conversation, or is it just to embarrass me?' I asked.

'I already told you, silly, I'm here to help. You need an informant, I'm your man. And woman, of course.'

I looked him up and down and wondered if he might be of use. With the collar of his trench coat turned up and a cigarette dangling from his lips, he certainly looked the part of a deepthroat (easy now).

'My other guy is the best,' I told the stranger. 'My usual source. A real oracle. You'd have a lot to live up to.'

'So where is he then, this other guy of yours?'

'Never you mind.'

'Oookay,' he said, seeing my hairs go up. 'Forget I asked. Just answer me this: can your other guy look like anyone, walk into any place, be a fly on the wall anywhere he damned well pleases?'

My failure to answer told him everything he needed to know.

'Then we're in business,' he replied. 'So how's this going to work? You get that I don't work for free, right?'

'What makes you so sure you've got the job?'

This time it was his silence that answered the question.

'Okay, you're on the payroll,' I said. 'And don't worry about money, I'm rolling in it.'

He'd seen the moolah I was flashing around at The Beehive, of which I had plenty more. And besides, it was generally accepted that where there were ghosts, there was sure to be money. For right or wrong, phantoms have a rep for stockpiling riches and leading the living to treasure troves. You know the drill: a man who amassed a fortune in cash/jewels/gold bullion (delete as appropriate) passes on and later leads some lucky breather to his fortune so they can enjoy the riches he never got to spend. There's a glut of urban legends on the subject, and in the Uncanny Kingdom, urban legends are more likely true than not.

'Okay then,' said the stranger, 'why don't you tell me exactly what it is you're looking for?'

I told him about the Ripper copycat I was chasing. Once I was done with that, I filled him in on the soul Vic Lords had me looking for, the one called Cimeries. He named his price, then said he'd ask around and get back to me.

'What do I call you, Mister...?'

'Fletcher. Jake Fletcher. You?'

'Shift.'

'A shifter called Shift? Didn't dig too deep for that one, did you?'

He cocked an eyebrow at me. 'Didn't I hear you call this tall drink of water FrankenJake, earlier?'

'He's my corpse,' I put in. 'We're the same bloody height.'

'Whatever,' he said with a flap of his hand. 'Go home and sober up, Jake Fletcher. I'll be in touch soon.'

We shook hands. It was only when my flesh met his that I discovered ghosts and shapeshifters can interact physically.

'Well, what do you know?' he said. 'Guess this means we might end up lovers, after all.'

I pulled my hand away and left the alley in big strides.

CHAPTER TWENTY: FRESH HELL

'Get your arse over here, Fletcher,' DCI Stronge squawked through the phone. 'We found the second body.'

It was first thing in the morning and my mouth tasted like Gandhi's flip flop. I rubbed some sleep from my eyes (can you call it "sleep" if you didn't actually get any kip?) and sat up straight in my chair. I'd spent the night in the funeral home's back office, slowly riding out the hangover, wide awake the whole time, as is my curse.

I got the details from Stronge, hung up, and made my way to the showroom, still in a state of soft focus.

'Wakey, wakey,' I told FrankenJake, who responded by sitting bolt upright in his coffin like something from a Hammer Horror. 'I've gotta hit the town. Can you be a good boy until I get back?'

'Braaaains,' he replied.

'Yeah, I thought as much.'

I conveyed him to the bathroom and cuffed him to the radiator. I wasn't taking any chances.

With Resident Evil secured, I headed off to the location I'd been given, a backstreet off Brick Lane. I was starting to get whiplash from all this going back and forth. As soon as I thought I'd sunk my teeth into one thing, off I went bouncing in another direction. The Ripper killings were a priority, I knew that, but it was hard jumping ship from the Vic thing knowing he had his mitts on Frosty. I could only hope that raggedy old git was still okay. I hadn't heard from Vic or his goon in a while, which I was taking for a good thing, based on nothing solid.

The crime scene was a small yard around the back of a curry house; the kind that specialised in mediocre vindaloos and over-priced bottles of Kingfisher beer. The area had been cordoned off, but people had started gathering around the perimeter of the police tape, mainly city boys on their way to work. SOCO were on the scene already, milling around in their boiler suits, looking like Hell's own Teletubbies.

I was attending the circus in my meat suit today, which was getting to be a habit of late. I didn't like having to borrow Mark all the time, but he was the established face of Jake Fletcher as far as Stronge's colleagues were concerned. Besides, so long as I was using Mark's body, he wasn't using it to give Hep C to some poor stripper. Win-win.

I saw Stronge among the throng and made a beeline in her direction, weaving through the milling crowd. She saw me making my approach and I nodded back to her, hands crammed into the pockets of my coat, too cold for a wave. It was an unusually crisp morning, and I was shivering like a shitting dog.

'Here, I got you one of these,' she said, handing me a Starbucks. 'Cup of rocket fuel.'

I thanked her and wrapped my hands around the coffee. I glugged down a bolt and felt the brown stuff light up my beleaguered brain. I hadn't had a shot of caffeine in a long, long time. It was a nice gesture on Stronge's part. Shame about the circumstances.

'You're sure this is the same killer?' I asked her.

The pattern was all wrong. Not only had the murder occurred early, it had also happened in the wrong place. The location of the original Ripper's second kill—the one the cops had been staking out—was a few roads over on Hanbury Street. If this was the same bloke, he was well off-piste.

'Trust me,' said Stronge, 'this is our guy.'

She led me beneath a corrugated plastic awning that jutted out from the back wall of the restaurant. A pile of large tin cans that once contained cooking oil were stacked three feet high. Next to that was a chest freezer: the kind the mafioso kept stoolies in before they cut them up and dispersed the pieces.

'And this is definitely the body the uterus in that video came from?'

Stronge nodded.

'Go on then,' I said. 'Let's have it.'

She took the freezer's lid by the handle and lifted it up. It opened with a gasp, releasing a cloud of frigid vapour. When it cleared, I saw the curled up body of a woman inside, her skin blackened by frostbite, her flesh slashed to pieces. Her wounds were a dead match for the description the guide on the Ripper tour had given of the body of Annie Chapman: throat severed, stomach disembowelled, intestines pulled free and slung over her shoulders like a pair of braces.

Edgar Allan Poe said the death of a beautiful woman was the most poetical topic there was, but I didn't see any poetry here. All I saw was a dead body in the middle of a big city; surrounded by millions of people yet utterly alone.

'Can you believe that?' asked Stronge. 'She's literally been fridged.'

'*Fridged*? Is that a thing now?'

'Don't worry about it,' said Stronge. 'It's after your time.'

Some pop culture reference that I was too out of touch to comprehend, no doubt. Yet more evidence that I was a relic of a bygone age. And now this prick...

'Jake fucking Fletcher. Shouldn't you be at the end of a pier gazing into a crystal ball?' Stronge's partner, muscling his way onto the scene.

'Insults really aren't your strong suit are they, Detective? Then again, neither is your actual suit...'

He reared up on me. 'Listen up, you sack of—'

'Leave it out,' Stronge told him. 'Start acting like a copper or you can go home.'

Maddox raised a finger to reply then thought better of it. 'Yes, guv.'

He shot me a death stare and stomped off.

Returning to the job at hand, I managed to drag my attention back to the contents of the freezer. Seeing the victim's ice-covered body reminded me of Frosty, which got me wondering, what had happened to this poor woman's ghost? There was no telling how long she'd been on ice, so it was possible she'd already gone feral and taken leave of the area. Or could she have taken the express train to Hell? Whatever the answer was, there had to be something to the fact that the bodies we'd found, both the victim of violent murders, had been discovered without their phantoms. That seemed like more than a coincidence. Could there be something supernatural behind these killings, or was I putting two and two together and coming up with a cheeseburger?

Best not to speculate. Better to work with the evidence at hand. What did we have? From a cursory look at the vic, the murder followed the pattern of the original Ripper's second kill, but only to a point. This murder didn't happen according to the Ripper map or timetable, which meant the copycat killer had rewritten the script. That didn't make sense to me. Surely the man who went to all the effort of reenacting JTR's first slaying would want to do likewise with the sequel? Unless they knew the law was on to them, so changed their plans on the fly. Was that why he adapted? Because he knew he'd get caught if he followed the second canonical kill to the letter?

Arriving on the scene and derailing my train of thought came Officer Pedersen, Chief Scene of Crime Officer.

'Ma'am,' he said, announcing himself to Stronge. 'Here to process the body.'

'Of course,' she replied, stepping away from the freezer and letting Pedersen do his thing.

He peered into the chest and regarded its contents like a magpie with its eye on something shiny. 'Oh my,' he said, licking his lips. 'It's going to take a while to thaw this one out.'

'What do you reckon?' asked Stronge. 'Do you think the murder went down here?'

'Hard to say at this point,' Pedersen replied, 'but it's not how I'd have done it.'

'That right?' I said. 'And how would you have committed this brutal murder, Officer?'

He didn't bat an eyelid. 'Well, for starters, I'd have paid someone trustworthy to do it for me. But if that wasn't an option, I'd want maximum control over my environment, so I'd have made sure the attack went down in a place I was accustomed to that wasn't within earshot of any witnesses. Once I'd taken the victim's life, I'd have removed her teeth and hands, being sure to do so in a room I could clean of trace DNA. After that, I'd dismember the rest of the body with a saw: legs, arms, torso. I'd make sure I severed the head with the body facing me. Most killers prefer it the other way around because they don't want to look in their victim's eyes, but it's a much harder cut from the back. Shall I go on?'

'No, thank you. That's very… informative.' The hair on the nape of my neck was standing to attention. I'm a ghost, but this guy even gave me the willies.

'But I didn't tell you how I'd get rid of the evidence yet,' said Pedersen.

'That's fine,' said Stronge, apparently unmoved by her colleague's incredibly vivid fantasy murder. 'Let's concentrate on this for now, shall we?'

Pedersen shrugged and went to work, activating the recorder on his phone and dictating his findings. Stronge and I stepped to one side, giving Pedersen the room he needed to carry out his investigation.

'Any witnesses?' I asked.

'Just one: a passer-by from last night, but he didn't see much,' Stronge replied. 'Said he saw a man with a big build come in here toting what looked like a gym bag.'

'That's not a lot to go on. What do we know about the victim?'

'Nothing much to say,' Stronge replied. 'Supermarket cashier, no known enemies, no criminal record; unless you count a minor driving offence from six years ago.'

The mention of the victim not having a criminal record got me wondering; so long as she'd lived a blameless life, what was the state of her disembodied soul? Her ghost wasn't here, but then again, if her murder had happened elsewhere, there was no reason for it to be. Chances were her ghost was beached in the same place that her body had been dismembered. Unless it had been dragged to Hell already. After all, not every sin gets captured in a police file.

'Anything else?' I asked.

'We did find this...' Stronge directed me to a yellow marker on the ground, next to which lay a pill pot. 'Medication. We're running a trace on the patient's name in case it belongs to the vic. I'm pretty sure we'll get a match.'

'What makes you so sure?'

'The pot's contents. Two pills. Lung medication.'

'I don't get it. So what?'

'So, Annie Chapman, the Ripper's second victim, was found with the same kind of medicine and the exact same number of pills.'

Interesting.

So, the killer was smart enough not to follow the Ripper's footsteps too closely, knowing that we were on to the copycat angle. The police had the second kill site staked out already, which made dropping a dead body there impossible, and yet our man hadn't let that stop him. Instead of giving up, he tweaked his plan and found a different way to ape the Ripper. A way that stayed authentic to certain historical truths without putting him too close to the firing line. Clever boy. Whoever it was that we were dealing with here, he had a brain in his head.

A brain full of wrong.

CHAPTER TWENTY-ONE: THE DEVIL IS IN THE DETAIL

I RETURNED my meat suit to his rack, collected FrankenJake from the funeral home, and headed to Ealing to meet Shift at The Beehive.

Given that Lenny didn't serve food, the pub was all but empty at lunchtime, inhabited by a handful of piss-heads slumped in their seats like marionettes with their strings cut. I caught a flash of blonde in one corner of the saloon and saw Shift sat in a booth by herself. She'd chosen to attend in female form today, and wore lipstick the colour of wet blood. I shuffled into the booth with FrankenJake beside me and took a chair opposite her. Before I could say anything, Lenny called over from the bar.

'Stop, I know this one… a ghost, a zombie, and a shapeshifter walk into a bar…'

'Fuck sake, Len. You knew all along, didn't you? You knew she wasn't really a bird?'

'You bet your arse I did,' he said, and off he toddled to the kitchen, chuckling as he went.

I know. All a bit "gay panic" this, isn't it? What can I tell you; I'm a product of my time. Please, bear with me, I do get better.

I turned my attention back to Shift. 'Can you change, please?'

'You don't like my outfit?' she asked, smoothing down the front of a polo neck jumper that strained valiantly to contain her ample chest.

'No, I mean can you change into a bloke?'

'Why?' she asked, leaning forward and setting her bosom on the table.

'Because this body's too... distracting. '

She laughed. It was a woman's laugh, but it had a man's edge to it. 'I think I'm gonna stay the way I am, thanks. You should be the one changing, Cookie, not me.'

'What's that supposed to mean?'

'It means, how about you try treating me the same way you would a man? You know, as an equal. Go on, it'll be good practice for you. Drag you out of the last century.'

'Oi, I didn't die that long ago.'

'Could have fooled me.'

If I had blood, my face would have flushed traffic light red.

'Braaaaains,' groaned FrankenJake.

'See, he gets it,' said Shift, reaching across the table and placing a delicate hand on the zombie's shoulder. 'That's the way you judge a person: by their mind, not by the way they look.'

'We don't have time for this, Shift. You called me here. What do you have?'

She ignored me. 'You know that's what Jeffrey Dahmer was doing when he drilled holes in the skulls of those homeless guys and poured in acid, right? Trying to make a zombie.'

'Did I really need to know that?' I replied, disgusted not so much by the story, but at the fact that I—an avowed true crime nut—wasn't already aware of it.

'Just showing you what a font of knowledge I am,' Shift replied with a twinkle in her eye. 'Another fun fact for you: old Jeff also had a real hard-on for *The Exorcist III*. Watched it over and over.'

'Yeah, well, I'm not really in the mood for horror stories,' I said, recalling the freezer behind the Indian restaurant. A crime that had crossed the line from "true" to "my problem".

'Fair enough,' she replied. 'How about we talk fashion, instead?'

'For the love of—'

'Come on, seriously,' she put in, 'your pal's a good-looking feller, so why is he dressed like a pile of dirty laundry?'

'That's what you're worried about?' I replied. 'Not that he's a zombie, but that he's dressed funny?'

She nodded sincerely.

'It's a disguise,' I huffed.

I told her about Vic Lords, explaining how he was using scrying magic to keep tabs on me, and that this was one of the precautions I'd taken to using in order to stay off his radar. This and holding strategy meetings inside The Beehive's magic-dampening bubble.

'What?' Shift cried. 'The guy who's forcing you to do his dirty work is spying on you, too? That's ridiculous. Here, take this…'

She snatched her trench coat from the seat beside her and thrust it into my hands. 'You can't keep running to The Beehive every time you need to hide from this lowlife,' she said.

'Right. And how's your coat meant to get Vic off my back?'

'That isn't just any old coat,' she replied. 'It's *electric*.'

This was a coded way of saying *magic*. If it were a regular coat, she would have referred to it as being *acoustic*. Sorry, but Uncanny slang can be just as confusing as the cockney kind.

Shift explained that the coat would shield me from Vic's gaze, meaning I could carry out my business without his evil eye boring into me. 'Think of it like that reflective coating you can get for your license plate. The stuff that's invisible to the naked eye, but reflects the flash from speed cameras.'

'Pretty sure that stuff's an urban myth,' I replied.

Not that it mattered. The speed camera spray might have been a fable, but I could feel just from touching it that the magic coat was real.

'So… an enchanted camo coat,' I said. 'Pretty sweet.'

'I like to blend in,' she explained. 'Sometimes being able to change shape isn't enough.'

Made sense to me.

I slipped my arms into the sleeves of the coat. It fit just right, which didn't make sense given that it belonged to someone who was—at present—a totally different build to me. It seemed the garment changed size according to the person wearing it. Handy.

I stood up and checked my reflection in a nearby Guinness mirror.

'Since you're a ghost, it'll be invisible to anyone without The

Sight, now,' said Shift, 'so you don't have to worry about freaking out any muggles with a floating coat.'

'Nice. Very nice.'

'It's got a range on it, too,' Shift noted. 'Good enough for you and your partner if he stays within a twenty-metre radius.' She gave her attention to FrankenJake. 'You hear that, handsome? No more living in the shadow of this old fossil.'

FrankenJake smiled, causing two ropes of saliva to droop from the corners of his mouth and slop onto the table.

'Maybe I should have brought a bib for you, huh?' she said, using a beer mat to scrape the drool pool off the furniture.

I ignored them and continued to regard myself in the mirror. The coat looked good on me. Made me look like Rick Blaine in Casablanca. Give me a fedora pulled down to one eyebrow and I'd look every bit the part.

'We'll always have Paris, kid,' I said in my best Bogey drawl.

I turned to check myself from the side and grinned at what I saw. A fashion change had been a long time coming. Like I said before, one of the many drawbacks of being a ghost is that you end up dressed the way you were when you died (don't ask me why, I don't make the rules). Lucky for me, I was done up like a dog's dinner the day God did a recall on me, but still, the same black suit every day, no matter the occasion? Fine for a night at the BAFTAs, but a bit formal for a Monday morning sat on my lonesome spinning old Iron Maiden CDs.

'Thanks for the clobber,' I said, shooting the coat's cuffs. 'Very swish.'

'It's got a back to it,' Shift replied.

'Eh?'

'What I mean is, it's a loan. You give it *back* when you're done using it.'

'Oh. Well, cheers, anyway.' A thought struck. 'While we're talking clothes, can you answer a quick question for me? Man-to-man.'

'Not a man, but carry on.'

'How does it work when you change? I mean, the gear you've got on now is pretty unisex and all, but… well…'

'Spit it out,' she sighed, no doubt aware of where this was headed.

'What about underwear?' I blurted. 'It's all well and good you changing from a bird to a bloke, but doesn't that leave you wearing a bra around your pecs?'

She offered a mischievous smile. 'I don't need a bra, I'm pert enough without one.'

I felt a confusing stir in my trousers and slid back into the booth before it became apparent. 'Let's get to work, shall we?'

'Okay then,' she said, still wearing an impish grin, 'moving on.'

She placed a manilla envelope on the table, one palm on top. 'I don't have any leads on your Ripper copycat yet...'

'Not a great start,' I replied.

'What I *do* have is some news about the soul you're on the lookout for; the one named Cimeries.' She tapped the envelope with a cherry red nail and slid it in my direction.

'Would you mind?' I asked, wafting a hand through the table to remind her that I lacked—to use her word—substance.

'Oh right, forgot about that.' She removed the contents of the envelope and fanned them out in front of me.

On the table: a couple of black and white photocopies. Next to those, a reproduction of an old woodcut drawing.

'Is that...? You're telling me *that's* Cimeries?'

'Afraid so.'

The man—well, monster—depicted in the woodcut was riding a black horse with giant bat wings. He carried a spear in one hand and a spiked chain in the other. His head was topped by two tall horns standing straight as car antennae. In short, he was a demon; an ancient and rather powerful one by the looks of it.

'Sometimes known as Cimeies, Cimejes, or Kimaris,' Shift added. 'He's the 66th demon of the first part of the Lemegeton, but we don't need to get into all of that hoo-ha.'

I recognised that last handle—Kimaris—from Anton LaVey's list of infernal names. Hardly a glowing endorsement.

Shift jabbed a finger at the photocopied texts. 'These are translated from an ancient Aramaic scroll I pulled from an off-limits back room of the British Museum. In case it isn't obvious already, this guy's not some lowly pit fiend. He's a prince. An arch-demon.'

I craned my head over the pages and began to read the text...

The earth opened up and belched out a horror that walked the land unfettered by Hell's chains. His countenance froze the hearts of those who stood before him, and buckled the sanity of even the strongest minds. The masses scattered before the darkness of his shadow as the harbinger of mankind's extinction threw back his horned head and...

You get the gist.

It was hard to imagine a creature that had loomed so large over history fitting into the tiny, fleshy pouch I'd been given to contain him, but so long as Cimeries' soul was bottled up and inert like Vic had promised, there was no reason this couldn't work. Which was good news for me, but even better news for civilisation at large. A demon like that running amok… well, let's just say we weren't ready for that kind of aggro.

Not since the London Coven fell, anyway.

The trio of witches who used to keep the balance around here was rubbed out a couple of years back, leaving our borders open to all sorts. It isn't all bad, though. Since the Coven's wards were dismantled, others have stepped up to protect the city from infernal invaders: a witch's familiar they left in their stead; a bureau of tweedy administrators calling themselves Myth Management; and of course, me. Not one of us had what it took to guard the realm from a demon of Cimeries' league, though. A monster like that, loose and unbound, could spell the end of everything.

'Right,' I said, looking up from the photocopies Shift had provided. 'So, a bit of a prick, this guy?'

'Oh yeah, but that's only the half of it. The story gets *way* better.'

I leaned forward in my chair, FrankenJake mirroring me. 'It does?'

'Well, not *better* exactly, but it goes on.'

I slumped back, arms folded. FrankenJake did the same. 'Go on then, get on with it.'

'I'm getting there!' she cried. 'Such a rusher. Honestly, what *must* you be like in bed?'

I held up my hands. 'Sorry.'

She continued. 'See, I started to wonder what this Vic Lords character wants with the soul of an arch-demon.'

I'd already started to wonder the same. What was Vic planning? Did he intend to resurrect the demon somehow, like he had my corpse? Give it form, bind it to him, use it as an enforcer? That would be a big upgrade on the disfigured goon he had doing his dirty work. Or did Vic have some other design? Perhaps he had plans to harness the demon's raw power and use it as a component in some black magic ritual. Who knew? The only thing I could be certain of was that he wasn't about to bung the thing on a mantelpiece alongside his snow globe collection.

Shift went on. 'I asked around, did some digging, scoped out some folks who've had dealings with your Mister Lords. Folks who might have a grudge to bear and a story to tell. I didn't have to look very far.'

I wasn't surprised by that. Vic was a family-sized tub of shit, after all.

Shift continued. 'Anyway, I found someone willing to spill on Vic for a price—that'll come out of my expenses, by the way—and what I found was real interesting.'

'Come on then, don't leave me dangling.'

There was that mischievous smile again. 'Are you ready? Vic Lords... sold his soul.'

'He what?' I cried, so excited that I pounded the table, forgetting my hand would pass through it.

'You heard me,' Shift replied. 'The old Robert Johnson special.'

I slapped my forehead, my hand making contact this time, and a bit too painfully for my liking. 'Of course.'

That explained how Vic had managed to level up the way he had. How a mere dabbler in the occult had suddenly learned how to walk through fire, make ghosts solid, turn his henchman into the Elephant Man, and, of course, reanimate the dead.

'Who did he sell his soul to?' I asked. 'Was it Old Nick himself?'

'Not according to my source,' Shift replied. 'Apparently, the devil he sold his soul to is called...' she scrolled through the notes on her phone, '...the Long Man.'

Hm. Didn't ring any bells.

'What do we know about him? Other than the obvious.'

'Not much. As far as I've been told, he lives in a pocket dimension of some sort, and collects souls that he plants in the ground to make something he calls his Forest of Souls.'

'Very emo. So let me guess – Vic's wanting to trade the demon soul he's got me hunting for in exchange for his own. That way he doesn't end up becoming part of the Long Man's goth orchard.'

'That would be my guess, yeah.'

'Right. So I suppose the only question now is, where do I find this Cimeries geezer?'

Shift pulled an expression that reminded me of a doctor in a TV show about to deliver a patient some very bad news. 'Ah, now there's the thing,' she said. 'I have absolutely no idea.'

'Great,' I sighed.

Lenny arrived at the booth and planted two anvil-sized fists on the table. 'Are any of you lot planning on ordering a drink, or am I going to have to sling you head-first through that door?'

I patted down the pockets of my new coat. 'Sorry, mate. Wallet's in my other jacket.'

CHAPTER TWENTY-TWO: DEATH'S DOOR

While Shift got to work finding out where the soul of this Cimeries prick was lurking, I went to reconnect with Stronge to see if I could help her with the Ripper case. The killer had taken two lives already, and we hadn't even come close to catching him. He must have felt like he was playing monopoly and sat on Free Parking. That pissed me off. Right off.

I was on my way out of The Beehive, phone in hand and just about to make the call, when the screen lit up with DCI Stronge's face.

Now, there are those in this world who'll tell you that these sorts of coincidences mean something. That these so-called "strokes of luck" are proof of a background machinery that we aren't privy to. An invisible, predetermined system that guides our every movement and lays to waste even our best-laid plans. And who knows, maybe they're right, but obsessing over it will give you a real pain in the thinker. You ask me, you're better off just rolling with the punches. Recognise these fluke happenings as happy little accidents, give a tip of the cap to the universe, and move on with your day.

'Kat?' I said, answering the call.

'Fletcher, you're needed.' She sounded out of breath. Was she running? 'Just caught a call from dispatch,' she went on, 'tenant in a high-rise phoned 999 to report blood soaking through his ceiling.'

That sounded promising. Well, unless you were the person leaking the red stuff.

'I'll fetch my meat suit and meet you there,' I told her.

'No time,' she wheezed. She was definitely on the move. 'Tenant reports footsteps upstairs. Looks like a crime in progress.'

So that's why she was in such a hurry.

'Give me the location,' I said.

Stronge gave me what I needed: an address on Bigland Street, Whitechapel. 'You know it?' she asked, aware that I could only bounce to areas I was already familiar with, or could see with my own two eyes (and no, Google Street View won't cut it). 'It's around the corner from Watney Market.'

'Don't worry, I can get there,' I replied. 'Hang tight, I'm on my way.'

I called back inside The Beehive and persuaded Shift to walk FrankenJake back to the funeral home. That meant giving her my home address, which I wasn't happy about, but needs must.

After that, I translocated to the Wimpy on the market road, which was as close as I could get to the location Stronge had given me. Getting to the high-rise took another four/five minutes on foot, but cutting the meat suit out of the route still made for a hell of a short cut.

I forged on to the rendezvous point, head tipped forward, jaw set, trench coat flapping in the wind behind me. The block of flats on Bigland Street loomed over me like a satellite branch of Mordor's Dark Tower. The outside walls were covered in graffiti, and the mountains of rubbish piled up in the courtyard suggested the local dustmen had either gone on strike or stopped coming to the area altogether.

DCI Stronge was waiting for me just outside of the building's entrance, stood up straight like a toy soldier, tapping an imaginary watch. 'What took you so long?' she asked.

'Keep your hair on, I'm here, aren't I?' I shot back, then detected a notable absence. 'Unlike your colleague, I see. Where is he? Where's Maddox?'

'He'll be here. Dispatch is on to him.'

'I thought you two were meant to be partners. Why isn't he here right now?'

'Just because we're partners doesn't mean we're glued at the bloody hip,' she replied.

'He's on his way, though, right? Tell me he's at least on his way.'

Stronge studied her shoes. 'He was out getting lunch when the call came through.'

I aimed a little shout of frustration at the sky.

This wasn't a two-man job. If the killer was up there—a killer capable of gutting people, a killer who ate human flesh—we needed all hands on deck.

'We can't sit on this,' said Stronge, sensing my hesitation. 'The longer we wait, the more chance he has of getting away. We need to get up there and make an arrest.'

I knew Stronge well enough to realise I was only moments away from being called chickenshit, so instead of wasting my time arguing with her, I stepped inside the building.

'Which floor?' I asked.

'Thirteenth,' she replied.

'Bit on the nose, isn't it?' I said, sensing another of those strange confluences best left ignored.

'Can we just get going, please?' she asked, pushing through the lobby in the direction of the lift.

'Out of order,' I said, noting the sign taped to the elevator door. It wasn't easy to read, given that the lights on the ground floor had either blown or been used for target practice, leaving the whole of the lobby oppressively dark.

'Stairs it is,' said Stronge, mounting the first flight.

I ran after her, struggling to keep up. I was impressed at how well she tackled the climb, bounding up the steps two at a time, her face a mask of pure conviction. As we clattered between floors, no one bothered leaving their flat to see what the fuss was about. People tend to keep to themselves in these vertical communities; they know better than to get wrapped up in someone else's affairs.

We arrived on the thirteenth floor, Stronge panting in hot spurts now, fingers digging into a stitch in her side. Given that I don't breathe (so didn't have a breath to be out of), my body was running like a metronome, slow and steady. If our situation had been reversed and I'd had to make that climb alive, I'm certain my heart would have exploded about halfway up.

Stronge leant against a wall, rasping like a sick Rottweiler, her hair hanging in two drenched wings. 'What's with the... anorak?' she wheezed, noting my new coat. 'You joining… the dirty... mac… brigade?'

'If you want to take a breather, just say so,' I replied. 'You don't have to cover up how tired you are by pretending to care about my outfit.'

'Fair... enough,' she said, taking a moment to collect herself before nodding that she was good to go.

Without any further delay, Stronge got back up to speed, pelting down a grey corridor, taking a corner, then a couple more. I followed until she pulled to a stop at a nondescript apartment door decorated with a brass number *132*. The door was ajar, its lock barrel bashed out with a hammer by the look of things.

'This is it,' Stronge whispered. Her nose twitched and she fanned some air from her face. 'Do you smell that?'

I shook my head. Seeing as I wasn't in possession of a set of nostrils, I couldn't smell anything. 'What is it? Dead body?'

She shook her head. 'No, worse. Smells like shit and rotten eggs had a baby.'

'I should pop in there and have a recce,' I said. 'See what's waiting for us.'

'No time. The vic could still be alive. We go in together,' Stronge replied, popping the safety clip on her hip holster and drawing her stun gun.

If the call from dispatch was right, the Ripper copycat might still be in there, which meant there was a small (*very* small) chance he hadn't yet finished the job. This was it. Our moment. Our chance to put an end to this freak.

Stronge fixed me with a look of steely determination. 'On my mark, you know the drill.'

I nodded. Stronge counted down from three with her fingers, then in we went.

'Police!' she shouted, Taser aimed straight ahead as we pressed forward into the hallway, past a tacky print of a sunset, checking doors left and right. 'Come out and show yourself, hands where I can see them!'

We rounded into the living room, although the room's function wasn't evident on first blush. The curtains were drawn, draping the room in a darkness like thick black velvet. It took a second for our eyes to adjust—to make use of the ambient light bleeding in through the now open door—and bear witness to the horror within.

A mutilated woman lay sprawled across the floor, rolled onto her side, her face turned to the far wall. Beneath her blossomed a great flower of blood, thick and red and wet. Above the woman, sat astride her torso like he was riding a horse, was her killer. In the scant light of the room, he was little more than a silhouette, a black hill rising above a body, a bloody knife in hand.

Of all the things I could have been thinking in that moment, here's the one that hustled its way to the forefront of my mind: *Why the living room?*

He could have dismembered the victim anywhere, so why had he chosen the living room floor to do it, knowing what a mess he'd make? There's a system for these things; a way the story plays out. When a killer seeks to take apart a dead body, they look for a place where the blood can be contained. Wiped up. Flushed away. The bathtub, that's where most dismemberments take place. Sometimes the kitchen. The living room? Almost never. Too many places for blood to hide. Too many materials to soak up evidence: carpet, cushions, soft furnishings. Then there are other factors to take into account: large windows overlooking the street (though not a factor here, thirteen storeys up), not to mention all those family photos leering down at you while you hack up the remains of their beloved daughter/niece/aunt/sister. Even the most poorly prepared, panicked killer will naturally find themselves gravitating towards a room with wipe-down tiles and easy access to running water. But not this one. It was almost as if he didn't care, as if he wanted to be caught in the act, blood up to his elbows.

The killer rose to his feet, slow and deliberate.

Stronge took aim at him with her Taser. 'Weapon on the ground,' she hollered. 'Right now!'

I could make the intruder out a little better now. He was a large man, though in the dim light it was impossible to tell whether it was muscle or fat he was carrying. I couldn't identify his clothing, either, save for the red balaclava he had on, which I recognised from the YouTube video Stronge had shown me.

'I said, drop it,' she cried.

To my surprise, the killer obeyed, letting the blade tip from his hand and clatter to the ground.

'You want me to take him?' I asked Stronge.

She shook her head. 'This is my collar.'

Stronge kept the stun gun trained on the killer with her right hand while she used her spare to reach for one of the zip-tie restraints she kept on her belt.

It was the moment the killer had been waiting for.

The second Stronge's focus wasn't on the gun, he pounced. Her finger tightened on the trigger, but the killer was quick, eating up the space between them in an instant and knocking her arm aside. As the Taser darts embedded harmlessly in the floor, the killer shouldered past her and into the hallway. I made a dive for him as he fled, but my tackle fell short, leaving me sprawled across the ground in his wake.

'After him,' Stronge yelled, clambering to her feet.

A set of bloody, red footprints extended into the distance, headed in the direction of the front door. Together, Stronge and I gave chase, racing out of the flat just in time to see the killer bouncing around the first corner of the staircase and disappearing to the floor below. I had to give it to him, he could shift. For a big man, he moved like shit off a shovel.

Stronge hit the call button on her radio. 'Pursuing suspect on foot,' she said. 'Urgent backup required.'

We put on a burst of speed, hurling ourselves down the first flight of stairs. As the killer ran, his heavy footsteps echoed up the dingy stairwell toward us like the sharp reports of a pistol. Combined with Stronge's cries for him to give himself up, the sound of our frenzied pursuit created a commotion loud enough to finally disturb the residents of the tower block, setting dogs barking and babies squalling.

I stayed by Stronge's side during the descent—was that for her protection or mine?—but no matter how fast she ran, she couldn't seem to close the distance on the killer. She was giving it her all, but she was slowing down. The bloody footprints were fading the further we dipped, vanishing from the steps like disappearing ink. If we didn't come up with something soon, the murderer was going to get away.

'Do your... ghost thing,' Stronge wheezed as we took the corner onto the eighth floor.

Translocate. That was the word she was grasping for. *Do your Mister Benn thing and cut him off at the pass*, she was saying, as if the thought had never occurred to me. I'd been trying to find the right angle to get ahead of the killer for the last four storeys, but the line of sight between the floors was tight, and every time I saw an opportunity, every time I caught a glimpse of a flight of stairs I could jump to, he was off taking the next one. I even considered translocating directly to the ground floor and cutting off the exit, but with the lights out down there, there was nothing I could latch on to, landing spot-wise.

'Can't,' I said, summing up the situation in a single word.

'Then jump,' she cried.

Take a dive down the central bore of the stairwell? Not as bad an idea as it might sound, actually. If I aimed right, I'd thread the needle and land on the ground floor unharmed and ready for action, despite the eight-storey drop. Benefit of being a ghost.

Of course, this raises the important question: why would I land on the ground in the first place? I mean, so long as ghosts are intangible and pass through solid objects, what would stop me going right through the floor and out the other side of the planet? In fact, why does the ground support ghosts at all, let alone stairs? Believe me, I've asked the same questions many times, and I'm still no closer to arriving at any real answers. My best guess is, whatever force it is that stops me plummeting through the Earth's molten core is the same one that lets me sit in a chair without falling flat on my arse. As for the nature or cause of that force, sorry, your guess is as good as mine. Unfortunately, being a ghost doesn't come with an instruction manual; you just have to figure it out as you go along.

But back to the jumping down the stairwell idea. One problem with that plan: what if the killer decided to exit the building via a different floor, say through the window of a first-storey flat? He might not want to go out the way he came in, thinking there was a good chance the police had that exit cut off already. Or worse still, he could decide he was done running, double back up the stairs, and confront Stronge head-on, taking her out of the picture altogether. And there I'd be, stranded on the ground, listening to her screams rain down from above. No, thank you.

'Don't worry, we'll catch him on foot,' I told Stronge.

She wasn't convinced. 'I need backup at my location, now,' she yelled into her radio. 'Right now!'

We carried on after the fleeing suspect, but with every new floor we reached, he only succeeded in gaining more ground. Soon enough, there were a good four floors separating us, and he was getting ever closer to the bottom floor, to the way out. I struggled to find the right angle to make a last-ditch jump to his location, but he was already too far gone. I craned my head over the bannister for one last look, but the only thing I saw of him was a blurred glimpse as he disappeared into the near-darkness at the bottom of the stairwell. All that was left of him after that was the maddening echo of his rapidly retreating footsteps.

'We're losing him,' Stronge cried, though she needn't have bothered, it was plain as day to see.

The next thing I expected to hear was the sound of the killer flinging open the lobby door as he bolted out of the building to freedom, but that wasn't the case. Instead, there came a commotion, the sounds of a scuffle, of loud grunts and heavy body blows. Had Stronge's backup finally arrived? Had they intercepted the perp trying to make his way out of the building and brought him down?

Stronge and I steamed down the last few flights, landing four-footed on the ground floor and expecting to see the killer knocked flat and surrounded by cops. But no. There was a man on the ground, but he wasn't the perp. He was the backup.

'Maddox?' Stronge blurted.

He was sat on his backside, nose flattened and split across the bridge, guttering blood down the front of his shirt. Behind him, the tower block's exit swung on its hinges.

'He came out of nowhere,' Maddox groaned, touching a finger to his nose and wincing.

Maybe he didn't see the killer coming, or maybe he froze, petrified by shock. Could the sight of another bogeyman rearing up from the darkness have been too much for him? Had it inflamed the buried memory of being attacked by that demon a while back, and triggered his PTSD?

Whether Stronge considered any of this, I have no idea. What I can say for sure is that she snapped to action in a heartbeat. Seeing that her partner wasn't in need of immediate medical assistance, she dodged around him, shoved open the exit, and scanned the forecourt outside, one hand over her eyes like a sailor scanning for icebergs.

There was no sign of the killer.

I could tell from the look on her face that she wanted nothing more than to jump in her car, light up the blues, and bury the pedal, but it would have been for nothing. She had no idea which direction the killer took off in. She could wear the tyres off that motor and still not find him. He was gone. Lost in the wind.

Stronge sunk to her haunches, one hand raking her hair in frustration, the other opening a channel on her police radio. 'Suspect still at large. Repeat, suspect still at large. Damn it!' She spun about and punched the wall behind her hard enough to break a couple of knuckles. 'Fuuuck!' she screamed, dropping the radio and clutching her wounded hand.

I looked from Stronge to Maddox—one bloodied, the other broken—and offered a clap so slow that it was almost imperceptible to the human ear. 'Good job, inspectors. Bravo. Top marks all round.'

And yet, I had hope. No, we hadn't caught the killer this time, but he wouldn't feel like he was sitting on Free Parking anymore. We'd taken that away from him, and that was something.

CHAPTER TWENTY-THREE: RIPPED APART IN THE DARK

BODY NUMBER THREE WAS TAGGED, bagged, and dispatched to the mortuary. As with the previous two murders, the victim's ghost remained mysteriously unaccounted for, which meant no witnesses to the crime. No one to question. So with no obvious leads to follow,

Stronge resolved to scour the crime scene with Maddox and report back to me with any new findings (once they'd seen to their injuries). For me, the case was on pause. Whoever it was hiding under that red balaclava, he was gone to ground for the foreseeable, leaving me in a holding pattern.

Might as well make use of the time I had before my phone rang again, I figured; check on the other plate I had spinning before that one came crashing down. Okay, I didn't know the whereabouts of Vic Lords' demon soul yet, but while I was waiting on Shift, I could at least pay Vic a visit and let him know I hadn't forgotten about him. That he was still a priority. A polite drop-in ought to buy me some time, plus I could check on Frosty while I was at it.

'Down, Fido,' I told the masked henchman guarding the entrance to Vic's establishment.

Kojo slid the peephole shutter closed, swung open the heavy door, and propped it with a steel-toe capped boot. His eyes swept left and right down the street to make sure I hadn't brought any reinforcements with me.

'Don't worry, I'm on my Todd,' I told him. 'The guvnor in?'

'What's with the long coat?' the henchman slurred through his demolished mouth. 'You got some watches you're trying to sell?'

'Very good,' I said. 'You know, if the goon thing doesn't work out, you should seriously think about getting into stand-up. I reckon you'd kill at the Fringe.'

He ignored me. 'This way,' he grunted.

I expected to be led upstairs to Vic's office, but instead, the goon escorted me all the way to the sex dungeon in the building's sub-basement.

Vic sat on a stool with his back to me, one hand resting gently on the wheel that tightened Frosty's torture rack. Old Frost was just as I'd left him, though a little longer than before, a little more stretched out. His brow, which was usually covered in a sheen of frozen rime, was pearled with sweat. I didn't know a ghost could sweat. I didn't know we could be pushed that far.

Vic took a puff on his cigar and blew out a smoke ring the size of a car tyre. He spoke without looking at me.

'The prodigal returns.'

I watched the smoke ring rise above him like a mockery of a halo. 'Always with the stogies, Vic. Just once I'd like to come in here and catch you doing something healthy for a change; eating a low-fat yoghurt, maybe, or doing a spot of yoga.'

The joke was about as well-received as my quip at the front door.

He took a languid drag on his cigar. 'Long time no see, Fletcher. What's been keeping you? You got lead in your shoes, boy?'

I took a couple of steps into the room, breaking away from the goon. 'Don't worry, Vic, I'm still working on finding you that soul. Just a matter of time now, you'll see.'

'Oh yeah?' he replied, still facing the other way, head tilted upwards, watching a fresh ring of smoke break apart on the basement ceiling. 'Taking your time, ain't you?'

'I'm not popping into a Burger King for a Whopper here. A thing like this, it's going to take a bit of finesse.'

'But you've made some progress, at least?'

'Yup,' I replied. 'Narrowed it down to a couple of possibilities,' I assured him. 'Just checking a few last things off the list then I'm good to go. You know me, Vic, softly, softly catchy monkey.'

He spun about in his stool, and for the first time since I entered the room, I saw the thunderstorm brewing behind his eyes.

'*Softly?*' he spat. 'What was it I said that made you think I had time for *softly?*'

I took a step back. 'Since when was there a deadline on this thing? You never said *when* you wanted me to fetch you the goods.'

His complexion turned the colour of an aubergine. '*Now,* that's when. You get the goods now—*right now*—or your friend here's brown bread, double-toasted.'

I looked to Frosty, his teeth gritted, in too much pain to answer back or defend himself.

'That wasn't the deal, Vic,' I said. 'You're moving the goalposts.'

He started a laugh that ended its life as a cough. 'Goalposts? What do you think this is, Fletcher? A Sunday afternoon kick-about down the park?'

He got up from his stool with a grunt and headed in my direction, cigar swaying in his hand, a look on his face like my eyeball would make a good ashtray.

'You're up to your neck in it, Fletcher. Don't think I don't know.'

'I've no idea what you're on about,' I replied, standing my ground.

Shit. What did he know? Did he know about FrankenJake? Did he know I'd been bunking off and chasing a serial killer instead of hunting down his errant soul? Had he been spying on me the whole time, tracking my every move? I hadn't felt the psychic prickle of his curtain-twitching magic, but then maybe I'd become numb to it.

He continued his tirade. 'While I've been sat here like a plum waiting for you to pull your finger out, you've been nosing around my business, ain't that right?'

'Steady on, Vic—'

'Digging up dirt on me, asking questions you don't need answers to. Oh yes, I've heard all about your new friend, the Yank: old two-face himself... or should I say *herself?*'

He knew about Shift, and that I'd used him (her?) to find out just why he was after the soul.

'What did I tell you, Jake? *Need to know basis,* wasn't that what I said? You couldn't help yourself, though, could you? Had to stick your oar in.'

He was within swinging distance of me now, rage roiling off him like heat from a mare's vagina.

'Here's the thing that's really bugging me, though,' he continued, 'it's that I can't seem to keep my eye on you. I look in my little scrying pool, trying to work out what rock you're scurrying about under, but it's like I've got cataracts or something. What's that all about, eh?' He studied me, his eyes glacier cold.

'I dunno, mate,' I replied with a shrug. 'Guess maybe you're not the almighty magic man you thought you were.'

Without warning, the fabric of Vic's civility frayed and tore. He raised his hands, his fingers curled into hooks, and with a sibilant whisper, unleashed a web of neon tendrils that latched on to my ankles and wrists, hoisting me into the air.

'The coat,' Vic thundered, his magic probing me, learning my secrets. 'That's how you did it: you got yourself a magic coat.' He clucked his tongue. 'Naughty naughty, very naughty.'

The neon tendrils stripped Shift's jacket off me and threw it to the floor. The coils holding me in place tightened, digging into my skin like hot razor wire.

'I got it for the job,' I rasped through the pain. 'You want me to bust into someplace and do a swifty with a soul? This is how it gets done. This is how I don't get rumbled: camouflage.'

The razor wire loosened, and Vic shot me a blistering scowl.

'You better not be feeding me flannel, Fletcher. Because if I find out you've been leading me down the garden path, things are going to get bad for you. Very fucking bad.'

It wasn't like Vic to snap like this. His threats were always measured, never this direct, never this vicious. I started to wonder what the rush was. Why was Vic so eager for me to nick this soul? Why did it have to happen yesterday? Let's say I was right, and Vic had sold his soul in exchange for a mystical level-up… presumably, the reason he wanted the soul of this arch-demon was so he could hand it off to the Long Man and save his own. Offer the buyer a trade-up, so to speak. But what if the buyer was impatient? What if he put a time limit on the deal?

'You seem worried, Vic. You on the clock, is that it? This Long Man geezer got the meter running?'

Vic growled and used his tendrils to hurl me across the basement, sending me flying through a whipping post and bouncing off the floor on the other side of the room.

Must have touched a nerve.

'You wanna play games, do ya?' he frothed. 'You wanna see what happens when you push a man too far?' He spun to face his henchman. 'Kojo, get rid of the tramp.'

'What?' the henchman replied.

'Kill him. Kill that filthy dosser, right now.'

Frosty swivelled his head my way and spoke in a voice laced with fear. 'Stop him, Fletch.'

I scrambled to my feet. 'Now, hang about, Vic, there's no need for that.'

The goon remained similarly unenthusiastic. 'Boss, I don't think we need to—' he started, but Vic snapped his fingers, causing him to double over in pain. Once again, he'd paid the price for giving Vic lip. I wondered what curse had been inflicted upon the poor bastard this time. What new disfigurement lurked beneath his clothing.

Vic grabbed the goon by the chin, a snarling animal. 'I said, kill him!'

The henchman tore off his mask, gasping for air. His face was tight, his skin stretched over his skull like the membrane of a snare drum. 'Please,' he begged, the flesh in the corners of his mouth splitting open as he spoke, carving a red grimace into his face. 'Don't.'

Vic raised his hand and pressed his thumb and middle finger together, readying for another snap. Sensing what was coming if he didn't obey, the henchman hobbled off in the direction of the torture rack, a whipped dog.

'Whoa whoa,' I said, eyes darting from Vic, to Kojo, to Frosty. 'Let's not get carried away, now.'

I had a bad feeling about where this was headed. This wasn't just Vic throwing his toys out of the pram. He'd been tapping on my shoulder for years, and every time I turned to look at him, I spat in his face. This wasn't just a threat. Not this time. This was payback.

The henchman did as instructed, taking the crank of the torture rack in one of his meaty fists.

'Wait!' I cried.

The henchman looked to his boss, who returned a nod that told him he should do as I requested. At least for the moment.

'Let's hear it, then,' said Vic.

Time to try some knife-edge diplomacy.

I stayed exactly where I was, afraid that the slightest twitch in the wrong direction would lead to Frosty's untimely end. Well, his end anyway.

'Okay, cards on the table, Vic, I *was* nosing around in your business. Yeah, I know you're looking to grab a demon's soul and do some sort of trade with another demon. That's it, that's everything I have. All told, I'd say I've snooped on you about as much as you have me, which I reckon makes us even. So how about this: you leave Frosty alone, and I go back to work. I get out there, I beat the long grass, and I get you your demon in a bottle. What do you say? Wanna shake on it?'

Vic took a breath, yanked down his tie, and loosened the collar of his shirt. The purple drained from his face, going back to its usual ripe Stilton colour. 'I'm not dense, Fletcher. I know I can trust you about as far as I can piss a brick, but I've got a soft spot for you, always have had.' He spat into his palm and extended his hand. 'You've got a deal.'

I reached out to shake his hand and felt his fingers dig into me like the talons of a bird of prey. He yanked me in close and pressed his mouth to my ear.

'You must take me for a fucking mug, mate,' he hissed. Keeping me in his grip, his head snapped in the direction of the goon. 'Do it. Kill the tramp.'

Frosty's mouth formed a silent scream of Munch-like proportions.

The henchman didn't hesitate this time. He whirled the crank, stretching Frosty's exhausted body beyond even its supernatural limits. I heard gears squeal in complaint, followed by a sound like paper tearing. It was a sound that made me glad I couldn't have nightmares.

I managed to pull myself free of Vic's grasp and run to Frosty's side.

'I'm so sorry, Frost,' I said, placing my hands on his broken body, feeling the sting of tears in my eyes.

'S'all right,' he wheezed, the last dregs draining from him. 'Been kicking around... long enough. Don't forget… you still owe me that keg...'

His eyes rolled back, his grey tongue lolled from his mouth, then he vanished to wherever it is that dead ghosts go. Gone, never to drop another pearl. He looked happy as he went, glad to be done with it all. I suppose it must have come as some kind of relief, finally getting out. That didn't mean Vic had the right to deliver him to the everlasting nothing, though. Not by a fucking long shot.

Vic offered me a disappointed shake of his head. 'Now, now, Fletcher, stop making that face. I told you there'd be consequences for mucking me about.'

I turned to him, white-lipped with rage. 'You're the one who messed up, Vic. Without Frosty, you're out of leverage. Now there's nothing you can do to twist my arm. Nothing to stop me from burying you.'

'Is that right?' he said, his voice somehow even oilier than usual.

He bobbed his head and his henchman responded by stepping behind the wicker changing screen in the corner of the room and producing a fresh victim.

Mark.

Mark Ryan, my unwitting meat suit.

With one meaty paw gripping Mark's man bun, the henchman frogmarched him to the torture rack in the centre of the room and tore a ball gag from his mouth.

'What are you doing?' Mark cried. 'Who are you people?'

'Keep your mouth shut,' I urged him. 'Let me handle this.'

But I was talking to myself. To a normal like Mark, I wasn't just invisible, I was set on mute. All he knew for sure was that he'd been taken hostage by a barrel of shit in a cheap suit and woken up in an underground sex dungeon. Any part I played in the conversation that preceded him being dragged out from behind that screen had been redacted from the record. As far as Mark was concerned, he was on his own, stuck in the middle of a pissing contest he had no hope of understanding.

'The dead tramp was a dog and pony show,' Vic told me, relighting his cigar. 'Let me down again and it'll be this one paying the ferryman next.'

I cocked an eyebrow in Vic's direction. 'This is how you finally convince me to be your dogsbody, is it? By torturing my school bully. The bloke who made my childhood a waking nightmare.' I forced a laugh. 'A real brain trust you've got going on here.'

Vic returned a jackal's grin. 'I know you won't let a man die, Fletcher, no matter how much he has it coming. That saviour complex of yours won't have it.'

The henchman took Mark's feet out from under him and strapped him to the torture rack that had only moments ago held Frosty. Mark fought the goon all the way, but it was like watching a tantruming toddler trying to stand up to an overbearing father three times his size.

'That's right,' Vic told his goon. 'Make him nice and comfortable.'

'This is low, Vic, even for you,' I said, 'dragging a civilian into this.'

'You left me no choice,' he replied. 'The way I see it, this is all on you.'

Mark's eyes searched for the person Vic was conversing with and found no one. 'Who are you talking to?' he begged. 'Are you on Bluetooth? Is someone paying you to do this? Because I can pay more!'

Of course, Mark Ryan thought money would be enough to buy his way out of this mess. Money had always been the solution. Money was like magic to Mark. To people who did what he did—playing the financial market—getting rich was just a shell game. They misdirected investors by lying about their returns and made huge sums of their income **poof** disappear. It might lack the in-your-face, razzle-dazzle that lighting a cigarette with a snap of your fingertips does, but that didn't make it any less magical.

Still, Mark's brand of sorcery had its limits, and Vic Lords was one of them. Vic didn't need Mark's money. What he needed was an arch-demon's soul to pay off his debt with the Long Man, otherwise, he was going to spend the rest of eternity screaming in his Forest of

Souls. Getting out of that pickle was the kind of abracadabra that money couldn't buy.

I watched Mark squirm and beg for his life, and wondered if he was really worth saving. The death of one hedge fund manager for Vic's eternal damnation sounded like a pretty sweet trade-off, considering. Maybe I should have left him at the mercy of his captor. Shown Vic that he was all out of playing chips, and resigned him to his fate. The idea certainly wasn't without its merits.

But no.

I had to get Mark out of this. Not just to keep the Big Man happy, but for my own sake. This was about more than saving my soul, it was about keeping my conscience clean. Mark was a world-class prick, a thief and a bully, but he wasn't a murderer, and he didn't deserve to die at Vic's hands for reasons he couldn't possibly fathom.

'This is your final warning, Jakey boy,' said Vic. 'One more strike, and the next time you see your friend here, he'll be floating face-down in the Thames.'

The henchman tightened the rack, drawing Mark to his full height, stringing him out as tense as piano wire. I don't think I'd ever seen a man so scared.

Vic arrived at Mark's side, a stub of cigar gripped between his forefinger and thumb.

'Hold him still,' he growled.

Vic's bully boy took Mark by the chin, fixing it in place like a vice while his boss aimed the lit end of his stogie at one of Mark's expensively moisturised cheeks. For a moment, I hesitated. Even with the terrified look in Mark's eye, I hesitated. Wasn't he the one who handcuffed me to a red-hot radiator and left me with a shiny pink bracelet of disfigured flesh that I wore until the day I died? Maybe he could stand to get a little burned. Maybe this served him right.

Finally, 'Enough,' I said.

'Enough what?' asked Vic, a picture of innocence.

'I'm on the job, okay? Just leave him alone and I'll fetch you your demon.'

Whatever it took. I'd do Vic this one thing, and once I was done doing it, I'd make it my mission to close the books on the old bastard.

The henchman loosened the rack and Mark went slack with a desperate gasp.

'Good man,' Vic told me, grinding the cigar under his heel and offering a grin that went wholly unreturned.

'You're going to let him go?' I said.

He laughed. 'What am I, touched in the head? Bring me the soul I'm after, then you can have your little boy toy. Not before.'

I had nothing to say to that. No ace up my sleeve. Nothing I could do to sway him one way or the other. Either I got Vic what he wanted, or Mark was plucking a harp with the choir invisible.

I did an about-face and headed for the door.

'Cheer up, mate,' said Vic, a wet chuckle rising in his throat, 'it might never happen.'

No reply seemed like the safest way to get out of there without anyone getting killed, so I bit my lip and kept walking.

CHAPTER TWENTY-FOUR: QUIET TEACHERS

'Afternoon, Cookie. How's life?'

'Don't *Cookie* me,' I told Shift, phone flat on my palm, braying into it like I was a contestant on *The Apprentice*. 'And don't, *how's life?* a dead man, either. Bad form.'

I'd just watched an old friend die and I was in no mood for Shift's cheery brand of gab.

'Jeez, what climbed up your butt and died?' he asked (he was a he at this point, which made it much easier to give him a telling off).

'I need to know where that demon soul is,' I said. 'My ears are thirsty, and all you've given me so far is a load of old chat.'

'Take it easy, would you?' he replied. 'I'm pretty sure I have the bead on what you need. Give me a few hours and I'll hit you up with the deets.'

'If you know where the soul's being kept, tell me now.'

'In a couple of hours, okay? I have some wrinkles to iron out first.'

'Wrinkles? Don't fuck me about, Shift.'

A pause. 'I can tell you're not your best self right now, so I'm going to forget you said that and hang up. Keep your phone switched on and I'll be in touch.'

The line went dead. It was all I could do not to toe-punt my phone over the horizon.

I took a breath (so to speak). Okay. All right. So long as I had some time going spare, I was going to use it. The Ripper case was still pending, and I'd be buggered if I was going to sit on my arse waiting on Stronge's next call. I scrolled through my contacts, found her number, and hit the big green button. She picked up before the third ring.

'What do you want, Fletcher?' she asked.

'How's the hand?' I replied.

'Just get to the point, will you?'

'Fine. I've been thinking about the case and something sparked. How did our killer know about the second victim's lung medication? He'd have to have access to medical records for that, which likely means he's a medical man—a doctor—like they say the original Ripper was. That's the angle we should be chasing.'

'Already on it,' she replied.

'Oh. Right then.'

'Pretty obvious line of enquiry, really,' she said. 'Was that everything?'

'No, there's something else,' I replied. 'I want to see the body of the last vic.'

A beat passed. 'What the hell for?'

'What do you think? To have a shufty and see if anything pops up.'

'We have people for that,' Stronge replied.

'Not with my expertise, you don't. Come on, look at the facts: three dead bodies and no ghosts on any of them. There's something spooky going on here, and that's where I come in.'

Stronge said, 'I'm the lead on this case. I decide how things get done.'

'We need to wrap this up before he does it again, Kat. The original Ripper killed five women. We're already three dominoes down; do you want to watch the next two take a tumble, or do you want to use all the tools in the box and catch this bastard?'

A long sigh. 'You are a tool, Fletcher, I'll give you that.' She clucked her tongue, thinking. 'Meet me at the morgue in an hour.'

'Wouldn't miss it for the world,' I replied.

St Pancras Mortuary was a cold, antiseptic, place; all stainless steel counters, white tiled walls, and polished metal sinks. A grim place. But then what do you expect? You don't go to a mortuary expecting party balloons and disco balls.

I was attending the autopsy of the Ripper's third victim. Inspectors Stronge and Maddox were there, the pair of them looking like they'd showed up to a knitting circle that turned out to be a fight club. A wide plaster decorated the bridge of Maddox's flattened nose, while Stronge wore a cast on her punching hand.

Upon seeing me, Stronge shot me a filthy look. She'd expected me to show up in Mark's body, but seeing as that wasn't an option, I'd chosen to attend au naturel. She obviously wasn't happy about my decision—having to deal with a disembodied voice with colleagues in the vicinity had always been a bugbear of hers—but given the situation, she was in no position to argue.

I looked at the empty metal slab before us and remembered how I felt the day I saw my body lying there, spread out in pieces: two legs, the bottom half of my torso, and the upper part, complete with head. A human life turned into four chunks of marbled fat and muscle. The day I saw that was the same day I decided to become a detective. My first case: the mysterious murder of Jake Fletcher. My first closed book, too.

The room's swinging doors flapped open, swiftly followed by an aluminium trolley bearing a naked, female corpse. It was the body of the Ripper's last victim, and escorting it was Dr Anand, the mortuary's Chief Coroner. Anand was a hard-working Indian woman that I'd never seen out the uniform she had on: a blue plastic apron, doctor's scrubs, and a pair of Croc shoes.

'Morning, campers,' she trilled, wheeling the trolley in and applying the brake next to the metal slab. She cut a glance to each of the detectives. 'Little help?'

She needed an extra pair of hands to help transfer the cadaver from the trolley, and going by the look on Maddox's face, the job would be falling to his partner. For a tough guy, the bloke had a weak stomach.

I stayed quiet and watched invisibly from the sidelines as Stronge stepped forward and helped Anand slide the body over to the slab.

'How do you want to do this, then?' Anand asked.

'Don't worry about us,' Stronge replied. 'You do your thing and we'll observe. Just act like we're not here.'

'Okay, but make sure you stand back from the splash zone,' she warned. 'The first three rows will get wet.'

I caught the look of revulsion on Maddox's face and felt the corners of my mouth turn up.

Dr Anand snapped on a pair of powdered latex gloves before handing the detectives a small orange bottle. They passed it around, emptying a jigger of the oil on their fingertips before dabbing it under their noses.

Anand switched on a microphone that hung from a cord above the cadaver. Having cleared her throat, she rattled off the date of the post mortem and a few other technicals. She circled the body, reporting into the mic, 'Caucasian female, no jewellery, displays no residual scars, identifying marks, or tattoos....'

To someone in Dr Anand's profession, corpses are quiet teachers. Each body that crosses her slab holds the secret of how its owner came to pass, but will only share its tale with someone fluent in the language of death. Thankfully, Anand is a gifted linguist and is able to coax secrets from what most would consider to be nothing more than a depersonalised shell.

'Blueish discolouration detected under the collarbone and to the right of chest. Dark brown spots on anterior surface of left chin. Lobe of left ear torn; old injury, possibly from forced removal of an earring, now healed.'

She went on like this until she reached the limits of what she could learn by sight alone.

'Commencing internal examination,' she said, her hand travelling to a tray of medical tools and selecting a gleaming silver scalpel.

While Anand went about her work on the copycat Ripper's third victim, Stronge and Maddox took a quiet sidebar.

'There's something I don't get,' whispered Maddox, eyes pointed at the ceiling, doing his utmost to make sure he didn't catch sight of the autopsy in even his peripheral vision. 'The other two killings both had a connection to the original Ripper's: the first was committed in the same location, and the second vic had that matching lung disorder.'

'And you want to know what the connection is with this one,' Stronge replied, her eyes not straying from the job at hand, carefully observing the dissection.

Maddox bobbed his big bald head.

Stronge said, 'I already worked it out. It's in the name. The vic there is Elisabeth Dotter.'

Maddox ceased his bobbing, a deep cleft appearing in his 360-degree forehead. 'But wasn't the OG Ripper's third victim called Elizabeth Stride?'

Anand cut in, arms crossed. 'Excuse me. Are you two here to watch or have a chinwag?'

The detectives waited for the doctor to return to work, then continued at a lower volume.

'Elizabeth Stride is what she called herself in London,' said Stronge. 'Back home, her name was Elisabeth *Gustafsdotter*. Swedish. The "Dotter" means daughter.'

'So what?'

'So the killer is telling us that Elisabeth Dotter there is the daughter of the original Ripper's victim.'

'You what? Her on the slab? She'd need to be over a hundred for that to add up!'

Anand shot them both evils. Stronge waited for the doc to carry on with her examination before she continued.

'Not *literally* her daughter,' Stronge whispered to her partner, her voice a mouse's squeak now. 'He's not saying the vic's an actual family heir, just a... successor. It's symbolic. He's using poetic license.'

Maddox seemed unconvinced, but the logic was sound enough for me. The link might have been tenuous and convoluted, but it was too unusual to be a coincidence. The dots were spaced far apart, but Stronge had managed to join them anyway.

'Pretty slick, Detective,' I said.

'Thanks.'

'Huh?' said Maddox, wondering who she was talking to.

Stronge dodged his gaze. 'Nothing.'

Anand spun on her heel, her blue apron now coloured with a red Jackson Pollock. 'If you two are done flapping your gums…'

She went on to give the detectives a run-down of the vic's wounds, not skimping on any of the details, much to Maddox's discomfort. She wrapped it up…

'The cause of death was a single clear-cut incision to the left side of the victim's neck, which severed the main carotid artery.'

'That makes the murder a dead ringer for the Ripper's third victim,' said Stronge, tilting her head to one side. 'We already suspected we'd see that. What else have you got?'

'What do you mean?' asked Anand.

'Anything else that can lead us to the culprit?'

Anand snorted. 'This isn't *CSI: Miami,* love.' She pointed at the gaping wound on the cadaver's neck. 'It's not like the perp left a murder weapon in there with his fingerprints on. Speaking of which, what did dabs have to say about the crime scene?'

I remembered the creepy SOCO guy, Pedersen. The bloke with the bowl haircut and the naked lady pen.

'Well?' Anand went on. 'Were any prints recovered?'

Stronge glared at her partner. 'Aside from the victim's, only one.'

Maddox threw up his hands. 'I took my gloves off for one second, okay? We all make mistakes. Jesus.'

Anand rolled her eyes at him. 'What's the matter with you, you dunce? Are you bleeding from the brain?'

A reasonable question. I sometimes wondered if Maddox had suffered worse than a fugue state when he tangled with that soul feaster. He should really have been declared unfit for work and sent packing by this point, but since Stronge signed off on his pay cheques, he stayed employed.

Shame heated Maddox's face. I suppose I should have felt sorry for the bloke. Instead, I leaned over to Stronge and spoke conspiratorially in her ear.

'I knew it. Prints on the scene – Maddox is our man. Called it, day one.'

She scowled and waved a hand through my face. When her partner shot her a curious look, she disguised the gesture by waving her hand again, swatting at an imaginary fly.

Anand concluded her analysis. 'Whoever your murderer is, he came wearing gloves and remembered to leave them on. That makes him smarter than at least one of the people chasing him.' She shook her head ruefully. 'This does not bode well for his capture...'

Stronge chipped in. 'There's a theory that the original Ripper was a surgeon. Do you think whoever did this had a medical degree?'

'Short answer: maybe, maybe not,' Anand replied. 'The killer shows some basic anatomical knowledge, in that he seems to have removed organs with a degree of skill, but he could just as easily be a butcher or a vet as a doctor.'

'What about the murder weapon, though? To be that precise, wouldn't he have needed a scalpel?'

'Not necessarily. A craft knife would have done the same job.'

Stronge rubbed her temples. 'So what you're telling me is, we're no closer to cracking this thing than we were at the start?'

'Pretty much.'

'There must be something,' said Stronge, digging her fingers into the skin on either side of her forehead so deeply that I expected her to leave divots. 'Is there anything else you might have picked up on, even if it seems like a total outlier.'

Anand considered this. 'There was something. It's gone now, but when I unzipped the body bag I smelled something rotten.'

'Don't corpses tend to smell that way?' asked Maddox.

'Not like this,' Anand replied. 'This smelled like a cacky nappy.'

She must have been picking up on the smell Stronge detected at the crime scene. How was it she described it?'

Like shit and rotten eggs had a baby.

'A cacky nappy?' said Maddox. 'That's funny.'

'That's not funny,' Anand replied. 'Funny is the time I hid a human ear behind the lungs of a cadaver so one of my medical students could find it during a mock autopsy. You should have seen his face!'

Even I was a bit appalled by that. No one knew quite where to look until the morgue door swung open to admit a technician in a white lab coat.

'Bloodwork came back,' he announced.

'That was quick,' Anand replied, impressed.

'We did a rush order on it, given the severity of the situation.' The technician placed a sheaf of paper-clipped documents on a nearby counter and exited, but not before adding, 'Skip to page seven. Freaky stuff.'

Anand snatched up the papers, peeled back the first few pages, and scanned the part she'd been directed to. 'That can't be right,' she said.

The look on her face; something was wrong.

Maddox piped up first. 'What? What is it?'

The doc delved a little deeper before replying, 'There were traces of blood found on the scene that don't appear to be human.'

'So what are we talking?' asked Stronge. 'Animal blood? A pet, maybe?'

'No,' said Anand, flipping through a series of photos picturing microscopically magnified cells. 'This is unlike any blood sample I've ever seen. The DNA profile isn't a match for a single species we have on file. It's... well, *freaky* is about right.'

I craned over Anand's shoulder and had a snoop at the documents on the sly. What I saw was exactly what I feared.

'Where does this leave us, then?' asked Maddox.

'We're going to need to run some further tests,' Anand explained. 'It has to be an anomaly, I'm sure of it. Let me look into it and get back to you.'

'How long?' asked Maddox.

'It'll be a few days before I can give you anything conclusive,' Anand replied. 'A week at most.'

'Great,' Stronge sighed.

She turned to her partner and gave him a nod that said, *Let's get going.*

Following that, there was a final bit of chit-chat, then the detectives and Anand parted company. I tailed Stronge and Maddox across the mortuary forecourt, through the car park, and to their vehicle. It was only once they stepped inside the car that I sidled into the back seat and made my pitch.

'Can I put a word in your ear?' I asked Stronge, who was sat at the wheel.

Maddox was still none the wiser that I was there, but Stronge decided to remove him from the picture all the same.

With a theatrical tutting noise, she announced to her partner, 'Shit. I forgot to ask for a duplicate of the bloodwork. Can you do me a favour, pop inside and grab a copy?'

Maddox sucked in a long breath, inflating his chest to barrel-like proportions, then finally popped the passenger door. 'Yes, guv.'

He made himself scarce, slouching off in the direction of the mortuary, leaving me and Stronge to talk in private.

She swivelled her head in my direction. 'What is it, Fletcher?'

'When the next round of lab results come back, the doc's not going to be any less stumped,' I explained.

'Why's that?'

'Because it's not animal DNA she's looking at. It's not anything from this world…'

'Please don't say what I think you're going to say…'

'...It's demon DNA.'

'How could you possibly know that?'

I could practically hear her teeth grind.

'Just working with the evidence. We've got a blood sample that doesn't belong on planet Earth, and then there's the smell...'

'Smell?'

'I didn't want to rush to conclusions before, but now the jury's in. That stink you described at the block of flats, the same one Anand just got a whiff of, it was at the first crime scene, too.'

'It was?' she asked, eyes narrowed.

'Yeah. We mistook it for a backed-up drain at the time, but we were wrong. It was sulphur.'

Stronge's chin hit her chest. 'Otherwise known as brimstone. The thing demons smell of.'

'You got it.'

The pair of us had faced down a demon before, and the encounter had left a deep impression on us both.

A scowl bent Stronge's face. 'Fuck!' She went to punch the steering wheel, remembered that her hand was already in a plaster cast, and pulled back before she did herself any further damage. She hollered at the roof of the car, flapping her arms like a trapped pigeon. 'Christ Almighty, Jake. How is it that every time you get involved in a case, a demon shows up? Whatever happened to good old-fashioned, bread and butter serial killers?'

'I'd like to remind you that you were the one who dragged me into this mess. I was just about to redecorate my new office before you came knocking on the door with a job I couldn't refuse.'

'So what are we looking at here?' asked Stronge, still red in the face. 'What's oozed through the cracks this time?'

'Not sure. It looks human, though, which means it's disguised itself as one of us. How exactly, I don't know. Could be that it's possessed someone, or it could just be using a glamour to appear normal on the outside.'

'If it's even done that,' Stronge replied. 'Hard to say what's going on, what with the balaclava. Our man could be hiding a real horror show under that getup.'

She had a point. Despite the video he sent us, we still had precious little to go on in terms of ID. Even our face-to-face with the killer had illuminated very little. For all we knew, only the thinnest of disguises masked the monster within.

Then again, how the demon was managing to cosplay a human wasn't the main thing playing on my mind. The real question mark stuck in my brain was the one asking this: what was a creature of the outer void doing in London, aping a bunch of dusty old killings from the Victorian era?

It didn't matter, though. Not yet, anyway. What mattered was stopping the bastard. Stopping him hard.

'What do we do next?' asked Stronge, a rare note of uncertainty in her voice.

I wasn't sure exactly, but I knew this much: it was up to the two of us to catch this freak and send it back to Hell before it chalked up victim number four.

'Don't worry,' I told Stronge. 'The Spectral Detective is on the case.'

CHAPTER TWENTY-FIVE: ANGEL OF THE NORTH

So apparently both of my jobs involved demons. Fuck my afterlife.

Since Shift wasn't proving much help with the Ripper, it was up to me to get on the front foot and find out just what it was I was dealing with. So long as my informant was drawing a blank, I should call in someone with specialised knowledge. Even if I really didn't want to get her involved.

I translocated to Reina's flat in Angel and rang the doorbell. The face that greeted me lit up with a smile the size of the Grand Canyon.

'Jake!' squealed the woman on the other side of the door.

Believe it or not, I'm not used to people being pleased to see me. I know, me with this knee-weakening jawline and an unending supply of hilarious quips. Who knew?

'Hey, Rei,' I replied, almost bashful. Anger, disdain, simmering resentment, these are emotions I can handle. Genuine warmth gives me the sweats.

'Get in here, you dead beauty!' she cried and led me inside.

Reina was an old friend. Well, not *old* old; she was actually in her early twenties, but when I first met her, she was just a teenager. I worked a case for her, back when I was still fairly fresh to this ghost detective malarkey. Something had murdered her parents, one of whom—long story short—turned out to be an angel. That's right, a genuine, holier-than-thou angel. This, in turn, made Reina part angel.

I know, an angel who lives in Angel; you couldn't make this stuff up.

Anyway, I ended up tracking down her parents' killer, a particularly nasty demon known as a harbinger, and cast it into Hell. Since then, Reina has been a trusted ally.

She steered me into her kitchen, which was an absolute state. The walls were grease-splattered, and the floor covered in curling linoleum. Where there wasn't a filthy, balled-up tea towel there was a chipped mug growing fungus.

'Jesus, this place looks worse than it did last time,' I said. 'I thought you Highway to Heaven lot liked to keep things spick and span.'

'Just because Mum was an angel, doesn't mean I have to live like one.'

I laughed. She certainly didn't look all that angelic with her multiple piercings and heavily tattooed cleavage. But then, who was I to judge?

She popped a limescale-barnacled kettle onto a scummy hob. 'Fancy a cuppa?'

'I'm fine, thanks,' I said, suppressing a grimace. She was only asking out of politeness, so there was no sense turning my nose up at her. It's not like I could actually drink tea, anyway.

She helped herself to a brew and we sat down at her wobbly kitchen table, which was loaded high with plates covered in mouldy leftovers.

'So what brings you round this way?' she asked.

'Hey, who do you think I am? Do I need a reason to drop in on my favourite half-angel?'

In this case, truth be told, yes. Reina had a talent that I had a real need for. Her angelic ancestry gave her a certain sensitivity to the Nether that had come in handy on more than one occasion over the years. With her help, there was a chance I could glean some important information about the killer I was tracking.

If you're going to do battle with a demon, you're going to want to know exactly what kind you're facing off against. Go toe-to-toe with a hellion thinking you're dealing with a common drude and expect to end your day in a lot more pieces than you started out with. But with so many varieties of demons to choose from, I needed specifics. It's the only way I was going to find the thing and beat it.

Reina saw through my ruse and pouted playfully. 'Aw, Jakey, you only come here when you want something.'

'Now, that's not true. What about last Christmas when I stopped by with that nice bottle of Bordeaux?'

'Wasn't that the time you wanted me to find a demon that was making pets tear out their owners' throats?'

A grim business, although I can't pretend I wasn't a bit impressed that one person managed to fall prey to his pet stick insect.

'There's a demon loose,' I said.

'There's *always* a demon loose.'

'This one's knocking off victims in the style of Jack the Ripper.'

Reina's brow creased. 'Huh. Weird for a demon to copy like that.'

'How do you mean?'

'They're a big-headed lot as a rule. Like to carve their own furrows.'

'Well, apparently this one doesn't mind digging up old ground. Three scalps on its belt so far. I need to find out what I'm dealing with and stop it before it takes a fourth.'

Reina sighed. 'You know it hurts when I do this, right?'

I really didn't want to involve Reina in any of this, which is why I hadn't called in on her sooner. She was a friend, and I don't like to see friends suffer. Unfortunately, the only other angel I knew—an actual full-blooded seraphim—was someone who wouldn't piss on me if I was on fire (the only reason I even knew the bloke was because he'd been sent to drag me in front of my Maker, back before He and I reached an understanding).

'I know it hurts,' I said, 'and I'm sorry, I'd only ask if I didn't have a choice.'

She smiled. 'I know, I just wanted to make you feel bad. Now, let's get to it, shall we?' She swept aside a stack of unwashed plates, hopped up on the table, and assumed a half-lotus position. 'What have you got for me?'

Reina's ability was helpful, but it was also limited. Chances were,

I wasn't going to learn the type of demon I was dealing with, its name, or where it was hiding, but she might find *something* of use. The info she came back with would likely be vague, but it could be the key to cracking the case wide open. I once clocked a demon disguised as a car mechanic because she told me it would be missing half a thumb from its left hand. Without that scrap of info, the creature would have butchered a lot more people.

'I'm looking for a very particular demon,' I told her. 'One with an interest in Jack the Ripper. One that can take human form, and only busted out of his realm recently.'

'Okay, not a whole lot to go on,' she said.

'I know, but I'm desperate here. This thing isn't playing by the Ripper's timeline anymore, which means another corpse could drop any second.'

She gave me a wink. 'I'll do what I can.'

She closed her eyes and let forth a long breath. After ten seconds or so, the air in the room became staticky, charging her hair with some alien electricity and making it stand up on end as though suspended underwater. She tilted her head back and her mouth fell open, releasing a stream of something like stardust. I heard the faint sound of choral music as the golden particles formed a glittering tendril that whirlpooled around her head, gaining speed until it was moving so fast that it looked solid. The golden ring rose to the top of her skull, where it hovered like a heavenly corona. A halo.

And then she began to glow.

I mean literally glow, as though her skin had been draped over a 100 Watt bulb.

This was it. She was shining her light on the Nether, scouring its darkest corners, illuminating its most shrouded secrets.

I sat forward, eager for Reina to open her eyes and smile, to tell me something I could use to take down this bastard. But when she opened her eyes, there was no smile. In fact, she would never smile again.

'No!' gasped Reina, reeling back, her eyes wide with terror.

'What? What's wrong?'

'Boobytrap. We need to—'

She coughed and blood erupted from her mouth. Not a splatter, not a glob, it was like a dam inside of her had broken.

'Rei!'

I reached for her, like there was anything I could do, but it was too late. For her and for me. The last I saw of Reina was her body exploding into a cloud of red mist, and then the world was pulled away from me.

...

'No...'

...

'Rein...'

...

I tried to form words, but everything was fragments, as if someone had taken a hammer to my brain. To my sense of reality. One thing I did know: Reina was dead. She hadn't had time to explain, but the word "boobytrap" was enough. The demon I was hunting had covered his tracks; made sure that anyone who poked their nose into his business tripped a hex. A hex that had blown up in Reina's face, and was taking me down, too.

I could feel myself unwinding, could feel the stitches that held me together popping one by one as the hex pulled me apart and made me less than nothing. The hex was attacking my body, my memories, my everything. It wasn't just killing me, it was trying to erase my existence entirely. Trying to wipe me out now, and in the past. Trying to make it so I never was or would be.

The hex raged through me, buffeting me in its fortean winds. There was no way of fighting it. I might as well have tried picking a scrap with a tornado.

Useless.

I was useless.

I couldn't save Frosty, couldn't stop the demon killing those women, and now, because of me, Reina was gone. Part of me wondered if I deserved this. If it was time to just let go. Another part of me yelled, *Like fuck it is! Don't go quietly into that good night! Fight! Scream! Gouge that hex's eyes out!*

The anger felt good. It blotted out my fear. Yeah, I was done—and no, there was nothing I could do to stop the hex doing what it had been created to do—but I didn't have to let it taste my fear. I could still go out strong.

Off I go.

Jake Fletcher has left the building.

. . . And then something unexpected happened.

I carried on existing.

I know. Came as quite a shock to me, too.

My essence was scattered so wide at this point that I was ready to disperse into thin air... then there was a flash of light and a deep rumble.

What?

I was no longer being pulled apart, I was being thrown around, fought over, and then. . .

...and then it was all over. Calm. Quiet. I looked around in shock. I was still alive! Well, not *alive* exactly, but you get the idea.

I let out a whoop of relief, my breath quick and ragged.

Wait. . . my *breath*?

I was breathing.

I had lungs. Lungs that pulled in air. And I could smell the dank of the room around me. Feel my nails digging deep into my palms. What the bloody hell was going on?

I opened my mouth to ask myself that very question, and you know what came out?

'Braaaiiins. . .'

Holy shit! I was in my old body. I was back at the funeral home and inside FrankenJake. I looked down at my hands. My actual, physical hands.

I felt like running around in a circle, half in panic, half in joy at actually being alive again. If I hadn't found myself handcuffed to a radiator, I probably would have done just that, but Shift had secured my wandering corpse as instructed.

So what happened?

I calmed down and tried to make sense of things. The hex had me, was scrubbing me from existence, so how did I end up here inside my old body? Best guess was that my situation confused the hex. I was dead, a ghost, but I was also alive physically—at least to an extent—in the form of my zombified corpse. The two parts of me existing like that must have short-circuited the hex in some way, so instead of killing me, it had plopped the two parts of me back together. Talk about a stroke of luck!

Scared.

What?

Scared. Want to stay.

A voice in my head. Was that me, or—?

Brains.

'FrankenJake?' I said.

Want to stay.

It was FrankenJake talking to me. Not in words as such, he wasn't actually talking, but I could sense how he was feeling. He was still here, inside my body. Whatever it was that made him what he was was still alive and kicking.

'This is my body,' I said.

A wave of sadness washed over me, but it wasn't my sadness, it was his.

'I'm sorry, big feller. This ain't my doing.'

What was I apologising for? This was my body first. And yet…

…I could feel him there with me. Feel his fear of being taken over, of being pushed aside. And then the truth hit me. This wasn't my body anymore. Hadn't been for a long time. I was an intruder.

I felt a familiar sensation like two magnets of matching poles repelling each other. It was the same sensation I felt whenever I stayed inside Mark for too long. The body I was in was about to eject me. I tried to hold on. It might not be my body, but it was once, and part of me didn't want to give it up.

Braaaaiinns, FrankenJake whispered in my head, and then it wasn't my head anymore. I was out of there.

I looked up from where I'd been deposited on the floor to see FrankenJake staring at me with complete bafflement. Okay, it wasn't much different to his usual expression, but this time I sort of felt it.

I stood and we eyed each other warily. Could I do that again? Could I take over my body? I impulsively dove right back at him, only to feel like I'd run headfirst into a brick wall. I tried again, and again, but it was no use. The hex had shoved me back inside my body, but there was no way I was getting in there again. Part of me felt guilty for even trying.

'All right, all right,' I said. 'Will you stop looking at me like that? I had to try, didn't I?'

Being judged by your own corpse, that was something new.

I slumped down on the edge of the bathtub, a real mix of emotions rolling around inside of me, but mostly relieved that I'd made it through in one piece. Then came the guilt.

Reina.

Dead.

All because I pulled her into this thing. The demon had taken her life, but I was the one responsible for walking her into his trap. Demons destroy; that's what they do. Blaming anyone but myself for what happened to Reina would be like blaming the floor for breaking a plate.

It was all too much to process right now. My grief would have to be put on layaway while I figured out my next step. While I concentrated on finding a way to avenge Reina's death.

Movement.

Footsteps.

FrankenJake pointed past me. I lurched to my feet and turned.

We weren't alone.

CHAPTER TWENTY-SIX: LIVE FAST AND LEAVE A BEAUTIFUL GHOST

'WHAT ARE YOU DOING HERE?' I asked. 'I thought I told you to cuff mouldy to the radiator and make yourself scarce.'

It seemed Shift had decided to hang around after delivering my corpse.

'You did,' he replied (he was a he today; the tall blond gent who first revealed himself to me back in that alley), 'but I liked the place and decided to stick around.'

I had a feeling that letting Shift know where I lived was a mistake the moment I gave him my address, and here it was, another poor decision, biting me square on the bum.

'We need to talk,' said Shift, taking a seat on the edge of the bath, 'and since neither of us is welcome at The Beehive right now, I thought this would be the next best place to have a chat.'

He had a point there. Although a barring rarely lasted long with Lenny, it was always best to let him cool down a bit before putting another show in.

'Go on then,' I said. 'Talk if you want to talk.'

'In a minute, Cookie,' he replied. 'Before we get to that, I can't help but notice you're not wearing my coat.'

Bugger. Forgot about that.

'Sorry, I don't have it right now.'

Which was a bit of an understatement given that Vic had stripped it off me and torn it to pieces.

Shift's voice dropped. 'Didn't I tell you that coat had a back to it?'

'Look, I'm really not in the mood for this,' I said, and I wasn't kidding. I'd just seen someone I cared about die horribly. Arguing over a coat seemed absurd. 'I'll get it back.'

'And if you don't?' he asked.

'Then I'll settle up with cash. Happy?'

'And this cash of yours, I don't suppose I could get a glimpse of it, could I? Just so I know you're on the up and up.'

Tell him where I kept my green? Fat chance. I barely knew the bloke, and I'd had enough of being mugged, thank you very much.

'Sorry, mate,' I told him, 'but that ain't going to happen. I've got your wonga; when the time's right you'll get it. Trust me, dead men tell no lies.'

He crossed one leg over the other and leaned forward. 'I'd prefer to see some proof if it's all the same with you. A show of faith, so I know you're not going to screw me over. Unless you don't want me to tell you the whereabouts of this arch-demon soul...'

Now it was my turn to lean forward. 'You know where it is?'

'Indeed I do,' he replied. 'But I'm not giving you bupkis. Not until I see some cheddar.'

'All right, all right, don't get your knickers in a twist.'

He rolled his eyes back so far he probably caught a glimpse of his own brain. 'Really? What kind of talk is that? Would you say that to a man?'

'You are a man!'

'Oh right, so I am,' he replied, looking down and finding his chest flat. 'Still, that's no way to talk. Not in this day and age.'

'Sorry, I guess I'm just old school.'

'You're not old school, Jake, you're pre-school.'

'Listen, mate, I'm really not in the mood for all this PC bollocks, so how about you concentrate on the job instead of handing out lectures?'

'This is for your own good, trust me. Do you really want to stay clinging to this outdated, macho way of thinking? Do you want to be a human time capsule, or do you want to get on the right side of history while you still can?'

'I dunno,' I said. 'Which one gets you off my tits and puts a demon in my pocket?'

He gave me an eye-tut. 'You're deflecting, when what you really need to be doing is looking inside yourself and embracing change.'

'Easy to say for a shapeshifter.'

He leaned back, arms crossed. Finally, he said, 'The money. Show me the green or I walk right now.'

What choice did I have?

'Stay there,' I told him.

In case he was otherwise inclined, I removed FrankenJake's handcuffs and instructed him to keep an eye on our guest. Leaving Shift in the bathroom, I visited the back of the parlour, stepped over the ruins of the demolished wall leading to the showroom's secret annexe, and whipped the dust sheet off the safe. I entered the combination, popped the lock, and removed a thick bundle of money.

'There,' I said, returning to the bathroom and showing Shift the dosh. 'Satisfied?'

He answered with a smile. 'You bet.'

Shift knew I was good for his fee now. I'd proved to him that the legend of the money-hoarding ghost still held water.

Satisfied that I had the goods, Shift revealed the whereabouts of Cimeries. 'He's being kept in the Museum of Souls,' he revealed, his voice lowered to a whisper.

'The what?' I replied, drawing a blank.

'Think of it as a sort of Uncanny Christie's,' Shift explained, 'an auction house run by a society of collectors who capture souls and sell them on to the highest bidder.'

'You're telling me this place trades demons like commodities?'

'Demons, people, anything with a soul.'

'*People*? What kind of people?'

'Famous ones,' Shift replied. 'Folks who left a dent in the history books.'

I was getting heated now. 'And they're just trapped there, stuck in this museum?'

'Until they get auctioned off, yeah.' He caught the dirty look I gave him. 'Hey, I'm not saying I condone it, okay, but I get it.'

'Get it how? What's to get?'

'People have always collected keepsakes of the dead,' he replied. 'Napoleon's doctor had away with the man's cock during his autopsy. Buddha's tooth was pulled out of a funeral pyre, and to this day, people come from miles around to pray to it. Christ's fingers are so popular that they're on display all around the world, more than thirty of them if you do the math... and most don't, obviously.'

I regarded him cooly. 'How come you know so much about all this stuff?'

He shrugged. 'It's like I told you: I'm a font of useless information. The point is, don't be surprised that this museum place exists. People fight wars to get hold of the relics of their dead heroes, of course they'd want to own their eternal souls.'

'They're keeping people in captivity and selling them on for a profit,' I fired back, livid now. 'That's slavery is what that is.' I felt my face tightening into a bulldog scowl and wondered if I looked anything like Stronge did when we let the Ripper copycat give us the slip at that block of flats. 'People think the dead are helpless,' I complained. 'That they can do anything they want with us. Well, I'm going to show them just how fucking helpless we are.'

'Loving that energy, big man. Use it.'

I ignored the daft bastard and barrelled on. 'Where is it? Tell me where this museum is and how I get in there.'

'The location I can give you, but getting inside is going to be a whole other beast. The place is locked up tighter than a Chinese finger trap. I'm talking security up the yin-yang.'

'There must be some way to bypass it? Some weak spot.'

'I don't know about that, but I can tell you who will know…' He produced a phone from his trouser pocket and held up a photo for inspection. It was a portrait of a bald, middle-aged man wearing a pair of spectacles. 'They call him the Curator. He runs the place. As far as I can tell, he always has. Get hold of him and you might just get some answers.'

I studied the photo closer, inspecting every last detail. And that's when I spotted it: my way in.

The corners of my lips hoisted into a smile. 'You're mine, sunshine. Oh yes, indeed.'

CHAPTER TWENTY-SEVEN: SOUL MATES

I WAS on my way to my next destination when I felt the psychic prickle of Vic's scrying magic. He was checking up on my progress, but he'd caught me at just the right moment: sans zombie and in the middle of running his errand. That meant Mark should still be safe. For now, at least.

Legerdomain, Jazz Hands' magic emporium; that was my next pitstop. I was heading there to kill two birds with one stone (a *twofer*, as Shift might say). For one thing, I wanted to follow up on a clue I'd seen in that photo of the Curator Shift had shown me. But I was mainly going there to get the dope on my monster in a man suit. It was personal between the Ripper and me now. I was going to end that fucker in a big way.

I arrived at Legerdomain to find Jazz Hands sat at the counter poring over a celebrity magazine.

'There's my little social butterfly,' I said, approaching the counter.

She didn't even bother looking up.

'You realise it's gone nine in the evening, right?' I asked. 'Shouldn't you have closed up by now?'

'Have you seen this?' she said, showing me a page from her gossip rag. 'Apparently, Cameron Diaz is having another skin flare up.'

'Wow. And I thought *I* had problems.'

She finally deigned to meet my eye. 'What is it?' she huffed, folding the magazine closed.

'Just looking for a bit of friendly advice.'

She studied me over the rims of her violet-lensed glasses. 'Of course. Heaven forfend you should come in here and make a purchase like a normal person.'

'Come on, Jazz, I'm up slack alley, here. I haven't got time to prat about.'

'Fine,' she said, rising to her feet and turning over the shop's Closed sign. 'Say your piece.'

I straightened my back. 'Demons,' I said. 'I need to talk to you about demons.'

I thought about the look on Reina's face as the hex tore her apart. The creature that did that wasn't going to stay a mystery. Not a cat's chance.

I filled Jazz in on the story so far, describing each of the copycat Ripper's kills and bringing her right up to the present, to the point we discovered that the killer had demon DNA. My guilt about what happened to Reina stopped me from sharing that part of the story.

'So let me get this straight,' she said, plonking herself down in her stool again and pushing her glasses up the ridge of her nose. 'Not only are you attempting to purloin a demon soul for a known gangster—which is ludicrous enough in and of itself—now you're attempting to run down a second demon?'

'I'm hoping one cancels out the other,' I replied.

Frustrated, she attempted to swipe a hand through her bird's nest of hair, but it got caught up in all the knots. She tugged it free, along with a small avalanche of dandruff.

'I'm looking for anything you can give me, Jazz. Anything I can use to bring this bastard down.'

She head-butted the shop counter a couple of times before returning to the conversation. 'Think about what you're asking, Fletcher. You're expecting me to identify the genus of a demon based on what? The fact that he's taken human form? Demons that can do that are ten a penny. I'm going to need more information if I'm to narrow this down.'

She was right. I was really pissing in the wind on this one, but I had to exhaust every avenue I had; for Reina, and for the rest of the dead women in the Ripper's bloody wake.

I remembered the dusty tome Jazz kept behind the till, and rapped a knuckle on the counter. 'How about we crack open the Monster Manual and figure this out?'

'*Monster Manual*? Is that what this is to you: a game of *Dungeons & Dragons*? I'll have you know the grimoire you are referring to is known as *Pseudomonarchia Daemonum*.'

'The Big Book of Demons; that's the one.'

'The *Pseudomonarchia* is an almanac that catalogues a comprehensive list of over one-thousand breeds of demon. People have died in pursuit of the knowledge contained within its pages. Show some bloody respect.'

Wearing a face like thunder, Jazz reached beneath the counter, hauled out a book the size of a paving slab, and dumped it in front of me with enough force to make the shop windows rattle. Without taking her eyes off me, she licked a finger, opened up the bestiary, and scanned its lengthy table of contents. 'Tell me everything you know about this killer of yours,' she said. 'Is he showing any obvious demonic traits? Budding horns? Scaly flesh? Perhaps he's doing the pea soup vomit thing that they're so keen on?'

'None of that, no,' I replied.

I needed to give Jazz something she could use, and it had to be better than what I gave Reina.

'Here's a thing,' I said, 'he gives off a brimstone smell.'

She nodded at me the way a nurse might respond to a demented geriatric. 'Pretty much all demons give off a trace amount of brimstone, Fletcher.'

'Okay, then how about this: when this one kills, he doesn't leave behind a ghost.'

'Again, that's hardly going to help us narrow our search, is it? There are plenty of demons that eat souls.'

She was on the money, of course. Some demons eat flesh, some eat corpses, but a whole lorry-load of them dine out on souls. Demons love to chow down on human spirits, obliterating them in much the same way I did back in my exorcist days, only with the full knowledge of what they're doing.

Jazz was right, I was going to need to give her more information if I wanted to figure out what kind of demon I was dealing with and how I could go about stopping it. Because the net I'd given her to throw out wasn't big enough to land a funfair goldfish.

'Are we done here?' she asked.

We were. At least as far as my little demonic line-up went.

'Actually, there is one more teensy little thing I could use you for…'

Her already granite-like expression somehow managed to harden even more. 'Out with it.'

I took a breath. 'I need your body, Jazz.'

She snatched up her magazine and swatted me in the face with it, though of course it passed right through.

'Let me be more specific,' I explained. 'I'm not looking for female company. What I need is a corporeal form.'

I told her about the Museum of Souls, and explained how she'd be just the disguise I needed to infiltrate the place and pilfer Vic's demon fossil.

She sniffed my breath. 'Please tell me you arrived at this ridiculous plan after several jars at The Beehive.'

'No, no. I'm perfectly compos mentis.'

'More like *compost* mentis.'

'Huh?'

'Shit for brains.'

Smack-talking me in Latin? Now, that's just mean.

'Okay, let's see if this sweetens the deal: you let me borrow your body for a couple of hours, and in exchange, I give your bag of bones a total spring clean. I'll get into all those hard to reach cracks, erase any unwanted memories you might have, even give you some new ones if you like. Just name it and it's gone.' I snapped my fingers for effect. 'Immaculate, wall-to-wall and floor-to-ceiling.'

She unrolled her celebrity magazine and resumed reading. 'Pass.'

'Maybe you don't get what I'm offering here. I'm talking about a complete mental detox. Put yourself in my hands and I'll have that blob of grey meat spruced up so nice it'll sparkle! You can't pay for that kind of service, Jazz. So come on, what do you say, old pal?'

Jazz looked up from an article about some woman who was apparently a royal, but—much like the demon I was hunting—

remained a total mystery to me. 'If you need a body so badly, may I suggest you use the one you brought in here last time?'

'FrankenJake? Tried it already; no joy.'

'Why not? He should be the perfect vessel.'

'I don't know why,' I replied, thinking back to my brief time of being reunited with my body, and my inability to stay that way. 'I guess we're just not compatible.'

'So even your own body doesn't want to know you. Why should I be surprised?'

I decided to let that one slide, too.

'Even if I could puppet the zombie, I doubt I could fool anyone into thinking he was alive. I need a breather if I'm going to make this thing work, and I can't just bring some rando into it. Too risky.'

'Oh, but you're perfectly happy putting my life on the line? Let me put this in no uncertain terms,' she said, leaning over the counter and pinning me with a cold eye, 'you're not leaving this place with my body, and if you try to take it without my permission, I'll have you circling the drain before you can say "very bad idea".'

'I thought we were friends, Jazz. I thought we helped each other out.'

'No, I help *you* out. You've never so much as made me a cuppa.'

I turned up the volume on my best smile; the one that always got me what I wanted. Well, most of the time.

Some of the time.

'It's just a quick loan. I borrow your body, I go into that museum, I come out with a demon soul.' I showed her the pouch of human skin with the bone clasp that I'd be using to transport the goods. 'Easy peasy, lemon squeezy.'

She looked at the fleshy purse with some distaste, then back to me. 'And what makes you so sure they're going to let you in just because you're wearing my face?'

I sighed theatrically. 'I really didn't want to do this, but you leave me no choice…' I produced my phone. 'See anything you recognise?' I asked, showing her the screen.

She peered over the rim of her glasses and studied the photo that Shift had given me. The picture of the man they called the Curator. She said, 'Doesn't ring a bell.'

'Oh no? I'm surprised. Because he *has* rung a bell. The one above your shop door, in fact.'

'What are you blathering on abo—'

She ground to a halt at the precise moment she recognised the glasses the Curator was wearing. The same kind that were perched on her own nose.

Spooktacles.

The violet-lensed specs Jazz manufactured that made ghosts visible to human eyes. The kind that only she made.

'This is the bloke who runs the museum I'm trying to get into. A real nasty piece of work. So do you wanna explain to me why you're supplying him magical loot?'

Jazz's face took on a distinct scarlet hue. 'I was just making a sale, that's all,' she protested. 'Besides, how bad can the man be if he makes a living keeping demons behind glass?'

'Not just demons, Jazz. This bloke cages human souls, too. Believe me, he's a towering prick.'

'How was I supposed to know?' she countered. Her voice had taken on a mild stutter, now. 'He was a customer like any other. I... I didn't ask what he wanted the goods for.'

I clucked my tongue. 'Yeah, I think the guy who designed the showers at Auschwitz said something similar.'

'You can't possibly be comparing me to—'

'I'm just saying, your hands are dirty and now's your chance to get them clean. Help me put a dent in this arsehole's operation and get yourself back on the right side of history.'

She sagged, defeated. She was going to give me what I wanted. I think a part of her knew that the moment I showed up.

'If I find so much as a ladder in my tights when you're done, you're dead to me,' she said.

I grinned. 'I'm a ghost, Jazz. I'm dead to everyone.'

CHAPTER TWENTY-EIGHT: SÉANCE FICTION

SINCE SHE INSISTED on her beauty sleep, I had to wait until the morning before Jazz Hands was ready to let me take her body for a joyride. I have to admit, she felt surprisingly sprightly for a woman of her age... assuming she was as old as I took her for. I could never tell exactly how much wear and tear had taken place beneath her mess of scarecrow hair and the jumble sale's worth of old rags she wore.

The loan of Jazz's body came with a long list of stipulations, chief of which were the following:

- I was to borrow her earthly form for a limited duration of no more than four hours (a number that was arrived at after no small amount of haggling).
- Nosing around or otherwise meddling with her memories was strictly forbidden.
- There would be no—REPEAT, NO—looking under her clothes (that one was written in bold print). If the toilet was required, it was to be done so in complete darkness, or with the aid of a blindfold.

I signed off on the agreement with every intention of keeping my promise. Though there were larger things at stake than upsetting Jazz Hands—saving Mark's life for one—I knew that God's wrath would be nothing compared to the sheer fury I'd find myself up against if I ticked off the woman whose body I was tooling around in.

I picked up the pace, nose pointed in the direction of the museum, Jazz's legs pounding a steady rhythm against the pavement. I wondered, was she the one to thank for the pep in my step, or was the get-up-and-go I was feeling simply down to the fact that I was inhabiting a physical body? I suspected the latter, and the thought immediately took the wind out of my sails.

When you think of a ghost, you imagine a wisp of a thing; an indistinct shape made of smoke and nothing. The reality of being a ghost is quite different. There's a heavy, leaden toll that comes with being a dead man. A lingering feeling of decrepitude that weighs on you every day. One that reminds you, no matter how alive you might feel, that you're long gone. It's like Jazz said before: technically speaking, my corpse is the real me. FrankenJake is made of bone and blood and brain. He's the person, I'm just an echo of one.

As if to underline this, my eyes landed on a poster plastered to the hoarding of a building site I was passing. The poster advertised a festival that was to be held at a nearby park the coming weekend, and was covered top to bottom in names of bands. I didn't recognise any of them. Not one. Not even the headliner.

But the assault on my relevance wasn't over yet.

Further down the road, advertised on the side of a bus stop, was a poster for Madame Tussauds. It trumpeted the unveiling of a brand new waxwork: a woman with caramel skin, tight denim cut-off jeans, and a microphone held high. The waxwork was surrounded by eager punters snapping selfies, and yet I had no clue who it was they were meant to be posing with. How could that be? Didn't you have to be a household name for them to make one of those? An icon?

I kicked a stray Coke can and sent it scuttling into the gutter. When did it happen? When did I get so out of touch? The world had slipped away from me and was gunning for the horizon at speed, moving too fast for me to ever catch it. Shift was right, I was yesterday's news. I wasn't becoming obsolete, it had already happened.

How could it not? How was I supposed to keep my finger on the pulse when I didn't even have one?

Shaking me from this stinking thinking was a noise coming from my pocket. The name on my phone said *Stronge*.

I projected my own voice through Jazz's lips and answered, 'What is it, Kat?'

'There's been another one,' came the reply.

The words stopped me in my tracks.

A fourth murder.

One more and the copycat killer was done. One more and he'd have the whole set; the Ripper's canonical five. The shit was piling up so high that I was starting to suffocate.

'He knows we're on his tail, so he's picking up the pace,' said Stronge. 'We have to stop him now. Right now. When can you get here?'

I was being pulled every which way. I had to stop the Ripper, but here I was in Jazz's body working another case. Lives hung in the balance no matter which path I took. What was I supposed to do?

'I can't. Sorry.'

A pregnant pause, then, 'What are you talking about? Stop pissing about and get your arse in gear.'

I didn't have time to explain what I was up to, so I just gave her this: 'I'm on another case. Give me a couple of hours and I'm all yours.'

'Will I, fuck,' she replied. 'There's a demon out there gutting women for fun. You got something more important on your plate than that?'

'Kat, I can't—'

'Let me stop you right there, Fletcher. I'm not interested in your excuses or hard-luck stories. Just get to the address I'm about to text you, or you and me are done. You got that?'

I took a breath. 'I got it.'

Stronge hung up.

She was right. I needed to get Mark free of Vic's clutches, but the Ripper job came first. A string of people had already died, and another was set to join the pile if I didn't act fast. I just had to bank on Vic having a bit more patience; just one solitary ounce. God help me.

The address Stronge gave me was all the way out in Walthamstow, the very arse-end of the Viccy Line. Normally, that wouldn't have been an issue, but since I was wearing Jazz and didn't want to lose her, I needed to travel the old-fashioned way. Give her back her body and she could decide that she was done being used as a human prophylactic. So, eastbound I went.

The crime scene was a run-down house in a part of the borough that had yet to be gentrified. No yummy mummies patrolling the streets with thousand-pound baby buggies here. No bouji cafes selling mashed avocado on sourdough for a tenner a pop. No art in your latte. The closest thing to a bit of colour I saw on these streets was a play park with a lone swing set held together by rust, and tarmac so cratered you'd think it hadn't been resurfaced since the Blitz.

Standing in the concrete front garden of the house were a couple of constables clutching the lapels of their hi-vis jackets like grey-wigged barristers posing for an oil painting (do they teach coppers to do that, or does it just come naturally?). Sawhorse barricades had been erected around the property, largely to keep out the general public, who had shown up like ants to a picnic. The whole area was teeming with rubberneckers, phones raised high, hoping to capture something clickworthy to display on their Instagram feeds. This, in turn, had attracted the press, who arrived in vans wearing fold-up satellite dishes on their roofs, parking on double yellows so they could get as close to the story as possible.

I later learned that the media had gotten wind of the spate of grisly murders occurring around London, and joined the dots between them. They'd even given the mystery killer a headline-friendly nickname: Jack the Rip-off. The front page of every scum sheet in town was decorated with junk theories as to who the killer might be and what his motives were. This was accompanied by rampant speculation regarding his choice of victims, much of which twisted the facts to fit the original Ripper narrative that the murdered women were sex workers. Diabolical stuff. If the men who own these rags don't end up knocking on damnation's door, there's no justice in this world or the next. Putting this case in the public eye only created more pressure, and where there was pressure, mistakes followed. Mistakes we couldn't afford to make.

A van door slid open and ejected a female reporter wearing trousers so tight that I could almost read the signature on the credit card in her back pocket. Accompanied by a cameraman, she hustled her way to the front of the crowd and thrust a microphone into the face of the nearest constable. He ignored her by pretending to focus on the indistinct chatter coming from his radio.

'Stay behind the barricade,' demanded his partner, obviously the more assertive of the two.

I elbowed my way to the head of the pack, past the reporter and the cameraman, and gave the constables a knowing nod, momentarily forgetting that I was wearing the skin of a middle-aged/elderly woman. Had I been wearing my usual meat suit, Mark, the officers would have recognised me and let me inside. I'd done the "psychic consultant" thing in their borough before when I helped Waltham Forest's finest track down an ice cream man who'd been snatching kids from the area. The perp turned out to be a gorger—a kind of gluttony monster—the unquiet zombie of a man who dies from overeating and comes back hungrier still... only this time his insatiable appetite craves food you won't find on any restaurant menu. Don't worry, that story wrapped with a nice, happy ending; Stronge and I stopped the gorger before he made chow out of the kiddie winks, and sent him to the Bad Place with no supper.

The reporter persisted, thrusting her mic across the police barricade like an air-to-air missile. 'Millie Sanders, ITV News. Can you tell us what's going on in there? Has Jack the Rip-off struck again?'

A plaster-cast hand swatted the reporter's microphone aside. 'This is an ongoing investigation, Miss Sanders. Now get behind that barricade before I slap the cuffs on you and give your cockroach friend here something actually worth filming.'

Stronge stood in the doorway of the house, hands on her hips, giving the reporter a look so hateful that it made her roll back on her heels. Suitably chastised, the lady took off, taking her partner with her.

Stronge tossed a glance my way. 'You, too, madam. Back it up right now.'

This new meat suit was really crimping my style.

I looked to the constables, then back to Stronge with a conspiratorial Groucho eyebrow wiggle. 'It's me, Detective. You know... JF.'

'JF?' Her eyes widened as the pieces slotted into place. 'Oh, right. JF. Of course. Come in, come in.'

Knowing better than to ask questions, the constables moved aside the barricade and allowed me through. The second I was past the blockade and inside the house, Stronge slammed the front door and shoved me up against it.

'What are you doing?' she hissed.

'Easy, tiger, you'll burst a blood vessel.'

She gave me a shake. 'Why, Fletcher? Why have you shown up in an old spinster's body?'

'Sorry, I didn't realise there was a dress code.'

She gave me another shove, hard enough to almost dislodge a painting of Krishna from the hallway wall. 'How am I supposed to explain you to my partner? To anyone? I've got a whole team of officers in there; who shall I tell them you are this time? The fucking tea lady?'

'What did you want me to do, Kat? My other suit's at the dry cleaner's, and I know how you hate me showing up au naturel.'

A cloud of impossibly smelly aftershave announced the arrival of DI Maddox, who barrelled over to us with his cue ball head and primate stoop. His eyes were panda black from the injury he sustained at the block of flats, and complemented by a white Adam Ant-style plaster fixed across his upper nose that made him look like he'd been run over by a road painter.

'Who's this now?' he asked his partner, looking at me.

Stronge quickly released her grip on my shoulders. 'This is... um...'

I extended a hand. 'Jamila Fabreze,' I replied, that being the best "JF" I could come up with in a pinch.

Maddox took my hand (Jazz's hand) and returned a wary shake. 'I see. And you are...?'

'A consultant. I'm here to help with the Ripper case.'

Maddox's eyes slanted over to Stronge. 'Please don't tell me you've brought another "psychic" in on this.' The speech marks were palpable.

Stronge faltered. 'No, not a psychic... she's a—'

'Spiritualist,' I cut in. 'Completely different beast.'

'A spiritualist?' Maddox growled.

'Yep, that's me,' I replied. 'Small medium at large.'

Maddox swiped a meaty paw down his face. 'Are you serious?' he asked his partner.

Stronge came back with an uncertain nod.

Blood heated Maddox's face. 'God Almighty. Are we running a circus here? First Fletcher, now this one?'

'Quiet down, Detective, or—'

'No, you listen to me. I've had about as much of this as I can take. This isn't a bloody TV show. The people I work with wear badges; people who swore an oath to uphold the law, not nutters with voices in their heads that you drag in from the street.'

'Detective—' said Stronge.

But Maddox was already making tracks, stomping off and muttering unsavoury words under his breath.

Quick side note here: I hate spiritualists just as much as Maddox does. Psychics, too. Don't get me wrong, I'm not talking about genuine channellers—those with real mystical powers—I'm talking about cold reading carny fuckos who pretend to be able to communicate with the spirit world so they can make a few quid off the bereaved. I've seen some heinous stuff in my time, but these guys stand top of the arsehole pyramid. It's not just that they're scammers, either, it's the way they spin their bullshit in plain sight that bothers me. To a rational person, a spiritualist is a con artist, plain and simple. They can communicate with the dead? Really? So why are they so closed-mouthed about it? Why are they always talking in riddles? Instead of all this, "I'm seeing the colour red; does that mean anything to you, madam?" bollocks, why aren't mediums telling it like it is? You think the dead are holding back? You think they don't want their relatives to know every single thing they're going through? Take it from a ghost; if these toss-bags could really act as inter-dimensional interpreters, they'd get more business than British

Telecom. Instead, they have nothing. *Are* nothing. And that's why I'd see every one of them wiped off the face of the planet if I had my way. Because only someone really hurting would buy what these scumbags are selling, and those who profit from pain deserve everything Old Scratch has to offer.

As Maddox took a corner at the end of the hallway, still muttering profanities, I turned to Stronge.

'I don't know about you, but I'm happy to see the back of him. What is that aftershave of his? Old Spice? Whatever it is, it could strip paint.'

The look Stronge gave me could have done the same.

CHAPTER TWENTY-NINE: UNFINISHED BUSINESS

Having dispensed with the unpleasantries, Stronge led me to the scene of the crime.

On the way to the kitchen—where I was told the body had been discovered—we passed a lounge decorated with ornately carved wooden furniture, vases of exotic flowers, and a miniature shrine to Ganesha.

The kitchen was your basic abattoir.

The room reeked of a sickly-sweet butcher shop odour that I hadn't been able to smell over Maddox's pungent perfume, but could already feel souring my insides. There was a trace odour of brimstone there, too. Our demon's signature scent.

Stronge and I stood in the kitchen doorway as SOCO dressed in white boiler suits photographed the scene, lifted prints, and packed anything that might be deemed suspicious into evidence bags.

The deceased was an Indian woman who looked to be in her mid-thirties, though the brutal disfigurements to her face made it hard to say for sure. She lay on her back with her head turned to the left, blood tracking from her wounds and pooling in one corner of the room; a product of the floor having been set at a slight slope. The woman's arms were frozen by her sides, palms upwards, fingers hooked into talons. As with the rest of the Ripper's victims, her throat was slashed and her intestines drawn from her belly.

I wondered when he'd done it. Had the demon been adding to his canonical five while Reina was being shredded by the hex he left to cover his tracks? Two bodies in one day?

'The neighbour called it in,' said Stronge. 'Got a delivery meant for the deceased and went to drop it off when he found the front door open and let himself inside.'

'What's the connection this time?' I asked.

So far, the links to the original Ripper killings had included a matching location/date, a shared medical history, and a correlating family name. So how did this fourth victim fit the picture?

'It wasn't easy to figure this one out,' Stronge replied, 'but I think I have it. It's about siblings. Catherine Eddowes, the original Ripper vic, was one of twelve kids. So was the woman on the floor there.'

I snatched another look at the body through the swarm of forensics officers.

'Really?' I asked. 'You think that's it?'

'How many people these days come from families that large? It's got to be.'

I had to admit, it did sound like more than a coincidence. Twelve was a very specific number. I wondered how many parents in all of London had that many offspring.

One of the forensics team sidled up to us and pulled down his face mask. It was Pedersen, Chief Scene of Crimes Officer.

He spoke to Stronge with that unsettling feral grin of his. 'Excuse me, Detective, but it's getting a little cramped in here. Would you and your friend mind waiting outside while we finish up?'

There was a definite whiff to the word "friend", but Stronge let it go.

'Of course,' she replied, and whisked me away so Pedersen and his team could get on with their job uninterrupted.

Outside, in the front garden, Stronge and I surveyed the gathering crowd. By now, the two constables in hi-vis jackets had moved from their post and taken position on the front line, manning the barricade that separated the murder scene from the masses. The whole area was abuzz with breathlessly-delivered news reports, speculative crowd chatter, and police radio squawks. The throng had doubled in size since I entered the house, and looked set to grow even bigger.

'Ghouls,' I muttered.

'That's rich,' replied Stronge, 'coming from a ghost.'

Just then, my eyes landed on a lone member of the crowd. He was a big lad, plenty of meat on his bones, and wore a neatly-trimmed beard. I couldn't make out much more than that at the distance he was standing, particularly as his face was partially obscured by the phone he was holding up. So many lit phones out there you'd think we were at a Spice Girls concert, and yet something about the way this guy wielded his made him stick out. It was the determination behind it, his arm a ship's mast, the device gripped in his hand like a dead man's trigger. The crowd buffeted him to and fro, but he stayed ramrod straight, not the faintest crook in his elbow as he filmed the scene. It was as though the footage he was recording was of the utmost value. A priceless artefact. A trophy?

'That bloke out there; does he look familiar to you?' I asked Stronge.

She gave him a squint. 'Not to me. Why, you seen him before?'

I studied him a little closer. He did look familiar, though I couldn't place him, not from so far away.

'Where are you off to?' asked Stronge as I moved for the front gate.

'To talk to him.'

'You're going to harass a member of the public? He's just a nosy parker, forget about him.'

Wasn't going to happen. Everything about the mystery cameraman set my alarm bells ringing, plus he was a match for our guy, build-wise. The least I could do was have a word with the bloke and eliminate him from our enquiries.

I reached out with Jazz's hand, threw the latch on the front gate, and made my way towards the barricades. For the first time since I started watching him, the mystery cameraman faltered. His attention moved from the screen of his phone to the woman making a beeline for him. To me. And that's when I clocked who he was.

The Van Dyke beard, the brown hair down to his shoulders, the silver crucifix necklace: he was the tour guide. The Ripper expert who led me and a crowd of others down the backstreets of Whitechapel. And here he was now, this murder aficionado, loitering on the edge of a crime scene. That couldn't just be a coincidence. Finally, a person of interest.

The tour guide's eyes widened and his arm went slack. I saw the phone fall to his side as he dithered on the spot, a rabbit in headlights. Moving as fast as Jazz's legs would carry me, I reached the barricade and bellowed at the constables to make a hole. The guide wasn't sticking around for questioning, though. The guide was making a run for it.

Off he went like the gingerbread man, threading his bulk through the crowd, shoving aside anyone who got in his way.

'Get back here!' I demanded, but my plea fell on deaf ears.

I squeezed Jazz's ample backside through the gap in the barricade and pegged it after the suspect. No one helped me. Not one member of the public did anything to stop the running man. Quick to stick their noses in, but not to stick out a leg.

The tour guide continued his escape, legs pumping, cheeks burning. I hauled after him as fast as I could, fully expecting to get left for dust, but Jazz's body proved to have some juice. Despite spending most of her time sitting behind a shop counter reading gossip magazines, she was surprisingly light on her feet.

The big man made big strides, but Jazz was quicker, tearing up the pavement, closing the distance, moving way faster than I'd thought her stumpy legs capable of. Pretty soon I was on the suspect, my breath hot on his neck, a hand hitched on his belt. I tried to drag him to the ground, but he threw back an elbow and cracked me in the jaw. Stunned, I put a hand to my mouth and came back with blood on my fingers. Balls. I'd only just pulled out of the rental place, and I'd already dinged the motor. Jazz wasn't going to be happy.

With fire in my belly—fire that seemed to come as much from my host as it did from me—I bolted after the guide. I wasn't letting him get the best of me. One way or another, this shithouse was going down.

The crowd continued to part as the burly guide barrelled away from me, but with each person he was forced to barge out of the way, he lost a little ground. Once again, I was catching up. A few feet more and I'd be on him. A few feet. Just a few feet more.

Wallop.

A blur from the fringe of the crowd, then the guide went shooting out of frame like he'd been yanked off stage by a shepherd's crook. In the blink of an eye, the suspect was on the ground, and on top of him, raining body blows, was DI Maddox.

Defending himself, the suspect took some swings of his own, one of which clobbered Maddox in the turnip. For a moment, I thought the detective had been sparked out, but the blow only served to piss him off. He gave the guide another clout, who traded one back, maintaining the scuffle. The two of them were both about the same size and evenly matched. Who knew how long the fight would have gone on for if it wasn't for Stronge intervening and showing the suspect the business end of her stun gun.

'You're under arrest for assaulting a police officer,' she told the suspect as her partner rolled him on to his front and applied the speedcuffs. It was obvious by the time she reached the *You do not have to say anything* part of the Right to Silence speech that his mouth was staying firmly shut.

For now, at least.

CHAPTER THIRTY: A LIKELY STORY

A BARE BULB illuminated the solitary metal table of the station's interview room, beneath which sat a plastic chair that looked as though it had been lifted from an inner-city high school. Perched in that flimsy chair was our suspect, tethered to the table by a sturdy cuff bolt. His face was a mess; one of his eyes swollen shut, his breathing laboured. I studied him with lethal intensity. Was there a demon in there, lurking behind that fleshy facade?

In this room, it was DCI Stronge's job to find out.

'I want my lawyer,' said the suspect, although the lumps he'd taken made it sound more like, *I want my liar,* which seemed about right.

The room was ripe. The suspect wasn't even sweating yet, but already smelled like a sour armpit. In any other room, someone would have cracked a window, but having the temperature turned up set the scene nicely for the grilling that was about to follow.

Across from the suspect, sitting on the opposite side of the interview table, were Stronge, Maddox, and me. Or as far as the latter detective was concerned, a slovenly-dressed woman of indeterminate age who had the gall to call herself a spiritualist.

Using the hand that wasn't cast in plaster, Stronge placed an ominous-looking folder on the table in front of her, leaving it closed for now. Written on the front of the folder was the suspect's name: Dennis Oberman.

'I wouldn't recommend a lawyer, Dennis,' she told the suspect. 'Having one present will only make you look guilty in the long run. You're far better off just speaking your mind and answering our questions.'

'You must think I'm a total idiot,' he replied, leaning forward in his seat, chair legs straining under his bulk.

Maddox craned forward in his chair, too, almost meeting the suspect's forehead, the two of them forming a human steeple. Their injuries made for a colourful contrast: the fresh red welts of Oberman's face complementing the murky greens of the detective's.

'You resisted arrest and assaulted a police officer,' said Maddox. 'The brains of Britain you ain't.'

'I did what I did in self-defence,' Oberman protested.

Stronge interjected. 'Forget about that for now. Just tell us why you ran.'

She asked the question like it was any other investigation. She didn't know for sure whether we were dealing with a demon or just Joe Bloggs, so she was playing this one by the book. Plus Maddox was in the room, which meant the supernatural stuff was off the table until we could get the suspect alone.

'I ran because I panicked,' Oberman replied, thrusting a finger in my direction. 'I saw a crazy woman screaming her head off and coming at me, so I took off. I didn't know she was a police officer.'

Neither of the detectives bothered correcting him on that score. I stayed quiet, too. The only reason Maddox had consented to me being in the room at all was on the understanding that I kept my trap shut.

'Let's start at the beginning,' said Stronge, drumming her fingers on the mystery folder laying in front of her. 'What were you doing at the crime scene in the first place, Dennis?'

The suspect hesitated. He knew full well that Stronge was baiting him, but couldn't resist saying his piece anyway.

'I got a push notification about it, okay? A news story about another Ripper murder. That's why I was there, to see what was going on.'

'Is that right?' asked Maddox. 'You a big fan of murder, then?'

'Not a fan, more… a scholar. It's my business.'

He explained to the detectives what I already knew: that he made a living teaching folks about the life and times of Jack the Ripper.

Maddox's nostrils flared so wide that I thought he was about to breathe smoke. 'I see. So it's not just evenings you spend wandering around in a murderer's footsteps, it's daylight hours, too?'

Oberman measured his words carefully. 'I'm a Ripperologist. I wouldn't be doing my job if I didn't take an interest in a killer replicating the Ripper's crimes.'

'And loitering outside a dead woman's house with a camera is doing your job, is it?' asked Maddox.

'For the purpose of reportage, I'd say so. Plus, the footage I captured today will drive a tonne of traffic to my blog.'

'Don't count on it,' Maddox replied with a distinct barb in his tone. 'Your phone's been impounded.'

'What? Why?' Oberman was sweating now, his breathing even more strained than it had been.

Maddox added, 'As evidence.'

The suspect forced a laugh. 'You've got to be joking! Now you're stealing my property as well as assaulting me? I can't wait for this to find its way to the courts; I'll have you done for police brutality for starters, and buy a hundred phones with the money I make.'

Maddox continued to fix the suspect with a dead-eyed glare, but I sensed disquiet there. He brought the cosh down hard on this bloke. Very hard. If we were wrong, and he turned out not to be the killer, Maddox would have to answer for that.

Was he a man, though, this suspect of ours? I wondered—not for the first time—if what we were looking at was a demon that had possessed a hapless member of the public, or using obfuscation magic to only *appear* human. That's if he was a demon at all and not just some gawker who found himself in the wrong place at the wrong time.

Stronge stepped in to play nice cop, meeting the suspect with a look of motherly concern. 'Listen, we want to help you here, Dennis, but consider things from our perspective. Here you are, a Ripper expert who just so happens to be in the proximity of a brutal killing carried out by someone aping the murders of Jack the Ripper. You've got to admit, that sounds a bit fishy, doesn't it?'

'Fishier than Billingsgate Market,' added Maddox.

Oberman's smile melted. 'This is a stitch-up. You don't know who killed those prostitutes, so you're trying to pin it on me.'

He looked concerned. Genuinely so. If he really was a demon playing the part of a human, he was giving an Oscar-worthy performance.

Stronge pushed on and read Oberman a date: the date of the first murder. 'Can you account for your whereabouts that evening?' she asked.

'I was at home,' he replied. 'With my mum.'

I can't think that I'd ever heard a twenty-something man announce that he lived with his mother with quite so much eagerness.

Stronge made a polite *hmm,* then offered something else from the calendar: this date lining up with the second copycat killing. Oberman answered the same way. As far as corroborating stories went, this bloke's weren't the most convincing.

Keeping the frustration from her voice, Stronge offered up two more dates. To no one's surprise, the suspect's alibi stayed the same each time.

'Didn't you say you worked evenings?' Maddox cut in.

'Not *those* evenings,' Oberman shot back. 'Why, do you work every day of the week, Detective?'

Sensing that her partner was on the back foot, Stronge wrested back control of the interview. Reaching for the folder, she ran a thumb under its seal and slowly emptied its contents, maintaining unbroken eye contact with the suspect as she did so.

'Officers with a search warrant took these about an hour ago,' she said. 'Care to tell us what we're looking at here, Dennis?'

Onto the table she placed a sheaf of photos taken around the suspect's home. The pictures featured a bookshelf stacked high with serial killer documentaries, a collection of murder-related keepsakes—hatchets, machetes, garrottes—and, curiously, a Texas Sheriff's badge.

'You want to talk about these?' asked Stronge. When the suspect didn't respond, she produced a final photograph. 'How about this one?'

The photo was of a paperback book penned by Oberman, bearing the ludicrously incriminating title: *Jack the Ripper, Villain or Hero?* (the book was self-published, naturally, and featured a cover that can only have been designed using MS Paint).

Oberman eyed the detective glacially, but stayed quiet.

'No?' said Stronge. 'Would you rather talk about your criminal record, Dennis?' Now she was fishing a rap sheet out of the envelope. 'I see a list of minor offences here—possession, drunk and disorderly, breach of the peace—all in the last couple of months. But what I'm really interested in is the headliner: stalking and harassment.'

A tic pulled Oberman's face into a scowl. 'That was commuted.'

'On a technicality.'

Oberman lit up with a hot rush of blood to the face.

Stronge clucked her tongue. 'Barmaid, wasn't she? Bet that stung. You, a learned man—a scholar no less—kicked to the curb by a woman who pulls pints for a living. Must have pissed you right off, that. I get it. But you can't get her, can you? Not since she got another job and moved out of the area, leaving you with this black cloud hanging over you.'

Oberman's face was crab stick pink now.

Stronge carried on laying down threads, weaving a tapestry. 'Word got around. A stalker, that's what they called you. So you thought to yourself, so long as they're going to call me that, maybe it's time I started acting like one. And who's a better stalker than your main man, Jack, eh?'

The narrative she was spelling out might have described a killer, but a *demonic* killer? I wasn't so sure. Demons lied and murdered, but they weren't really known for coveting. What they wanted they took. The idea of a demon going on a killing spree out of jealousy, out of unrequited love… it didn't add up.

Of course, none of that was rattling around Maddox's big bald head as he circled the suspect like a dog looking for the perfect place to take a shit. 'You said it yourself, pal: murder is your business. Nothing wrong with mixing business with pleasure, right?'

'That's enough,' growled Oberman, leaning over his paunch, the chain of his handcuffs drawn tight against the restraining bolt. 'I want my lawyer. I want my lawyer, right now.'

'What's the matter?' gloated Maddox. 'We were just getting friendly.'

But Oberman was saying nothing. He'd wised up and clammed up.

'Fine,' said Stronge. 'Have it your way, Dennis.'

The detectives rose to their feet, and I followed suit.

'We'll be back in a bit,' said Stronge.

Without a further word spoken, the three of us turned and exited the room. Stronge closed the door behind us, leaving the suspect on his lonesome. From the adjoining suite, we observed Oberman through a reinforced pane of one-way glass.

'What do you reckon?' Maddox asked his partner, though it was barely a question.

'Are you kidding?' Stronge replied. 'I like him for it. A lot.'

Since the interview had concluded, for the time being at least, I decided I was okay to join the conversation.

'So what happens now?' I asked the detectives. 'Are we just going to leave him in there?'

'We'll let him stew for a bit,' Stronge replied. 'In the meantime, we're going to run this up the ladder and see what the bosses think.'

She looked to Maddox, who took the hint, bobbed his head, and headed off to set the wheels in motion. Stronge continued to peer through the one-way glass at Oberman, who sat frozen, muscles tense as overtuned guitar strings, the collection of incriminating photos still fanned before him. After a while, she turned back to me.

'Why are you looking at me like that, Fletcher?'

'Like what?' I replied.

'Like you've got something to say and you don't know how.'

The woman earned a crust as a detective, but sometimes I forgot just how good she was at her job.

'I don't know,' I said, scratching my borrowed chin. 'Something about him ain't right.'

'No shit.'

'You don't get it. What I'm saying is, I think you're barking up the wrong tree.'

Stronge gave me a look that could have drawn blood. 'What are you talking about? He's a dead cert. We even caught him returning to the scene of the crime. What do you need, fingerprints on a candlestick?'

'He said *prostitutes*. That's who he thought the victims were. *Prostitutes*, like the newspapers are saying. The real killer would know better.'

Stronge scoffed. 'So he chucked some bullshit our way to throw us off the scent. What about the criminal record?'

'Way too human for a demon. Except for the stalking stuff, there's nothing on Oberman's rap sheet that I didn't get up to at uni; the only difference is, I didn't get caught doing it.'

'What about the fact that all of the offences are clustered into the last couple of months?' said Stronge. 'Doesn't that sound like possession to you?'

'Not necessarily. Could just be that he went a bit doolally when this barmaid gave him the cold shoulder. And anyway, if there was really a demonic entity inside Oberman, I'd expect to see way blacker marks on his record. Satan's minions aren't exactly known for subtlety.'

Stronge chewed on a fingernail. 'Okay, so what about the book he wrote?' she tapped the glass separating us from the interview room. 'The love letter to Jack the Ripper. You're telling me that's *human*?'

'That's exactly what I'm saying. That bloke in there isn't a murderer, he's just a fanboy. So he's got a stiffy for the Ripper; so what? Just because someone checks Mein Kampf out of the library, doesn't mean they're going to invade Poland.'

I was a true crime nut too, remember? Didn't make me a serial killer.

For the first time since I'd begun sowing doubt, Stronge stopped to properly consider what I was saying, hashing my argument out in her head. 'Okay then, let's say you're right so far. There's still the DIY slasher kit we found. Explain the weapons.'

'Junk he bought off eBay to goth up his bedroom. None of it matches the murder weapon we're looking for. And what about what we *didn't* find? What about the red balaclava; where did that get to?'

She'd given up listening to me again, and had taken to shaking her head instead. 'He lives with his mum, Fletcher. They *always* live with their mum.'

The conversation was in a spiral.

'Kat, no one wants this killer in the clink more than I do, but just because a feller can't afford his own place, doesn't mean he's carving up women. Not in this economy. Also, there's something else that doesn't fit: the perp we chased at that tower block outran the both of us.' I gestured to the body I was occupying. 'This bloke got run down by an old woman. He was out of puff long before Maddox blindsided him. You heard the way he was breathing back there; he sounded like a hog hunting for truffles.'

Stronge examined the suspect through the glass. 'You're pretty cocksure about this.'

'More than cocksure,' I replied. 'Cock*certain*.'

Stronge wasn't having it. 'I don't care. This isn't the time for your low-rent Dick Tracy bit, okay? I called you in because shit's gone all Scooby-Doo, and I need you to pull the bad guy's mask off. If you really want to help me, just tell me whether the guy in there is a demon.'

'There's no way of knowing for sure.'

'Then what good are you?' she cried, doing that trapped pigeon thing again, flapping her arms in frustration. 'Didn't you used to be an exorcist? Can't you just go in there and splash some holy water about; get him doing the spinny head thing?'

'I wish it was that simple. Exorcising a demon ain't a picnic. It's a ritual that takes a colossal amount of effort, and if it's buggered up, it can do untold damage. I won't risk it; not without ironclad evidence.'

Stronge finished flapping and folded her arms. 'Fine. You want evidence, go get it. Get inside him like a human turducken and pull some answers out of his brain.'

If only it were that easy. Given enough time, I might—*might*—have been able to root around inside the suspect's head and find out if he was a demon, or at least playing host to one, but doing so would have taken forever. Demons are notoriously good at keeping out of sight, and I didn't have time to run around playing hide and seek. I couldn't waste my hours sitting in a police station when I had a life out there to save. Mark was on the chopping block, and every second I spent not fetching Vic that soul was a second the axe might fall. No, I had to stick to my guns on this one. Convince Kat that she was wrong and get her to move on.

'Listen to me; I don't have to spend hours trawling through the muck in that bloke's skull to know there's too much evidence telling us he's not our demon.'

'There you go again. What *evidence*?'

'Well, aside from the list I already gave you, there's the smell. Oberman doesn't have it.'

'What are you talking about? The bloke stinks.'

'He's not exactly Mister Hygiene, I'll grant you that, but we're not on the lookout for BO, it's brimstone we're after.'

Stronge considered what I was saying, but only for a second. 'You're giving the brimstone thing too much weight. What if the demon can turn his smell off somehow?'

'Selective smell? With all due respect, Kat, if you want me to lay off the detective stuff, maybe you should stay out of my area of expertise. Bottom line is, I don't think the man you've got cuffed to that table is a demon. He's a murder buff, not a murderer. I'm telling you, you're pinning the tail on the wrong donkey.'

'So I should just let him go? Is that what I should do?' She brushed past me, heading for the door. 'You're wrong, Fletcher. Dead wrong. That man—that demon in there—is the one who killed those women, and by the time I'm done with him, he'll never see sunlight again. End of.'

She slammed the door behind her. She was angry; I got that. Four bodies had gone through the morgue, and here I was telling her she was no closer to finding the killer than when she started.

I studied the suspect through the one-way mirror, but no matter how hard I looked, I couldn't find the first sign of a demonic infestation. If anything, he looked even more human than he had from the other side of the glass. Since we started the interview, he'd gone from looking a bit dewy to turning his shirt transparent with sweat. I was right about him, I was certain of it. But could I prove that to Stronge before another body dropped?

CHAPTER THIRTY-ONE: LIGHTS, CAMERA, AUCTION

DETECTIVE STRONGE NEEDED a chance to cool down and get her head straight before I went at her again. In the meantime, I had the Museum of Souls to think about. I borrowed Jazz Hands' body so I could give the place a shufty, and yet I'd spent the last four hours tied up with the Ripper case. According to our deal, I should have been returning Jazz to her shop about now, but she'd have to stick with me for the time being. Saving Mark was too important to let that rule stand.

A bolt of pain pistoned through my head, almost knocking me flat. The body I was inhabiting started to tremble uncontrollably, making me look—to anyone in the station forecourt paying attention—like an alien whose human suit had malfunctioned. Either Jazz was fighting me or she was having convulsions, and I didn't recall her being prone to fits.

'There's a life at stake here,' I pleaded, aiming my words inward. 'I'll have you back behind your counter in a jiff; just give me a little more time.'

The pain subsided as Jazz retreated to the passenger seat. She was giving me an extension on the loan, at least for a little while.

'Thank you,' I said, clutching the bony cradle of her head as I staggered off in the direction of the museum.

As it had been described to me, the Museum of Souls was one part menagerie, one part auction house. I'd managed to secure an official invitation to the institution by posing as a merchant interested in sampling the museum's goods. Of course, the invite wasn't made out to Jake Fletcher, it was addressed to my host, Madame Olena (AKA Jazz Hands), a known dealer of arcane curiosities. The invite wasn't hard to obtain. Surprisingly easy, actually.

The Museum of Souls was situated in Holborn, tucked away down a street I'd never visited before. Its exterior was a black marble facade. Above its entrance were the letters "MoS" engraved in a tasteful serif typeface. I took a breath, readied myself, and stepped into the zoo of disembodied souls.

Inside was not what I expected at all. When I hear the word "museum", I expect chandeliers and parquet flooring and antique furnishings. This place was far more voguish, with its bone-white walls, polished concrete pillars, and wall-to-wall skylights. More like a gallery for contemporary art than a dusty old exhibition house.

As I entered the reception area, I was instructed by a security guard to pass through a metal detector. Fine. I hadn't come packing, let him go ahead and have his rummage (just not so deep that it offended Jazz's delicate constitution).

Having passed the bodycheck, I arrived at the reception desk to be met by a chic young woman with a body so matchstick-thin that she looked more like an X-ray than a human being.

'Please take a seat and you'll be seen shortly, Miss,' she instructed.

For a split-second I bristled at the "Miss", at least until I remembered I was cross-dressing.

I nodded politely, found a seat, and plonked myself down. From my vantage point in the waiting area, I took in the lay of the land. There wasn't much to look at. This part of the Museum displayed nothing in the way of decoration: no wall hangings, no vases of flowers, sod all. Even the light fittings on their ceiling were recessed: little gophers too scared of getting whacked to risk popping their heads out. Certainly, there was no evidence of the Museum's merch on show. Then again, I suppose the enslaved spirits of the dead don't exactly complement a nice glossy catalogue.

I sat in my seat twiddling my thumbs until I was greeted by a tall man with a shiny pate and the body of a praying mantis. The man wore a smart midnight blue suit with spotless white gloves. A pair of thin spectacles sat perched atop his imperious nose. In short, he looked like the type of bloke who dabbed his cock with a silk handkerchief after he took a piss.

'Madame Olena, I presume?'

'That's me,' I replied.

I went to scratch a nervous itch on my chest and ended up copping a feel of Jazz's not inconsiderable bosom. She'd want words about that later, no doubt.

'Welcome to the Museum of Souls,' said the white-gloved man. 'I am the Curator, the custodian of this venerable institution.'

I stood up to greet him and received a limp handshake for my trouble. As I drew closer to the man, I caught a flash of violet in the glass of his spectacles and remembered they were the kind used to detect phantoms. Not this phantom, though; I was invisible so long as I stayed hidden behind my meat shield.

'I hope you don't mind a couple of my men joining us on our tour,' said the Curator.

Immediately, he was flanked by two security guards the size of Ben Nevis. Each of them was draped in a standard-issue black suit and tie, but—and this stuck out as quite unusual—wore a thick iron chain around his neck adorned with a bulky antique padlock.

I thought it best not to enquire.

'What brings you to us today, Miss Olena?' asked the Curator, leading me away from the reception area and into the guts of the Museum.

I proceeded as planned. 'I'm on the lookout for new stock,' I explained. 'Fresh inventory.'

Of course, the Curator already knew of Jazz Hands' establishment, having purchased his spooktacles there.

'I see,' he replied, smiling warmly. 'In that case, I hope I can be of service. Please, come with me.'

His burly lackeys steered me around a corner and through a set of large double doors. Inside was a generously-sized hall full of rows of folding chairs occupied by collectors. An auction was taking place. The Curator gestured for me to join him at the back of the hall where we could observe the proceedings.

'They're bidding on the soul of Amenhotep the Third, an

Egyptian pharaoh,' he whispered. 'Also known as Amenhotep the Magnificent. A most impressive piece.'

Set on a raised platform to the right of the room was a six-foot tall glass vitrine. It reminded me of a Damien Hirst sculpture, only instead of a bisected cow, it contained an ethereal dark-skinned man made up with green eyeshadow and black kohl eyeliner. The man was dressed as he'd died, wearing a wraparound skirt with leather sandals, and dripping with gold jewellery. His hands were pressed palm-flat to the inside wall of his prison, his dark-rimmed eyes roaming the crowd outside with malicious intent.

Next to the soul prison, standing behind a wooden rostrum, was a smartly-dressed man with a gavel. He spat words in rapid-fire succession as paddles went up and down in the crowd.

'Do I hear four-point-two, four-point-three, four-point-four? I see four-point-nine!' He turned his attention to the high-roller who'd jacked up the price of the lot and gave the man a congratulatory nod. 'Well done, sir'.

Those present were swept up in the drama like the crowd at a close-run horse race, sat forward in their seats, knees jiggling, eyes bulging.

The auctioneer scanned the crowd for any further interest. 'That's four-point-nine on the net, four-point-nine on the net.' His head whipped to a hesitant bidder whose paddle twitched in his lap but didn't meet the sky. 'I think you're going to regret this, sir,' the auctioneer told him. 'That's four-point-nine. Last time. Going, going…' The gavel came down and the deal was sealed. 'Sold to Mister Giles L'Merrier. Congratulations, sir.'

No one stood up to cheer. Only the winner of the auction got to his feet, rising slowly to take a shallow bow, fingers interlaced across his stomach. He was a solid, stocky man, dressed in floor-length robes decorated with sewn-on symbols of arcane protection. Positioned to his rear, I couldn't make out his face; instead, I was treated to the back of his polished bald head and a bulging roll of neck fat.

I'd heard of Giles L'Merrier. He was the proprietor of a cobwebbed antique shop off Portobello Road that sold anything from silverware and old perfume bottles to the taxidermied hearts of creatures that shouldn't exist. As well as being in the antiques business, L'Merrier was also rumoured to be the most powerful wizard in all of London, perhaps even the whole of the Uncanny Kingdom.

Four-point-nine million quid he spent on that canned mummy. Big money, whatever business you're in. I was busy wondering what plans Giles L'Merrier had for the poor, trapped bastard inside the glass box when he took off to collect his prize. Despite his considerable girth, L'Merrier moved with practiced grace, seeming to glide rather than walk. With a snap of his fingers, a dogsbody with a pallet truck was summoned, and the vitrine was removed from the auction floor, its ancient occupant raging silently within.

With a sharp rap of his gavel, the auctioneer returned to business. 'Don't be disheartened, ladies and gentlemen, we still have plenty more lots under the hammer today.'

A fresh vitrine was wheeled up onto the platform beside him, this one containing a young woman dressed in a black habit.

The auctioneer continued. 'I have here the late Sister Maria Crocifissa della Concezione, otherwise known as the "Possessed Nun". Bids begin at eighty-thousand pounds. Do I hear eighty-thousand?'

Paddles shot skyward as another sick display was set in motion.

The Curator placed a hand on the small of my back and offered a rictus grin. 'Come,' he said, 'I have something *very* special to show you.'

And with that, he led me from the auction house and on to part of the Museum that few got to see.

CHAPTER THIRTY-TWO: SPECTRE COLLECTORS

THE GOONS with the strange padlock necklaces stayed at my heel as the Curator guided me through several more layers of security, and finally to a curtained-off back room.

'This is where we house our permanent collection,' he explained.

The room was large and circular, and far more elegant than the staging area that had preceded it. The rotunda was just what I expected from a museum: dark-walled, sombre, and almost punishingly quiet. Well, quiet except for the discordant squeak of cloth rubbing against glass.

A man in blue overalls was busy polishing one of many vitrines set into the nooks spaced around the room's curved wall. No, not a man, an *eaves*. And not just any eaves, either. This was the very same eaves I'd run into at the Beehive the time I went there looking for an informant – the mole man I made a job offer, but who turned me down flat. For a moment I panicked, thinking he'd recognise me, but of course, he wouldn't. Not while I was hidden inside my meat suit. Then again, I suspect I'd have been a stranger to him even without the disguise. While the sight of a ghost tends to have a lasting effect on most people, to the Uncanny, we're mostly thought of as little more than a stubborn energy that persists after death. Nothing to concern yourself about. Yesterday's fish wrap.

The Curator produced a pocket watch from a cavity in his waistcoat and checked the time. 'This room was meant to have been cleaned fifteen minutes ago,' he huffed at the eaves, making no attempt to disguise the contempt in his voice. 'Now go. Kindly make yourself scarce, and report to my office at the end of your shift.'

'Yes, sir.'

The janitor's shoulders slumped and he skulked out of the room, taking with him his mop and bucket.

I felt sorry for the bloke, but more annoyed than anything. I'd been willing to make him my trusted tipster, and he'd blown me out to... what, push a broom around this place? I'm telling you, you try to do good in this world, but there's just no helping some people.

With the janitor out of the picture and the henchmen flanking the exit, the Curator gave me the tour, moving clockwise around the rotunda and stopping briefly at each vitrine to describe its occupant: a Medieval king; a Roman centurion; and a couple of historical figures I was obviously supposed to know, but who meant nothing to me. The prisoners looked out at us from their glass cells as we passed them by, some cow-eyed, others wearing masks of pure rage.

'We call them soul cradles,' said the Curator, choosing to ignore the captives' torment and discuss their prisons instead. 'Once the subject is inside of one, they're there until we choose otherwise.'

Which was never, I guessed.

'Very impressive,' I said, playing the part, acting like I wasn't disgusted. Whatever I needed to do to avoid arousing suspicion, and get closer to the demon soul I'd come for.

We continued our circuit of the room, taking in the rest of the collection. Most of the souls belonged to ancient history, but a few were from more recent times. In fact, one particular prisoner was alarmingly contemporary: a beehived pop star who'd only recently gone extinct from alcohol poisoning.

'Isn't that...?' I started.

'Yes it is,' the Curator replied.

He produced a slim steel remote control and aimed it at the dead diva's prison. The controller was decorated with a number of buttons and toggles, including a knob that looked very much like the kind you'd find on a Marshall amp.

'Would you like to hear her sing?' he asked. 'She's quite the songbird... when she behaves.'

He shot the prisoner a look, and she cast her eyes to her feet.

I felt my stomach turn. This poor woman: denied her place in the afterlife and forced to perform like a concert hologram; a plaything for the amusement of the ultra-rich.

I wanted to give the old scrote in the white gloves a punch in the bracket, but managed to keep my cool.

'I have a business question,' I said, swallowing the bile rising in my throat. 'Trafficking in ghosts... surely it must carry some legal ramifications?'

'It's what you might call a grey market,' the Curator replied matter-of-factly, 'but rest assured, we are fully compliant with all Uncanny codes and practices. The commodities that change hands here may not be regulated or sanctioned by the state, but their sale and distribution is entirely lawful.' He snickered. 'Just about.'

'What about Him Upstairs?' I asked. 'I wonder what God would make of an establishment that trades in human souls.'

I mean, so long as I was stuck in purgatory for an honest mistake, what did this bloke have in store? Red-hot pokers up the arse in perpetuity, that's what I was thinking.

The Curator responded with a fishhook-thin smile. 'He'd have to know of us first. Believe me when I say that the things that go on inside the walls of this Museum are a mystery to those out there. Unless we extended an invitation, God Himself couldn't get inside this place.'

We'll see about that, I thought, and on went the tour.

Having almost completed the circuit, we arrived at the second to last vitrine. Unlike the rest of the pieces in the exhibition, the occupant of this one was concealed by a red velvet curtain. Upon reaching it, the Curator drew to a halt.

'This, Miss Olena, is the star of the show. Our most valuable acquisition.'

Engraved upon a brass plaque next to the vitrine was a single word...

Cimeries.

Rider of the black horse. The marquis of twenty legions. The demon prince himself.

At last, the prize was in sight. The key to Mark's salvation—my debt to Vic paid in full—and the only thing standing in my way was an old drape and a bit of glass.

'Can I see it?' I asked.

The Curator's face split into a wide grin. 'But of course.'

He pulled on a cord and the red curtain slid aside to reveal the vitrine behind. Right away, I noticed something unusual about this particular cell.

'It's empty,' I noted.

'Not so,' the Curator replied with a knowing chuckle. 'Take another look, why don't you?'

I leant closer to the glass and peered inside, but saw nothing. Were those spooktacles the Curator was wearing allowing him to see something I couldn't, or was he just taking the piss?

Then I saw it.

Not a demon, but a swirling, greenish fog. The eerie vapour behaved as if it had a mind of its own, changing direction at will, forming shapes so distinct that they seemed almost solid until they dispersed, seeped away, and appeared elsewhere to create new, nebulous structures.

'To say this particular specimen is a dangerous one would be a *vast* understatement,' the Curator explained. 'For this reason, we prefer to keep it in a state of semi-stasis. It can observe us, even hear us, but the cradle ensures it remains in a gaseous state. For safety reasons, you understand.'

Blimey. And I thought I had it bad, stuck between life and death, a thong in the arse-crack of existence. This poor bugger had nothing, absolutely nothing; no body, no freedom, no voice. A prince of fuck all. A total non-entity.

'I get that he's a demon,' I said, still peering into the glass cell, trying to make out something, anything, of the prisoner inside, 'But isn't that a bit barbaric?'

'Oh, we don't keep it in this state all of the time,' replied the Curator, using a white-gloved hand to brush a piece of lint from his shoulder. 'Unlike this one, we're not monsters.'

A seed of anger took root in my belly and blossomed big and red. *Not monsters.* This goat's anus had the cheek to stand there and tell me that he was imprisoning people for all eternity, and yet to his mind, he was a businessman like any other.

'We allow the exhibit an hour's respite per day,' the Curator went on. 'It's an opportunity for it to experience its ethereal form fully and have a stretch of its legs, at least within the confines of the soul cradle. We call it "yard time". Without it, the soul would lose all integrity and be lost to the ether.' He pushed his specs up the bridge of his nose. 'A costly error that we're in no hurry to repeat; not since a similar oversight caused us to lose the first emperor of the Qin Dynasty.'

He spoke about the man's destruction as if he were talking about an expensive vase that had been elbowed off a sideboard. Absolute death chalked up as an unfortunate loss of property. A mark in the loss column.

The Curator checked his pocket watch again. 'I do believe you're in luck, Miss Olena. The time has come for our guest to have his exercise. Would you like to observe?'

He didn't even give me a chance to answer before he flicked a switch on his controller, causing the shifting greenish smoke to immediately firm up.

Two huge fists pounded against the inside of the glass like a couple of lump hammers, so loud that I almost jumped out of my skin (well, technically Jazz's skin). The explosive entrance was followed by the appearance of a pair of cruel eyes, which emerged like some dire warning. They stared out at me with an overpowering animosity, lit by infernal light.

'Christ,' I gasped.

Though if God's eye couldn't penetrate this place, what chance did his offspring have?

The demon's muscular black body just about filled the vitrine wall-to-wall, its whip-like tail writhing behind it, leaving scorch marks on the glass. A toxic smog escaped the creature's nostrils as it bellowed thunder from its fanged mouth. He made the woodcut Shift showed me look like a Disney princess. Any sympathy I might have had for a creature kept in suspended animation immediately evaporated.

'Look at him,' said the Curator, raising his voice to be heard over the demon's roar. 'Isn't he a magnificent find? Worth a king's ransom.' He took aim at the prisoner's vitrine and turned the dial on the metal controller he was carrying. Cimeries was instantly muted. 'Bit of a loudmouth, though.'

Cimeries continued to rage, spraying flecks of black ichor against the glass of his cell. Offended by the sight, the Curator drew the velvet curtain, blotting out the demon's vulgar display.

'Apologies. I should have known he'd get himself all worked up.'

The Curator absent-mindedly set the controller down on a nearby pedestal.

'On behalf of the Museum, I sincerely hope you have enjoyed this tour. We've certainly enjoyed having you visit us.'

And yet there was one more vitrine to go. Why had we skipped over it? I supposed it didn't really matter—the only soul I'd come to the Museum for was the one behind that velvet curtain—and yet it bugged the shit out of me. I tried to make out the occupant of the final vitrine, but it was recessed into a nook like all the others, and I didn't have the angle.

Wearing that painted-on smile of his, the curator wrapped up his farewell speech. 'Thank you very much for coming in today, Miss Olena. We'd be only too happy to furnish you with a calendar of our upcoming auctions if you're interested in joining us as a bidder next time. Now, if you'd like to follow me to reception…'

He turned around, the tails of his jacket swishing in his wake. I realised for the first time since we entered the room that the Curator's eyes weren't on me, so naturally, mine twitched to the remote control he'd forgotten to tuck back into his pocket. The one sat on the pedestal that regulated the vitrines containing his precious exhibits. The same one that might very well allow me to free Cimeries from his cell and get him inside my pocket; into the pouch made of human flesh that Vic had armed me with.

I'd only come to the Museum to eyeball the place, but maybe this was my chance, my one shot at walking out of there with the demon in hand. It was a crazy, spur of the moment idea, but it had some merit. I mean, I was there, wasn't I? On the inside, within the hallowed walls of the Museum's sanctum sanctorum. I'd seen the layers of security keeping people out of the room I was standing in, heard how it was hidden even from the Lord Almighty. If that was true, what were the chances of me getting into this part of the Museum a second time, even in my spectral form?

Then again, let's say I made it to that controller fast enough to free Cimeries and get him into the pouch, where would I go from there? I was wearing Jazz Hands' skin, and even though she hadn't specifically forbidden me from getting her brains bashed in by a pair of over-enthusiastic security guards, I had a suspicion that she'd prefer I didn't.

The Curator turned on his heel to face me. 'What's the matter?' he asked, grinning like a Cheshire cat, still. 'Aren't you coming?'

I was pretty sure that going for his controller was a terrible idea, but wiping that soppy look off his mug was enough to persuade me to do it anyway.

Once again, my eyes flicked to the device, only this time the Curator caught me.

'Careful, my friend. This isn't a petting zoo.'

'What do you mean?' I replied, like butter wouldn't melt in my mouth.

'I think you know very well what I mean... Mister Fletcher.'

That really put me on a tilt.

The two guards flexed in the background.

How did he know? How could the Curator possibly be savvy of the fact that I was a ghost occupying a living woman's body? He wasn't Uncanny, and the glasses he had on weren't able to penetrate the shell I was wearing. How he knew my real identity was a total mystery.

'Nice to meet you,' I replied, acting like I hadn't stepped in a giant shit. 'Just out of curiosity, what tipped you off?'

'The security gate you passed through on your way into the building isn't for detecting metal, Mister Fletcher, it's for sensing supernatural intrusions. That includes residual necroplasmic entities such as yourself.'

Huh.

'Okay, so you know I'm a spook,' I replied, 'but how come you know me by name?'

The Curator's cheery disposition had faded now, replaced with a look of cool reptile indifference. 'A simple deduction. Who could possibly be better positioned to have breached our walls than your host's well-known cohort, the so-called "Spectral Detective"?'

I hadn't realised that me and Jazz Hands were considered "cohorts", but there it was. I'd been picked out of the identity parade, and there was no stepping back in line now.

'I suppose it's your business to catch out loose souls, isn't it?' I replied. 'Right before you bottle them up and sell them for profit.' I gave that last part a real twist of pepper.

The jumped-up prick produced a fey titter. 'I didn't catch you out because you're a ghost, Mister Fletcher. I'm sorry to say your subterfuge was doomed from the off.'

'What are you banging on about?'

He tented his fingers the way that arseholes do. 'If there's one thing I know even better than the dead, sir, it's the living. And no woman alive, at least outside of a situation comedy, would allow *that* to happen.' He made a motion with his finger—the kind you give someone when you want them to give you a twirl—and I realised I'd made an unforgivable mistake.

My skirt was tucked into the back of my knickers.

Somewhere inside the body I was occupying, an angry shop proprietor screamed blue murder. Maybe if she hadn't insisted on me wearing a blindfold to the toilet...

'I don't get it,' I said. 'If you knew who I was, why give me the guided tour? And while I'm at it, why haven't you had Tweedledum and Tweedledumber over there give me a going over?'

The Curator's smile returned, brighter than ever. 'Because I find you fascinating, Mister Fletcher, that's why.'

'Uh, okay,' I said, feeling strangely exposed. 'Fascinating how exactly?'

He let me walk in off the street to view his merchandise knowing full well that I was up to no good. Clearly, I was there for a reason.

'Just look at yourself.' said the Curator. 'An exorcist turned phantom. The residue of a man who used to hunt the very thing he has become. Why, it's almost Shakespearean.'

'I dunno about that,' I said. 'The Bard's ghosts got other people to avenge their murders. I caught the tosser who put me in a box.'

'Of course you did, my friend. You truly are a magnificent specimen.'

Specimen?

With a hooked finger, the Curator led me to the last of the vitrines, and I finally got to see what I was missing.

Nothing.

The cell was empty and awaiting an occupant. An occupant whose identity had become all too obvious.

I squared my fists at the guards, daring them to come at me.

'Please, Mister Fletcher,' said the Curator. 'You're embarrassing yourself.'

I didn't care. If this was going to end in a fight, I was going down swinging.

The guards took positions either side of me, and I suddenly wondered how exactly they planned to turf me out of the body I was occupying and stuff me into that vitrine. As if reading my mind, the Curator explained.

'These men are no regular guards,' he said. 'We stewards of this institution are a proud brotherhood; an ancient order that stretches back for millennia. The men flanking you are known as collectors. They are trained to capture ghosts, and are equipped with specialised apparatus designed explicitly for this purpose.'

'Oh yeah?' I fired back. 'What have they got; a couple of those Hoover thingies the Ghostbusters are fond of?'

'In a manner of speaking, yes.'

He gestured to one of the collectors, who took a bow and lifted the thick iron chain he was wearing over his head. The Curator took the necklace by its padlock and presented it to me.

'We call them soul siphons,' he explained. 'They allow us to capture and contain disembodied spirits until such time as we are able to transfer them to a more fitting environment.' He nodded to the empty vitrine by way of demonstration. 'Think of the siphons as a sort of spirit trap. An activation word is spoken, then the soul is drawn into the contraption and locked inside. Allow me to demonstrate...'

Before I could voice an objection, the Curator used a white-gloved hand to draw a long, slim key from inside the padlock. A spot of blazing white light leaked out of the keyhole, searing my retinas like the spark from an arc welder's torch. I was sure the next thing I heard was going to be that activation word, then that would be that. Sayonara sucker. So long, and thanks for all the fish.

It was hard to imagine a worse fate than ending up an exhibit in this bastard's morbid collection. Being marooned on the material plane was something I'd learned to tolerate, but ending up confined to one of those glass cages for the rest of my days was a fresh kind of hell. At least when I was alive and hunting ghosts, I dealt with them humanely. What I did was wrong—I know that now—but it was final. The disembodied spirits who found their way into my crosshairs never knew pain, never knew suffering. There was no incarceration, only extinction. Sweet oblivion.

I winced, steeling myself for the end, but the Curator had other ideas. Instead of unleashing the power of the soul siphon, he slid the key back into the padlock and returned the necklace to his goon.

He chuckled. 'What's the matter? You didn't think I'd actually use this, did you? That wouldn't be very sporting now, would it?'

'So that's it, is it?' I asked. 'After all that, I get to just... go?'

'For now, yes,' he replied.

I had trouble believing that, but he insisted.

'You are quite free to leave this place, but know in coming here that you have earned our attention.'

The implication wasn't lost on me. The jaws of the trap I'd stepped into had been hinged apart just this once, but out there, in the wild, I was fair prey. So long as I roamed free, it was ghost season in London Town. I could practically hear the trumpet of the hunting horn. He knew what I'd come for—knew it the second he saw my eyes stray to Cimeries' cell—but he didn't care. As far as the Curator was concerned, I was already mounted on his wall.

'The guards will escort you from the building now.'

The one closest to me bobbed his head in the direction of the exit, but I wasn't ready to leave; not quite yet.

'Before I make myself scarce, I've got a question.'

The Curator's eyes narrowed into two ten-pence pieces turned on their side. 'Of course. What is it?'

'How much?'

'How much what?'

'How much would I sell for at one of your auctions?'

He made a wet chuckle. 'Oh, Mister Fletcher, I assure you, you would fetch a *handsome* bounty.'

'Oh yeah? Humour me. How much are we talking exactly?'

'Easily north of two-million pounds,' he replied.

I blew a long, thin whistle. 'Not too shabby,' I said, genuinely impressed.

The Curator's thin mouth curved into a wolfish grin. 'Have a safe journey, Mister Fletcher. I'm sure we'll run into each other again soon.'

I took one last look around the exhibition hall—around the soul prison—before the guards showed me the door. As I was led out, I brought to mind the Curator's superior smile and formed one of my own. Of all the wrong-'uns it had been my displeasure to meet, he was surely one of the worst.

Which was only going to make breaking into his "venerable institution" and filching the crown jewel of his collection all the more fun.

CHAPTER THIRTY-THREE: HOW THE OTHER HALF DIE

WITH MY INITIAL investigation of the Museum concluded, it was time to restore Jazz Hands to the stool behind her shop counter. I can't say I was particularly relishing the prospect of letting her have her body back, least of all her mouth. I may be made of smoke and nothing, but that wouldn't stop Jazz doing her best to whittle me down to a nub with her razor-sharp tongue.

'How dare you?' she seethed, pounding the till with her fist and accidentally ejecting the cash drawer with a raucous *kerching*. 'How bloody dare you?'

I'd broken the rules. Not only had I flashed her arse in public, I'd exceeded our agreed rental duration by quite a margin. Then again, I hadn't poked my nose into any of her private brain space, so I hadn't broken *every* rule. That had to be worth something, right?

Right?

I raised my phantom hands in supplication. 'I'm sorry, okay? Things took a turn. Why don't you let me know what that extra time's worth and I'll make it up to you?'

'What do you think I am?' she screeched, testing the shop's acoustics. 'A bloody overdue video cassette that you need to return to the shop? You think you can pay a late fee and make this right?'

I changed tack. 'You were there, Jazz. You saw what I was up against. The only reason I ran late was because another poor cow ended up slashed to bits. Would you rather I just let that slide?'

She pursed her lips, ready to spew some fresh invective, but settled on a menacing scowl instead. 'If you wanted to renew the terms of our agreement, you should have given me a choice in the matter. You should have asked my permission.'

I nodded solemnly. 'Like I say, I'm sorry. It won't happen next time.'

'Next time? You should be so lucky! That's the last time I let you talk me into loaning you anything. Do I make myself clear?'

'As a bell.'

At which point, as if by magic, the bell above the shop door chimed. Shift stepped into the store, dressed in female form.

'Bang on time,' I said, impressed.

'I'm sorry,' said Jazz, sitting up straight on her stool. 'What's going on here?'

'Forgot to mention,' I said. 'I need a favour.'

Jazz stared at me like I'd taken a shit in her shoe. 'Come again.'

'This is my friend,' I announced, placing an arm around my blonde companion's shoulder. 'She's been doing a bit of work for me.'

'I'll bet she has,' said Jazz, eyeing Shift sourly.

'Not like that,' I scoffed, recalling the shapeshifter as she was the time I'd run into her outside of The Beehive—the tall drink of water with the five o'clock shadow and the Adam's apple—and giving her an involuntary shove in the opposite direction. 'Shift isn't some bit of totty. She's on the payroll.'

For some reason, informing Jazz that money was changing hands did nothing to improve her opinion of my buxom new friend.

Sensing the animosity in the room, Shift extended a slim hand in Jazz's direction. 'It's a pleasure to meet you, Miss Olena. May I just say what a charming store you have here.'

I cast a look about the filthy shop and its collection of scuzzy merchandise, most of which you wouldn't want to handle without using a pair of tongs.

Shift continued to mount her charm offensive. 'It's so refreshing to visit a boutique that isn't part of some faceless corporate chain. And I *love* what you've done with the decor. So... original.'

Jazz's frown melted. After a second's contemplation, she shook Shift's hand. 'It's a pleasure to meet you, too, Miss…'

'Just call me Shift.'

'Shift?' she replied. 'What an unusual name.'

'Probably the least unusual thing about me, Cookie,' she said, offering a sly wink, 'once you get to know me.'

Jazz was beaming. She turned to me. 'I like this one! You be good to her, you hear? She's a keeper.'

I was about to explain that I didn't have any romantic intentions towards Shift, but thought it best just to move the conversation along.

'Shift isn't here for a social call,' I explained. 'She's escorting a friend.'

I rapped a knuckle on the grimy shop window and a second visitor entered the premises. FrankenJake lumbered into Legerdomain, drooling like a hungry bullmastiff.

Jazz lit up as if a butterfly had flown in through the door and landed on her shoulder. 'Come here, you!' she cried, slapping the front of her thighs. FrankenJake hurried over to her, and she ruffled his hair, repeatedly asking, 'Who's a good boy?'

She really did love that mutt. I had to admit, since I briefly inhabited him—since I connected to how he actually felt—I was starting to take a shine to the big lug myself. Now our minds had touched, I knew for a fact that he was alive. Sort of. Maybe, eventually, I'd be able to train him not to be a danger to others. Except for Vic Lords, that was. With him, he could be as dangerous as he liked.

'So I was thinking,' I started, capitalising on Jazz's good mood, 'since you two get on so well, whether you wouldn't mind doing a bit of dog sitting for me. Shift would do it, but she's got other stuff to be getting on with.'

Jazz reluctantly turned her attention to her least favourite version of me: the actual me.

'I don't know, Fletcher. Of course, I'd love to, but where would I put him?'

'I was thinking he could stay in the lock-up you've got round back. It'll only be for a little while.'

She harrumphed. 'I've heard *that* before.'

I put my hands together in prayer. 'Please?' I begged. 'If I could pour myself into his head and make him do what he's told, I would. But since I can't, he needs a kennel, and I really don't want to have to chain him up in my bathroom again.'

'Good Lord,' she shrieked, placing her mitts on either side of FrankenJake's head as if to protect his delicate ears. 'Is that where you've been keeping him?'

'What choice did I have?'

Jazz turned to Shift. 'How *do* you put up with him?'

'Sometimes, I really don't know,' she replied sportingly.

Jazz gave the zombie a scratch behind the ear. 'Okay, fine. Go do your thing, but I want you back here before I open up tomorrow. Are we clear?'

'Braaaains!' mooed my cadaver, so excitedly that for a moment I thought he was going to stick out his tongue and lick Jazz's face.

I gave Shift a nod that we should get out while the going was good, and the pair of us backed quietly from the shop, leaving Jazz to roughhouse with my former body.

I PARTED ways with Shift feeling pretty good about myself, at least for a little while. I was about to send Vic Lords a text to let him know I was making inroads on his demon soul when my phone turned into a jumping bean. I answered the call.

'Kat?'

'He did it,' replied Detective Stronge, her voice cold as a chisel. 'He fucking did it.'

'Did what?'

'The Ripper. He got the last one. The canonical five.'

I felt the phone weigh heavy in my hand. 'He what?' The question was a reflex; it didn't need an answer. I pictured all the victims so far. I pictured Reina's eyes as she realised she was about to die.

'Where are you?'

'On my way to the crime scene,' she replied. She sounded tired. Exhausted, even. As though she was wearing a hod of bricks on her back.

'Tell me where.'

She did, and I made my way to her, hurrying through the rapidly approaching dusk.

How could I have let this happen? While I was busy doing Vic's dirty work, another innocent woman had ended up gutted. Chances were the demon was done now. With the Ripper's legacy honoured, he'd most likely jump ship and return to the place he crawled out of. Off in the wind.

I could have stopped him. I'd let those women down; let Reina down. If I hadn't been pulling double duty—if I hadn't let Vic sink his hooks into me—I could have knocked this demon on the head days ago. I was sure of it. But then Mark would have been broken on Vic's wheel, and I'd have had another body on my conscience. There was no winning. Whatever choice I made, whichever path I took, there were dead bodies at the end of it. Sometimes, I think that's my whole life: just a steadily mounting pile of corpses.

The location Stronge gave me was a well-to-do house out Fitzrovia way. There were no gawkers lying in wait this time, and the press had yet to be tipped off about the latest Ripper murder. Small mercies.

The house was the kind a person invested in when they were worried they had too much money going spare. The property was built like a fortress, surrounded by ten-foot-tall walls and more security gizmos than a military compound. It was the type of place that required you to state your business before you got anywhere near the front door.

None of which meant anything to a ghost, of course.

I breezed through the perimeter wall, past a neatly manicured hedge, and emerged onto the house's sweeping gravel driveway. If only breaking into the Museum of Souls could be this easy, I thought, but there was no chance of that.

I was busy admiring an Aston Martin parked under an aluminium lean-to when Stronge's car arrived at the exterior gates. She applied the brakes, wound down the driver's window, and hurriedly tapped a passcode into a terminal outside. Soon enough, the gates scraped open, smoothing down the shingle driveway like a pair of giant shovels. The detective pulled up next to me and gave the handbrake a tug with her good hand.

Stepping out of the motor, Stronge greeted me with a terse, 'Fletcher.'

She didn't even bother bitching about me showing up in phantom form this time; just ushered me to a spot around the side of the house where we could talk privately, and brought me up to speed.

'The body's upstairs. Maddox was first on the scene. SOCO are on the way.'

Those were the headlines. For the rest, I'd have to accompany her to the first floor where the body had been discovered.

'I guess this puts the tour guide out of the frame, anyway,' I said.

'Not it doesn't,' Stronge replied, 'not until we've established time of death. Far as I'm concerned, Oberman's still on the hook until we can confirm he didn't do this before we brought him in.'

I was dead sure that wouldn't be the case, but I didn't press the matter. Not yet.

CHAPTER THIRTY-FOUR: MORTAL REMAINS

STRONGE LED me into the house, which was grand, tastefully decorated, and uncomfortably quiet. At least until DI Maddox blundered into the fray.

'She's in the bedroom,' he said, talking to his partner, no clue that I was there. 'Masseuse found the body when she stopped by for the vic's weekly appointment.'

His injuries were looking better. The nose plaster was gone, the exposed cut mending nicely, the surrounding bruises faded to a sallow yellow colour.

Stronge nodded. 'Paramedics?'

'Ambo's on the way,' Maddox replied. 'For all the good they'll do.'

'Right then,' said Stronge, picking up her feet, 'let's get on with it.'

The detectives climbed the stairs to the first floor, past a row of framed family photos, guided upwards by the gentle arc of a brightly-polished bannister. I followed them to the landing and on to the master bedroom.

Maddox wafted a hand in front of his face. 'We haven't worked out where it's coming from yet, but the bedroom reeks of it.'

Stronge's nostrils twitched and her face took on a look of instant familiarity. 'Sulphur,' she whispered.

The only thing that surprised me about that news was the fact that she could smell anything over the cloying stench of Maddox's aftershave.

The detectives arrived at the bedroom and stood at the threshold, peering in through the doorway. They stopped short of entering so as to preserve the integrity of the crime scene. Maddox would have established that the victim's wounds were fatal already – beyond that, there was no sense trampling the room any more than strictly necessary. Let SOCO be responsible for the delicate stuff. That said, the room could have been dusted wall-to-wall with flour and I wouldn't have left a mark, so there was nothing to stop me from having a crafty butcher's.

The bedroom was big enough that you could ride a motorbike around it and not knock over a single stick of furniture. The dying sunlight that bled through the floor-to-ceiling window was dampened even further by a pair of half-drawn curtains, but compared to the crime in progress we'd stumbled into at the tower block, this place was practically a solarium. I could see the layout of the room clearly: the cluttered make-up table, the floor-length mirror propped against the far wall, even the bluebottle zig-zagging around the room, banking at impossible corners, drawn by the smell of fresh carrion.

But what really stuck out was the room's king size bed, draped with the pale body of the Ripper's fifth victim, its crisp white sheets peeled away and tossed angrily to the pinewood floor. The victim's right arm lay across her stomach, fingers splayed wide. Her legs were spread in a way that would have seemed like an open invitation had this been any other bedroom scenario. There was no ghost present, but then I'd come to expect that. Nothing in that room but a dead body and a big lack of God.

While I inspected the scene for evidence, the detectives talked.

'Do we have any idea what the connection to the original Ripper's fifth victim is?' Stronge asked.

'Mary Jane Kelly,' Maddox replied, impressing his partner for once. 'Not seeing a parallel just yet, no.'

And there went the respect.

I took a couple of steps towards the deathbed so I could study the victim closer. The mattress beneath her was swollen with blood—heavy as a fed tick—though I wasn't clear where exactly it had escaped from. Mary Jane Kelly was carved up like a Christmas turkey; by comparison, this woman had got off lightly. The wounds I could see from the angle I was viewing her from looked mostly superficial and decidedly non-life-threatening. I saw slash marks across her hands, her face, her thighs, but not one of them cut as deep as the horrific injuries inflicted upon the original Ripper's final victim.

I was about to move in to get a closer look when heavy footfalls on the floorboards of the landing heralded the arrival of a familiar face.

'Detectives,' said Pedersen, the creepy SOCO Chief.

He was out of breath, and greeted Stronge and Maddox dressed in his civvies. Nipping at his heels was the team of forensics officers he commanded, who swarmed the landing, setting down equipment and stuffing themselves into blue boiler suits. In a matter of seconds, the house had gone from being oppressively quiet, to louder than a three-ring circus.

'You're late,' Maddox grumbled.

'Sorry, I got snarled up in traffic,' Pedersen replied. He made a face. 'What is that smell?'

'We were hoping you could tell us,' said Maddox.

Stronge decided to steer the conversation in a new direction. We already knew the brimstone smell came from a demon. What we needed to know was *who* the demon was.

'The body's in there,' Stronge announced, aiming a finger into the bedroom.

Pedersen angled his head around the door jamb. 'Goodness,' he said flatly. 'What a mess.'

He said it like he's stepped out of his house to find a fox had gotten into the bins.

Without further ado, Pedersen zipped himself into his boiler suit, tugged on a disposable face mask, and traded his street shoes for a pair of rubber slippers.

'Let's have a look then, shall we?' he chirped, sidling his heavy-set frame through the bedroom door and whipping open the curtains, demystifying every corner of the massive room.

The rest of the forensics officers followed his lead, fanning out and combing the area for prints, fibres, and DNA. Pedersen, for his part, produced an SLR camera and started taking snaps of the victim. As far as I knew, that job belonged to a professional crime scene photographer, which made me wonder where the pictures he was taking were going to end up: on a police database, or tucked away in a personal hard drive?

Determined to establish how the victim had met her end before Pedersen got his grubby hands on her, I craned over the body, searching for the fatal wound. Even with just a few centimetres separating us, the cause of death still wasn't clear.

I turned to Stronge. 'It's weird,' I told her. 'Jack the Ripper's victim was completely disembowelled, her throat cut right down to the spine. So far the wounds dealt to Jack the Rip-off's bodies have been completely consistent with his, but from what I can see here, this one just has a few shallow cu—'

I stopped talking when I saw the look on Stronge's face. It was the look of a lamb tangled in barbed wire watching the slow, inevitable footfalls of an approaching wolf.

I followed the direction of her horrified gaze, which sailed over my shoulder and pinned itself to the bed.

'Christ,' she moaned, a dry click in her throat, forcing me to spin around and face whatever it was that had turned her face fishbelly white.

The victim was sat up on the bed. Sat bolt-upright.

'What the...?'

I watched her blood-caked eyelashes spring open, then her mouth, which let loose a sound that should only have existed within the walls of an insane asylum. As the cry ripped out of her, the woman's whole body went into violent convulsions, writhing, flopping, bouncing up and down. She threw herself about the mattress like a lover in the throes of passion, only anything but.

I jumped back as if I was about to be sucked into the gears of a combine harvester. She was alive! It made no sense—none at all—but somehow she'd pulled through.

The effect of the woman's surprise resurrection was explosive, sending some of the officers scattering like quail, and others rushing to the convulsing victim, who was bleeding a red waterfall from her back.

'Get some pressure on that!' Stronge cried, her own blood returned to her face now, her training taking up the reins.

One of the female SOCOs snatched up the discarded bed sheet and applied it to the victim's wound, while two more held her against the mattress to stop her from causing herself any further damage. And all the while, Pedersen stood by snapping pictures, unfazed, aloof, a dispassionate robot eye recording the event for posterity. And the line of his mouth… was I imagining it, or was he grinning under that face mask?

'Move aside!' came a new voice.

As if by some divine intervention, the paramedics finally made a show, one male, the other female, both dressed in green polyester and stepping boldly into the heart of the hurricane to attend to the victim. The medics peeled plastic wrap from their needles so they could dose the screaming woman with sedatives and see to her wounds.

Meanwhile, Stronge read Maddox the riot act.

'You idiot,' she cried. 'Did you even check for a pulse? What kind of a bloody detective are you?'

Maddox was first on the scene, so checking that the victim wasn't in need of medical assistance should have been his top priority. Number one on the checklist before any kind of analysis or securing of evidence was preservation of life. I'm not a copper, and even I know that. This really was one colossal fuck-up. Maybe Dr Anand was right; maybe Maddox was suffering a brain bleed.

Deathly pale, he stammered the beginnings of an apology. 'I just assumed—'

'Oh, you assumed? You fucking *assumed*?'

Stronge continued to tear shreds off her partner, dressing him down in front of the whole squad, who were all looking for a distraction from the shock they suffered and seemed to find Maddox's embarrassment just the tonic. As this was going on, the paramedics busied themselves with the job of stabilising the victim, and yet still found time to join the dogpile, throwing even more scorn on Maddox.

'I've never seen police work that lax,' said the female medic, using her teeth to tear the cap from a fresh hypodermic and spit it on the floor. 'Never in my life.'

Maddox tried to deflect. 'Yeah, well, maybe if you'd gotten here sooner and done your jobs—'

'Sooner?' she yelled back. 'We thought we were coming to pick up a cadaver, not treat a casualty!'

'It's a wonder she's still alive,' her partner said. 'The only reason she didn't bleed out was because she clotted against the mattress.'

Maddox stood there, shamefaced, bearing the barrage as it bombarded him from all angles.

And me? On any other day, I'd have been front row centre to Maddox's public undressing, but the truth is, I tuned out pretty fast. My mind was already on higher things, like how was it that the victim had been allowed to survive in the first place? Our killer wasn't known for leaving things unfinished, so why did he take off with the job half done? The only reason I could think of was that something had spooked him before he could wrap things up. Given that we almost caught him at the block of flats that time, he'll have been on high alert on this occasion. I supposed it could have been just about anything that set him running. We may never know what triggered his escape, but we did know this much: the fifth victim was alive.

The Ripper was one canonical kill short.

'I need to talk with her.' Stronge's voice, cutting through the chaos.

'You're joking, right?' replied the female paramedic, who, along with her partner, had just finished securing the victim to a stretcher, ready to be conveyed to the ambulance outside. 'Look at her, she's not up to that.'

'I need to get her statement while it's still fresh in her head,' said Stronge.

'Fresh in her head?' said the male medic, incredulous. 'We just shot her with enough midazolam to take down an elephant. Her head's mashed potato.'

Stronge ignored him and took a knee by the victim's side. The paramedics objected, but Maddox, no doubt eager to redeem himself after shitting the bed so badly, stepped in and kept them at bay.

'Hello there,' said Stronge, addressing the victim softly but firmly. 'Can you hear me okay?'

The woman looked up from the stretcher, her glassy eyes staring clean through the detective.

Stronge tried again. 'I need you to tell me what the man who did this looked like. I know it's painful, but the more you can tell us now, the better our chance of catching him.'

The woman showed no sign of life, which only served to make the paramedics all the more aggravated.

'She needs urgent attention, and you're in the way,' said the male medic.

'She needs to be in a hospital!' chimed his partner, doing her best to elbow past Maddox, who refused to give way.

Tempers flared. The medics made angry demands for badge numbers, and in return, Maddox made retaliatory threats to arrest the ambulance crew for obstructing a police investigation.

'It was red,' said the victim, her thin voice bringing the escalating row to a crashing halt.

The room fell library silent.

'Can you say that again?' asked Stronge, placing a hand on the pale woman's shoulder.

'The man… a red mask.'

'That's good,' said Stronge, urging her on. 'That's very good. Can you tell us anything else? Anything at all?'

'Of course she can't,' said the male medic, still riled up. 'She doesn't even know what bloody year it is.'

And yet despite the sedatives in her system, the woman said, 'A badge. Had a badge. That's… that's how he got in.' A delta of tears tracked down her cheeks.

'What kind of badge?' asked Stronge.

'Metal star.'

Stronge reached into her pocket, plucked out a black wallet, and flipped it open. 'Like this?'

The victim tried to nod, but her head was braced, so she answered out loud instead. 'Yeah.'

Her eyelids fluttered and closed. For a moment I thought she'd had it, but I could hear the sound of her breathing over the pin-drop silence that followed.

Stronge stood up and nodded to her partner, who stepped aside, allowing the paramedics to scrape up the stretcher and lug the victim out through the bedroom door. The male medic grumbled something unsavoury as he went, but no one was really listening to him. The only thing anyone in the room was thinking about was that badge.

With heads no doubt full of wild speculation, Pedersen and his team returned to their jobs, scouring the room for anything out of place. Maddox went to join his partner, saw he wasn't wanted, and skulked away with his tail between his legs. All of which gave Stronge and me a chance to hold a private sidebar in the corner of the spacious bedroom.

'Can you believe this?' she asked, one hand cupped over her mouth to disguise her lips moving. 'What a fiasco.'

'Tell me about it.'

It felt good to be part of the conversation again, even though being outside of it was a pretty common part of the job. A regular detective might spend a chunk of his days idling away in an unmarked car staking out perps, but a spectral detective has it so much worse. Way too much of my time is spent standing in a corner with my trap shut while people who know less than I do play tennis with idiot ideas.

'So what are we thinking?' I asked Stronge.

She answered before I even finished speaking. 'There's no way a cop did this,' she said, only just managing to keep her volume in check. 'The tour guide did it. We know that.'

'*You* know that.' I wasn't surprised by the dismissal, just the speed it arrived at. 'So let me get this right; you're saying Oberman came here with a fake badge pretending to be a copper?'

Her eyes took on an eerie light. 'Wait... didn't our boys find a phony badge when they tossed Oberman's place?'

'That was a Texas Sheriff's badge.'

'Yeah, well who's to say he doesn't have other fake IDs?'

'Okay, then why didn't we find anything when we went through his pockets at the station?'

'Maybe he dumped it before we could get to him.'

Stronge was working way too hard to make Oberman fit the picture. Taking whatever crumbs she could get her hands on.

'Okay, how about this,' I said. 'Are you telling me Oberman murdered the vic out in Walthamstow, came here to bump off another, then went all the way back to the other side of London to lurk outside of an old murder scene? All of that in the space of a single day?'

'He's a serial killer,' Stronge hissed. 'Don't go looking for rational decision-making.'

'Are you okay, Detective?' asked Pedersen, who'd caught wind of Stronge's one-way conversation and become concerned.

She coughed, embarrassed. 'Just... checking in with the station,' she vamped, showing him her police radio. 'Over,' she said, fake signing off.

Pedersen shook his head then returned an eye to the viewfinder of his camera and continued documenting the scene.

Stronge released a shoulder-sagging sigh before turning slowly in my direction, her volume dialled way down now. 'How about this: the guide had blue balls because he didn't get a chance to finish off here, so he went back to the Stow for a sniff of the old murder magic? That would work.'

'Come on, Kat. Really?'

Her pet theory was crumbling and she knew it. The idea that the tour guide had been responsible for both attacks was looking like wishful thinking at best.

'All right then, smart arse,' said Stronge, making a pretzel of her arms, 'if it wasn't Oberman, who did do it?'

I had no idea. The only thing I knew for sure was that I wasn't ready to take a U-turn at the avenue Stronge had built her roadblock on.

'I don't think we should rule out a cop,' I told her. 'I know you don't want to hear it, but someone on the force would be a good fit for the killer. They'd have easy access to people's homes, they could even get their hands on medical records. Plus they'd know how to clean up a crime scene.'

'What about motive?' asked Stronge.

'Don't forget, we're not talking about a cop here. Not really. This is a cop with a demon at the wheel.'

Even though she got that, I could tell she was having a hard time picturing one of her own butchering a bunch of innocent women, possessed or not.

I decided to give her some space so she could come to terms with the notion, and took the opportunity to make a final circuit of the room. SOCO were doing a fine job of tagging and bagging, but it never hurt to have an extra set of eyes on things.

I approached the bed. Its mattress was pooled with a gory scarlet silhouette; a haemophiliac's funeral shroud. The blood was still wet in places, wet enough that I could see my reflection staring back at me, a vision in red.

And then…

What was that?

Something in the blood. Something submerged. Could that be...?

The motherlode.

I whirled about to Stronge. 'Ask Pedersen for a pen.'

Why? she mouthed.

'Just do it!'

She did.

'A pen?' said Pedersen, patting himself down but coming up empty. 'Sorry… must be in my coat. Give me a sec.' And off he went, heading downstairs to retrieve it.

'What was that about?' Stronge whispered.

I didn't answer. Instead, I played poltergeist, pushing over the floor-length mirror on the other side of the room and shattering it to pieces on the floorboards. While dabs were distracted by that—Christ, you should have seen their faces—I pointed Stronge to a set of tweezers sitting in a compartment of one of the SOCO's open kit bags.

'Grab those,' I said. 'Quietly.'

Confused but going along with it, Stronge snuck the tweezers from the kit and gave me a look that said, *Now what?*

I pointed to the thing I'd found in the victim's blood. 'Right there.'

Checking she wasn't been watched, the detective used the

tweezers to poke around in the blood. While she worked, I hovered at her shoulder, urging her on.

'Chop chop,' I said, aware that the diversion I'd created wouldn't last much longer.

Being forced to work with her left hand wasn't helping matters. Stronge got a grip on the mystery object, only for it to slip from the tweezers and sink beneath the blood, unidentified.

'I'm working as fast as I can,' she hissed back.

Heads were beginning to turn her way. The distraction was losing its effect. She'd be rumbled soon enough.

'Come on!' I snapped.

Finally, Stronge got a hook on the submerged piece of evidence and fished it out of the gore.

'Are you all right over there, Detective?' asked one of the SOCO team.

Stronge quickly stuffed the evidence into the sleeve of her plaster cast. 'All good,' she said. 'Found some dropped tweezers where they shouldn't be. You lot should be more careful.'

The team bristled at that, but knew better than to argue with their Senior Investigating Officer. The SIO was top dog; feared and revered.

Stronge handed the tweezers to the nearest officer. 'Okay, that's enough for now,' she said, talking to the room. 'Good job, everyone. Clear out, grab a bite, and we'll pick this up in a bit. You too, Maddox.'

Only too happy to take a break, the officers did as told and headed downstairs, leaving the room to me and Stronge.

There was a heavy pause, then, 'What's with all the bloody secret squirrel stuff?' she asked, casting aside any pretence of cool.

'Why don't you take a look and see?' I asked.

Still grousing, Stronge slid the purloined evidence out of her cast and wiped a stripe of blood off it. As she turned the object over in her hand, a cocktail dress vanished, revealing a naked lady beneath.

Pedersen bowled through the door, minus the pen he'd been searching for. 'Jeez, Louise,' he said, seeing smashed glass spread all over the bedroom floor. 'What happened in here?'

CHAPTER THIRTY-FIVE: IF THE SPIRIT MOVES YOU

I STOOD INVISIBLY by Stronge's side as we peered through the one-way mirror of the station's interview room. Inside sat Pedersen, hands tapping out a jaunty tune on his knees.

'What does he think he's in there for?' I asked.

'I told him I wanted to discuss his job performance. Made it sound like he had a commendation coming his way.'

I chuckled. 'You could almost feel sorry for the bloke.'

The demon had spent all night finishing up in Fitzrovia, only to be pulled into the station under the pretence that he was getting a pat on the back for his sterling work, when what he was really getting, was destroyed. While Stronge had waited for him to show, I made use of the spare time and acquired a fresh set of exorcism tools to replace the ones I lost in the office fire. As soon as we had his confession, it was bye bye birdie.

Stronge frowned. 'Don't get any ideas, Fletcher. Just because Oberman probably didn't do it, doesn't mean Pedersen did. For all we know, his pen fell out of his pocket while he was investigating the scene.'

'If that's true, how exactly did it get where it was, especially since the closest Pedersen got to the bed was taking pictures of it from six feet away.'

We'd both seen it: Pedersen snapping away with his camera like he was at a Calvin Klein photoshoot instead of a crime scene.

'I think he's been messing with us from the start,' I said. 'I should have seen it. I knew he was a creepy fucker the first time I clapped eyes on him.'

'Just because he's a bit off, doesn't mean he's a serial killer.'

'*Off*?' I bleated. 'Did you hear the way he talked about that second vic? Telling us how he'd have done it if he was the murderer, pissing right on our shoes. And who the hell brings a naked lady pen to a homicide, anyway?'

I was flapping, but Stronge was calm.

'What's that saying?' she asked. '*Death and humour are close companions*. That's the way people are when they work with dead bodies for a living. You heard Dr Anand and her ear behind the lungs autopsy story, right? Gallows humour. It gets them through the day. Look at you, you're around corpses all the time and you're always cracking jokes.'

'Yeah, but my jokes are funny.'

I ignored what Stronge's eyebrows were doing and went on.

'This is different, Kat. I've heard Anand say some messed up stuff, but Pedersen's something else. When he's around a dead body he's practically glowing.'

Stronge massaged her temples. She knew I wasn't going to let up with this Pedersen theory.

'Then you've got his build,' I added, 'which is a dead match for the killer. Look at him. A bloke his size could do some real damage.'

'Circumstantial,' said Stronge, shooting me down yet again.

Christ. It was going to be easier freeing a caged demon from the clutches of a megalomaniacal spirit collector than it was turning this woman around.

'And he arrived late to the scene, didn't he?' I continued. 'Why? Because he'd only just washed the blood off and made himself presentable, that's why.'

Stronge pursed her lips. 'You're reaching, Fletcher. Big time.'

'Says the woman who tried to convince me that the bloke she locked up ran a murder marathon right across London.'

The little pads of gristle that worked Stronge's jaw tensed involuntarily. 'Pedersen's an expert in his field. If he attacked this woman, why would he leave a big fat piece of evidence lying around at the crime scene?'

'We all make mistakes,' I replied, nodding to her plaster cast.

While it was true that the demon would have had access to Pedersen's memories and skills, that didn't make him infallible. He was only human, even if he really wasn't.

She frowned. 'What about the smell then? If Pedersen's a demon in disguise, why doesn't he stink of brimstone?'

Now who was giving the brimstone thing too much weight?

'Tell me one time you've been around Pedersen and *not* smelled brimstone,' I said.

'That's different,' Stronge replied. 'That's only because we've been at crime scenes that already stank of the stuff.'

I showed her my *Aha!* finger. 'That's what we *thought*. We assumed the smell was something the demon had left in his wake, but we were wrong. Every time a dead body showed up, the demon was with us, right there in the room.'

Stronge scrutinised Pedersen through the one-way mirror. 'If he stank of sulphur, he'd have a nickname at least. The kind that gets around. It's a small circle we move in; I'd know about it.'

I laughed. 'That's what you've got? A missing nickname? You wanna stack that up against my blood-soaked ballpoint?'

The pen was my smoking gun, and there was no way I was going to let Stronge smother it with that old flannel. I was ready to gamble my left nut that Pedersen owned a red balaclava, but wild bets weren't going to cut it with this detective. Maybe if I talked to her in her own language...

'With everything we've got on him, are you telling me that you're not prepared to go in there and at least eliminate Pedersen as a person of interest?'

Stronge raised a perfectly plucked eyebrow. 'Which episode of *The Sweeney* did you get that bollocks from?'

That stung.

'Maybe it's time you stopped treating me like I won this job in a competition, Kat. I had to solve my own murder to get where I am.'

Seeing she'd touched a nerve, she softened her tone. 'Look, it's not as simple as just walking in there and asking him a bunch of questions. Pedersen's a fellow officer. Do you have any idea how much of a shitstorm this could bring down on me?'

That one didn't require a response, just a look. A look that said, *You're telling me you're ready to let this slide because it could hurt your job prospects?*

Stronge placed her hands on top of her head, fingers laced. 'At least let me gather some more evidence first.'

'There's no time.'

The demon was one kill from the full set. We'd never get this lucky again. If we let him walk now, he was sure to claim victim number five.

'This isn't the way we do things, Fletcher.'

'Kat, take a look around. You're stood here talking to a ghost about a demon. I think it's fair to say you stopped following official procedures a while back.'

Her arms dropped to her sides. 'This is insane. Oh God, I'm going to lose my job over this.'

'You're not. I promise you, this is our man. The gun's already loaded, you just need to go in there and pull the trigger. If you're too scared to do it, just give me your body and I'll take the shot for you.'

She threw me the evil eye. 'Try it and see what happens.' She took a deep breath and wrapped her fingers around the handle of the interview room door. 'How the hell did I let you talk me into this?'

'I dunno,' I replied. 'Must be the old Fletcher charm.'

She headed inside and I followed.

Time to play good cop, invisible cop.

CHAPTER THIRTY-SIX: WHEN THE DEVIL TAKES HOLD

'Do you mind if I ask... why this room?' enquired Pedersen as Stronge took a seat opposite him and slid a cup of coffee his way. 'Is your office being redecorated or am I on the wrong end of an interrogation?'

He added a dry chuckle.

Stronge didn't join in.

'Can I get you something from the snack machine to go with that coffee?' she asked.

'I'm fine, thanks.'

Stronge nodded. Since Maddox was in the doghouse, typing up a very long and very boring report, she had Pedersen to herself. She placed her phone on the table and activated the recorder.

'This is DCI Katherine Stronge interviewing Chief Scene of Crimes Officer, Giles Pedersen.'

The recorder was just for effect; nothing that happened here would be admissible as evidence. Stronge was just using it as a shorthand to let the suspect know she meant business. It worked.

'What is this, Detective?' asked Pedersen, getting fidgety. 'Why am I here?'

Stronge answered the question, if not directly. 'Officer Pedersen, can you account for your whereabouts during your off-duty hours over the last week?'

No messing around. Straight to the point.

Pedersen measured Stronge with his eyes. 'Are you asking me for an alibi?'

'Just answer the question, Officer.'

He squeezed out a sick laugh. 'This is ridiculous.' He pointed to the one-way mirror. 'Is there a camera behind there? Is that it? Am I being pranked?'

Stronge's expression remained unchanged; grim to the point of funereal. If it was a punchline Pedersen was after, he'd be waiting an awfully long time for it.

Stronge spoke to her recorder. 'Note that the Officer chose not to account for his whereabouts.'

Now Pedersen was really agitated, his forehead folded like a concertina. 'Listen, I don't have to sit here and—'

'The Fitzrovia victim said her attacker gained access to the property using a police badge. You carry a badge, don't you Officer Pedersen?'

He did. I remembered seeing it the first time we were introduced. It had *Police Staff* written on it, which distinguished him from actual police, but I doubt a civilian would have caught that detail.

Pedersen placed a black wallet on the table and opened it up to show the badge inside. 'There. Happy? Would you like to check it for bloodstains?'

'You want to talk about blood?'

Stronge produced a plastic baggie from her jacket pocket. Inside was Pedersen's pen, caked red with claret. His face dropped at the sight of it. Must have come as some shock, seeing the evidence of his deeds sealed inside one of the tools of his trade.

'Where did you get that?' he asked, shocked.

'Where do you think?'

His pupils flicked about like a couple of pendulums. 'I must have dropped it while I was processing the scene.'

'Really?' Stronge replied, using a pair of tweezers to remove the pen from the bag as if she were fishing out the final cards in a game of Cluedo. 'So how do you explain how it came to be *underneath* the victim?'

'I don't know,' he fired back, eyes fixed on the pen now, lying on the table in front of him. 'But I do know the DPS are going to have a field day with this.'

The Met's internal affairs department, the Directorate of Professional Standards. The rubber heelers would definitely have something to say about an unauthorised interview of a senior officer based on an item of evidence removed unlawfully from a crime scene. No, this investigation couldn't be allowed to make it that far. What we were doing had to end in this room. If this case went before some herbert in a white wig, it would fall apart quicker than a Hollywood marriage. With the scant evidence we had, even the Uncanny Courts would have declared a mistrial. We needed a full confession within these four walls. Only then could punishment be meted out.

The mention of the DPS gave Stronge pause. She glanced at her recorder, aware that the conversation it was documenting was more incriminating of her than it was the person sitting in the hot seat.

'What are you doing, Kat?' I asked. 'Don't give up on him now. Take your foot off the brake.'

'Is that everything?' Pedersen asked. 'You're telling me you dragged me in here based on a single piece of inadmissible evidence? Are you really that desperate to tie a ribbon on this thing?'

Stronge went to say something but nothing came out.

'I heard you were a hell of a detective,' said Pedersen, shaking his head, 'but here you are, ready to throw one of your own under the bus just so you can rise up the ranks.'

The demon had taken the upper hand. I looked to Stronge, who was visibly wavering now, a stubborn tic playing in the corner of her eye.

'Are you just going to sit there and take that?' I asked her, my hands turning into claws, ready to throttle the demon out of Pedersen if need be.

'I didn't just pull your name out of a hat, Pedersen,' Stronge croaked. 'I know the risk I'm taking. If I wanted things easy, we wouldn't be having this conversation. If all I wanted was the collar, I'd have pinned this on the suspect I've got locked up downstairs.'

'Oh, so it's two of us you've wrongly accused is it?' said Pedersen.

'Good job, Detective. Talk about hedging your bets!' His shoulders bucked with laughter. He was enjoying this.

'Lay into him,' I told Stronge. 'Rile him up. Blow a hole through his bullshit!'

Demons have a tendency to be aloof and short-tempered. If Stronge could provoke him just right, she could force him to break character. To reveal his true self.

But Stronge had nothing. She was used to grilling common criminals, not unhallowed darkspawn. In the face of this crook, she was a kid wearing a suit two sizes too big for her.

I felt like a boxing coach sat in the corner of the ring watching his prizefighter get whupped by a guy half his size. It was agonising.

Pedersen was still laughing. He was Ned Kelly at his last stand, rising up behind his clueless assailants and opening fire, police bullets zinging harmlessly off his iron-plate armour. It wasn't normal, this laugh, but the demon didn't care. The demon was untouchable.

Something inside of me snapped. I was so tired of being a voice on the wind. So tired of having to stand by and watch helplessly from the sidelines. I was going to take control of this situation, and I wasn't going to ask permission this time. I was going to take this demon down, even if it meant doing something I'd regret forever.

Knowing I was doing wrong, but knowing I had no choice, I poured myself into Stronge's body, taking charge of it, making it mine. She fought like mad, but there was nothing she could do to stop me taking the reins. Her senses flooded into mine, giving me the whole room, right down to the smell of vending machine coffee.

Without skipping a beat, I shot to my new feet and pounded a fist on the metal table, making a sound that was practically apocalyptic.

'Be a man and admit it, Pedersen,' I said. 'You killed those women. You made that sick cooking video. You're Jack the Rip-off!'

The sudden change of temperature took him by surprise, but he kept his cool. 'You've got nothing, Detective,' he smarmed. 'Less than nothing.'

I turned off Stronge's recorder and smiled back at him. 'Oh, I've got something. I've got a demon who thinks he's smart enough to fool me into thinking he's a man.'

Pedersen's face quirked. 'What? What are you talking about? Are you mad?'

I stared back at him with absolute conviction.

'Okay, now this isn't funny,' said Pedersen, placing a palm on the table and levering himself to his feet. 'You've lost it, Stronge. You need help.'

'You're the one who needs help,' I said. 'From me.'

Quick as a flash, I slapped one half of Stronge's handcuffs to his wrist, and the other to the table's cuff bolt. Now I had him. Short of chewing Pedersen's hand off, the demon would just have to sit there while I proved his guilt. While I made him confess to his crimes; what he did to Reina, what he did to those other women.

I could feel Stronge rebelling in the back of my head, but I swept her aside. I had Pedersen right where I wanted him. This was my room now. It was only a matter of time before I pressured the demon into surfacing.

Or at least it would have been if DI Maddox hadn't come charging into the room like a wounded rhino.

'What is going on here?' he cried.

'Get out, Detective,' I said. 'That's an order.'

But Maddox wasn't playing Fido this time, dog house or not.

'That's a fellow officer you've got cuffed to the table. I'm not going to just stand by and—'

'And what?' I countered. 'Mess this investigation up even worse than you already have?'

His eyes flicked to Pedersen straining at his cuffs, then back to me. Back to his partner. 'Why are you doing this, Kat? Who put this idea in your head? Was it one of those freak psychics you've been hanging around with?'

My ears were burning. 'Your judgment hasn't exactly been spot on lately, Maddox,' I said, as calm as I could manage, 'so why don't you do me a favour, go back through that door, and forget you were here.'

'You know I can't do that.'

He produced a key from his duty belt. It was a standard key; the kind that would open most police-issue handcuffs.

'Don't!'

I tried to block him, but Maddox pushed past me with ease. Stronge was half his size and presented zero challenge to him physically. He crammed his key into the cuffs and gave it a twist. Pedersen immediately pulled free of the bracelet, but instead of rubbing his wrist and giving me a piece of his mind, he did what demons do.

He snatched the bloody ballpoint from the table, grabbed Maddox by the neck, and pressed the tip of the pen into the soft flesh of his jugular.

The detective let out a strangled yelp. He walked into that room with the intention of exonerating an innocent man, and ended up being taken hostage by him. I can't imagine that was written anywhere on Maddox's vision board.

Pedersen's eyes were two pools of ink now. The thin patina of respectability that disguised the demon had dissolved; now he was there for all to see. Or at least he was to me. Maddox wasn't afforded the luxury of being able to turn his head.

'Pedersen, what are you—?'

The detective wasn't able to finish his sentence before the demon dug the pen deeper into his throat, cutting him off.

I felt a sudden spike of pain in the back of my head as Stronge screamed with violent complaint.

The pen drew a bead of blood from Maddox's neck the colour of a matador's cape. You wouldn't think a thing like that would make for much of a weapon, but in a demon's hands, it could go through muscle like it was made of candy floss.

'*You*,' said the demon, the word scuttling out of his mouth like a cockroach across a cellar floor. 'You think you have the right to interrogate me, human?'

Maddox squirmed. '*Human?*'

Of course it had fallen to me to save the dozy sod's life. Obviously, it had. 'Belt up,' I told him. 'Just keep your mouth shut.'

I wanted to move, to act, to do something, but my feet were breeze blocks. All I could do was bear witness as the demon mocked me from behind his human shield. I was powerless. I had the tools for the job, but to use them, I needed the demon immobilised. Since DI Maddox had freed him, I had no chance of dragging the scumbag into the trash basket before it painted the walls with the contents of Maddox's carotid artery.

How are you gonna dig yourself out of this wet ditch, Jakey boy?

Searching for another weapon to use against the demon, I remembered Stronge's Taser, but what good would that do? I didn't have a clear shot at him, and chances were the stun gun's electrified darts would only give a demon the hump. I left the weapon in its holster but held my ground. The only weapon I had left now was my wits.

The demon regarded me with its obsidian eyes and spoke in a voice loaded with acid. 'You think I don't see you, playing your little games, running your silly scams. Oh, but I see you. I *see you*, ghost.'

The demon wasn't talking to Stronge, he was talking to me directly. I suddenly felt very exposed. How Maddox felt about a psychopath referring to his partner as a ghost I could only imagine, as for once he'd chosen to take my advice and keep his gob shut.

'Do we know each other, mate?' I asked the demon.

The corners of Pedersen's mouth stretched far beyond the point of comfort. 'I don't need to know you to take your measure. To me, you are the same as any other human: simple, arrogant, convinced that you are the centre of all things. You think you can make a difference in this world. That the future is putty in your hands. I am here to show you the true power of destiny.'

It was obvious that the demon had no intention of backing off. If anything, he was ramping up to something. Something awful. An idea surfaced like the bloated body of a drowned man. There was nothing I could do to defuse this situation. One of us wasn't leaving that room alive.

No, don't give up. Think, Jake, think.

I did a couple of mental cartwheels. What if instead of possessing Stronge, I ditched her and jumped into someone else? But who? The demon wouldn't share Pedersen's body, and making the leap to Maddox wasn't going to improve the situation. There was nothing I could do in his body that Maddox couldn't do himself... not with the sharp end of a pen digging into his throat.

Keep him talking. So long as the demon's talking, everyone stays breathing.

'You're trapped and you know it,' I bluffed. 'If that pen goes one millimetre deeper, there's nothing to stop me going Rentokill on you.'

I raised my hands and set them dancing, muttering mysterious words of power that set my fingers aflame. The idea was to kid the demon into thinking that I was preparing to repel an ancient evil, when in fact I was just employing a bit of petty pyromancy.

A cocktail dress slid off as the demon adjusted his grip on the pen, angling the business end down, ready to ram it through Maddox's thick neck so deep that it got lost in the middle.

'Don't you get it, Detective? I already beat you.'

I scratched my chin. 'Yeah, I'm going to need to see your working on that one, pal.'

The demon's grin remained unbroken. 'For days you've been hunting me, and now, in this room, you had your one chance to force my confession. Except you didn't. The only reason I'm showing myself now is because I choose to. Because I want to take off the mask and look you in the eye before I finish what I started...'

He made his move, but it wasn't the one I expected. Instead of ventilating Maddox's neck, he grabbed him by the back of his bald head and drove him into the interview room table hard enough to leave a portrait. Maddox bounced once and flopped to the ground, out cold, the cut across his nose reopened and gushing blood.

It was at this point that I realised it had never been the demon's plan to kill Maddox.

The demon raised Pedersen's arms in the air, crucifix-style, and began walking him backwards towards the interview room's fifth-storey window.

'No!'

I pedalled after the possessed man, fingers searching.

Too late. The window came apart in a thousand glittering fragments. Time seemed to dry up as Pedersen tipped through the opening and hung suspended in the air, surrounded by a rabid swarm of freeze-framed glass.

I saw a foot slip out of view, and Pedersen was gone.

Silence—a horrible, sinking silence that seemed to drag for an eternity—then a cold howl as the invading wind filled the room with its annihilating roar. I rushed to the shattered window, my teeth biting into Stronge's lip hard enough to draw blood, and craned over the edge to see what had become of Pedersen.

Strawberry jam. That's what he looked like. Dead on impact.

The demon must have jumped free of his host before he painted the pavement. If he hadn't, he'd be dead. If a demon is still inside its host when the host expires, they suffer the same fate.

The demon was right. He beat us. He came here to get his jollies, then he flew the coop before we could do anything about it. He'd be back in the Nether right now, bragging to his fellow hellspawn how he chalked up a slate of homicides and made idiots of a couple of humans.

It was all over. Just like the man he was plagiarising, Jack the Rip-off got away with it.

'That's it for you and me,' said Stronge.

I hadn't even realised I'd slipped out of her body until I caught her voice in my ear.

'You hear me, Fletcher? We're done. Now get out of here and don't come back.'

CHAPTER THIRTY-SEVEN: A GHOST OF A CHANCE

I CAN ONLY IMAGINE how the conversation between Stronge and Maddox went after I left the station that morning. I can only imagine, because I was no longer part of the discussion. Stronge had frozen me out. I'd taken control of her body without her permission, and for that, I'd been made a pariah.

I got it.

How could she trust me after a thing like that? Our friendship—a rocky one at best—was based on mutual respect. She trusted me to guide her through the city's shadow world, and I trusted her to keep me on the straight and narrow. Currying favour with the Big Tuna never felt like even the remotest possibility until I met Kat Stronge, but with her by my side, I knew I'd earn my wings one day.

At least I thought I would.

Now I was back to being alone, all because I betrayed the trust we had. Kat relied on me to keep her one step ahead of the monsters, but when push came to shove, I'd behaved no better than the creatures we fought. So that was that. Bridges burned. The capstone on another perfect fucking day.

But I didn't have time to dwell on that mess. Not yet. Not with another life still on the line. Mark Ryan was strapped to a rack, and he wasn't getting off it until I showed up at Vic's place with an archdemon in my pocket.

As if by magic (and for all I knew, magic was a contributing factor), my phone chimed and Vic's name appeared on the screen. Too risky not to answer. I picked up.

'Till Midnight,' said Vic. 'That's how long I'm giving you to bring me that soul.'

Of course it would have to be midnight. It wouldn't do to schedule a date with destiny at the brunching hour.

I heard a *ping* and checked my phone to find a video of Mark being drawn to full extension. He was shaking so badly that it looked like the fear alone would seize him up dead. I remembered what that rack had done to Frosty, and knew Vic's threat wasn't an idle one.

I went to speak, but the line had already gone dead. Vic had no interest in hearing what I had to say. He was set to transmit, not to receive.

There followed a text message with a set of instructions I needed to follow once I had the soul in my possession. I was advised to bring the pouch directly to Vic's office, where I would hand it to his right-hand man, Kojo. So long as the deformed goon was satisfied that I'd brought him what his master had asked for, the hostage would be exchanged, and Vic and me would be square.

No funny stuff.

The message made that quite explicit. Kojo had been taught to identify the soul of Cimeries. If I tried to fob him off with anything less than primo product, the contract I had with Vic would be torn in half, along with Mark. After how badly I'd botched the Ripper case, I couldn't let that happen. I needed a win. Something to lighten the heavy load bearing down on my shoulders, even if just a little.

It was Sunday and the Museum of Souls was closed, so I wasted no time getting down to business and translocating inside the building

Or nearby the building, anyway.

I tried to pitch my landing in the exhibition hall—the place the Curator kept the institution's most valuable souls—but it wasn't happening. Instead of bypassing the Museum's security and arriving in the heart of the building, I found myself stood outside on the street. No big surprise there. Shift already told me the place was locked up tight, so I wasn't expecting this caper to go down that easy. That said, I'd be a fool not to use every tool in the box, so I tested the walls to see if I was able to filter through that way. Once again, no joy; the shell of the building was rock solid, even to a ghost. I wasn't beaten yet, though. After all, this wasn't my first time on the rob.

A bit here about my nefarious past. When I was younger, I used to enjoy testing the law. A bit of light burglary here, a spot of joyriding there, you know, youthful indiscretions. Not exactly spelunking into the abyss, but enough to leave me with a record that made getting a regular job nigh on impossible. Which is how I came to be an exorcist, and how I learned about the Uncanny. It was also my route into magic, specifically, the kind of magic that could be used to break into places, thereby bringing the whole saga full circle.

I balled my fists and pressed them to my temples. I needed to see what I was up against if I was going to figure out how to bypass it, and that required a spot of the old kleptomancy. I whispered an invocation, piecing the magic together in my head, making the impossible real. The spell I was casting wasn't to pick a lock this time, but to get a glimpse of the lock's inner workings. To open it up and find its flaws, to identify any weaknesses I could exploit. I closed my eyes, and when I opened them again, the world had transformed.

I could see now that every brick of the Museum was illuminated with a glowing sigil: a warding symbol specifically engineered to prevent the ingress of sub-mortal metaphysical phenomena. In other words, the whole building had been rubbed with ghost garlic.

No wonder I got bounced when I tried taking a shortcut. The only way an apparition was getting into the Museum was through the front door, except the entrance was locked today, and protected by its own warding sigil. The people who built this place weren't taking any chances. They made the Museum a fortress, and with merch that valuable, who could blame them?

My ghost powers weren't going to get me into the exhibition hall, and neither was my magic. No degree of kleptomancy was going to make a chink in that kind of armour. There had to be some way to breach the place. The Museum couldn't be totally airtight. I just needed to come at it from a different angle—

I looked down at my feet, and when I didn't find the thing I wanted right away, I began a circuit of the building until I did. There it was, tucked away around the west side of the building, an inconspicuous alley, and at the end of that, a lone sewer plate.

It couldn't be that easy, could it? Was there any chance that the Museum's architects had neglected to add those warding sigils to the underside of the building? There was only one way to find out.

CHAPTER THIRTY-EIGHT: DOWN IN A FAE-HOLE

By the time Jazz Hands arrived, the day was in full swing and the people of Holborn were settling into their offices. I'd counted on that. It made escorting a zombie through the streets that much easier.

'Another promise broken,' said Jazz, arriving in the back alley I'd steered her to and reuniting me with my walking corpse. 'Didn't you swear to me you'd collect this one before I opened up this morning? Now I find myself delivering him to you like some bloody courier.'

She was agitated, and understandably so. She wasn't accustomed to being outside of her shop, much less creeping around in a back street.

'I know, Jazz, I'm the worst. The absolute worst.' Sometimes it's best to just agree with someone when they're angry at you. Leaves them with nowhere to go.

She gave me a hooded look. 'So what exactly is the plan here?'

'FrankenJake is going to help me get inside that place,' I explained.

I showed her the manhole at my feet.

Jazz laid a look on me. 'You're insane to even think about going in there. Do you know what you are? A baby seal willingly throwing himself into a shark's mouth.'

'A baby seal with back-up,' I replied.

To get my point across, I instructed FrankenJake to remove the manhole lid, which he did by ripping it free and tossing it to the opposite end of the alley like a frisbee.

'See? I'm in safe hands.'

Jazz wasn't convinced. 'Need I remind you that there are dangerous things lurking beneath this city?' She reeled off a list, no doubt catalogued within some dusty tome she kept under her shop counter. 'I can think of two dozen creatures just off the top of my head: redcaps, scrats, shamblers, clabbernappers, screaming skulls—'

'Yep, that's enough examples for now, I reckon,' I said, halting her with a flat palm.

I already knew things could get hairy down there. There were all sorts of supernatural creatures that called the sewer their home. Creatures that could harm even ghosts.

'—And that's without even mentioning fairies,' Jazz added, undeterred.

I gave FrankenJake a playful jab in the short ribs. 'I've seen this geezer tear down a brick wall bare-handed. Imagine what he'll do to a titchy little fairy.'

I was making light of a serious situation. The fairies that infested London's underworld weren't the kind that carried magic wands and turned pumpkins into fancy carriages. These fairies had claws.

'You're talking about our friend here as if he were a wrecking ball,' said Jazz.

'So what?'

'*So what?*' She shook her head in frustration. 'Have you listened to nothing I've been telling you? He might not seem it, but this man is as much a person as you or I. You can't just boss him around and treat him like a slave.'

I cast a glance at FrankenJake, who stared back at me in a vacuous daze. I knew Jazz was on the money. Inside FrankenJake was a mind that feared the end of its own existence. That made him more than just a walking corpse.

'This'll all be over quick sharpish,' I assured her. 'Ten minutes and I'll be coming up under that place like a randy gopher; bingo bango. Now get back to your shop and I'll give you a tinkle as soon as I get home.'

Her eyes betrayed maternal concern, even if the rest of her body language said she wanted to batter me.

She gave FrankenJake a kiss on top of his head then side-eyed me. 'Bring him back in one piece,' she made me promise, and I did.

Jazz and I said our farewells, then it was off to work. Being out in the open with FrankenJake was risky. There was no telling when Vic might choose to use his scrying magic to rub his peepers on me, and then my big secret would be blown. I had every intention of employing the zombie he lumbered me with as a secret weapon—one that I'd use to cave in his skull the moment his guard was down—and I'd hate for anything to ruin that surprise.

I gave FrankenJake a nod. 'After you, pal.'

Through the manhole and down the slimy ladder he went, disappearing into the darkness. I wondered what he was thinking. Was he feeling fear in that moment, like he did when I piloted him and he thought I was trying to push him aside? Were his thoughts that complex, or had what I experienced just been an animal reflex?

When the ladder stopped shaking, I followed him down, one slippery rung at a time.

I know what you're thinking: *How come a ghost can use a ladder?*

No idea, mate. Not a sausage. Tell you what, though, as soon as someone writes a peer-reviewed paper titled *The Physics of Phantoms,* I'll be sure to let you know.

I stepped off the last rung next to FrankenJake, who greeted me with a soft groan. I took a look around the cramped space. My eyes struggled to adjust to the piss-poor light, which amounted to a loosely-spaced trail of dingy lamps strung to the sewer wall like the world's most depressing Christmas lights. Beyond that, all I could make out were the tunnel's walls, smeared with ancient layers of oil and grease. The sewer was a giant clogged artery, coated in cholesterol.

A look at my feet showed me that I was standing on a narrow brick walkway that ran alongside a lumpy river of effluence. There wasn't much room to manoeuvre. One wrong step and I was going face-first in the muck, and even though shit doesn't stick to ghosts, I could do without the visuals.

I clapped a hand on my companion's shoulder. 'I hope you see in the dark better than I do, mate.'

A gentle shove and away we went, heading off into the great unknown.

It turned out that FrankenJake made for a pretty decent guide. If it weren't for me using him as a seeing eye dog, I'd definitely have taken a tumble twenty yards down the tunnel where a chunk of walkway had crumbled away to nothing, turned soft as wet gingerbread by decades of urban decay.

I gave FrankenJake a pat and thanked him for saving my bacon. We stepped over the gap in the walkway and carried on through the sewer. We shuffled forward another ten yards or so when I realised there was something missing.

Life.

The tunnel should have been teeming with it. The last time I was brave enough to venture into the sewers, it was like walking over a furry brown carpet, the rats were so many. Now, not a squeak. Literally. No life at all. Just a couple of dead men doing a funeral march.

After a swift bit of navigational calculation on my part, we chucked a Ronnie at the first junction and headed for the area of the excrement-caked catacombs that lay beneath the Museum. As we inched our way along, the darkness pressing in on us like grave dirt, I did my best to concentrate on the positives of being down in the sewer.

Um...

Well, there was one thing. So long as I was underground, I couldn't be spied on. The magical energy thrown off by fairies and the like acted as a kind of mystical chaff, which would shield me from Vic's scrying magic. That gave me a pretty decent window of invisibility, which was exactly what I needed to keep my long game with FrankenJake quiet.

Then again, the benefits of fairies were definitely outweighed by the bad stuff they brought with them. As if seeking to illustrate this point, one of FrankenJake's feet came down on the brittle bones of a human skeleton.

'Jesus.'

I crouched down to get a better look at the remains, which were piled up on the walkway in a manner that suggested the person they belonged to had died with his back propped against the tunnel wall. Some poor bastard had come down here to escape the world up there, and this had been his reward: murdered by fairies.

I said before that fairies—real ones, not the Disney variety—were bad news, and I wasn't joking. Sewer fairies are tiny parasites that feast on waste and breed by the thousands. They do this by preying on sleeping vagrants, piercing them with their stingers and pumping them full of fairy seed. Unknowingly impregnated with their evil little brood, the down-and-out wakes up with their guts tied in knots. A day later, their stomach bursts like a rotten pumpkin and they vent a swarm of new fairies, ready to repeat the cycle on some other poor sod.

The bones were piled close enough to one of the tunnel's lamps that I was able to inspect them with some degree of scrutiny.

'Here, have a dig about in there,' I instructed FrankenJake.

He followed my lead, rummaging around the pile and locating a skull among the remains.

'That's weird.'

The top of the skull had been cracked open like a coconut. There were claw marks visible inside the cranium, too large to have been made by fairies.

'No braaaaiins,' groaned my companion, and for once, he was bang on the money.

The victim's skull had been hollowed out and picked clean, and yet fairies didn't eat brains. The only thing I could think of that lived in a sewer and did was—

'Oh shit—'

A brown blur blasted from an overhead outlet and struck me in the side of the face. It wasn't sewage. No, this was something far worse.

The blur landed on the walkway with a sickening squelch. At first, it looked like a squashed log, at least until it unfurled and became something vaguely humanoid. Limbs peeled away from the creature's trunk, trailing webs of sticky brown ooze. The thing rose on a pair of squat legs, its body twisted, its back crooked, giving it the appearance of something that had been expelled rather than born. The beast turned our way, its eyes clamping on to mine, two deep-set yellow dots. Its mouth was a simple horizontal tear filled with a riot of fangs. It had no nose, but then if I was made of human filth, I wouldn't have wanted one either.

This was a dunnie.

Dunnies are what happens when magicians lay down roots in a metropolitan setting. See, here's the thing: every time a spell-slinger channels the primordial energies that we call magic, their bodies become congested with a certain amount of supernatural debris. That debris, like any other debris a person takes into their system, needs an exit. Yeah. It's something that most magic-users don't even consider as they're going about their **ahem** business.

And so their supernatural waste arrives here, down underground, where it mingles with other magically-charged excretions in the diabolical cauldron of the sewer. And on rare occasions, when some of that waste combines with certain other kinds, an alchemical reaction occurs that gives birth to something new. In this case, a dunnie: a walking blob of septic shock with a taste for brains.

At least now I knew why the sewer was so quiet. The fairies, the rats, anything with a scrap of grey matter in its head, had no doubt wound up inside of this thing's belly.

The dunnie let rip a ragged blood-flecked scream and launched its attack. I cocked a fist, but I wasn't fast enough. The creature came at me like a feral mongoose, snarling, slashing, a full-body weapon. The dunnie's claws raked my cheek, drawing four lines of ectoplasmic blood. Yet another critter that could hurt me. Wonderful. You'd think being a ghost might give a man a bit of relief from being smacked about, but no. The list of things that could do me a mischief was getting longer by the day.

I threw the dunnie a dig, but it dodged my swing with ease and threw a low blow that landed right in my meat and two veg. Agony. I folded in half and staggered backwards, pitching over the edge of the walkway and landing in the river of foulness below.

I didn't even make a splash. To a ghost, liquid presents about as much of a physical obstacle as air does you. Don't get me wrong, landing in a bubbling stream of raw sewage was no picnic, but at least I wouldn't have to worry about the dry cleaning bill. I managed to find my feet and get my head above the effluence, which I realised now was only waist-high. I came topside with a cough and splutter, but for no real reason – the reaction was purely psychosomatic. Don't worry, nothing got in my mouth.

I was still swaying when the dunnie launched its next attack, leaping from the walkway and screeching like a knackered fan belt. He came at me like something from a Bruce Lee movie, fly-kicking me in the face and landing on the other side of the channel. My feet came up and the rest of me went down, back to the sewer bed, buried beneath the muck. I was getting the tar knocked out of me. If the bookies were to take bets on the outcome of this fight, it wouldn't come down to who won; the smart money would be on which direction my body fell.

I wasn't going to win this thing fighting mano-a-mano. The only way I was coming out of this scrape was by tagging in a partner. I caught my balance and went to push back above the surface of the brown water, but the Dunnie wouldn't let me. I only managed to make it to my knees before the bastard thing leapt onto my back and sunk its claws into the meat of my shoulders.

I screamed for FrankenJake, but I was still underwater, and the sewage smothered the words. No matter how hard I tried to get the zombie's attention, my voice refused to break the sludgy surface (in case you're finding the science of all this hard to swallow—*why would a ghost's voice be affected by being submerged in liquid when his body isn't?* —I would once again refer you to the as-yet-unwritten *Physics of Phantoms*).

I struggled to right myself, but the dunnie was pressing down too hard for me to get my head above water. This presented a major problem. While I wouldn't drown beneath the muck, I was effectively on mute, and since FrankenJake only responded to simple instructions (when he responded at all) that meant I was on my own.

I reached up behind my head and grabbed the dunnie by the scruff of its... Jesus, I don't even want to think about what it was I was grabbing, but I got a fistful of it and pulled as hard as I could.

The creature was going nowhere.

Its claws were embedded so deep that any attempt to dislodge it hurt like a fresh tattoo on an open wound.

I'm going to die in this place. Thanks to some Presto the Magnificent crimping one off and flushing it down here, I'm going to cark it in a sewer pipe at the hands of a shit golem. And they say the detective game ain't glamorous.

Ectoplasmic blood leaked freely from my shoulders. I screamed, but no one heard me. The bone phone was calling my number. *Ring ring. Ring ring.* I felt a scraping on the side of my neck—the dunnie's pin-sharp fangs—and realised the little fucker was about to chew my throat out.

My entire field of vision turned bright white.

What is that? Is that death's pale flag? Is it Heaven? Have I finally earned my day in the sun?

No chance.

It was spume: a foamy madness as the thrashing dunnie turned the brown water into frothy white suds. I felt the monster's claws eject from my flesh, felt its weight lift off my back. When my head broke the froth of sewer scum, I saw FrankenJake craned over me, the dunnie's head gripped in his mitt like the prize in a fairground claw machine.

'Not... hurt!' he groaned, much to my astonishment.

Since when did he say more than just "brains"? And more to the point, did this mean he actually *cared* about me?

The zombie hoisted the frenzied dunnie to shoulder-height, levelled a fierce roar at the thing, and hurled it at the tunnel wall hard enough to turn it into a smear.

'Go on, my son!'

He did it. He saved me. And he did it without being asked. Despite everything I'd done—insulting him, imprisoning him, almost killing him, even—that slack-jawed diamond came through. I wondered why. Was it because he *was* me, in a way? Did he do what he did to save a piece of himself? Or had our brief time cohabiting the same body connected us on some deeper level?

The zombie reached down a paw and pulled me out of the muck.

'Thanks,' I said, checking my wounds and realising I'd survive the damage I'd taken. 'I owe you one, FrankenJake.'

That name... it wasn't enough. I dubbed him that back when I thought of him as a brainless burden, something I had to drag around and make excuses for. It was no good. Not now. He deserved better than some clumsy portmanteau.

'Frank. That's what I'm going to call you from now on. Just Frank.'

He gave me one of his lopsided smiles. 'Braaiiiiins.'

I swiped some drool off his chin. 'Sure thing, pal,' I said returning the same smile, only a tad more symmetrical. 'Whatever you say.'

CHAPTER THIRTY-NINE: LET'S GET SMALL

There are these things called desire paths. You'll have trodden one before, whether or not you're familiar with the term. Every time you take a short cut across some flattened grass, or nip through a gap in a hedge in favour of a route that some city planner designed, you're walking a desire path.

It doesn't make you a maverick.

All it means is you're following someone else's script. Making yourself a footnote to some other guy's story. Walk that path enough times and it becomes a routine. Something you do without even thinking about.

So really, "desire" isn't the word.

The only person who gets to stake that claim is the person who flattened the grass, who made the hole in the hedge. He's the one going against the grain. The one who disobeyed. All you've done is ride his coattails.

In a way you've become a ghost: the kind that walks through walls, not because he's a nonconformist, not because he's trying to freak anyone out, but because it's all he knows. The route he's threading isn't a new one, it's the same he's always used, since he was alive, even. So what if the next generation remodelled the house around him? So what if they put up new walls? Old habits die hard.

Well, not for this ghost. While others follow paths out of habit, I carve fresh ones. I create new grooves through this world. Or at least I try to.

Another twenty yards down the tunnel and I was staring up at the ceiling, eyes trained on a glowing warding sigil.

'Bollocks.'

The sigils were spread all along the tunnel roof, spaced out evenly, leaving no margin for error.

'Bollocks!'

I was spitting feathers. Whoever it was that had designed the Museum, they'd had the foresight to ensure that it was completely bulletproof, top to bottom. The soul-jack was a bust. Another perfectly good plan, chucked in the fuck bucket. Was it too much to ask that I get one solitary break? One little chink of light in the void? I mean, seriously, I survive a fight with a monster made of shit and spite and this is what I get? This is my reward?

Frank gawped at me with that puppy dog expression of his.

'You're right,' I said. 'Dry your eyes, Jake. This ain't over yet.'

I reached up to the tunnel ceiling. It was low enough that I could get my hands to it, so I did, and confirmed that it was solid to the touch. And yet not *too* solid. Just like the crumbling walkway we passed back near the manhole, it was spongy in places.

'Hm.'

I looked, to Frank, then to his hands, which were curled up in fists by his sides. Jazz had used the phrase "wrecking ball" when she talked about him earlier. I wondered if there was something to that. I'd seen him bring down a brick wall before, and he wasn't even trying then. Could his hulk-like strength be used to tear a hole through the crumbling tunnel roof and burrow into the museum? Okay, it wouldn't make for the most elegant break-in, but the idea could have some merit. If in doubt, give it a clout, right?

'Ach, what am I thinking?'

The only reason Frank was able to do that kind of damage at the funeral home was because it was just a flimsy bit of false wall he was knocking down. And he lost a finger doing it, let's not forget that. Tunnelling through the foundations of a building... his arms would be a pair of stumps before he got anywhere near breaking in. That's if he didn't bring a landslide down on himself and end up stuck under two tonne of rubble.

No.

I couldn't put another life at risk just to convenience one of my schemes. I did with Reina, and look what happened. I shouldn't have used her as a means to an end, and I wouldn't do the same with Frank. He pulled my arse out of the fire back there, and I wasn't about to show my thanks by burying him alive.

And so the pair of us continued our patrol, heading further along the tunnel, hoping to find a gap among the warding sigils. A dent in the armour. Some oversight we could make use of. We were almost past the foundations of the Museum, straddling the boundary to the next building along, when I saw a possible access point overhead: a smaller sewer duct feeding into the main pipeline. Not exactly what I was after, but then what else was I expecting? A convenient stepladder leading to a trapdoor that opened directly into the exhibition hall?

My eyes went back to the sewer duct. Going by its angle, it led back the way we came, suggesting that it serviced the Museum's plumbing. The duct was spaced just far enough between two sigils that the discrete zones of warding magic they gave off wouldn't provide any protection against it. Trouble was, the artery was only a foot wide, if that. Big enough for a dunnie, but way too small for me to fit in. I'm six foot tall; six-one if I blow dry my hair. To make it through an opening that size, I'd need to be a whole other shape.

Then again…

Who was to say I had to be *any* shape? I'm a ghost; residual necroplasmic energy, according to the Curator. Technically, I only existed in human form out of habit. This was the body I had while I was alive, and so I'd returned in the same shell. But that shell wasn't made of flesh and bone. The energy a ghost is composed of is far more elastic. I remembered Frosty, stretched out like taffy in Vic's dungeon, his limbs pulled impossibly thin. And then there were those padlock traps the Curator's guards wore; able to shrink down and contain a soul the size of an arch-demon. So long as a dislocated soul could be forced to alter its size and shape, was that something I could will upon myself?

It seemed possible. Likely, even. I wasn't made of memory foam, I was an apparition, a thing of smoke and nothing. I wouldn't even need to change my form all that much to pull this stunt off, just slim myself down enough to squeeze through that pipe and pop out of the other side. If I strung a kleptomantic incantation together in the right order, if I performed the correct somatic gestures, I could force myself to take up less space and carve a desire path right into that place.

They say God loves a trier, don't they? Then again, how does that other saying go... every corpse on Mount Everest was once an extremely motivated person? Something like that.

And yet I had to try, no matter the risk. A life hung in the balance, and my debts were far outweighed by what I owed. I couldn't have Mark's death in my ledger. What I needed was karma, not drama.

Please let me do a better job of robbing that demon than I did of putting a stop to the other one.

Letting the Ripper get away with it was a stain on my soul that would never come out, but if I could just get in there and save Mark's life, at least I'd feel a little better about myself.

'You hold the fort here, Frank. I'm going in.'

If I only felt as confident as I sounded. The fact was, anything could happen to me if I tried this. I could come apart at the seams and drift away like celestial ether. I could destroy whatever vital force I was made of and discorporate myself for good.

Then again, fuck it.

I closed my eyes and concentrated, calling forth the necessary magic and raising my potential to the nth power. I was going to change myself, reconstruct the very fibre of my being, make my body into something malleable. Come hell or high water, I'd find a way to rewrite the script and squirt through that shit pipe. Ugh. I knew doing this job was going to mean getting my hands dirty, but I had no idea.

Don't lose your bottle now, Jake. In for a penny, in for a pound. Let's crack this piggy bank wide open.

I heard a sound in my head like an orchestra tuning, then I was gone.

CHAPTER FORTY: BONES IN THE WALL

IT WAS PAINFUL. Gordon Bennett, it was painful, but I did it. I moulded my essence into a brand new shape, blasted through a sewage pipe like a cylinder through a pneumatic tube, and emerged from a crapper inside the Museum.

When I arrived in the toilet stall, I was me again; six feet tall, two feet wide, one hundred percent Jake Fletcher. How I managed to cheat the laws of physics like that, I'm still not entirely sure, but then supernatural physics are built on some pretty shaky foundations. I had to hand it to myself, though, I was really starting to level-up, magic-wise. And without blagging it. Unlike Vic Lords, I didn't have to sell my soul to make my gains.

My idiotic idea had paid off.

I was in like Flynn.

Hey, if it's stupid but it works, it ain't stupid.

Here was my chance. I had everything I needed to get what I came for. I stepped out of the toilets and moved invisibly through the bowels of the museum, travelling along a corridor that I recognised from my last visit. I listened out for any sign of another presence, but heard nothing. Satisfied that I wasn't being watched, I continued along the corridor until I reached the circular exhibition hall. The rotunda had no windows, and the overhead lights were turned off, so the only illumination came from the room's dim emergency lighting, which threw long green stripes across the polished glass of the soul cradles.

There he was.

The arch-demon Cimeries; less a demon than a swirl of fog in his current state, but a demon nonetheless. I reached inside my pocket and cupped the pouch Vic had equipped me with, fleshy and warm in my palm.

I saw the remote that controlled the vitrine's settings, sat on the pedestal where the Curator had left it. Firming up a hand, I aimed the remote in the direction of Cimeries' cell and searched for the release button. There were so many, and none of the buttons made any sense to my Luddite brain. I'd have needed an enigma machine to crack the poxy thing. Not that it mattered. Making use of the remote was an option that was about to be swept a long way off the table.

A whisper of fabric, the sound of shoes scuffing marble, then...

'Mister Fletcher, as I live and breathe.'

The Curator stood in the doorway, flanked by two of his padlock-wearing cronies; the ones he called collectors. With a white-gloved hand, he flipped a switch on the wall, throwing me under the spotlight.

'I must confess, I don't recall instating an open door policy,' he said.

'And yet here I am,' I replied, 'like a dog to vomit.'

He laughed. 'Didn't I tell you we'd meet again? I rather expected the encounter to be out in the wild, but I'm quite comfortable with you bringing the mountain to Mohammed, so to speak.'

He could have bagged me before, but that wouldn't have been sporting. This time I was fair game.

I'd run into a bit of an obstacle it seemed, but I wasn't ready to roll over just yet. To a good detective, "obstacle" is just another word for "inspiration".

I rushed the closest collector, intending to fuse with his corporeal form and turn the tide on my would-be captors. Have a guess how well that went. It was like trying to force my way into a Russian nesting doll, every layer I peeled back only revealed another layer. No, this nut would not be cracked. Same for the other guy. Some kind of magical shielding I guessed, or maybe they were just bred that way. I mean, you're not going to get very far as a ghost hunter if your body's an open goal for every spook on the spectrum.

'Not today, my sticky-fingered friend,' said the Curator, wagging a white finger at me. 'And before you get any ideas...' He showed me the inside lining of his waistcoat, sewn into the fabric of which was all manner of runes and glyphs. Protection magic: the kind I had no hope of defeating.

'Tuck your ego away, mate,' I told him, 'I'd rather be seen in a Skoda than driving you about.'

His lip curled just a little. Good. That was a hit.

'What shall we do with you?' he asked, tapping his chin as he stepped right up to me. 'Since I find you trespassing on private property, I suppose you are rather at my mercy.'

'Easy, sunshine. Just because I'm dead, doesn't mean I don't have rights.'

No lie. Technically speaking, civil liberties still apply to ghosts. When it comes down to it, we're really just like you, only with less density.

Then again...

'My dear Mister Fletcher. In this house, your rights are worth about as much as a chocolate teapot.'

I was about to fire off another barb, but since I got the feeling that the Curator was ready to trade witticisms all night, I decided on a more direct course of action. This showdown was only going to end one way; so long as he wanted me in one of those vitrines, we were heading for a spot of aggro.

The Curator read my face. 'I would advise against acting upon that anger. I assure you, this garment protects me against anything you might wish to throw at me.'

'Anything, huh?'

He nodded, but not out of affirmation. The thing that set his head bobbing was my fist connecting with the bridge of his nose.

'No protection against that, eh?'

He rocked back a step, stupefied.

It was only a glancing blow. I didn't get to feel the satisfying crunch of broken cartilage, but it was enough to break his spectacles in half and leave him with a face like a smacked haddock. Sweet Jesus, that felt good. I finally got to land a punch, and on a creature even slimier than the walking turd that attacked me in the sewer.

Of course, the guards didn't hang about after that, so I planted my feet and put up my dukes. Don't get me wrong, I'm no Jackie Chan, but I'm better at scrapping than you might expect. Not that I've had any official training. For me, fighting isn't about boxercise classes or karate lessons. The only way to get good at fighting—the real kind, the kind that happens in a pub car park or beer garden—is to do lots of it, and thankfully, my youth provided me with plenty of opportunity to brush up on the subject. Walking around town wearing eyeliner and a long black coat when everyone else is listening to acid house and wearing Hi-Tec trainers was apt to send trouble my way, and I've never been a shrinking violet.

I grabbed the first collector by the chunky iron chain he was wearing, hammered the top of my skull into his face, and landed a Glasgow Kiss with enough force to tear the jewellery free of his neck.

A strong opening, but I had nothing to follow it up with. After my hit landed, his mate got to trade one back, and his did more than give me a bit of a wobble. His was like a grenade going off. The blow left me on my ear, then came the three Os: outnumbered, overwhelmed, overcome. The collectors held me down, pinning me to the ground like a pair of anvils.

The Curator produced a handkerchief from the pocket of his waistcoat and dabbed some blood from his nose. 'Oh, dear, Mister Fletcher. Bad luck. You know, you really do bring a whole new meaning to the phrase "thick as thieves".'

He instructed his goons to hoist me to my feet, then had them march me in the direction of the rotunda's empty soul cradle. It was the one he showed me before, only with a slight difference: now it wore a brass plate engraved with my name.

I did my best to think of some clever way out of the mess I was in, but my mind was an engine that wouldn't turn over, sparking again and again but refusing to kick into action. I was scared. Proper scared. I've died once already, so threats to my person generally ring hollow, but not this one. I couldn't end up in that cell. I just couldn't.

The Curator had his men hurl me to the ground.

'Kindly show Mister Fletcher to his room,' he said.

One of the collectors removed the key from the padlock hung around his neck, setting its keyhole ablaze. He uttered an activation word that sounded as if it had been nicked from a bit of Zoroastrian scripture, then the light punched out of the padlock's keyhole, so bright that I had to turn away to the soul cradle to stop from being blinded. I began to unravel, to dissipate. One moment I was there in the room, the next I was gone; captured, bricked up, the last chink of light all drowned out.

CHAPTER FORTY-ONE: MESSAGE IN A BOTTLE

What happened to my hands? Where are my arms? Is there anything left of me at all?

These were the first questions I asked myself when I regained my senses and discovered that I'd been transformed into an indistinct, swirling fog. The soul cradle had turned me gaseous. I was no longer able to hold a human shape. Now I was a storybook phantom; a pale wisp of nothing that didn't even have the substance to bemoan its pitiful fate. At least not out loud.

It was the demon's hex all over again, only instead of rubbing me out of existence, now I was forced to live in it forever, a silent witness to eternity.

With immense effort, I could just about gather enough of myself to create a flash of something visible, but nothing you'd call solid. Nothing I could use to break through my container and spill out of the other side. Any time I succeeded in creating an approximation of matter, I felt myself being pulled apart again, turned to smoke in the wind.

What about my ghost powers? Could I translocate to the other side of the glass and break free that way? I'll give you two guesses, but you'll only need one.

I could think and I could see, and that's all I was getting.

Or was it?

A man in blue overalls ambled into the rotunda carrying a basket of cleaning products. No, not a man, an eaves. *The* eaves. I was more than familiar with this one by now, having spoken with him at The Beehive, then heard him getting told off by the Curator in this place.

He approached my vitrine with a bottle of Windowlene and gave the glass a couple of squirts before wiping it down with a damp rag.

Hello? You remember me, right? Jake Fletcher, we met at the boozer.

No answer. No wonder. I had no voice. No form. The words I was speaking existed only in my head. Actually, I don't know how they existed at all, seeing as I didn't have a head to contain them. Once again, science was left crying in the corner.

The eaves leaned in with his mole rat face. For a moment I thought I'd succeeded in getting his attention, but he was only checking to make sure he'd not left any streaks on the glass. Satisfied that he'd done his job properly this time, he went about checking his sharp yellow teeth in the vitrine's mirror finish and digging out a scrap of trapped lettuce.

Oi, Roland Rat, listen up! Get me out of this thing and I'll make sure you never see another bottle of Windowlene in your life. You hear me? Just name your price!

Another failed attempt to get the guy on my side. Another plea falling on deaf Spock ears. So long as I was kept intangible, so long as I was denied a voice, I had no way of recruiting this potential ally. And yet I needed help. I wasn't getting out of this hole on my own. I had to find some way of getting a message into a sympathetic ear.

My next thought was Frank. I left him under the Museum awaiting my return, but what if instead of idling away down there, I could get him up here? A quick word in his shell-like and I could have him do to the Curator what he did to that dunnie, I was sure of it. How exactly he was going to make it past security and find his way into the heart of the Museum, that was a question for later. First of all, I had to figure out a way to talk to the feller.

Think think think.

Some kind of psychic link; that's what I needed. As far-fetched as it might sound, the idea wasn't completely crackers. I had something similar going with my main meat suit, Mark. Okay, I couldn't communicate with him remotely—not exactly—but I did always have a handle on his whereabouts, which was proof of some kind of supernatural bond. Then again, the only reason I had that was because I'd possessed him so many times. These days, getting inside Mark's brain was so easy that he might as well lay out a welcome mat. No wonder I could predict where the bloke was parked at any given moment – his mind was an open book to me (nothing worth getting excited about, mind you; a real beach read).

On the other hand, I had been inside Frank once, and I felt like we made a connection. Also, we were, essentially, two parts of the same person. Maybe, if I was lucky, I'd be able to reach him. A psychic link, that's all I needed. If I could just push my thoughts through some glass, a few layers of concrete and a human skull, I could beat this thing. I managed to cram my whole body through a U-bend already, how hard could it be to smuggle out a couple of simple instructions?

Find the right words, Jake. Send your mind questing outwards. Break free of this prison.

I imagined a piece of string with a paper cup on each end, one end over my mouth, the other over Frank's ear. I imagined my words vibrating along that length of string and crawling inside Frank's head. I imagined him crashing through the rotunda wall and punching a fist through the soul cradle. Then reality reasserted itself and I realised I was going nowhere. Two parts of the same person or not, I was exactly where I started, trapped behind glass, a helpless, shapeless essence.

I was stuck. Cursed to spend the rest of my days as fog in a jar, the world passing me by like time lapse photography as the days flicked on and on and on.

And then…

A tall man in a midnight blue suit entered the exhibition hall. The Curator looked to my vitrine, then to the eaves janitor.

'Give us the room,' he instructed the lackey. 'You may return to complete your duties once I'm done.'

The eaves offered a respectful nod, then a decidedly less respectful middle finger once his employer's back was turned. I wondered if the eaves knew us prisoners could see him do that. I wondered if he cared.

The Curator's thin face appeared on the outside of my vitrine. He aimed his remote control at my cell and pushed a sequence of buttons, then suddenly I was me again; hands, arms, legs, the whole kit and caboodle. I was whole, or at least as whole as a ghost could be.

'Yard time, Mister Fletcher,' said the Curator. 'Do feel free to stretch your legs.'

His words sounded muffled, as though they were coming from behind a closed door. He wore a smile that made his head look like a split watermelon. What he didn't wear were his spooktacles, which I'd demolished when I laid one on his smug bonce earlier. This left him unable to see me, and so his eyes roamed the vitrine like a blind man's, searching for my voice.

'All right, mate,' I said, careful to keep my words bright and silvery. 'Any chance you've got the time?'

The Curator considered my request for a second, then decided there was no harm in sharing and produced his pocket watch. 'It's just gone 6 p.m. Why, do you have somewhere you need to be?'

I did: a meeting with Vic Lords at the Cinderella hour that I really couldn't be late for. Not that I divulged this. No sense brightening that smug look of his.

'You should know that I'm aware of the little trick you pulled earlier,' said the Curator, tapping the glass of my cell like a kid at a reptile house winding up the cobra. 'A clever bit of sleight of hand, but I realise now that you pocketed my colleague's soul siphon before you were captured.'

I did. When I head-butted the goon during that scuffle and saw his padlock necklace come off, I decided to hang onto it.

'It won't do you any good,' the Curator went on. 'Tomorrow you're going to be released, and the trap will be returned to us.'

'I'm getting out?' I said. 'How'd I earn parole so fast? Is it because I'm too pretty for jail?'

His grin opened wider still. 'While you are no doubt a handsome specimen, Mister Fletcher, that is not the reason. Tomorrow morning you are being put up for auction, and since several parties have already expressed a great deal of interest in acquiring you, I don't expect you to be part of our collection for much longer. Sad as that may be.'

Expressed an interest? Who had? Some soul fancier with more money than sense, or someone from my past who liked the idea of getting his mitts on my soul eternal? I've made a lot of enemies over the years. A lot of people who'd take real pleasure in popping me on a shelf and letting me go dusty.

So now I had two deadlines. If I didn't make it to Vic's place by midnight with a demon in hand, Mark was gone for a Burton. On top of that, if I hadn't figured a way to jailbreak my cell by sunrise, I was going to end up trucked out of here, a curiosity in the corner of some rich fuck's living room. A talking point. A party ice breaker. Christ. With this much darkness and pressure in my life, you'd think I was a frigging deep-sea fish.

'Listen,' I said, addressing my captor in a respectful tone for a change. 'You and me got off to a bad start, but that doesn't mean we can't still be friends.'

That caught his interest. He leaned in, close enough that his breath steamed up the other side of the glass.

'You're obviously a smart geezer, so you'll know wherever there's a ghost there's a treasure trove not far behind. Well, I'm no exception, mate. This ghost is *minted*. Let me out of here and I'll make you rich as a sultan. I'm talking yachts-in-yachts money. So what do you say, pal? You wanna sell me off for a few measly crumbs, or do you wanna make some real mullah?'

He moistened his lips as he considered my offer, until finally he delivered his verdict. 'Has anyone ever told you that you talk too much, Mister Fletcher?'

With a stab of his remote control, I was placed on mute. I cried out in protest, but no sound emerged. I bashed my fists against the glass, but it was futile. The Curator was up on his brogues, then with a final *toodle-oo*, he was gone.

I felt a bitter sting of defeat, but the sensation was only a passing one. I may have been silenced, but I was me now, and soon the eaves janitor would be back to finish his rounds. So long as I could be seen, I'd figure out a way to communicate with him, to persuade him to free me from my cage. I saw how the Curator mistreated the bloke – I saw that middle finger. How hard could it be to whip him into a fervour? To convince him that we were on the same side? Just two working-class stiffs, sticking it to the man.

But the Curator was no one's fool.

Bleep-bleep-bleep—

The noise was coming from the vitrine.

Bleep-bleep-bleep-bleep—

The mechanical warning sounds were getting closer together, more insistent. And with each new *bleep* I could feel myself losing substance. Becoming vapour again.

Bleep-bleep-bleep-bleep-bleep—

Yard time was running out. Soon enough, I'd be paralysed, my jaw wired shut. I had to find some way of making my mark before that happened. Some way of sending the eaves a message.

I'd write him a note.

But where was the ink coming from? Or the paper, for that matter? My mind started sparking again, but this time the engine turned over and revved.

Blood. I'll write the message in blood. I'll smear the words on the glass like a vengeful phantom spelling out a grudge on a bathroom mirror.

Ghost blood would be just as visible to an eaves as ghost skin or ghost hair. All I had to do was work out a way of getting the stuff out of my body, but not so much of it that I turned up my toes. I needed something sharp, but what? I was surrounded by glass, but if I could smash through that, I'd have no need to stick around and write an SOS.

I patted down my pockets. I had my phone, my wallet, a few pieces of lint, but nothing close to a knife. Then I rewound the tape to the eaves checking his reflection in the glass of my cell, and pictured his fangs. I had fangs... well, teeth. A whole mouthful of tiny knives.

I hoisted up a sleeve and began gnawing on my wrist, going at it like a dog on a pork chop, but I couldn't bring myself to puncture the skin.

Bleep-bleep-bleep-bleep-bleep-bleep—

I was unravelling again. In a moment or two I'd have no blood left to give. Fuck it. I bit down on the inside of my cheek until I tasted copper. Pain followed, but I didn't have time for it. I was too busy digging around the inside of my mouth, loading a finger with blood and using my head as a madman's inkwell.

'Come on, come on...' I muttered as I hastily daubed my plea on the inside of the cell.

GET ME OUT

I didn't have time to write the message backwards; I had to trust that the eaves had the brains to reverse it.

Bleep-bleep-bleep-bleep-bleep-bleep-bleep—

The alarm was almost a flatline now. Just a couple more words...

BIG £ REWARD

Bleeeeeeeeeeeeeeeeeeeeeeeeeeeeeeeep.

And I was gone. Reduced to a swirling, yet somehow conscious, fog.

Had I done enough to capture the eaves' interest? Would the knight in shining armour rescue this fair maiden from her ivy-covered tower? Sadly, I had no fingers to cross.

CHAPTER FORTY-TWO: TWILIGHT SLEEP

I WAITED. And waited. Inside the soul cradle, I quickly lost sense of my surroundings. The room beyond the glass was so still that it looked like a photograph, giving me nothing to mark the passage of time. Minutes passed. Maybe hours for all I knew. Was I already too late? Had the eaves clocked off for the night and left me to my fate?

All I needed was ten seconds of his time. So long as he saw that message, I had him. I made the mistake of offering him a taste of magic before, but I was flashing the wrong currency. Sure, eaves couldn't get enough of the old hocus pocus, but this one knew I was bullshitting him. I should have kept things simple and led with cash. Of course, back then I wasn't aware that he pushed a mop around this place. If I were, I'd have known he was obviously in dire need of the stuff, and who could resist parting a ghost from his treasure?

The lights went out.

Not in the room, but inside my head.

One second my focus was trained on the door the janitor had left through, my mind desperately willing him to make a return visit, the next, a black curtain descended. My brain just... switched off.

When I came to, the room had changed. I was in the exhibition hall still, but the lights were turned on now, each of the exhibits picked out by a brass gallery lamp. It took me a moment to realise what had happened.

The cradle put me to sleep.

It had been so long since I'd experienced the sensation that I just assumed my brain had temporarily gone on strike. But no. I'd been artificially put under. It seemed the pod I was contained in could control more than just my physical state, it could flick my consciousness off, too. Every facet of my existence was regulated. Climate-controlled.

What time was it now?

I could only guess at how long I'd been out of it. Forget about minutes or hours, whole days might have passed since I was KO'd.

No. That couldn't be right. The Curator had gloated about an auction taking place in the morning, and since I was still at the Museum and not in the hands of some private collector, that meant we couldn't have seen sunrise. There was hope yet, at least so long as the clock hadn't ticked past midnight.

I was vapour, still—Scotch mist—but my SOS was where I left it, freshly daubed on the wall of my cell. I just had to pray the janitor reappeared and gave it a read. He'd see the message, see my name on the plaque, and be spurred into action. Then, once he'd set me free, I'd half-inch the demon, hotfoot it out of there and—

Someone was coming.

And it wasn't the janitor.

A tall bald man in a long overcoat entered the rotunda, wending his way around the circular room and towards my cell.

The Curator.

'Oh dear, oh dear, Mister Fletcher,' he said.

Pure terror surged through my insides, sending icy daggers straight to my fog heart. The eaves had grassed me up. My plan was scuppered.

The Curator drew his remote control from the pocket of the coat he was wearing, and tapped a quick sequence into it. I felt a familiar sensation as the smog I'd been reduced to coalesced into my walking form. You'd think being whole again would have perked me up a bit, but it only served to make the dread I was feeling all the more real. All the more heavy.

'As I'm sure you've guessed already, your little Mayday was intercepted,' said the Curator. He spoke to me with his head tilted to one side, talking like a priest at confession.

Buggeration. If I ever got my hands on that eaves I'd... do absolutely nothing, because I was stuck inside a glass prison until kingdom come.

'How long?' I croaked. 'How long did you knock me out for?'

'Why, Mister Fletcher, I regret to say that you were in stasis for quite some time.'

'Don't bullshit a bullshitter, mate. We both know I wouldn't still be here if that were true.'

'Ah, yes, the auction.' He sucked some air through his teeth. 'It seems I rather overestimated your market value. Vastly, if I remember correctly. Forgive me, the debacle was so long ago that I'm afraid it's become something of a blur.'

Long ago?

'How long?'

'Close to three-hundred years,' he replied.

I bit back a scream. 'What?'

'I'm sorry, but your failure to sell was something of an embarrassment to this institution. Given the circumstances, we thought it best to mothball you.'

No. No. This can't be happening.

Three-hundred years. Where did that leave me? Were people flying around with jetpacks out there?

None of these questions was really worth an answer. The only thing that mattered was that I'd failed. I couldn't stop the Ripper, and I couldn't stop Mark dying. Or Frosty. Or Reina. I was at a complete dead end.

The Curator pulled a pantomime sad face. 'Come along now, Mister Fletcher, what did you expect? Did you really think your silly little scheme would work?'

A snappy comeback, a threat, even a plain old "fuck you" would have sufficed, but my larynx felt staple-gunned together.

'It did work, by the way,' said the Curator. 'Your little scheme. Like gangbusters.'

He produced a pack of Winstons and lit up a cigarette. For the first time since he entered the room, I realised he wasn't wearing his customary white gloves.

'What's up, Cookie?' asked the Curator, speaking with a distinct Yankie twang.

...

'Shift?' I cried.

'Bingo.'

His laugh took on a new pitch as he mutated into a familiar, blond-haired man.

With a couple of button presses, he used the remote control to activate my soul cradle, which slid open with a breathy hiss. I staggered out of the glass box like a convict pardoned from death row, giddy with excitement, my world transformed.

Of course it had been Shift. Something was off from the start; the overt cockiness for one. He must have copied the Curator's face from the picture he showed me, and fudged the rest. The mad genius bastard.

'Come here, you!'

I laid a smacker on him; a big sloppy one.

'I thought you were old-school,' said Shift, doing his best to wriggle free of my embrace. 'Don't you care that you're kissing a dude?'

'Nope.'

'Well, that's progress, I suppose,' he said, pushing me to arm's-length. 'Now, the next lesson is going to be a little thing called "consent".'

A thought struck.

'Wait a sec… if you could mimic the Curator, why didn't you say so? Why did I need to come here at all?'

'You think I'd put my neck on the line unless I absolutely had to? No way, Jose.'

Another jolt of anger.

'And what was that bullshit story about me losing three-hundred years? You scared the bejeebers out of me!'

He snorted. 'I was only yanking your chain, Cookie. Don't be mad.'

'Bit late for that.'

Shift slapped his knee. 'Boy, I can't *believe* you fell for my fake Limey accent. Call yourself a detective...'

'It was hard to hear inside that box, okay? And you… you… you utter bastard!'

But my annoyance was quickly replaced by a question: *how*? How did Shift get word that I was trapped here?

'You can thank the eaves,' he said, saving me the bother of asking out loud. 'After he saw your message, he came looking for me at The Beehive.'

That sort of made sense. The eaves had been there the night I first met Shift, so he knew we were acquainted. Then again, Shift had been in female form at the time…

'The two of us go way back,' said Shift, continuing to fill in the blanks. 'His name's Gary, by the way. Great guy. Hell of a chef, too. One time he cooked me this chicken and quinoa casserole that blew my freaking—'

'Shift, just FYI, if you don't tell me how you pulled this off right now, this conversation ends with you gargling blood.'

He rolled his eyes at me. 'Fine. So Gary shows up at The Beehive and tells me this crazy story about a rich ghost who needs breaking out of jail. Trouble is, even though Gary wants to get paid, he doesn't have the clearance to crack this ghost's cell. So he says to me, "Hey, buddy, wanna help a brother out?"…'

As Shift's story went on, I suddenly remembered that I had other places to be.

'Shit, what's the time?'

He checked his phone. 'Just gone eleven.'

The news pinned me to the spot. I had less than an hour left before Mark was torn in two.

Shift saw the alarm on my face. 'It's cool, I told the guards to take off for the night. We're on our own here.'

'I don't care about that!' I cried. 'I have to get a demon soul to Vic Lords, and I'm standing here listening to you gab away like a little girl.'

In a less than macho display, Shift clamped his hands on his hips. 'Hey, you're the one who told me I'd be gargling blood if I didn't talk.'

'Christ, I don't have time for this!'

I strode to the other side of the rotunda and arrived at the soul cradle Cimeries was kept in. The arch-demon wasn't much to look at in his current state; just a nebulous green haze that I had to bust out and ferry to Vic ASAP.

'Over here with the remote,' I told Shift, my voice hiked high with tension.

He crossed his arms like a sullen teenager. 'You might consider asking a little nicer if you want me to operate this thing. Especially since I doubt you could operate a toaster.'

'Shift, listen—'

'No, you listen to me, Cookie. Gary did his bit, but I was the one who risked his ass breaking in here. I expect to get paid for that.'

'You'll get paid.'

'Mad paid?'

'Mad paid!'

He unfolded his arms, raised the remote, and took aim at Cimeries' cell. Meanwhile, I reached inside my jacket pocket and pulled out the soul siphon.

'By the way,' I grumbled, 'I knew you weren't the real Curator. Clocked you coming a mile off.'

Shift smiled. 'Bullcrap, you did.'

CHAPTER FORTY-THREE: FREE SPIRIT

GETTING out of the Museum of Souls was a whole lot easier than getting in. Once I'd siphoned off the arch-demon, all I had to do was head for the front door and walk out of the place. Piece of piss.

Speaking of which, my next stop was the sewer, where I collected a very happy-to-see-me Frank. I wasn't taking Vic on alone this time; not after what happened before, when he almost exorcised me. I needed the demon soul to get close to him—to trick Vic into dropping his guard—but I wasn't going to just hand it over and let him have his way. If he wanted to claim his prize, he'd have to fight for it.

I had it all figured out. The demon soul would get me through the front door, but the second Kojo checked the pouch and slid back the bolt, I'd send in Frank and have him juggernaut his way inside. I reckoned there was a fifty/fifty chance of Vic making good on his side of the deal and exchanging Mark, or screaming psalms at me until I was wiped off the face of the Earth; all depended on whether he had any further plans for me. Either way, it didn't matter, because before he knew what hit him, Frank would have his cold, dead claws around his throat, and that would be that.

I could not *wait* to see the look on Vic's face when he found out I'd turned his own weapon against him. Seeing his rotten soul claimed by the Long Man would just be the cherry on the trifle after that.

I gave Frank a friendly pat on the back as we made our way to Camden. I'd run through the plan with him already, but I wanted to make sure he grasped it.

'You ready for this, son?'

He nodded, though it wasn't clear whether he understood, or whether he just liked agreeing. After what happened in the sewers, though, I was banking on the former.

God, I hoped he was up to this. Could Frank really follow my instructions? Yes, he did a good job in the sewer, but was he just acting on instinct, dealing with something right in front of him? Taking Vic down was going to be a lot harder than flushing a dunnie. I tried to rope Shift into helping me with Vic, but he made it pretty clear that he'd already done his bit. The next time I saw him, he'd be collecting his paycheque.

I checked my watch. An hour and change to put the arch-demon in Kojo's hand and turn the tables on his master. Plenty of time. I cradled the pouch in my pocket. It seemed ludicrous that the thing capable of saving Vic's eternal soul was small enough to fit in my jacket and weighed less than a bag of sugar, but there it was. Not that Vic was getting it. As soon as Frank had throttled the life out of that jumped-up gangster, I was having the pouch and its contents destroyed. No one was getting that soul. Not Vic Lords, not the Long Man. *No one*. Getting rid of it wouldn't be easy, but I felt sure Jazz Hands would know a way to destroy the—

'Damn.'

I promised Jazz I'd call her as soon as I made it out of the Museum. I dialled her number, pressed the phone to my ear, and heard the line trill. She picked up before the second ring.

'Is he all right?'

'What?' I replied. Then it dawned on me. 'You mean my corpse?'

'Yes, yes. Did he make it out okay?'

'He's fine. Thanks for asking after my well-being, by the way. Really touching.'

'Of course you're okay, you goon, you're the one I'm talking to.'

She had a point. God, I hated when she had a point.

'I got the demon soul,' I told her.

'Well done,' she replied. 'Just make sure the clasp on that pouch stays done up.'

I patted my pocket. 'Take it from me, this arch-demon ain't going nowhere.'

'That isn't what I'm worried about. If the pouch isn't properly sealed it could leak the stench of brimstone everywhere. Just because you don't have a nose, doesn't mean you shouldn't spare a thought for others.'

A nose.

I was struck by a memory: the smell of vending machine coffee served in a styrofoam cup. The interview room where the Ripper demon made his last stand... when I took control of Stronge's body, it wasn't brimstone I smelled, it was coffee. There was too much going on at the time for me to have grasped the significance of that detail, but now...

A thought went tinkling through my brain like a coin in one of those maze machines you used to see at the arcade.

'Jazz, is there such a thing as a demon that can turn its brimstone smell on or off?'

She scoffed. 'Selective musk? Ludicrous. Whatever put that idea in your head?'

How about the fact that I shared a tiny, unventilated room with a demon that I knew for a fact smelled of brimstone, and hadn't caught so much as a whiff of the stuff?

What was this? The demon was inside Pedersen. He confessed. He jumped out of a window for Christ's sake.

Pedersen had to be the demon.

Pedersen couldn't be the demon.

'Jazz, I need you to go behind your counter and fish out your Big Book of Demons.'

'You mean the *Pseudomonarchia Daemonum?*'

'You know what I mean,' I snapped.

I waited while she reluctantly fetched her grimmest of grimoires.

I had to be sure that Pedersen was the demon. Not 99.99% sure; 100% sure. I was unhappy enough with the way the Ripper story had ended already, without adding further doubt.

Finally, Jazz returned to the phone and said, 'What is it you want to know?'

'I need you to identify every type of demon that gives off a brimstone smell.'

Why Pedersen only seemed to give off the smell periodically, I had no idea, but if I could find out exactly what kind of demon it was that had possessed him, maybe I'd find my answer.

'Didn't we go through this once already?' said Jazz. 'There are over a thousand demons in the *Pseudomonarchia*—'

'Just go with me on this.'

I had new information now. A third clue to narrow the search.

She sighed into her phone so loud that it sounded like the receiver was being blasted by a force nine gale. 'Let me just check the index…'

I waited. And waited.

'Jesus, Jazz, did you ever think about getting that book on a database so you can search it a bit quicker? Get with the times.'

'Seriously? I'm getting advice about living in the now from a bloody ghost?'

Getting her back up wasn't going to help. I needed to take the slack out of this chat.

'I'm sorry, okay. Carry on checking your index. Please.'

I heard her mutter some word-vomit in Latin: a spell of intuition to help speed up the search.

'Fine,' she said. 'In answer to your question, I can see seven-hundred and forty-two demons that exhibit your required characteristic.'

'Great. Now I need you to cross-reference those with demons known to eat human souls.'

As I walked, and Jazz continued to whittle the list down, I watched a line of drool swing from Frank's chin like the pendulum of a grandfather clock.

'One-hundred and twenty demons remain,' she reported.

Now we were getting somewhere.

'One more question. Do any of those demons have black eyes?'

I thought back to the showdown in the interview room when the demon showed his true colours, right before he threw Pedersen out of the window.

I listened to Jazz hum and haw for a bit before she delivered her verdict...

'Zero. There are no demons that exhibit all three of those characteristics. Not one.'

I stopped in my tracks. 'That can't be right. There must be demons that aren't in that book.'

'This is a comprehensive rogue's gallery of infernal invaders. If it was born in the Nether, it's listed in this bestiary.' I heard her finger stab the book.

'That doesn't make sense.'

The three attributes I fed Jazz were definitely on the money, even if one of them—the brimstone thing—was apparently a bit spotty. Something had been overlooked. Something vital. It was as though I had all the pieces of the clock laid out on a sheet in front of me, but one cog was missing.

'Oh, there is this, though,' said Jazz, her voice brightening, 'in regards to your third observation.'

'What?'

'Well, while there is no such thing as a demon that smells of brimstone, eats souls, and has black eyes, there is one that comes close. A thrall demon.'

I'd never heard of such a thing, but then that came as no huge surprise. While I'd done a certain amount of research on the topic, I was nowhere near Jazz's league. When it came to demons, the woman really knew her onions.

'While a thrall demon doesn't have black eyes, it does exhibit a related attribute,' said Jazz. 'The creature is able to enslave mortals by touch, and when it does so, its victim's eyes—and I'm reading off the page here—*become two bottomless wells, dark as an Alaskan winter*. The language is a bit fruity, but you get the idea.'

'You're telling me this thrall demon can make a person do its bidding while it stays hidden in its host?'

'For a limited time, yes.'

There it was: the final cog. And now the clock was ticking.

Stronge had been right all along. I got it into my head that she'd been getting in my way this whole time, but the opposite was true. I had it wrong. She'd been the one doing the detective work, I was chasing a crackpot theory.

Pedersen wasn't the demon. He was just a patsy. A slave.

And I had a pretty good idea who was cracking the whip.

CHAPTER FORTY-FOUR: THE WRONG ARM OF THE LAW

I HUNG up and made a beeline for the cop shop. Despite the urgency of the Vic job, priorities had shifted. I just had to hope I could pull this off and still get to Mark in time.

It was ten past eleven when I got to Kentish Town Police Station. According to a notification on my phone, there had been an all-officers-on-deck-shooting at a nearby nightclub, so I wasn't surprised to find the station pretty much empty. Only a couple of higher-ups remained, scattered over the building's five floors. DCI Kat Stronge was one of them.

I translocated directly to her immaculate office, where I found her sitting at her desk drinking coffee with her good hand, and one-finger typing a report with the other. She was working on her laptop. A laptop that—the second I burst onto the scene like the Ghost of Christmas Past—became filled to the brim with vending machine cappuccino.

'We got the wrong man,' I blurted.

'Jesus Christ, Fletcher,' yelled Stronge, using a napkin to pad down her soaking-wet keyboard, 'you really are making bold strides in the field of being a dick.'

'Didn't you hear me? Pedersen didn't do it.'

'Didn't you hear *me* when I said I never wanted to see you again?'

'You're not listening, Kat.'

She rose to her feet, marched over to me, and jabbed a finger into my chest (literally, into).

'Don't *Kat* me. We both watched that demon take a dive, remember? You were looking through my eyeballs at the time.'

Clearly, she wasn't over the whole possession thing, but then I already knew that.

'I'm sorry that happened—you've no idea how sorry—but I promise you, the Ripper is still out there.'

She chuckled bitterly. 'Is that right? So who is it then? And don't say the tour guide, because we released him right after Pedersen offed himself.'

I shook my head. 'Oberman was no one.'

'Right. And Pedersen confessed for the fun of it.'

'No. He only did that because he was possessed.'

Stronge's stare just about burned a hole through my head. 'Am I missing something here? Of course, he was fucking possessed.'

'This was different. The demon wasn't inside him. It took control another way.'

I explained to her what Jazz Hands had told me: that there was a creature called a thrall demon that could enslave a human host just by touching them.

'What a load of bollocks,' said Stronge, turning away and straightening something on the wall. 'Way too complicated. Face it, we lost. The demon was in Pedersen, and now he's gone.'

She was furious. She had every right to be. Once again, I was stood in front of her arguing against myself. I identified Oberman as the killer then argued in his defence, now here I was doing the exact same thing.

'Pedersen was just a pawn,' I said.

'How convenient,' replied Stronge, rounding on me. 'So, sticking with your "tag, you're it" theory, I suppose the real Ripper could be absolutely anyone?'

'Not just anyone.'

'Go on then, Poirot,' she seethed. 'You've got me in the drawing-room. Why don't you tell me whodunnit?'

'Okay, but you might want to sit down for this.'

'I'm fine standing, thanks.'

She sat anyway.

'Okay, just hear me out here, Kat. That godawful aftershave your partner wears... has he always worn it?'

She raised a finger to tell me off, then wavered. 'What's that got to do with anything?'

'I think he's using it to mask something. To disguise the smell of brimstone.'

Stronge threw back her head and let forth a full-throated shriek of laughter. 'Maddox? You think Maddox is behind this? He's a prick, Fletcher, but he's no killer.'

I showed her my palms. 'That's not what I'm saying. Not at all. I'm saying he's demonically possessed.'

'Oh yeah? And when did that happen exactly?'

'Best guess: during his last psychiatric break.'

Demons like to go after people when they're at their weakest. They're a lot like Christians that way.

Stronge got up from her desk and placed her hands flat upon its surface like Jesus posing for Da Vinci's Last Supper (only decidedly more pissed off). 'If you're going to accuse my partner of being a demon, you'd better have a lot more than that.'

I laid it all out: the matching physical description, the fact that Maddox would have access to protected information such as medical records, his dabs being present at the third crime scene.

'Don't you see? It all adds up now. It wasn't Pedersen's badge the fifth vic identified, it was Maddox's.'

Stronge returned an unblinking stare. Come to think of it, had I ever seen that woman blink?

'That's what you've got, is it? Jesus, I don't know where to start. There are so many heavy-set men in this city that I'm not even going to touch that one. Maddox contaminating the crime scene; that was just a professional fuck-up. As for the badge, any old tin star could have given the killer enough cred to get inside that house, so long as it was flashed quick and with conviction.'

Down went my ducks, *bang bang bang*.

'What about this then?' I countered. 'How did the conversation between you and your partner go after Pedersen threw himself out of the window?'

'What do you mean?'

'Maddox heard a bunch of loony bin stuff in there about "ghosts" and "taking off masks" and "the power of destiny". You're telling me he wasn't the least bit interested to follow up on that?'

She waved the notion away. 'He had bigger things to worry about. He'd just suffered a major concussion.'

Stronge wasn't the only one pissed off now.

'You need to believe me. Maddox wasn't the hostage in that room. He was the hostage-*taker*.'

I'd figured it out. The demon was using Pedersen to voice his own words; standing behind him and using his thrall powers to work him like a glove puppet.

Stronge was just about to throw water on that theory when we both heard a *ping* noise from outside the office.

'Was that the lift?' I asked.

'Yeah,' she replied. 'Cleaners.'

I saw a gap in the conversation and decided to fill it.

'I know you don't want to hear it, but Maddox has been playing us from the start; messing with our heads. We let him blend into the background after Pedersen, and now he's going to finish what he started.'

'Finish what? According to you, Jack the Rip-off already got his five kills: four women and Pedersen.'

'But not the *canonical* five. Think about it; what was the connection between Pedersen and the original Ripper's fifth victim? I'll tell you: there wasn't one.'

Neither was there a connection to Reina, who was just collateral damage to the demon.

Stronge's eyes drilled into mine. 'Yeah? And what makes you so sure you're right about that?'

'Don't you get it, Kat? Because the fifth victim is *you*.'

There was that shrieking laughter again. 'Get fucked, Fletcher.'

'I'm telling you, it's why the demon chose to possess Maddox in the first place. So he could get into your orbit.'

'Why? What could I possibly have to do with any of this?'

You want Poirot? I'll give you bloody Poirot.

'It's your name,' I said, aiming a finger at the plaque hanging from

Stronge's wall. 'Your middle name: "Mary Jane". Same as Mary Jane Kelly, Jack the Ripper's final kill.'

Stronge's face dropped. Her eyes shot to a wall clock.

'What's the matter?' I asked.

'The cleaners don't start their shift for another hour.'

Ping.

And with that, the lift arrived on our floor.

CHAPTER FORTY-FIVE: OFFICER DOWN

STRONGE HURRIEDLY DREW a key from her pocket, unlocked a desk drawer, and thrust her good hand inside. When it came out again, it was wrapped around a gun. And this gun wasn't of the stun variety.

I wondered what Stronge was doing in possession of a firearm, but only for a second. After all, if you were a police officer who knew demons walked among us, wouldn't you want to keep a shooter handy? In any case, the question of why Stronge had a black market weapon in her desk had to take a backseat to the real thinker: was I right about Maddox being the one to step out of that lift, or had this all been some horrible mistake?

'Guv? What are you still doing here?'

DI Maddox, right on schedule. Here to topple the last domino and feast on Stronge's soul. Of all the times for me to be right about something, why did it have to be now?

Stronge exited her office and strode over to the lifts. 'Stay where you are,' she insisted, taking aim at Maddox.

Something about the lack of conviction in her voice made it sound like a joke.

He stuck up his hands. '*You'll nevva take me alive, koppa!*' he joshed.

Stronge pulled back the pistol's hammer. 'I'm serious, keep back.'

Maddox took a step forward and reached out. 'Where did you get that thing? It looks really real…'

I shot out a hand. 'Don't let him…'

Bang.

If Maddox had any hair on his head, Stronge would have parted it.

'Holy shit!' he cried, spinning around and seeing the bullet hole in the wall behind him. 'What the hell are you doing?'

The words, 'I told you to stay back!' punched their way out of Stronge's throat.

'That's right,' I said. 'Keep a bead on him.'

She rounded on me. 'Will you shut up?'

Maddox didn't react to me at all. Instead, he stayed frozen, still as a billboard model. 'Kat, what's going on? Why are you doing this?'

'Did you do it?' she shot back.

'Do what?'

'Did you murder those women?'

'Did I...?' He looked genuinely perplexed. 'The Ripper murders? Is that what this is about?'

With his bashed-up face and generous helping of upper lip sweat, Maddox was doing an award-winning impression of an innocent man. If I wasn't careful, he was going to appeal to the part of Stronge that wanted me to be wrong about him, and throw her off guard.

I took a spot by Stronge's side. 'Kat, why don't you let me try possessing him? If I see a demon in there, you can unload the rest of that clip into him.'

It would mean killing Maddox, but what choice did we have? Desperate times...

'I'm the detective here,' she hissed. 'Stay out of this.'

'Seriously, I can put this to rest right now if you just let me—'

She answered with such force that I flinched. 'No! I can't just take your word for it. I need to know.'

'Okay, okay, have it your way,' I said. I had a chance to make it up to her. To mend the bridge I'd burned. I wasn't going to throw that away. Not unless I absolutely had to.

Maddox hadn't moved an inch since the bullet ate a hole through the wall behind him, but he dared a step forward. 'Listen, Kat, it's me, your partner. I don't know what's going on with you, but this has to stop. You're hearing voices. The stress has gotten to you.'

'Tell me you didn't do it,' said Stronge. 'I want to hear you say it.'

'Pedersen did it,' he replied. 'We know that.'

She wrapped a finger around the trigger.

Maddox held his hands up in self-defence as though they had some magical, bullet-stopping powers. 'Fine,' he said. 'I didn't kill anyone, okay? Now will you put down the gun so we can talk?'

But the gun wasn't going anywhere.

'Think about what you're saying,' he said. 'What about the tower block? Look at my face.' He pointed to the mess of his nose, busted during his visit to the block of flats, then again in the interview room. 'The person who killed those women did this. Pedersen. Did. This.'

As Stronge took a moment to process this information, she realised her pistol was sagging and righted her aim. From the side of her mouth she said, 'Go on, how do you explain that?'

'He did it to himself,' I replied. 'Both times.'

'What?'

'He never ran into the killer at the tower block, he just pretended to. It was dark, remember; all we saw of the bloke we were chasing was an outline. I'm telling you, if there was any CCTV footage of that lobby, we'd see Maddox stuffing a red balaclava into his pocket before he head-butted a wall. Same with the interview room; a diversion to throw us off his trail.'

Stronge gave me a flinty look. 'That's a big bloody stretch.'

Sensing that he was gaining ground, Maddox did so literally and took another step toward Stronge. 'You realise there's no one else here, right? It's just you and me, Kat. Your partner of eleven years.'

Stronge's eyes darted to mine. 'How would he know that?'

'Same way he knows everything: he has access to Maddox's memories.'

His hands were down by his sides now. He could see Stronge beginning to falter and was milking it for all it was worth. 'I'm worried about you. You're not well. Trust me, I've been there, I know what it's like.'

She chewed her lip.

'Ignore him, he's messing with you,' I said. 'Come on, Detective, use your loaf. He just shows up here in the middle of the night for no reason? He's come to do you in.'

'I never said this to anyone besides my shrink,' Maddox told his partner, 'but since I took that hit on the job a few years back, I've been to some dark places. Really dark. Even thought about… you know... a couple of times.'

Stronge loosened her grip on the gun. Was she really buying into this sob story?

'Get it together,' I told her. 'That's the killer, right there.'

The atmosphere was so thick you could have planted a Union Jack in it.

Finally, after a pregnant pause that ran to its third trimester, Stronge told Maddox, 'Get on your knees.'

'Kat, will you stop a second and think about what's going on here? Just look at the facts and tell me your thinking isn't muddled right now. You've been breaking protocol, involving weirdos in our investigations; now you're talking to yourself and waving a gun about? Can't you see something's wrong?'

Another step.

Stronge took aim at his head. 'I said, on your knees!'

'Don't let him get any closer,' I said.

I was itching to take a run at him, but there was no outcome there that worked in my favour. Either I was right and Maddox was the demon, which meant I had no means to possess him; or Stronge was right, and the only thing I'd accomplish would be to completely torpedo an already broken friendship.

Maddox squared his shoulders. 'Okay, that's enough, Detective. You're going to give me that gun and we're going to talk this out.'

'Last warning…'

'Come on, give it here....'

He thrust out a hand, grasping for the weapon.

'No!'

A flash ate up the room and Maddox went spinning.

Stronge meant to wing him—at least I think so—but she wasn't used to firing a gun, least of all wrong-handed.

DI Maddox went down.

Hard.

CHAPTER FORTY-SIX: PAST SINS

STRONGE WAS the first to move.

'Maddox?'

The detective's sizeable bulk laid face-down on the floor, still as a rock. Dead still.

Stronge dropped to the floor by his side, grabbed him by the shoulder, and hauled him onto his back. The front of Maddox's shirt was drenched red, the bullet hole positioned to the right of his chest, just below the shoulder.

His lips were moving but nothing was coming out.

'Stay still, Maddox,' said Stronge.

'Hurts...' he wheezed, his voice so meek that he sounded like a little boy.

Stronge whirled in my direction. 'I think I got him in the lung.'

If the demon was in there, a single round shouldn't have done that kind of damage. To be honest, I was thinking *glass half full* when I suggested a whole clip would have taken him down. Had I got it wrong? Oh God, please tell me I was right and I didn't have another death at my feet.

A weak cough rattled Maddox's throat. 'Please… don't let me…'

'I'm getting help,' said Stronge. 'Just stay with me.'

Maddox's eyes bulged, then his head rolled off to one side.

'Maddox?'

Stronge gave him a slap to the cheek. He didn't respond. The rise and fall of his chest ceased. His body had shut down.

'Maddox? Detective Maddox!'

But Maddox wasn't there anymore. His body was empty. A depersonalised shell.

Desperate, Stronge searched her pockets for her phone. 'This is your fault,' she spat. 'You turned me against him.'

With the right side of her body patted down and no phone found, she placed her gun on the ground and switched to the other hand.

Big mistake.

Maddox's hand shot out at viper speed, grabbed the pistol, and crushed it like tin foil.

'What the…?'

Before Stronge could finish her sentence, his other hand came up as a fist, catching her under the chin and landing hard enough to lift her whole body into the air. She struck the lift door with such force that she left a dent, then slumped to the ground, face pressed to the station's cheap tile carpet.

Instantly, Maddox was on his feet, a leer of sheer insanity spread across his face. The demon was in there; he'd just been playing possum.

'Hello Jake,' said the Ripper. 'So nice to finally speak to you in person.'

I heard a *clunk* and looked down to see a metal slug land at Maddox's feet. He ripped open his shirt to show me the bullet wound Stronge had dealt him, which fused together before my eyes.

'First of all,' he started, 'let me say sorry for that hacky "destiny" speech I gave in that interview room. I just needed something that sounded a bit *demony* to throw your way, and that was the first thing that popped into my head.'

I smiled, playing it cool, while under the water the swan's feet were frantically churning. 'Why Pedersen?' I asked. 'Why add a second suspect to the mix when the tour guide was already in there?'

'Ah, Oberman,' the demon recounted wistfully. 'Wasn't he perfect? Down he dropped like a penny from Heaven… not that Heaven owes me anything!'

While the demon got nostalgic, my eyes flicked to Stronge. She was out for the count, but breathing.

'Oberman was a nice bit of distraction, but he never really stood up as a suspect,' said the demon. 'You knew that, and you'd soon have convinced the detective here likewise.' He gave Stronge a nod. 'No, what I needed was a viable fall guy. Someone who really fit the bill.'

'But why Pedersen in particular?' I asked.

The demon favoured me with a cold smile. 'Oh, you can thank yourself for that.'

'Don't put this on me.'

No way. I had enough black marks next to my name without another ink spill.

'I saw the way you looked at him,' said the demon. Saw the disgust written all over your face. It was already in your head that Pedersen was the killer; I just made it real.'

He was right. Pedersen had set my alarms ringing, and the demon had played on that prejudice.

'One stolen pen and it was done,' said the demon. 'You had your man.'

'So why kill him?' I asked. 'You made him confess. Why not let us stick him in some draughty madhouse?'

'I couldn't let that happen,' replied the demon. 'Given time, you'd have figured out Pedersen wasn't the culprit, either. You're good at your job, Detective. Better than I took you for.'

'Good enough to suss you out,' I said.

The demon laughed. 'About that... what was it that gave me away?'

'In the end? The aftershave.'

He snapped his fingers as if to say *"rats!"*

'Didn't have a choice on that one,' he said. 'Best I could do to pass the old smell test. Not that it did me much good when I got all murdery. Nothing like a spot of bloodshed to open up the glands.'

Gross.

'You know,' I said, stalling for time as much as anything, hoping for Stronge to come around and pull something out of the hat, 'before this gets physical, I have one question left. What's with the copycat shit? Why mimic the Ripper killings?'

The demon gave me the kind of grin that lowers the temperature of a room. 'Finally! You know, I was starting to think you'd never ask...'

As discreetly as I could, I gave Stronge a quick eyeball. Her breathing was getting stronger, her extremities starting to twitch. It wouldn't be long before she came to.

'Fancy a cuppa?' asked the demon, jerking a thumb over his shoulder in the direction of the break room. 'I can tell you all about the Ripper stuff, but it's a bit of a saga.'

'Ghost,' I reminded him.

'Of course,' he said, slapping his forehead. 'You're so full of life that I plum forgot. You should take that as a compliment.'

'Yeah. Can we skip ahead to the Ripper stuff?' I asked, tapping my watch.

I was happy for him to drag his story out, but I didn't want to come across as suspicious. Standing there and politely following his story wasn't exactly on brand. Besides, I could only stay here for so long. Even if I somehow managed to survive my encounter with the thrall demon, I still had Vic's soul to deliver.

'Spoilsport,' he replied. 'But all right, I suppose I can cut to the chase.'

'My lucky day.'

'Okay, are you ready, Jake, because here comes the big reveal...' he drew it out like a game show host preparing to announce whether I'd won the million quid or I was going home empty-handed... 'I'm not a Ripper copycat,' he said, 'I'm the *actual* Ripper.'

Okay, fair play, that was actually worth the build-up.

'You're JTR?' I asked.

The demon answered, 'The very same.'

'So... Jack's back?'

'Think of it as a vacation. A sort of busman's holiday. Every century I visit this charming little realm of yours, kick off my shoes, and have my fun.'

So that's what this demon was: a wide-eyed tourist, taking in the sights, taking lives.

'You know, if it's a holiday you want, I hear Blackpool has loads to offer.'

He chuckled. 'Oh, Jake. You are a card.'

A question occurred. One for the ages.

'Just between the two of us, who was it? I mean, I get that you're the Ripper, but whose body did you borrow the first time around? A butcher? The Queen's surgeon? That painter bloke?'

The demon cupped a hand to his mouth. 'Actually, I used a woman. Much easier to get close to victims that way. Kinda sexist of you not to consider that. Bit disappointing.'

Even more disappointing was the fact that the gobby Yank on that Ripper tour had been right with her wild *Jill the Ripper* theory.

'Aaanyway,' said the demon, 'that was just one of my wee sprees. I've taken possession of so many people over the centuries, committed murders all over the globe. You name them, I've been them: Giles de Rais, Peter Stumpp, Sarah Malcolm, Thug Behram, Son of Sam.'

Christ. If what he said was true, he'd been doing this schtick since the 1400s.

'That Son of Sam outing was a real disappointment,' the demon went on. 'Can you believe they got me on a parking ticket? Shocking. So, I decided to revisit a classic and do the Ripper thing this time. And let me tell you, it's been a total blast.'

'I'll bet. So what happens now?'

'Well, first of all I'm going to kill that woman down there, and then… I don't know, how do you fancy a team-up?'

There was no trace of irony in his voice. Not a hint of guile.

'Come on, Jake, I've been watching you. Don't act like you're better than me; you sock puppet these meat bags just like I do. All I'm saying is, why don't you have some fun doing it for a change? Live a little!'

'Thanks for the offer, but I'm looking to send my soul the other way.'

He shrugged. 'Suit yourself. Well, it's been fun—real cat and mouse stuff—but all good things must come to an end…'

He took a step toward Stronge.

'Wait,' I said, my voice coming out a lot more feeble than I'd intended. 'That's it? You complete your canonical five and then you just go home again?'

The demon placed a hand palm-down on his chest. 'Whatever made you think I'd stop at five, Jake? The only reason I did that last time was because the woman I was using died of cholera before I could make it to six.' His eyes blazed with terrible intent. 'This time I'm going to really go for it. Create a whole new canon. Up and down the country, I'll go, a real Ripper roadshow.'

He tapped his chin, taken with a thought. 'You mentioned Blackpool before. Maybe I'll start there. I've always liked the seaside at wintertime.' His eyes landed on the unconscious detective. 'Just as soon as I've tied up this little loose end...'

Stronge groaned and rolled onto her knees, one hand massaging her jaw. She spoke in a drowsy, sunken voice. 'Where... what...?'

'Speak of the devil,' said the literal demon.

I firmed up a hand and grabbed Stronge by the wrist. 'Come on, Kat. We have to go.'

A grin lit up the demon's face. 'Oh, I do love a chase.'

CHAPTER FORTY-SEVEN: STITCHED UP LIKE A RIPPER

I RAN LIKE THE CLAPPERS, Stronge quick-stumbling behind me. Demons could kill ghosts just as easily as they could kill the living; this I knew from bitter personal experience. Dead or alive, we were both on the menu today.

We rounded a corner and ploughed ahead, stumbling through the office bullpen.

Stronge went heavy in my grip and wheezed, 'Stop... can't...'

From blacked out to a hundred-metre sprint; this was too much for her. Much as she wanted to go on, she couldn't will her legs into action. She needed a breather.

A quick glance over my shoulder told me the thrall demon was taking his time. He hadn't even rounded the corner into this part of the building yet. Building up an appetite, no doubt.

'Here...'

I steered Stronge into the bullpen, where we took cover amongst a forest of cubicles.

She settled into a squat, gasping in short, plosive breaths.

'Come on, Kat, keep your head on.'

'Can't you just... exorcise him?' she heaved.

I patted down my jacket, only to discover that my exorcism tools were gone. They must have shaken loose of my pockets during the fight in the sewer.

'No can do,' I replied.

In any case, to perform an exorcism, I'd need restraints and time to go with the tools, and even if I did have the whole trinity, there was no guarantee that I could banish an entity of that strength. The thrall demon was ancient. Even on a good day, chances were I'd be useless against a creature with his kind of power. A water pistol squirting into a volcano.

I stuck out my neck and dared a peek through the partition wall of the cubicle we were hiding in. We were still alone. Perhaps the demon had gotten lost and wandered off in the wrong direction. Or maybe he'd moved on to another floor. Gold star for optimism, right?

'Kat, there's something I've been meaning to ask,' I whispered.

'Is this really the time, Fletcher?'

'Given that we're both probably about to die, yeah, I reckon.'

She tipped back her head and rested it against the partition. 'Fine. Speak your truth.'

I didn't appreciate the way she teed me up, but I wasn't going to miss this chance.

'Okay, here it is. Why have you been so closed-off with me lately? What happened?'

I felt a bit mushy asking, but I had to know. We used to be a team. A good team. What turned her against me?

'*You're* what happened,' she replied, her breath rapid still. 'You and the lunacy that comes with you.'

'You're a copper,' I replied. 'Loony's part of the job.'

'Not like this! Before you came along, what I did made sense. Now look where we are: trapped by a frigging demon and about to get our souls eaten.'

'Kat, keep your voice down—'

'No, I won't! What's the point? You're going to get me killed anyway, so why bother?'

She was freaking out, her chest going up and down like an oil derrick. I'd never seen her like this. Never seen her so scared. She placed her hands over her face in frustration, and for the first time, I noticed how abused her fingernails were; chewed to the bone despite the rest of her being presented just so. No wonder she'd taken to toting a gun.

Sometimes I forget how big a deal dying is to the living. To some degree, I've become deaf to the drumming on death's door. Don't get me wrong, I've no wish to have my flame extinguished, but when it happens, I'll be ready.

I stole another glance across the bullpen and caught a glimpse of a shadow on the other side of the office. The demon was making his approach. We had to move, but not before I said my piece.

'Kat, I would never have brought you into this world if I didn't think you could hack it. You're the toughest person I know. I promise I can beat this demon, but not without your help. Now, are you with me?'

Stronge's chest settled, finally. She'd found her breath. 'I'm with you, you soppy shite,' she said. 'Now pick up your toes, we have to go.'

A quick exchange of smiles, then we bolted from the cubicle and tore across the office floor, heading for the stairs. What neither of us realised when we set out was that the demon had made it there before us.

'Detective Stronge. We haven't been properly introduced,' he said, stepping out from behind a vending machine and extending a hand.

'Thanks for the offer,' she replied, 'but seeing as the last time I saw that hand it was punching me in the face, I'm going to say no.'

'Sorry,' he said, making a face like he was sucking on a lemon, 'but you know, I can't claim one-hundred percent responsibility for that.' He tapped the side of his head. 'There's an angry little man in here, and he is *not* happy with you.'

Stronge laughed. 'Don't think you can put that on Maddox.'

'I wouldn't be so sure,' said the demon. 'He's been watching you, you know? Sat in the passenger seat during your whole investigation. How do you imagine that felt? Knowing that his own partner couldn't tell him apart from a demon. But then why was he surprised by that? You never made the effort to know him before I took his body.'

'That's not true.'

'Isn't it?' He studied Stronge like she was a bit of fluff he'd plucked from his navel. 'You realise that cookery video I sent you was filmed in his kitchen? Oh no, of course you didn't, because you've never taken the time to get to know the man. If you'd broken bread with him just once in the eleven years you've been working together, this whole thing could have been over days ago.'

He was baiting her. Trying to trick her into losing control again. And it was working.

Stronge scooped up an office chair and swung it at the demon—

Who caught it with ease, tossed it aside, and grabbed her by the throat.

'Kat!'

The demon held up a hand to halt me. 'What are you going to do, Jake?' he asked, closing his fingers around Stronge's throat and making her eyes bug out like a pair of door knobs.

'Me?' I replied. 'I'm not going to do anything.'

But someone was.

A fist landed so hard on the demon's head that I'm surprised he wasn't driven through the floor. He toppled sideways, going down like a sack of spuds and releasing his captive. Stronge landed on her back, eyes aimed upwards at her saviour.

'Braaaaaaaiiins.'

Stronge scrambled backwards on her heels. 'What the fuck is this now?'

'Kat, meet Frank.'

Seeing as I couldn't bring him with me when I translocated here, I asked Frank to make his way to the station by foot. Showing up behind the demon the moment he got hold of Kat... that was just a stroke of Fletcher luck.

The demon had already made it onto his hands and knees, and was wobbling about like a dog drunk on fermented crab apples.

'Frank, can you do me a favour and keep him down for a bit?'

He did so without objection, heaving the vending machine over his head and dropping it on the demon with an almighty crash.

That would hold him. For a little while, at least.

'Come on,' I told Kat, 'I've got an idea.'

Her eyes strayed from me to my dead doppelganger.

'What's the matter, woman? Never seen a zombie before?'

The vending machine groaned like a sinking battleship and shifted to one side. The demon was already getting up.

CHAPTER FORTY-EIGHT: DEAD RECKONING

I PUNCHED OPEN the door beneath the green exit sign and ushered my companions through.

'Where's your evidence locker?' I asked as we took the first flight of emergency stairs. Here we were again, I thought, me and Stronge, pelting down another stairwell. Only this time, we were the ones being chased.

'Fourth floor,' Stronge replied. 'Why? Shouldn't we be getting the hell out of here?'

'We can't. We have to finish this now or we'll never see the Ripper again. If this doesn't end tonight, he'll just start over in a new town.'

We alighted on the fourth floor and followed Stronge to the evidence room.

'Can I ask… why is your dead body with us?' she enquired, refusing to turn her back on the zombie shambling along in our wake.

'Let's just say I've been keeping some skeletons in my closet,' I replied. 'Or more accurately, a zombie in my casket.'

The cogs shifted in Stronge's head as she thought back to her visit to the funeral parlour. '*That's* what you were hiding!'

'Don't stress about it,' I said. 'You've got nothing to worry about.'

'Braaaaaiiiins,' said Frank.

Stronge's eyes widened.

'You should probably ignore that,' I suggested.

We arrived at a serious-looking metal door. The evidence locker. Stronge tapped a string of numbers into a nearby keypad and the door opened with a meaty *kerchunk*.

We stepped inside quickly and locked the door behind us.

The room was lined with row upon row of towering metal racks stacked high with all manner of contraband.

'What are we doing?' asked Stronge. 'We're just meant to hide in here? I thought you said we were going to take that demon down.'

'This isn't hiding,' I replied, 'this is a final stand.'

The room was well fortified, but nothing was going to stop the demon from getting in here. Not with Stronge so close to joining his gallery of atrocities.

'Quickly, get yourself tooled up,' I said.

I was banking on the evidence room being stocked with confiscated weapons we could use to defend ourselves, and I wasn't left wanting. A quick rummage from Stronge turned up a machete the size of a Medieval broadsword.

She weighed it in her hand. 'How are we going to fight back against this bastard without hurting Maddox?'

'Let me worry about that,' I said, 'you concentrate on twatting him with that thing.'

If the demon could spit out a bullet, he could certainly take a few whacks with a machete. The main thing was to keep the bastard distracted long enough that Frank could pin him and figure out what to do next.

Stronge and I took positions on either side of the door. Frank stayed where he was, awaiting instructions, his eyes so vacant that they seemed almost hopeful in light of our bleak predicament.

'Are you sure about him?' Stronge asked.

'Frank? Don't worry, he's good as gold.'

Stronge didn't seem convinced. 'At some point, I'm going to want to know what you're doing hanging around with your own dead body.'

We waited. And waited some more. I checked my watch. Thirty minutes to be done with this thrall demon, then a quick scoot to Vic

Lords' place to smash his evil empire and rescue Mark from a fate worse than death. Simple as that. Nothing to it, really.

Stronge placed an ear to the door. 'Maybe he's given up,' she said.

'He'll be here, trust me.'

Stronge's nose twitched. 'Is it just me, or do you smell Old Spice?'

I heard a crack of fibreglass behind us as ceiling tiles gave way and the demon came crashing down through the roof.

He landed in a perfect three-point crouch and tilted his head our way, his face etched with a malignant leer. 'Humans,' he scoffed. 'Look at you. Nothing more than primates with anxieties.'

He came at us fast—too fast—jerking in our direction like something off a scratched DVD. His attack was aimed at Stronge, who didn't even have a chance to raise her chopper before the demon was on her. I've no doubt that would have been the end of DCI Kat Stronge, had Frank not caught the demon like a wedding bouquet and hurled him back where he came from. If Stronge had any doubts over the zombie being an ally, they must surely have evaporated by this point.

The demon struck the ground hard but righted himself quickly. Stronge didn't wait for him to get his bearings, and launched at him, screaming like a wounded Valkyrie. Down came the machete, but the demon managed a side-step, which left the blade embedded in one of the evidence shelves. Not before it sliced through a large bag of impounded cocaine, though. Stronge choked down a giant cloud of marching powder, her face iced white as freshly-fallen snow.

'Don't stop now, Kat,' I cried.

But she wasn't waiting on my encouragement. Fired up on God knows how much booger sugar, she went at the demon like a wet cat trying to claw its way out of a bathtub. Taken by surprise, the creature could only raise its guard and gird itself against her onslaught. Slash after slash found its mark as Stronge swung the blade so fast it's a wonder it didn't lift her off the ground like a helicopter's rotor.

'Die, die, die!' she screamed.

Sweet Baby Jesus, the woman was practically breathing fire.

'Okay, easy there, Scarface,' I said.

I considered asking Frank to step in before she did some damage to Maddox that the demon couldn't heal, but the look on his face told me he wasn't getting anywhere near that mess. He might not have been the brightest bulb in the box, but even Frank knew better than to get in the way of a coked-up copper waving a machete around.

While the detective continued to hack lumps out of the intruder, I ransacked the shelves for anything I could use to deport his malignant spirit. If I could just scrape together a bible, some salt, maybe a couple of candles, there was a chance I could perform a rite of exorcism on the weakened demon. This not being the Vatican, though, the shelves were rather light on holy weapons, and my desperate search failed to turn up so much as a drop of blessed water. Typical.

I turned back to the rumble to find Stronge gripping the machete in both hands and drawing a swathe of meat from the demon's shoulder. For a moment I worried that she was going to dole out some damage that Maddox wouldn't be able to come back from, but then the demon turned the tide.

With a stinging backhand, he lifted Stronge off her feet and deposited her halfway up a rack of shelves. She struck it so hard that the metal crumpled as she tumbled down the rack, then the entire unit teetered and toppled, crushing her under its weight. Even if she had managed to stay conscious—which she hadn't—her body was trapped, pinned like a framed butterfly.

'Frank, twat him!'

Wasting no time, Frank steamed in, fists windmilling, but this time the demon was ready. Snatching up the fallen machete, the creature drove the weapon through the zombie's shoulder, bulldozed him across the room, and nailed him to the wall. Frank tried to pull himself free, but he was fixed in place, fingers clawing uselessly at the air.

The demon turned slowly in my direction. His wounds were already on the mend. The injuries that Stronge had inflicted were rapidly knitting together, leaving behind nothing but a lattice of silvery scars. Her assault had seemed so savage, so final, but as far as doing our aggressor any real damage, it had been another wet firework.

'Now, where were we?' asked the demon, his eyes practically pyrokinetic.

He marched over to me, gathered up a fistful of shirt, and drove me into the ground.

'You know what I'm going to do now, Jake? I'm going to dispatch your soul to Hell, tear your friends to pieces, and once I'm done with that, I'll be visiting you on the other side. We're going to have some fun, you and me. So much fun.'

I caught a flash of Frosty, fastened to Vic's torture rack, his body stretched to inhuman proportions. At the time, his suffering had seemed so interminably drawn out, but compared to the barrel I was looking down, his death had been a kindness.

'Are you ready to die?' asked the demon.

A laugh burst out of me. 'I don't die. I'm a survivor. I'm a weed growing out of a concrete crack in Chernobyl. People keep trying to bury me, but here's what you don't get... I'm a seed. I just keep on growing.'

'Nice speech,' said the demon. 'Tell me, were those your final words?'

'Nope.' I turned to Frank, pinned to the wall still. 'Can I get a hand, mate?'

The demon smirked. 'What a waste. Can't you see your commands are useless?'

'You're missing the point.' I fired back. 'I'm not commanding him. I'm *asking* him.'

With a triumphant roar, Frank pulled himself free of the wall, the hilt of the machete passing through his chest and out of his back with a messy *schlurp*. Grabbing the demon with both hands, he hoisted him off me and slammed the creature against a concrete pillar hard enough to make the room shake.

The demon wasn't having that.

He struck back, damn near knocking the zombie's head off his shoulders. Frank slid across the floor, rolled once, and flopped onto his front, stunned.

With a contemptuous sneer, the demon returned his attention to me. 'Let's get this over with.'

His fingers went for my neck, but I pulled the chicken switch and translocated to the other side of the room before he could get there. I'd only be able to grease-pig my way out of his clutches for so long, though. I could pinball about as much as I liked, but as soon as he got his hands on Stronge, it was game over.

I had one opportunity to defeat the demon, but making it work meant taking a hell of a gamble. Still, what did I have to lose? Given my options, the only play I had left was what Shift might have called a Hail Mary Pass: a desperate risk with little to no chance of success, but a chance all the same.

I translocated again, but this time it wasn't to maximise my distance from the demon. This time I had a very particular target in mind.

Frank.

If I was going to stand any chance against this demon, I needed to pool my strengths with his. If I could unite our souls and combine my mind with Frank's body, I believed we'd have something stronger than the sum of its parts. Maybe even strong enough to take on this monster.

We combined once by accident, but now I had to do it deliberately, and this time I had to make it stick. It's like Jazz Hands had been saying all along: I needed to get simpatico with my twin. Except what I was attempting here wasn't a regular possession. I wasn't trying to take control of Frank, I was trying to become one with him, and only now did I realise what that required.

I needed to ask his permission. Get his consent.

Frank's head turned my way as I appeared by his side.

'Room for a little one?' I asked.

He gave me a nod.

'And you're sure you're okay with this?' I asked.

Frank smiled. 'Frieeeeeends.'

The demon snarled and stomped my way, teeth bared.

I stepped into Frank's body and immediately locked into place. We were two pieces of the same puzzle, coming together with a crisp snap. I felt the summoning of blood in my veins, felt sinews stiffen, felt muscles bunch in my shoulders. I was complete again. I was whole.

Frank had been the key all along. I'd been treating him like a dead weight, but I was dead wrong. Frank wasn't an anchor. He was a kite. And this time, there was no fear or confusion in him. This time, we were a team.

I asked Frank to move, and his body answered the call. Our constituent parts were working in perfect concert. I could feel the extra power, the extra strength, my zombified body had, and I was ready to use it. The demon came crashing down on us, but we succeeded in vaulting him over our shoulder, bearing our weight upon his, and overpowering him completely. We fixed our hands either side of his head and held him there like the jaws of a vice. One twist of the crank, that's all it would take.

The demon only laughed.

'What's so funny?' I asked.

If I killed Maddox's body with the demon inside, the demon would die. Right now, his only chance for survival was fucking off back where he came from, pronto.

'You won't do it,' he said. 'The Spectral Detective isn't going to kill a human being just to settle the score with a demon.'

'Try me, mate. I never got on with Maddox at the best of times, and besides, what's one life compared to stopping an immortal serial killer?'

'You're bluffing.'

'Wanna slide all your chips in on that?'

I squeezed with hulk strength and felt the bones in Maddox's skull shift like tectonic plates.

Was I bluffing? I'm not even sure I could answer that. Either way, the demon certainly didn't think so.

'Fuck you, Jake,' he growled.

'Yeah, I get that a lot.'

I increased the strength of my grip, hard enough to make Maddox's eyes stand out on their stalks. He squirmed and thrashed and threatened, but it was no use, I had him now and I wasn't letting go. With a sick grinding noise, his jaw hinged open impossibly wide, then the thrall demon poured out of Maddox's mouth like a tanker of crude oil performing a gravity-defying spill. In a moment of panic, the demon had deserted his host's body, fleeing back to his realm, tail between his legs.

I won. Lopped the demon's murderous spree off at the knees. The Ripper was no more.

I checked my watch. Twenty minutes to get to Vic. Twenty minutes to stub him out like one of his foul-smelling cigars.

I checked Maddox and found a pulse. His injuries were all gone. Good. I made myself vertical, levered up the rack of shelves pinning Stronge, and tossed it to one side. Her face was pancake-white from the ruptured cocaine, her heart hammering like a humming bird's. She looked into my eyes with pupils the size of pinpricks.

'Christ!'

Correction: Frank's eyes.

'Easy, Kat. It's me, Jake. No one wants your brains.'

'You scared the shit out of me,' she said, and followed with a tell-tale sniff. 'Is Maddox okay?'

'He's fine.'

'Thank God,' she replied, crawling over to him. 'But he's going to need a bloody good brain scrub after all this.'

'Don't worry, I've got it.' I reached out a hand to help her to her feet. 'Now, who's up for a nice trip to the detox clinic?'

CHAPTER FORTY-NINE: THE WRONG SIDE OF MIDNIGHT

FRANK ESCORTED Stronge to the local hospital, where she was treated for multiple concussions and a possible drug overdose.

Maddox, I dealt with myself. Having possessed the station's snoozing night guard and used him to wipe the evening's CCTV footage, I took ownership of the detective's brain and made the necessary tweaks to his memories. I started off by scrubbing his hard drive from the point the demon had taken control of him, filling the interim with some general work-a-day cop stuff, and removing any trace of otherworldly possession. I capped the whole story off with a killer scene in which Maddox valiantly and single-handedly saw off an armed intruder caught in the act of robbing the station's evidence locker. A story he later related so convincingly to his superiors (including the easily swayed DCI Stronge) that he ended up earning a commendation for valour. You're bleedin' welcome, Maddox.

With that done, I had less than ten minutes to hoof it across Camden and rendezvous with Vic Lords. I was running out of time; when all four digits of the clock turned into zeroes, Mark was a dead man. Just as well I was able to translocate to my destination in a heartbeat.

My surroundings were pulled away like a magician's tablecloth, then I was standing at Vic's front door with minutes to spare. I knew now that my past plan—to have Frank kick his way inside the building and take Vic on with brute strength alone—was doomed to failure. Vic had too many goons on the payroll; with the best will in the world, a full-frontal assault would have just seen Frank overwhelmed. No, I needed to go this one alone. No backup, just me. Make the trade, rescue the captive.

It was time to put an end to this Punch and Judy show. I firmed up a fist and hammered on the door. The peephole shutter slid open before I could even lower my arm. A masked man looked back at me: Kojo, Vic's deformed number one.

'Cutting it fine, Fletcher,' he said in his Elephant Man drawl.

I shrugged. 'I've got the goods and I made the cutoff. Call it an A-minus.'

The goon's eyes narrowed. 'Hand it over,' he demanded.

I produced the pouch containing the demon. For a moment I wavered, then thought better of it and passed the offering through the slot. I had to play this just right. One wrong move, one dead meat suit.

Kojo rolled his mask up so the lower portion of his ruined face was showing. A face that—thanks to the curse placed upon him by his master—looked like it had been sculpted by fists. He put the pouch to his crooked nose and drew in a deep breath, going at it like an addict huffing a paper bag full of glue.

'Ahhh, I love the smell of brimstone in the morning,' he said with a broken smile that would have given hardened criminals nightmares.

I'd never seen him happy before. Not once. This was new.

I heard a series of bolts slide open, then the reinforced door swung inwards.

'Come with me,' said Kojo, rolling his mask back down.

Instead of heading upstairs to Vic's office, he led me into the bowels of the building, past a procession of heavies and indentured molls. Another flight of steps and we were back in the sub-basement sex dungeon where Mark was being kept. I found him strapped to the rack still, emaciated, unconscious, but alive.

Vic Lords stepped out of the darkness trailed by a thick snake of cigar smoke. He was dressed in the red velvet robe he'd been wearing the day he burned down my old office.

He grinned at Kojo. 'Why, is that an arch-demon in your pocket, or are you just pleased to see me?' He laughed. At least, I think that's what it was. It could just as easily have been gas escaping his rotten innards.

Kojo placed the pouch on Vic's upturned palm.

'This legit?' asked Vic.

Kojo nodded.

Vic had his goon lead me to the other side of the room where a pentagram awaited, scrawled across the wall in red chalk. Apparently, Vic was up for a spot of wizarding, no doubt preparing to make his offer to the Long Man.

'Well, Vic, I reckon this is where you and me part ways,' I said. 'You get your demon, and I get my meat suit. I'd say it's been a pleasure doing business with you, but I'd be lying.'

Vic remained unmoved. 'You didn't really think this would be the end of it, did you, Jakey boy? You reckon I'd let you out of my sight before the deal's done? Not bloody likely.'

'What are you talking about?'

'You're coming with me,' he growled. 'You're going to stand in front of the Long Man, and you ain't going nowhere until the ink's on the dotted line. Any funny business, and I'll see to it that your man there leaves this place in two bin bags.'

I turned to Kojo, who backed his boss up with a pointed nod. What choice did I have?

'So where is it we're going exactly?' I asked.

Vic removed a leather sheath from the pocket of his robe and withdrew a small knife. 'A place called Drayeadran,' he replied.

'Never heard of the gaff. What is it; south of the River?'

Vic didn't answer. Instead, he used the knife to slash open his palm, then held up his wounded hand, twisting it this way and that until it was gloved red. Satisfied, he pressed his palm into the centre of the chalk pentagram, painting it with a bloody handprint. With his dark sacrament complete, a hole opened in the wall: an interdimensional breach, a portal into another place.

'After you,' said Vic, flicking his cigar through the hole.

I took one last look at Mark, and off I went, herded through the portal like a cow on its way to the abattoir.

Drayeadran was a harsh, desolate place. The kind of place where nightmares are born. The sky was grey and mirrored by barren, scorched rock without a whisper of colour to break up its monochrome palette. Dotted here and there like pimples on a backside were the brittle husks of tree stumps, and all was still save for a light breeze that eddied around loose ground stones, stirring up the parched earth.

'Get a wriggle on,' said Vic, urging me onwards.

We walked for what felt like miles until we reached a forest of large, twisted trees with bark the colour of charcoaled skin.

'I'm going to take a wild stab here and say this is the Forest of Souls. Am I right?'

Neither Vic nor his goon favoured me with an answer. Instead, they shepherded me into the woods, and on we marched.

Densely-packed trees rose into the sky, their leafless branches splayed like talons ready to strike. It was dark. So dark that I had to squint to see by the scant light trickling in from above the forest canopy.

Eventually, the woods opened out into a grey glade decorated with a few choice saplings. A creature rested on its knees, carefully pruning branches from a particularly delicate specimen. The creature was enormous—at least thirty feet tall—and looked as if it had stepped straight from the pages of *Fangoria* magazine. This was the Long Man; a gaunt giant with a leering skull face and a body built from exposed, glistening muscle. The top of his head was decorated by a pair of thick spiral horns, and his clawed hands were the size of JCB digging buckets.

The monster climbed to his feet, swivelled our way, and regarded us with the endless hollows of his eyes.

'At last,' said the beast, 'my soil is thirsty for a fresh soul.'

CHAPTER FIFTY: WE'RE NOT IN CAMDEN ANYMORE

THE LONG MAN wasn't The Devil, just *a* devil. And yet, looking up at his gargantuan frame, looming over us like a wave about to break, I felt every bit as awestruck as I would if I were in the presence of the Dark Prince himself.

Vic dropped to his knees, eyes pointed to the dirt in reverence, and his goon did likewise. Me, I stayed standing. It's not that I wasn't scared, but by this point, demons were starting to seem like things that were just part of my day. In any case, bowing and scraping wasn't going to achieve anything. If the Long Man wanted me dead, I'd be dead.

'I bring you your gift, O Lord,' Vic beseeched, holding the pouch aloft like some sacred offering. 'The demon's soul in exchange for mine. My humblest apologies for the delay.'

Delay? But I showed up on time. Unless... was that why Vic had me running around town like a blue-arsed fly; because he'd already let the Long Man down once? Had he tried to acquire the demon soul by his own means and crapped out? Questions without answers.

The Long Man didn't even bother looking at Vic's offering. Instead, he turned to the one person not grovelling: me.

The demon spoke in deep, sepulchral tones. 'Each of these trees is a soul that was promised to me,' he said, slowly moving from sapling to sapling, touching them tenderly. 'I plant the souls in the dirt and they grow.'

I didn't quite know what to say to that, so I opted to stay schtum.

'At night,' the Long Man went on, 'when the moon is at its apex, the trees are given voice and scream in eternal, orgasmic torment.'

The Long Man dropped to a crouch and regarded Vic's offering. 'The arch-demon Cimeries will make a handsome addition to my orchard; a fair exchange for the paltry gifts I have bestowed upon you.'

'Thank you, Lord,' said Vic, his nose buried in the black earth. 'I am unworthy of your generosity.'

Using two huge claws, the Long Man plucked the gift from Vic's hands and carefully undid its bone clasp. With the utmost delicacy, he drew apart the pouch's fleshy folds and peered into the void within.

The forest seemed to grow darker.

'This is not the soul I was promised,' he boomed.

'What?' cried Vic, eyes lit with panic. His head whipped in my direction. 'What's happening? What the fuck did you do, Fletcher?'

I smiled. 'Nothing good. At least not for you.'

I didn't give Vic any more information than that, but you... you can have the lot.

Thing is, when I said I handed Kojo the demon at Vic's front door, I didn't actually say *which* demon. Truth be told, the creature I passed through the slot wasn't Cimeries at all, it was—you guessed it—the thrall demon.

Yup, the old switcheroo.

So how exactly did I swap out the Ripper for Cimeries? Well, technically, I didn't. Cimeries was never in the pouch in the first place. When I siphoned him from his cradle at the Museum of Souls, I wasn't using Vic's doodad, I was using the padlock I lifted from the Museum's spectre collector.

I guess I left that detail out at the time, same as I didn't mention the thrall demon being sucked into the pouch at the point he bolted from Maddox in the evidence room. What can I tell you? I said he made a break for Hell when he leapt out of Maddox's mouth, I didn't say he got there. Sorry if you feel a bit cheated by my selective storytelling, but if you knew I trapped both demon souls, you'd have seen this caper coming a mile off, and where's the fun in that? Ask yourself what you'd rather have: a precise account with all of its parts told in strict chronological order, or a ramshackle yarn that skips a few details in service of a satisfying surprise? I mean, isn't that what you really want? Killers shown justice. Bad guys made to account for their crimes. All that good stuff. Can you imagine the thrall demon just getting away with it after he killed all those people? Balls to that. Instead, you get this...

The Long Man emptied the contents of the pouch into his giant hand, and for the first time, I saw the true eldritch horror of the thrall demon. A draconic head with amber eyes and slanted nostrils sat atop a pale, stringy body shot with spidery purple veins. The demon looked at me with dread in its eyes like it couldn't believe things had turned out this way. Like it couldn't believe a lowly human had doomed its immortal soul.

The Long Man closed its hand into a fist, turning the thrall demon into bone and paste. When the fist opened, four balls of bright white light emerged, the four human souls taken by the Ripper. They circled for a moment, then off they went like seeds blown from the head of a dandelion, soaring upwards, Heaven bound.

There, isn't that better?

But the best is yet to come...

Because you weren't the only one I kept in the dark about my little shell game. Vic didn't have a clue, either. If he'd been able to use his scrying magic to spy on me, this little ruse would have fallen flat at the first hurdle, but circumstances made that impossible. The Museum of Souls was shielded from all forms of arcane penetration, and the thrall demon gave off enough supernatural static to fuzz up any picture.

The Long Man towered over Vic, a heinous bailiff, come to claim his debt. 'You will pay for your insolence with your soul,' he roared, loud enough to leave cracks in the scorched earth beneath our feet.

Vic could only cower on the ground, terrified, shattered. He turned to his right-hand man and spoke with a tremor in his voice. 'You told me the demon in that pouch was legit.'

Kojo tugged off his mask and smiled. 'I lied.'

Kojo was the key to this whole thing. I couldn't have pulled off the con by myself; to fool Vic, I needed an accomplice. But how did I make an ally of Vic's right-hand man without so much as an eyebrow wiggle? Another bit of artistic license on my part? A phone call I neglected to mention? Not this time…

Here are two things I knew about Kojo: Number one, he'd been trained to identify the soul of Cimeries, so I wouldn't be able to fob him off with a cheap substitute; Number two, he was probably the only person on Earth who despised Vic Lords as much as I did. That gave us common ground, and in that ground we planted a united flag.

I'd done Kojo no favours, and he killed my friend, Frosty, but Vic was someone we could both rally against. All Kojo needed was opportunity, so when I came knocking with my poisoned chalice, he answered the call. Our cooperation went unsaid. The moment Kojo opened the door to me, I knew we were in cahoots. It was the way he smiled when he huffed that pouch. The look of joy on his face when he caught a whiff of Vic's imminent annihilation. That was the pivot point. That was the moment I realised that trusting Kojo wasn't even a risk. Of course, he went along with it. This was his chance to take Vic Lords down, and in the most gruesome way imaginable.

The Long Man reached out an arm, casting an ominous shadow across the mortal who had dared wrong him. Vic tried to move, but the only body parts he could will into action were his hands, which only agreed to shield his terrified face.

I held up a finger. 'Oh Vic, before you get slaughtered, you should know that me and that zombie you sent my way are best pals now. Okay, bye.'

The Long Man touched the tip of a single claw to Vic's cranium, and that was the end of him. He screamed and screamed as his skin sloughed off in sheets and gnarled branches pushed their way out of his dying body. And yet he still found it within himself to commit one final atrocity before he was lost completely.

'Judas!'

With his dying breath, he snapped his fingers—or were they twigs now?—and dealt his right-hand man a fatal curse. Kojo's spine made a sickening crunch and he fell to the ground, the rest of his bones cracking, snapping, bending limbs in impossible directions.

And yet Vic fared no better. His body was gone now; a mess of shredded flesh piled on the dusty ground like discarded lunch meat. Only his soul remained; a crooked sapling among the Long Man's orchard. I'd always thought of Vic as a root I needed torn out of my life, so there was a satisfying irony in seeing him perish this way. Seeing him planted. A thing that would exist forever, and only to feel pain.

Vic told me that I had a saviour complex. That I wouldn't let a man die, no matter how rotten. He was wrong.

'That was for you, Frost,' I said.

I heard a ragged, wet slurp, and realised that Kojo was still breathing. His flesh was torn open, wide rips unzipped across his joints where his limbs had folded back on themselves.

'How did you know?' I asked. 'How did you know Vic wouldn't check the pouch and make sure I brought him the right demon?'

Somehow, Kojo managed to answer. 'His ego was... too big. He never... saw you coming.'

I thought this goon had the IQ of a Heinz baked bean, but it turned out he was a canny sod.

'You must have known this was a suicide mission,' I said.

The clouds broke and a great luminous pearl of a moon chromed the harsh lines of Kojo's mangled face.

'Wanted... out. Sick of living... like a freak. Vic... had to die...'

Not just die. He needed Vic's punishment to be the worst kind of suffering. Hell was too good for that man.

I looked to the thing that Vic had become: the sinuous, deformed topiary tended to by the Long Man. The thing that flinched from the demon's touch.

'Mission fucking accomplished.'

Kojo laughed and creased with pain. 'Feels nice to... have the air... on my face.'

He opened his mouth to say more, but the only thing that came out was blood.

The forest screamed as he died.

Mixed thoughts here. The bloke saved Mark's life, but he also took Frosty's. When all was said and done—when the final score was toted and tallied—what was *his* ledger going to look like?

The Long Man rose from the Vic tree and turned his attention to me.

'Did you think I had forgotten about you, ghost? Now it is your turn. You too will join my forest and become agony eternal.'

'Actually,' I said, reaching under my shirt and fishing out a padlock necklace, 'I was thinking we might do a deal.'

'What is this?' asked the Long Man, cocking his giant skull head.

'It's the soul you were promised,' I replied. 'The arch-demon, Cimeries.'

The necklace weighed heavy, but was it loaded with potential, or was it an albatross around my neck?

'What sort of deal did you have in mind?' asked the demon.

'I was thinking even Stevens.'

The Long Man smiled.

CHAPTER FIFTY-ONE: POST MORTEM

Fletcher & Fletcher, Paranormal Investigators: that's what I had stencilled on the frosted door of my new office.

The refit was done on the quick, and was worth every penny. The private contractor who did the work had some reservations—why did our dealings have to happen strictly over the phone? Why was I converting a funeral home into a 1940s style detective agency? Did I have permission from planning regs to be making these alterations? —but nothing a well-placed bribe couldn't satisfy.

Everything was perfect. I had the Venetian blinds, the chiaroscuro lighting, even the bottle of Bushmills sat on my office desk (just for the look). I was really doing it. I was going to be an actual PI. No more making it up as I went along—that's how I messed up being an exorcist—I'd learn the trade and become a bona fide detective this time. Not just a wannabe, the real deal.

'Well, would you look at this?' said a familiar voice.

Shift was here, acting on my invitation and visiting in female form.

'You like it?' I asked. 'Really puts the "home" in funeral home, doesn't it?'

She ran a finger over the new mouldings. 'Must have cost some dough. Hope you saved a slice for me.'

'Sorry. Nothing left after I squared up with your pal, the eaves.'

She cut some eyes at me.

'Okay, fine. Hey Frank, would you be a lamb and fetch the lady her money?'

'Braaaaaaiiiins.'

He did as asked and sloped off to the safe to collect Shift's cut.

She tucked a stray wisp of blonde hair behind her ear. 'You know, I look around this place and I worry about you, Jake.'

'What for?'

'All this old-timey junk; it tells me you're stuck in the past. How are you gonna go on in this world if you're not capable of change?'

I showed her a smile. 'When I first met you, I didn't like you one bit. Now I do. Tell me that ain't change.'

She laughed, boisterous and unladylike. 'The reconstructed man you ain't, Cookie, but you're heading in the right direction.'

Frank showed up clutching an envelope of cash.

Shift took it in her cherry-red nail-polished fingers. 'Why, thank you, young man.'

'Enough in there for your services, and to cover the cost of your coat,' I said.

She trousered the money without counting it and headed for the door. Before she left, she turned and took in the room again, seeming to appreciate it this time. 'It's like Bogey said: "I think this is the beginning of a beautiful friendship".'

I waved her goodbye and took a seat at my desk, which was decorated only by the aforementioned bottle of whiskey, a green glass reading lamp, and a push-button telephone. A real one; none of this hands-free, touchscreen bollocks.

Things were looking pretty good for old Jake Fletcher. I thought back on the events of the last few days...

I'd snatched Mark Ryan from the lion's den and returned him home safely, his mind scrubbed and pumped full of sunshine, same as with Maddox. You might take a dim view on all this messing with people's heads, but I like to think of my brand of brainwashing as the benign kind. I get rid of dirt. Tidy up mess. Give those old grey globs a nice spit polish. And besides, I was done using Mark as my meat suit. Seeing as I could merge with Frank now, I had no further use for him, which was probably for the best. It's like Shift said: it was time I stopped living in the past. I had to move on. Mark Ryan had paid his debt. What was done was done.

Talking of "done", Vic's operation shuttered pretty much the moment he got flicked off the game board. With no successor to take the Lords throne, the only thing he left in his wake was a dirty great hole. No doubt some even bigger scumbag would step in to fill the vacuum, but that was a problem for another time. For now, at least, the world was a little bit less shitty.

And Vic's business wasn't the only one to take a hit. I received word through the grapevine that the Museum of Souls had also closed its doors. From what I heard, a bunch of halo-wearing heavies raided the place and cleaned out the whole building. Apparently, their entire inventory was confiscated and guilty parties perp-walked off the premises in white handcuffs. It seems someone Up There had decided that the Museum couldn't continue to exist, and sent in the God squad. The fact that this only came about after I had my run-in with the "venerable institution" can't have been a coincidence. Someone had chosen to finish the job I started. Was this the way it was going to be from now on? I turn over a rock to expose the ants, and God pulls out the magnifying glass?

A knock on the office door. A woman's silhouette through the frosted glass. Two ladies in one night? Jake Fletcher, you old dog, you've still got it.

DCI Kat Stronge swanned into my office loaded with uncharacteristic cheer.

'Oh, it's just you,' I grumbled.

She ignored me. 'If it isn't the gruesome twosome,' she said, eyes flicking from me to my sidekick.

'Very clever,' I replied.

'Braaaaaaiiiins,' Frank agreed.

Stronge plonked herself on the corner of my desk. 'Well, look at you two. The Dynamic Duo: Deadman and Rotting.'

I gave her an exaggerated laugh. 'That your lot, or have you got any more in the hopper?'

'No, I'm done,' she said. 'I spent the whole ride here thinking those little gems up.'

She sniffed and dabbed at a nostril with the sleeve of her coat.

'That better not be—'

'Hay fever,' she pinged back. 'You think I can afford a habit like that on a cop's salary?'

'Whatever you say, Officer,' I said, tapping my nose. 'So what can I do you for? Here about a new case?'

'No, just stopping by,' she said. 'Loving the decor, by the way. Very you.'

'Cheers. Thought it was about time I went legit. You really like it?'

'Yeah. Except it's missing something…'

She reached inside her coat and pulled out a gift-wrapped package.

'For me? Why, thank you. Frank, would you do the honours?'

While Jazz Hands had been kind enough to enchant the office appliances and such, I still struggled with regular solid objects, at least when I wasn't borrowing someone else's digits.

Frank fumbled the package open and placed its contents on the desk.

'A plaque?'

'One of those things they give actual detectives,' said Stronge. 'Call it a moving in present. Or a peace offering. Your choice.'

I pointed Frank to a spot on the wall and had him hold the plaque up so I could inspect it.

'*Certified Private Detective, Jake Fletcher*,' I said, reading the inscription.

'It's not real, obviously,' said Stronge. 'It's kind of an honorary thing.'

'I thought I was just an old relic. Isn't that what you said?'

'Maybe,' she replied, 'but you've got integrity, and that's something that never goes out of fashion.'

Yeah, it was a cheesy line, but it warmed my phantom heart.

'So what do we do now?' I asked. 'Hug?'

Stronge shook her head and made off the way she came. 'Goodbye, Fletcher.'

'Don't leave it so long next time, yeah?' I shouted after her, but she was already gone.

Well, would you look at that. It seemed that me and Stronge were back on level footing again. At least until the next time I pissed her off.

I turned to Frank, who was holding on to my new plaque with a look on his face like, *Where's my housewarming gift?*

'Don't worry, mate, you get a pressie, too.' I pointed to the top drawer of my desk. 'Go on, fill your boots.'

A dopey grin sprang up on Frank's mug as he bungled the drawer open and dug out a big lump wrapped in brown paper and tied with a piece of string.

'Braaaaains!'

He tore into the parcel, scooped out a great big fistful of grey matter, and stuffed it into his mouth like it was filet mignon.

Before you get yourself all wound up, don't worry, it was just a pig brain I got from the butchers. I wasn't about to go feeding Frank human body parts. Not until his birthday, anyway.

I looked at him there, sat on the other side of the desk, my new partner, the muscle to my brains. Working with a colleague was going to be a whole new way of doing things, but I could learn to adapt. I mean, I adapted to dying, didn't I? And besides, having Frank about was going to make some things a whole lot easier. After years of wishing I had a body, I finally did, and even better, it was the one I was actually given. When I merged with Frank, I felt like the Jake I used to be. Like I'd regrown an amputated limb. Like I was whole again.

Frank smiled at me with bits of brain in his teeth, and I smiled back. A zombie and a ghost, living in harmony; who'd have thunk it? I came to this place looking for somewhere to hide, but what I found was friendship.

I put my feet up on the desk and raised an imaginary glass to my new partner. 'Here's looking at you, kid.'

Before Frank came along, I was having a real unlife crisis. Being a phantom is hard work. When most people die, it's lights out then on to the next place, but not me. I get to stick around knowing that the universe continues to roll along without me, indifferent and increasingly indistinguishable from the one I left. I was starting to feel like less of a person than a residue of one. An old Polaroid fading away in the sun.

And then the events of the last few days took place and made me realise that I was worth something. Made me realise that I could still make a difference in this world. Because a ghost isn't a copy of a former human being. There's no real me some other place; I'm here, and I'm not going anywhere. And yeah, I may have some old-fashioned ideas rattling around in my head, but that doesn't make me obsolete. I can still cut it in the modern world. I may not be a "reconstructed man" just yet, but I'm doing my best. Because I realise now that my life didn't stop the day I watched my office burn down. That wasn't an end, it was a baptism by fire. When I walked out of that blaze, I was reborn. To a fashion, anyway. Born dead, but more alive than ever.

Frank sucked down the last morsel of brain and whisked his tongue around his lips.

'I guess it's true what they say. A mind is a terrible thing to waste.'

I hoped that was okay with the Big G; feeding a brain-hungry zombie. It's really all guesswork where that guy's concerned. I didn't even know for sure if I'd scored points by bumping off that thrall demon, or for ending Vic's reign of terror. Like I keep saying, there's no rulebook for living in limbo.

I looked to the window and saw motes of dust dancing around in the silvery slants of streetlight that razored in from outside. When I looked back to my desk, I saw something new. A hardback book had appeared as if from nowhere.

My head whipped to Frank. 'Did you put that there?'

But it was obvious he hadn't. Not just because of the look on his face—which was even more gormless than usual—but because the book was giving off a pale glow accompanied by the ever-so-faint sound of choral music.

'Is it just me, Frank, or is that thing giving off a real "Heaven" vibe?'

Following my instructions, Frank opened the book and revealed the first page, which was stamped *The Case File of Fletcher & Fletcher.*

He was watching. The Big He. And He was telling me to carry on doing what I was doing.

With a smile upon my lips, I reached into the desk, plucked out a pen, and handed it to my partner.

'Take this down, would you, Frank? Heading: *Case File Number One...*'

Apparently, the bit of my old brain that knew how to write was still intact, as Frank was able to follow my dictation. His penmanship wasn't the greatest, and he moved like he was underwater, but we were in no rush. We had all the time in the world.

Hands behind my head like a sunbather, I rattled off the date and dictated Frank the first paragraph...

'Night-time. Smoky shafts of neon light filtering through the slats of a Venetian blind. A shady lady with legs up to her armpits and lipstick the colour of wet blood. That's how detective stories are meant to start...'

LEAVE A REVIEW

Reviews are gold to indie authors, so if you've enjoyed this book, please consider visiting Amazon to rate and review.

STILL HAVE QUESTIONS?

Like, how did Jake die?

Who owned the funeral home that became Jake's office?

And what exactly was his nefarious past with Vic Lords?

For answers to all of these questions, sign up to the *Uncanny Kingdom* mailing list and become an Insider. Membership includes the free mini-story, *Deathday,* which kicks off the first Jake Fletcher series. You'll also get the complete *London Coven* saga, which intersects with Jake's story.

Sign up at...
WWW.UNCANNYKINGDOM.COM

ALSO SET IN THE UNCANNY KINGDOM

The Spectral Detective Series
Spectral Detective
Corpse Reviver
Twice Damned
Necessary Evil
Deadly Departed

The London Coven Series
Familiar Magic
Nightmare Realm
Deadly Portent
Other London

The Hexed Detective Series
Hexed Detective
Fatal Moon
Night Terrors

The Uncanny Ink Series

Bad Soul
Bad Blood
Bad Justice
Bad Intention
Bad Thoughts
Bad Memories

The Dark Lakes Series

Magic Eater
Blood Stones
Past Sins

The Branded Series

Sanctified
Turned
Bloodline

The Myth Management Series

Myth Management

uncannykingdom.com

Created with Vellum